Rafael Sabatini, creator of s⸻ was born in Italy in 1875 and educated in both Portugal and Switzerland. He eventually settled in England in 1892, by which time he was fluent in a total of five languages. He chose to write in English, claiming that 'all the best stories are written in English.'

His writing career was launched in the 1890s with a collection of short stories, and it was not until 1902 that his first novel was published. His fame, however, came with *Scaramouche*, the much-loved story of the French Revolution, which became an international bestseller. *Captain Blood* followed soon after, which resulted in a renewed enthusiasm for his earlier work.

For many years a prolific writer, he was forced to abandon writing in the 1940s through illness and he eventually died in 1950.

Sabatini is best remembered for his heroic characters and high-spirited novels, many of which have been adapted into classic films, including *Scaramouche*, *Captain Blood* and *The Sea Hawk* starring Errol Flynn.

TITLES BY THE SAME AUTHOR
ALL PUBLISHED BY HOUSE OF STRATUS

Venetian Masque

Rafael Sabatini

HOUSE OF
STRATUS

This edition published in 2001 by House of Stratus, an imprint of Stratus Holdings plc, 24c Old Burlington Street, London, W1X 1RL, UK. Also at: Suite 210, 1270 Avenue of the Americas, New York, NY 10020, USA.

www.houseofstratus.com

Typeset, printed and bound by House of Stratus.

A catalogue record for this book is available from the British Library.

ISBN 1-84232-837-9

Contents

CONTENTS

Chapter 1

The White Cross Inn

The traveller in the grey riding-coat, who called himself Mr Melville
was contemplating the malice of which the gods are capable. They
had conducted him unscathed through a hundred perils merely, it
seemed, so that they might in their irony confront him with
destruction in the very hour in which at last he accounted himself
secure.

It was this delusive sense of security, the reasonable conviction
that having reached Turin the frontiers of danger were behind him,
which had urged him to take his ease.

And so in the dusk of a May evening he had got down from his
travelling-chaise, and walked into the trap which it afterwards
seemed to him that the gods had wantonly baited.

In the dimly lighted passage the landlord bustled to inquire his
needs. The inn's best room, its best supper, and the best wine that it
could yield. He issued his commands in fairly fluent Italian. His
voice was level and pleasantly modulated, yet vibrant in its
undertones with the energy and force of his nature.

In stature he was above the middle height and neatly built. His
face, dimly seen by the landlord under the shadow of the grey sugar-
loaf hat and between the wings of black hair that hung to the collar
on either side of it, was square and lean, with a straight nose and a
jutting chin. His age cannot have been more than thirty.

1

Accommodated in the best room above-stairs, he sat in the candlelight contentedly awaiting supper when the catastrophe occurred. It was heralded by a voice on the stairs; a man's voice, loud and vehement and delivering itself harshly in French. The door of Mr Melville's room had been left ajar, and the words carried clearly to him where he sat. It was not merely what was said that brought a frown to his brow, but the voice itself. It was a voice that set memories dimly astir in him; a voice that he was certainly not hearing for the first time in his life.

'You are a postmaster and you have no horses! Name of God! It is only in Italy that such things are permitted to happen. But we shall change that before all is over. Anyway, I take what I find. I am in haste. The fate of nations hangs upon my speed.'

Of the landlord's answer from below a mumble was all that reached him. That harsh, peremptory voice rejoined.

'You will have horses by morning, you say? Very well, then. This traveller shall yield me his horses, and in the morning take those you can supply. It is idle to argue with me. I will inform him myself. I must be at General Bonaparte's headquarters not later than tomorrow.'

Brisk steps came up the stairs and crossed the short landing. The door of Mr Melville's room was pushed open, and that voice, which was still exercising him, was speaking before its owner fully appeared.

'Sir, let my necessity excuse the intrusion. I travel on business of the utmost urgency.' And again that pompous phrase: 'The fate of nations hangs upon my speed. This post-house has no horses until morning. But your horses are still fit to travel, and you are here for the night. Therefore...'

And there abruptly the voice broke off. Its owner had turned to close the door, whilst speaking. Turning again, and confronting the stranger, who had risen, the Frenchman's utterance was abruptly checked; the last vestige of colour was driven from his coarsely featured face; his dark eyes dilated in an astonishment that gradually changed to fear.

He stood so for perhaps a dozen quickened heart-beats, a man of about Mr Melville's own height and build, with the same black hair about his sallow, shaven face. Like Mr Melville he wore a long grey riding-coat, a garment common enough with travellers; but in addition he was girt by a tricolour sash, whilst the conspicuous feature of his apparel was the wide black hat that covered him. It was cocked in front, à la Henri IV, and flaunted a tricolour panache and a tricolour cockade.

Slowly in the silence he recovered from the shock he had sustained. His first wild fear that he was confronted by a ghost yielded to the more reasonable conclusion that he was in the presence of one of those jests of nature by which occasionally a startling duplication of features is produced.

In this persuasion he might well have remained if Mr Melville had not completed the betrayal of himself which Fate had so maliciously conducted to this point.

'An odd chance, Lebel,' he said, his tone sardonic, his grey eyes cold as ice. 'A very odd chance.'

The Citizen-Representative Lebel blinked and gasped, and at once recovered. There were no more illusions either about supernatural manifestations or chance likenesses.

'So it is you, Monsieur le Vicomte!' The thick lips tightened. 'And in the flesh. Faith, this is very interesting.' He set his dispatch-case on a marble-topped console beside Mr Melville's conical grey hat. He uncovered himself and placed his own hat on the dispatch-case. There were beads of perspiration glistening on his brow just below the straight fringe of black hair. 'Very interesting,' he repeated. 'It is not every day that we meet a man who has been guillotined. For you were guillotined – were you not? – at Tours, in ninety-three.'

'According to the records.'

'Oh, I am aware of the records.'

'Naturally. Having been at such pains to sentence me, you would not be likely to neglect to make sure that the sentence had been executed. Only that, Lebel, could give you security of tenure in my lands. Only that could ensure that when France returns to sanity, you will not be kicked back to the dunghill where you belong.'

Lebel displayed no emotion. His coarse, crafty face remained set in impassivity.

'It seems that I did not make sure enough. The matter calls for inquiry. It may bring some heads to the basket besides your own. It will be interesting to discover how you come to be a ci-devant in two senses.'

Mr Melville was ironical. 'Who has better cause than yourself to know what bribery can do among the masters of your cankered republic, your kingdom of blackguards? You, who have corrupted and bribed so freely, and who have so freely been bribed and corrupted, should find no mystery in my survival.'

Lebel set his arms akimbo, scowling. 'I find a mystery in that a man in your condition should take that tone with me.'

'No mystery, Lebel. We are no longer in France. The warrant of the French Republic doesn't run in the dominions of the King of Sardinia.'

'Does it not?' Lebel chuckled maliciously. 'Is that your fool's paradise? My dear ci-devant, the arm of the French Republic reaches farther than you suppose. We may no longer be in France, but the Republic is master here as elsewhere. We have a sufficient garrison in Turin to see that Victor Amadeus observes the terms of the Peace of Cherasco and to do what else we please. You will find the commandant very much at my orders. You'll realize how a French warrant runs here when you are on your way back to Tours, so that the little omission of three years ago may be repaired.'

It was at this point, in the sudden annihilation of his confidence, that Mr Melville was brought to contemplate the cruel ironies of which the gods are capable. This man, who once had been his father's steward, was perhaps the only member of the government personally acquainted with him, and certainly the only one whose interests would be served by his death. And of all the millions of Frenchmen in the world, it must be just this Lebel who was chosen by Fate to walk in upon him at the White Cross Inn.

For a moment a wave of anguish swept over him. It was not only that his own personal ruin confronted him, but the ruin at the same time of the momentous mission to Venice with which Mr Pitt had entrusted him, a mission concerned with the very fortunes of civilization, imperilled by Jacobin activities beyond the frontiers of France.

'A moment, Lebel!'

His cry checked the Frenchman as he was turning to depart. He turned again; not indeed to the request, but to the quick step behind him. His right hand slid into the pocket of his riding-coat.

'What now?' he growled. 'There is no more to be said.'

'There is a great deal more to be said.' Mr Melville's voice miraculously preserved its level tone. In his manner there was no betrayal of the anxiety consuming him. He side-stepped swiftly, putting himself between Lebel and the door. 'You do not leave this room, Lebel. I thank you for warning me of your intentions.'

Lebel was contemptuously amused.

'Perhaps because I am a lawyer I prefer things to be done for me by the law and in proper form. But if that is denied me by violence, I must act for myself in kind. Now, will you stand away from that door and let me pass?'

His hand emerged from his pocket grasping the butt of a pistol. He proceeded without haste. Perhaps it amused him to be deliberate; to observe the futile struggles of a victim, trapped and helpless at pistol-point.

Mr Melville was without weapons other than his bare hands. But there was more of the Englishman in him than the name. Before the muzzle of that slowly drawn pistol had cleared the lip of Lebel's pocket a bunch of knuckles crashed into the point of his jaw. The blow sent him reeling backwards across the room. Then, his balance lost, he toppled over and went down at full length with a clatter of fire irons which his fall disturbed.

He lay quite still.

Mr Melville stepped forward, swiftly and delicately. He stooped to pick up the pistol which had fallen from the Citizen-Representative Lebel's hand.

'Now I don't think you will send for the commandant,' he murmured. 'At least, not until I am well away from Turin.' He touched the fallen man with his toe contemptuously. 'Get up, canaille.' But even as he issued the command, his attention was caught by the queer, limp inertness of the body. The eyes, he perceived, were half-open. Looking more closely, he saw a spreading flow of blood upon the floor. And then the spike of an overturned andiron caught his eye. It was tipped with crimson. He realized at once that Lebel's head had struck it in his fall, and that it had pierced his skull.

With a catch in his breath, Mr Melville went down on one knee beside the body, thrust his hand inside the breast of the coat, and felt for the heart. The man was dead.

He came to his feet again, shuddering, nauseated. For a moment, the shock of finding himself an unintentional murderer turned him numb. When presently he recovered the use of his wits, physical nausea was supplanted by panic. At any moment the landlord or another might walk into that room and find him with the body; and the body that of a man in high authority among the French, who, as Lebel had informed him, were virtually, if not officially, the masters here in Turin. He would have to face the French commandant, after all, and in no whit better case than if Lebel had summoned him. There were no explanations that would save or serve him. Investigation of his identity, if they troubled about that, would merely provide confirmation of the deliberate murderous intent with which it would be assumed that he had acted.

Only instant flight remained, and even of this the chances were dismayingly slender. He could announce that he had changed his mind, that he would pursue his journey that very night, at once, and demand his chaise. But whilst the horses were being harnessed and the postilion was making ready, it was unthinkable that no one should enter his room, that there should be no inquiry for the French representative who had gone to interview him. His very action in calling for his chaise must excite suspicion and inquiry. Yet he must take this monstrous chance. There was no alternative.

He stepped briskly to the door, and pulled it open. From the threshold, whilst putting out his hand to take his hat from the console, his eyes, those grey eyes that were normally so calm and steady, wandered in a last glance of horror to the supine form with its head by the hearth and its toes pointing to the ceiling.

He went out, mechanically pulling the door after him until it latched. He clattered down the stairs calling for the landlord, in a voice the harshness of which almost surprised him; and because of the confusion in his mind, French was the language that he used.

As he reached the foot of the stairs, the landlord emerged from a door on the left.

'Here, citizen-representative.' He advanced a step or two, and bowed with great deference. 'I hope the English gentleman has been persuaded to accommodate you.'

Mr Melville was taken aback. 'To... to accommodate me?'

'To yield you his horses, I mean.'

The landlord was staring at him. Instinctively, not knowing yet what capital might be made of this unaccountable mistake, Mr Melville averted his countenance a little. In doing so he found himself looking into a mirror on the wall, and the landlord's mistake became less unaccountable. He was wearing Lebel's wide-brimmed hat cocked à la Henri IV with its tricolour panache and tricolour cockade.

He braced himself, and answered vaguely: 'Oh, yes. Yes.'

Chapter 2

Dead Man's Shoes

In a flash Mr Melville perceived all that he had contributed to the confusion of identities. His height and build were much the same as Lebel's. Like Lebel, he wore a grey riding-coat, and the landlord evidently overlooked the lack of the representative's tricolour sash. Both he and Lebel had arrived at nightfall, and had been seen only briefly in the dimly lighted passage. The most distinguishing feature between them so viewed was the panached hat of the representative; and this Mr Melville was now wearing. Also, whereas on arrival Mr Melville had spoken Italian, now, in summoning the landlord, he had used the language in which he had lately been speaking to Lebel. Therefore, even before seeing him, the landlord had persuaded himself that it was the Frenchman who called him.

All this he perceived in a flash, between saying 'Oh, yes,' and adding the second 'Yes.' From that perception Mr Melville passed instantly to consider how best he could turn the landlord's error to account. The most imminent danger was that of an invasion of the room above-stairs whilst he was waiting for the chaise.

He must begin by averting this, and hope that in the leisure gained he would discover the next step. To this end he spoke promptly.

'You may order the horses to be harnessed and the postilion to be ready. I shall be departing presently. But first this English traveller and I have business together. A very fortunate meeting. We are not on any account to be disturbed.' He turned on the stairs as he spoke. 'You understand?'

'Oh, but perfectly.'

'Good.' Mr Melville began to ascend again.

A waiter appeared, to inform the landlord that he was ready to serve the supper ordered by the gentleman above. Mr Melville, overhearing him, paused.

'Let that wait,' he said, with the peremptory curtness that Lebel had used. 'Let it wait… until we call for it.'

Back in the room above-stairs, with the door now locked, Mr Melville took his square jutting chin in his hand, and those cold, thoughtful, wide-set eyes of his considered the body at his feet without emotion. What was to do he by now perceived. Precisely how to do it might be suggested, he hoped, by the papers in the representative's dispatch case.

He made a beginning by transferring the sash of office from Lebel's waist to his own. In adjusting it, he surveyed himself in the long gilt-framed mirror above the console. He took off the big cocked hat, and pulled his long black hair a little more about his face, so as to deepen the shadows in it. Beyond this he attempted no change in his appearance, and when it was done he went to work swiftly, and, all things considered, with a surprising calm. There was not a tremor in the hands with which he searched Lebel's pockets. He found some money: a bundle of freshly printed assignats, and a small handful of Sardinian silver; a pocket knife; a handkerchief; and some other trivial odds and ends; a bunch of four keys on a little silken cord; and a passport on a sheet of linen-backed paper.

Proceeding with method, he next emptied his own pockets, and from their contents made a selection of passport, notebook, soiled assignats and other loose money, a handkerchief, and a silver snuffbox engraved with a monogram of the letters MAVM which agreed nearly enough with the name on the passport. These objects he bestowed suitably in the pockets of Lebel.

To his own pockets he transferred all that he had taken from Lebel's, with the exception of the little bunch of keys, which he placed on the table, and the linen-backed passport, which he now unfolded. His eyes brightened at the terms of it.

It bore the signature of Barras and was countersigned by Carnot. It announced that the Citizen Camille Lebel, a member of the Council of the Cinque-Cents, travelled as the fully accredited representative of the Directory of the French Republic, One and Indivisible, on a mission of state; it commanded all subjects of the French Republic to render him assistance when called upon to do so; it warned any who hindered him that he did so at the peril of his life; and it desired all officers of whatsoever rank or degree, civil or military, to place at his disposal all the resources within their control.

It was not merely a passport. It was a mandate, and probably as formidable as any that had ever been issued by the Directory. It showed Mr Melville the heights to which the dead rogue had climbed. A man to whom such powers were entrusted must himself be ripe for election as a director.

A description of the bearer was appended: Height 1.75 metres (which was within a couple of centimetres of Mr Melville's own height), build slim, carriage erect, face lean, features regular, complexion pale, mouth wide, teeth strong and white, eyebrows black, hair black and thick, eyes black, distinctive signs none.

In all details save only that of the colour of the eyes, the description fitted Mr Melville. But the eyes offered an awkward obstacle, and he did not see how the word 'noirs' was to be changed into 'gris' without leaving obvious and dangerous signs of tampering penmanship. Inspiration came, however. Writing materials were on the table. He sat down and made experiments. The ink was stale and deep in colour, a shade deeper than that on the document, he thinned it with water from a carafe, adding drop by drop until he was satisfied. Then he chose a quill, tested it, cut it, tested it again, and rehearsed with it on a separate sheet of paper. Finally satisfied, he addressed himself with confidence to the passport. It was a simple matter to lengthen the first limb of the *n*, so that it became a *p*; he appended a stroke to the *o*, so that it became an *a*, and added a circumflex above; he passed on to join the dot with the body of the next letter, so that the i was transformed into an *1*. Then a little curl above the *r* made it look like an *e*, arid the final s remained intact. He let it dry, and then examined it. A magnifying-glass might reveal what had been done, but to the naked eye 'noirs' had been impeccably transformed into 'pâles'; a neat compromise, thought Mr Melville.

He had proceeded without haste, and therefore a little time had been consumed. To make up for it he went now to work more briskly. He unlocked Lebel's dispatch-case. A swift survey of its contents was all that the moment permitted. But here he was fortunate. Almost the first document he scanned disclosed that Lebel was the creature of Barras, dispatched by Barras to exercise surveillance over Bonaparte – that other creature of Barras' – to check the young general's inclination to go beyond the authority of his position, and to remind him constantly that there was a government in Paris from which he must take his orders and to which he would ultimately be answerable.

For the moment this was all that he required to know. He thrust back the papers and locked the case.

His eyes moved slowly round the room in a last survey. Satisfied, he drew a sheet of paper towards him, took up a pen, dipped it, and wrote swiftly:

Citizen – I require that you wait upon me here at the White Cross Inn without an instant's delay on a matter of national importance.

He signed it shortly with the name Lebel, and added below the words: 'Représentant en mission.'

He folded it, and scrawled the superscription: 'To the Commandant de Place of the French Garrison in Turin.'

Out on the landing, in the harsh, peremptory tones the Frenchman had used, Mr Melville bawled for the landlord. When he had curtly ordered him to have the note conveyed at once, he went back and shut himself into the room again; but this time he did not trouble to lock the door.

It was a full half-hour before voices, a heavy tread on the stairs, and the clatter of a sabre against the balusters proclaimed the arrival of the commandant.

The officer, a tall, gaunt, sinewy man of forty, his natural arrogance and self-sufficiency inflamed by the curt terms of the note he had received, flung the door wide, and walked in unannounced. He checked at what he beheld upon the floor. Then his questioning glance travelled to the man who, pencil in hand at the table, sat as unconcernedly busy with some documents as if corpses were his daily companions.

The truculent eyes of the soldier met a sterner truculence in the eyes of the gentleman with the pencil. He heard himself greeted in a rasping tone of reproof.

'You make yourself awaited.'

The officer bridled. 'I am not at everybody's beck and call.' With a soldier's ready sneer for the politician, he added: 'Not even a citizen-representative's.'

'Ah!' Mr Melville poised his pencil. 'Your name, if you please?'

The question crackled so sharply that the commandant, who was himself full of questions by now, answered it almost unawares.

'Colonel Lescure, Commandant de Place in Turin.'

Mr Melville made a note. Then he looked up as if waiting for something more. As it did not immediately come, he added it himself.

'Entirely at my orders, I hope.'

'At your orders? See here. Supposing you begin by telling me what this means. Is that man dead?'

'You have eyes, haven't you? Take a look at him. As to what it means, it means that there has been an accident.'

'Oh! An accident! That's simple, isn't it? Just an accident.' He was full of obvious malice. Behind him the landlord showed a round white face of fear.

'Well, perhaps not quite an accident,' Mr Melville amended.

The colonel had gone forward, and was stooping over the body. In that stooping attitude he looked round to jeer again: 'Oh, not quite an accident?' He stood up, and turned. 'Seems to me that this is a police affair; that a man has been murdered. Supposing you tell me the truth about the matter.'

'Why else do you suppose I sent for you? But don't raise your voice to me. I don't like it. I met this man here tonight by chance. I distrusted his looks and his manner. For one thing, he was English; and God knows no Frenchman today has cause to think well of any member of that perfidious race. An Englishman in Turin, or anywhere in Italy, may be an object of suspicion to any but a fool. Foolishly I announced the intention of sending for you that he might render a proper account of himself before you. At that he drew a pistol on me. It is there on the floor. I struck him. He fell, and by the mercy of Providence broke his head on that fire-iron, on which, if you look, you will find blood. That is all that I can tell you. And now you know precisely what occurred.'

'Oh, I do, do I? Oh, I do?' The commandant was laboriously ironical. 'And who is to confirm this pretty little tale of yours?'

'If you were not a fool you would see the evidence for yourself. The blood on the fire-iron; the nature of the wound; the position in which he is lying. He had not been moved since he fell. He will have papers that should speak to his identity as an Englishman, named Marcus Melville. I know that he has, because he showed them to me under my insistence. You will find them in his pocket. You had better have a look at them. And at the same time, it may save words if you have a look at mine.' And he proffered the linen-backed sheet.

It checked an outburst from the empurpling colonel. He snatched the passport, and then his manner changed as he read those formidable terms, which might be said to place the entire resources of the State at the bearer's service. His eyes grew round. The high colour receded from his cheeks.

'Bu…but, citizen-representative, why…why did you not tell me sooner?'

'You did not ask. You take so much for granted. You seem so ignorant of the proper forms. Do you know, Colonel Lescure, that you do not impress me very favourably? I shall have occasion to mention it to General Bonaparte.'

The colonel stood dismayed.

'But name of a name! Not knowing who you were… In dealing with a stranger…naturally… I… '

'Silence! You deafen me.' Mr Melville recovered the passport from the soldier's nerveless fingers. He stood up. 'You have wasted enough of my time already. I have not forgotten that I was kept waiting half-an-hour for your arrival.'

'I did not realize the urgency.' The colonel was perspiring.

'It was stated in my note to you. I even said that the matter was one of national importance. That to a zealous officer should have been enough. More than enough.' He began to replace his documents in the dispatch-case. His cold, hard, inflexible voice went on: 'You are now in possession of the facts of what happened here. The urgency of my business does not permit me to be detained for the convenience of the local authorities and their inquiries into this man's death. I am already overdue at General Headquarters in Milan. I leave this matter in your hands.'

'Of course. Of course, citizen-representative. Why, indeed, should you be troubled further in the affair?'

'Why, indeed?' Ever stern and uncompromising he locked the dispatch-case and turned to the awed landlord. 'Is the chaise ready?'

'It has been waiting this half-hour, sir.'

'Lead the way then, if you please. Good night, citizen-colonel.'

But on the threshold the commandant stayed him. 'Citizen-representative! You – you will not be too harsh with an honest

soldier, who was seeking to do his duty in the dark. If now...
General Bonaparte... '

Eyes light and hard as agates flashed upon him sternly. Then a
chill, tolerant smile broke faintly on the features of the citizen-
representative. He shrugged.

'So that I hear no more of this affair, you shall hear no more of it,'
he said, and with a nod went out.

Chapter 3

The Dispatch-Case

The real name of this escaping gentleman who rolled out of Turin that night, in a jolting chaise, was Marc-Antoine Villiers de Melleville.

In manner and air he was as French as his real name when he spoke French, but as English as that name's present anglicized form when he spoke English. And he was not merely bi-lingual. He was bi-national, lord of considerable estates both in England and in France.

He derived his English possessions of Avonford, from his grandmother, the Lady Constantia Villiers, who had been so bright an ornament of the court of Queen Anne. She had married the brilliant Grégoire de Melleville, Vicomte de Saulx, who at the time was French Ambassador at the Court of Saint James's. Their eldest son, Gaston de Melleville, had further diluted the French blood of his house by an English marriage. Himself as much English as French, he had divided his time between the paternal estates at Saulx and the maternal inheritance at Avonford, and it was actually at Avonford that Marc-Antoine had been born, one degree more English than his half-English father before him. When the troubles grew menacing in France, Gaston de Melleville's definite departure for England can hardly be regarded in the light of an emigration.

He placed his affairs in the hands of his steward, Camille Lebel, a young lawyer educated at the Vicomte's own charges, and putting his trust in this man whom he had raised from the soil to the robe, he confidently left him to steer the fortunes of the estates of Saulx through the dangerous political waters of the time.

Upon his father's death, unintimidated by the condition of things in France, and actually encouraged by his English mother, a woman who placed duty above every consideration, Marc-Antoine crossed the Channel to go and set affairs in order at Saulx.

His estates, like those of all emigrated noblemen, had been confiscated by the State, and had been sold for the benefit of the nation. They had, however, been purchased for a bagatelle by Camille Lebel with Melleville money which had come into his hands as the intendant of the estate. No doubt crossed Marc-Antoine's mind even when he found Lebel of such republican consequence in Touraine that he was actually president of the Revolutionary Tribunal of Tours. He assumed that this was a mask donned by that loyal steward the better to discharge his stewardship. Disillusion did not come until, denounced and arrested, it was actually by Lebel that he was sentenced to death. Then he understood.

One great advantage Marc-Antoine possessed over other unfortunate nobles in his desperate case. Wealth was still his, and wealth that was safe in England and could there be drawn upon. This weapon he was shrewd enough to wield. He had perceived how corruptible were these starvelings of the new régime, and to what lengths corruption could go. He sent for the advocate he had employed, but whom Lebel had silenced, and what he said to him induced the lawyer to bring the public prosecutor into the business. Lebel, his work done, had left Tours for Saulx, and this rendered possible the thing that Marc-Antoine proposed. Against his solemn pledge and his note of hand for some thousands of pounds in gold redeemable in London, his name was inserted in a list of persons executed, and he was spirited out of prison and supplied with a passport that bore him safely back across the Channel.

Until their chance meeting that night at the White Cross Inn in Turin, Lebel had remained in the persuasion that no hereditary proprietor of the Saulx estates survived ever to rise up and claim them even should the monarchy be restored. How far that meeting, instead of the catastrophe he had accounted it, was actually destined to further Marc-Antoine's present aims, he was not to realize until he came to a closer scrutiny of Lebel's papers.

This happened at Crescentino. He reached it towards midnight, and since, according to the postilion, his horses had also reached the limit of endurance, he was constrained to put up at the indifferent house that was kept by the postmaster. There, late though the hour and weary though he was, he sat down to investigate, by the light of a couple of tallow candles, the contents of Lebel's dispatch-case. It was then discovered to him that Lebel had not been crossing merely the path of his travels when they met, but also the very purpose of his mission to Venice.

On his escape from France in '93, Marc-Antoine bore with him the fruits of shrewd observations, as a result of which he was able to convey to King George's watchful government a deal of first-hand information. The authority which he derived from his social position, the lucidity of the expositions which he was in a position to make, and the shrewdness of his inferences from the facts, caught the attention of Mr Pitt. The minister sent for him, not only then, but on subsequent occasions when news more than ordinarily startling from across the Channel rendered desirable the opinions of one as well-informed upon French matters as Marc-Antoine.

From all this it had resulted that when, in the spring of this year 1796, the Vicomte had announced that his own affairs were taking him to Venice, Mr Pitt displayed his trust in him by inviting him to assume a mission of considerable gravity on behalf of the British Government.

The successes of Bonaparte's Italian campaign had appeared all the more dismaying to Mr Pitt because so utterly unexpected. Who with the facts before him could have imagined that a mere boy without experience of leadership, followed by a ragged, starveling horde, inadequate in numbers and without proper equipment, could successfully have opposed the coalition of the Piedmontese with the seasoned army of the Empire under the command of veterans in generalship? It was as alarming as it seemed fantastic. If the young Corsican were to continue as he had begun, the result might well be the rescue of the French Republic from the bankruptcy on the brink of which Mr Pitt perceived it with satisfaction to be reeling. Not only was the exhausted French treasury being replenished by these victories, but the ebbing confidence of the nation in its rulers was being renewed, and the fainting will to maintain the struggle was being revived.

A republican movement which was almost in the nature of a religion was being given a new lease of life, and it was a movement that constituted a deadly peril to all Europe and to all those institutions which European civilization accounted sacred and essential to its welfare.

From the outset William Pitt had laboured to form a coalition of European states which should present a solid, impregnable front to the assaults of the anarch. The withdrawal of Spain from this alliance had been his first grave setback. But the rapid victories of the Army of Italy under Bonaparte, resulting in the armistice of Cherasco, had changed mere disappointment into liveliest alarm. It was idle to continue to suppose that the successes of the young Corsican, who, as a result of a piece of jobbery on the part of Barras, had been placed in command of the Army of Italy, were due only to the favour of fortune. A formidable military genius had arisen, and if Europe were to be saved from the deadly pestilence of Jacobinism, it became necessary to throw every ounce of available strength into the scales against him.

The unarmed neutrality declared by the Republic of Venice could be tolerated no longer. It was not enough that Austria might be prepared to raise and launch fresh armies more formidable than that which Bonaparte had defeated. Venice, however fallen from her erstwhile power and glory, was still capable of putting an army of sixty thousand men into the field; and Venice must be persuaded to rouse herself from her neutrality. Hitherto the Most Serene Republic had met all representations that she should definitely take her stand against the invaders of Italy with the assumption that the forces already ranged against the French were more than sufficient to repel them. Now that the facts proved the error of this assumption, she must be brought to perceive the danger to herself in further temporizing, and out of a spirit of self-preservation, if from no loftier motive, unite with those who stood in arms against the common peril.

This was to be the Vicomte de Saulx's mission. The very laws of Venice, which forbade all private intercourse between an accredited ambassador and the Doge or any member of the Senate, called for something of the kind.

Virtually, then, the Vicomte de Saulx travelled as a secret envoy-extraordinary, charged with a method of advocacy paradoxically impossible to the avowed British Ambassador by virtue of his very office. And since he had set out, the need for this advocacy had been rendered increasingly urgent by Bonaparte's crushing defeat of the Imperial forces at Lodi.

Now Lebel, it appeared from the papers which Marc-Antoine perused with ever-increasing interest and attention, had the same ultimate destination, and went in much the same capacity to represent the French interest.

The elaborate, intimate notes of instruction in Barras' hand confirmed that complete confidence in Lebel which the powers bestowed upon him already announced.

Lebel's first errand was to Bonaparte, from whom he was enjoined to stand no nonsense. He might find – and there were already signs of it – that the general's successes had gone to his head. Should Bonaparte display any troublesome arrogance, let Lebel remind him that the hand that had raised him starving from the gutter could as easily restore him to it.

There were minute instructions for the future conduct of the Italian campaign, but in no particular were they so minute as in what concerned Venice. Venice, Barras pointed out, was dangerously poised, not merely between armed and unarmed neutrality, but between neutrality and hostility. Pressure was being brought to bear upon her. There were signs that Pitt, that monster of perfidy and hypocrisy, was active in the matter. A blunder now might fling Venice into the arms of Austria with sorry consequences for the Army of Italy.

What exactly this would mean was made clear by a minute schedule of the forces by land and sea within Venetian control.

It must be Lebel's task to insist with Bonaparte, and to see that he complied with the insistence, that Venice should be lulled by protestations of friendship until the time to deal with her should arrive, which would be when the Austrian strength was so shattered that alliance with Venice could no longer avail either of them.

The instructions continued. From Bonaparte's headquarters at Milan, Lebel was to proceed to Venice, and there his first task should be thoroughly to organize the revolutionary propaganda.

'In short,' Barras concluded this voluminous note, 'you will so dispose that Venice may be strangled in her sleep. It is your mission first to see that she is lulled into slumber, and then to ensure that those slumbers are not prematurely disturbed.'

An open letter from Barras to the Ambassador Lallemant, presenting the bearer and asserting in unequivocal terms the powers that were vested in him by the Directory, made it clear that Lallemant and Lebel were not personally acquainted. This fact came to nourish and fertilize the notion that was already taking root in Marc-Antoine's mind.

His tallow candles were guttering and flickering at the point of exhaustion and day was breaking before Marc-Antoine with a hectic flush on his prominent cheek-bones and a feverish glitter of excitement in his eyes flung himself, half-dressed as he was, upon his bed. And then it was not to sleep, but to survey the prospect spread before him by all that he had read.

Chapter 4

The Ambassador of France

Marc-Antoine first beheld that loveliest and strangest of the cities of the world in all the golden glory of a May morning. He came by boat from Mestre, where he had lain the night, and from afar as they approached the Canareggio it seemed to him that there floated before his gaze not indeed a city, but some vast fantastic jewel, compounded of marble and gold, of coral, porphyry and ivory, set in a vaster jewel of sapphire lagoon and sky. His black gondola swung from the Canareggio into the Grand Canal and glided between splendours of palaces blending the arts of East and West in a voluptuous beauty startling to his Northern eyes. He leaned forward under the canopy to feast his wonder on the Romanesque marvel of the Ca' d' Oro and the great arch of the Rialto Bridge with its burden of shops all glitter and movement of colour and of life.

The gondola gliding like a black swan through the water-traffic, threaded its way across the canal, past the Erberia, where all was noise and bustle of men and women about the piled stalls of fruit and flowers and about an unloading barge. It slipped into the quieter, narrow waters of the Rio delle Beccherie, to bring up at last at the water-lapped steps of the Osteria delle Spade, the Inn of the Swords, as the crossed blades of its sign announced.

Marc-Antoine landed and consigned his person and luggage into the care of the rubicund little landlord Battista, who welcomed him volubly in the Venetian dialect, which to Marc-Antoine sounded like a mixture of bad French and bad Italian.

He was lodged on the piano nobile in an ample salon, sparsely furnished and cool with a stone floor and clumsily frescoed ceiling where cupids of unparalleled obesity rioted in an incredibly gaudy vegetable kingdom. A bedroom with a vast canopied bed, and a powder-cupboard adjoining, completed his lodging.

He installed himself, unpacked, and sent for a hairdresser.

He had travelled straight from Turin, and he had accomplished the journey in two days. In this he had been extremely fortunate, for the movements of the battered Austrian troops about the country east of the Mincio might easily have hindered and delayed him. As it was he had missed them, although the ugly signs of their passage were not wanting. He had reached Mestre unchallenged, and now in the ease and peace and dignity of Venice it seemed difficult to believe that the hideous stress of war could be anywhere within a thousand miles of them. Gay laughter-laden voices floated up to his windows from the canal below, and more than once whilst his hair was being dressed there came, to the accompaniment of the swish of oars and the gurgle of water under an iron-headed prow, snatches of song as if to stress how carefree were the people of the Lagoons.

The assumption, upon which he had decided, of the role of the dead Lebel, imposed upon him the necessity of journeying at once to Milan where Bonaparte had made his triumphal entry and had just established his headquarters. But he had shirked a course that was fraught with so much risk, and had contented himself with writing to the French commander. Thus he created with Barras the impression of having represented the wishes of the Directory to Bonaparte, and he could leave Barras to suppose that this had been done orally.

It would be some three hours after his arrival, when having made a careful toilet and with his glossy black hair carefully dressed and tied, but free from powder, he went below, and called for a gondola to carry him to the French Legation.

Reclining in the shade of the felza he was borne westwards up the Grand Canal, where with the approach of noon the water-traffic was becoming brisk, and then, by a network of lesser channels that lay in shadow between tall dark palaces, to the Fondamenta of the Madonna dell' Orto in the north. Alighting on the quay, he came by a narrow alley into the Corte del Cavallo, a little square scarcely larger than a courtyard. On the corner stood the residence of the ambassador of France, the Palazzo della Vecchia, a roomy but comparatively modest house for a city of such splendours.

The Citizen-Ambassador Lallemant was at work in the spacious room on the first floor which he made his office. He was interrupted by Jacob, the middle-aged, rustily clad, alert Semitic secretary, who could never forget that during the interregnum three years ago he had been for a season chargé d'affaires.

Jacob brought the ambassador a folded note, which he said had been given to him by the door-keeper Philippe.

Lallemant looked up from his papers. He was a man in middle life of a comfortable habit of body and a full, kindly, rather pallid face that like a pear was wider at the base than at the summit. The lethargy of his double chin was belied by the keen shrewdness of full dark eyes, set prominently on his face.

He unfolded the note and read: 'Camille Lebel, representative on mission, requests audience.'

He frowned in silence for a moment. Then he shrugged. 'Bring this man in.'

In the representative when he was introduced Lallemant beheld a man above the middle height, prepossessing of countenance, slimly built but with a good width of shoulder, elegantly dressed in a long black coat above spotless buckskins and boots with reversed tops. He wore a very full white neckcloth, carried a tricorne hat tucked under his arm, and bore himself with an air of consequence and authority.

The ambassador scrutinized him searchingly as he rose to greet him.

'You are welcome, Citizen Lebel. We have been looking for your arrival since the last letters from the Citizen-Director Barras.'

The newcomer frowned. 'We?' he echoed. 'Do you say "we"? May one know whom you include in that pronoun?'

Lallemant was taken aback by the hard tone and the cold, hard glance of those light eyes in which he read displeasure and reproof. Resentment was to succeed his momentary confusion. But it was in this confusion that he answered.

'The pronoun? Oh! I but use it officially. A form of speech. So far no one shares with me the secret either that you were expected or that you have arrived.'

'You had better see that no one does,' was the dry injunction. 'I do not propose to be found one morning floating in one of these picturesque canals with a stiletto in my back.'

'I am sure you have no cause to be afraid of that.'

'I am not afraid of anything, citizen-ambassador. It is simply that the thing is not among my intentions.' He looked round for a chair, found one, thrust it nearer to the ambassador's writing-table, and sat down. 'Don't let me keep you standing,' he said, tone and manner plainly conveying that he accounted himself the master here. 'If you will look at this you will learn our exact relationship.'

He placed Barras' letter on the table before the ambassador.

That letter made abundantly clear the formidable authority with which Lebel was vested by the Directory. But it did not suffice to conquer the annoyance aroused in Lallemant by his visitor's hectoring manner.

'To be frank, citizen, I do not quite perceive what you are come to do that I could not have done. If you...'

He was interrupted by the abrupt opening of the door. A florid young man bounded impetuously into the room, speaking as he came.

'Citizen-ambassador, I am wondering whether you would like me to...' He broke off, perceiving the stranger, and presented every appearance of confusion. 'Oh, but my apologies! I thought you were alone. I... If... Perhaps... Oh, I will return later.'

Nevertheless, he did not depart. He remained swaying there, undecided, and all the while his eyes were very busy upon the visitor.

'Since you are here, what is it that you want, Domenico?'

'I should never have intruded if I had dreamed… '

'Yes, yes. You've said so. What do you want?'

'I was wondering whether you would allow me to take Jean with me as far as San Zuane. I am going to the… '

Lallemant cut him short. 'Of course you may take him. There was no need to break in on me for that.'

'Ah, but then you see, Madame Lallemant herself is not at home, and… '

'Oh, yes, yes. I've said that you may take him. To the devil with your explanations. You see that I am engaged. Be off.'

Mumbling excuses the young man backed away; and all the time his eyes continued to play over the visitor, from his fine boots to his sedulously dressed head.

When at last the door had closed upon him, Lallemant's lips were compressed into a little scornful smile. He glanced over his shoulder at an open doorway and a small room beyond.

'Before that interruption I was about to trouble you to accompany me in there. You were a little hasty in accommodating yourself, my friend.' He moved from the table, and waved a hand in the direction of that doorway, a tinge of sarcasm in his manner. 'If you please.'

Mystified, the visitor complied.

Lallemant left the communicating door open, so that from the inner room he commanded a view of the larger outer chamber. He advanced a chair, and explained himself.

'In here we shall be safe from eavesdroppers. It was not my intention that anything of importance should be said out there. That pleasant young man, so innocently concerned to take my son for a walk, is a spy placed in my house by the Council of Ten. By tonight the circumstance of your visit and a description of you will be in the hands of the inquisitors of state.'

'And you tolerate his presence? You leave him free of your house?'

'He has his uses. He runs messages for me. He helps to entertain my son. He makes himself pleasant to my wife, and frequently acts as an escort for her when she goes abroad. Also, since I am aware of his real trade, I take him into my confidence now and then, and disclose to him as political secrets just those matters which it suits me that the inquisitors of state should believe.'

'I see,' said Marc-Antoine, readjusting his ideas concerning this phlegmatic-looking ambassador. 'I see.'

'I thought you would. Believe me, he learns nothing here that can profit his employers.' Lallemant sat down. 'And now, citizen-representative, I am at your service.'

The false Lebel proceeded to disclose his mission. He began by congratulating himself and all Frenchmen upon the glorious victories which were attending French valour and French arms in Italy; victories which in themselves simplified the task upon which he came. However, the end was not yet reached. Austria disposed of vast resources, and none could doubt but that she would employ them freely and endeavour to re-establish herself in Lombardy. The odds against France were heavy enough already, and it was his business to see that they were rendered no heavier. Venice must at all costs be held strictly to her unarmed neutrality.

'Unless, of course,' Lallemant interrupted him, 'she could be brought into alliance with us against the Empire.'

The cold eyes stared at him. 'That is unthinkable.'

'Not to General Bonaparte.'

'General Bonaparte? What has General Bonaparte to do with it?'

Lallemant's thin smile made its reappearance. 'Only this: he has sent me just such a proposal to place before the College.'

The representative became haughty. 'And since when have such matters concerned the military? I was under the impression that General Bonaparte was in command of the forces in the field. Let me ask you, citizen-ambassador, how you propose to deal with his proposal?'

'Why, to be frank, it seems eminently reconcilable with our interests.'

'I see.' The representative got to his feet. His tone was bitter. 'And so, you, Citizen Lallemant, the accredited representative here of the French Government, are proposing to take your orders from the General in the field! Really, sir, it seems that I arrive no more than in time.'

Lallemant made no attempt to vent his irritation. 'I don't see why I should not act upon orders which I judge to accord with the best interests of France.'

'I say again that I arrive no more than in time. An alliance, sir, sets up obligations, which are not in honour or even in decency afterwards to be evaded. France has very definite views on the subject of Venice. Venice is to be delivered from her oligarchic government. It is our sacred mission to carry the torch of liberty and of reason into her territories. Are we to enter into an alliance with a government which it is our object to destroy? It is our business – the precise business on which I am here – to see that Venice is kept rigidly to her unarmed neutrality until it is time to strike this oligarchy into the dust. Understand that clearly, citizen-ambassador.'

Lallemant looked up at him without affection. Then he shrugged with a plain and careless display of ill-humour.

'Since the Directory has sent you here to meddle, my responsibility is at an end. But will you tell me what I am to say to General Bonaparte?'

'Say to him that you have referred the matter to me. I will deal with him.'

'You will deal with him! Ha! I wonder do you know what manner of man he is.'

'I know what manner of position he holds. If he is in danger of getting above it, I shall know how to repress him.'

'One sees that you are of a sanguine temperament. The man who with the ragged army under his command could win the battles he has won in the last two months, against well-disciplined, well-equipped forces twice as numerous as his own, is not easily repressed.'

The representative was supercilious. 'I have no wish to detract from the merit of which he has given proof as a soldier. But we will preserve, if you please, a sense of proportion where this young man is concerned.'

Lallemant smiled broadly. 'Shall I tell you something about him? Something that I had from Berthier himself. When this little Corsican went to Nice to take up the command which Barras had procured for him, the generals of division of the Army of Italy were enraged that a boy of twenty-seven should be placed over them; a parvenu as they called him; a general off the streets; the man contemptuously known in Paris as the mitrailleur, since the only action known to his credit was to have swept away a mob with grapeshot. It was even said of him – I am merely repeating the words of others – that he was given his command as the price of having made an honest woman of one of Barras' mistresses. Those generals prepared to give him a reception that should make him think twice about remaining with the Army of Italy. Augereau, masterful and violent, was loudest in how he would put the upstart down. Bonaparte arrived. You know what he looks like. A starveling wisp of a fellow, frail and pallid as a consumptive. He walked in amongst them, and whilst buckling on his belt issued his orders, curt and sharply, without a wasted word. Then he walked out again, leaving them speechless, stunned by a force within him which they could not define, but in the presence of which not one of them had retained the courage to make good his boast.

'That is Bonaparte. Since then he has won a dozen battles, and smashed the Austrian might at Lodi. Conceive if he will have become easier to deal with. If you can dominate him, citizen, there should be a great future for you.'

But the representative remained unimpressed. 'It is not I who will dominate him. It is the authority of which I am the mouthpiece. And, anyway, as to these proposals of his, you will understand that the matter is now in my hands, and need concern you no further.'

'Oh, but gladly, citizen-representative. It is a responsibility of which I am very ready to be relieved.'

There was sarcasm in his tone, and it was met by sarcasm in the reply.

'So that you perceive at last a purpose in my presence here in Venice.' He sat down again, crossed his legs, and, descending a little from his loftiness of manner, came to matters which Lallemant found even more startling than anything that had gone before.

He announced that in the furtherance of the purpose responsible for his presence, and so as to study Venetian intentions at first hand, he proposed to go into the enemy's camp, representing himself as a secret agent of the British. He asserted that it was a part he was well-equipped to play before any audience, even at need an English one.

Nevertheless, Lallemant's amazement was only partly allayed.

'Do you know what will happen if they unmask you?'

'I count upon so disposing that there will be no unmasking.'

'Name of God! You must be a very brave man.'

'I may or may not be brave. I am certainly intelligent. At the outset I shall inform them that I am in relations with you...'

'What?'

'That I have imposed myself upon you by pretending to be a French agent. I shall establish my good faith by dealing with them precisely as you deal with this spy of theirs who has been installed in your house. I shall give them some scraps of information about the French, which, whilst worthless and perhaps even quite false, shall have all the appearance of being valuable and true.'

'And you imagine that this will impose upon them?' Lallemant was scornful.

'But why not? Surely it is no new thing for a secret agent to appear to be working on both sides. In fact, no secret agent ever succeeded either in serving his side or keeping his life who did not take the pay of both parties. A government so experienced in espionage will recognize this without explanations. I incur one serious danger. At a whisper that I am Camille Lebel, a secret agent of the Directory, and the stiletto and the canal to which I have alluded will probably close a career of some distinction and great utility to France.' He paused there, to cast a glance through the open door at the empty room beyond. Then he added with peculiar emphasis: 'It follows, therefore, that the secret of my identity, which lies at present between you and me, Lallemant, is not to be shared with any other single soul. You understand? Not even your wife is to suspect that I am Lebel.'

Lallemant again betrayed that suspicion of strained patience. 'Oh, very well. As you please.'

'I mean it to be as I please. We touch upon a matter of life and death. My life and my death, pray observe. They are matters about which you will admit my pre-eminent right to dispose.'

'My dear Citizen Lebel…'

'Forget that name.' The representative rose, suddenly dramatic. 'It is not to be used again. Not even in private. If we are really private in a house in which spies of the Council of Ten are at large. Here in Venice I am Mr Melville, a flaneur, an English idler. Mr Melville. Is that clear?'

'Certainly, Mr Melville. But if you should get into difficulties…'

'If I get into difficulties I shall be beyond any man's assistance. So see that you create none for me by any indiscretion.' His clear eyes were sternly upon the ambassador, who, utterly browbeaten, inclined his large head in submission, 'That, I think, is all at the moment.'

Lallemant was instantly on his feet. 'You'll stay to dine. We shall be alone: just Madame Lallemant and my boy and my secretary Jacob.'

Mr Melville shook his impeccably dressed head. 'I thank you for the courtesy. But I could not wish to embarrass you. Some other day, perhaps.'

Not even the anxiety to conciliate could lend reality to Lallemant's air of disappointment. His expressions of regret rang so hollow that they almost betrayed his satisfaction in being rid of this overbearing fellow.

Mr Melville delayed yet a moment to inquire into the progress being made by the French agents charged with Jacobin proselytizing.

'I have nothing,' he was answered, 'to add to my last report to the Citizen Barras. We are well served, especially by the Vicomtesse. She is very diligent, and constantly widening the sphere of her activities. Her latest conquest is that barnabotto patrician Vendramin.'

'Ah!' Mr Melville was languid. 'He is important, is he?'

The ambassador looked at him in astonishment. 'Do you ask me that?'

Instantly conscious of having taken a false step, Mr Melville carried it off without a flicker of hesitation.

'Well – do you know? – I sometimes doubt his consequence.'

'After what I have written about him?'

'It is only the Pope who is infallible.'

'It does not need the Pope to know the extent of Vendramin's influence. And the Vicomtesse has all but made him fast. It is only a question of time.' He laughed cynically. 'The Citizen Barras has a great gift of disposing of his discarded mistresses to the nation's profit as well as to his own.'

'I'll not stay to hear scandal.' Mr Melville took up his hat from the table. 'You shall know what progress I make. Meanwhile, if you want me, I am lodged for the moment at the Inn of the Swords.'

On that he took his leave, and went his ways, wondering who might be the Vicomtesse, and who this Vendramin who was a barnabotto.

Chapter 5

The Ambassador of Britain

If the manners of Mr Melville had ruffled the feelings of the ambassador of the French Republic, One and Indivisible, they were almost as severely to ruffle those of the ambassador of His Britannic Majesty, upon whom he waited that same afternoon. There was, however, a difference. Whilst the overbearing tone assumed with Lallemant had been purely histrionic, convincingly to colour the role assumed, that which he employed with Sir Richard Worthington was a genuine expression of his feelings.

Sir Richard, a stocky, sandy, pompous man, hung out those inevitable banners of a poor intellect: self-sufficiency and suspicion. Prone to assume the worst, he was of those who build suspicions into convictions without analyzing their own mental processes. It is a common enough type, readily identified; and within five minutes of being in the ambassador's presence Mr Melville was aware in dismay that he conformed with it.

He presented to the ambassador a letter from Mr Pitt which had travelled with him from England in the lining of his boot.

Seated at his writing-table, Sir Richard left his visitor standing, whilst with the aid of a glass he slowly perused the letter.

He looked up at last and his greenish eyes narrowed in scrutiny of the slim straight figure before him.

'You are the person designated here?' he asked in a high-pitched voice that went well with his receding chin and sloping brow.

'That would seem to follow, would it not?'

Sir Richard opened his eyes a little wider at the tone.

'I did not ask you what would seem to follow. I like direct answers. However... Mr Pitt says here that you will state your business.'

'And he requests you, I think, to afford me every assistance in the discharge of it.'

Sir Richard opened his greenish eyes to their utmost. He set the letter down, and sat back in his tall chair. There was an edge to his thin tone. 'What is this business, sir?'

Mr Melville stated it briefly and calmly. Sir Richard raised his sandy brows. A flush was creeping up to his cheek-bones.

'His Majesty is already quite adequately represented here. I fail to perceive the necessity for such a mission.'

It was Mr Melville's turn to be annoyed. The man was a pompous idiot. 'That observation is not for me; but for Mr Pitt. At the same time you may tell him of something else that you fail to perceive.'

'If you please?'

'Something that suggested to him that he should supplement you. Representations of the kind that expediency now suggests should be made to the rulers of the Most Serene Republic, to be effective are not to be made in public.'

'Naturally.' The ambassador was sharp and frosty. 'You will not have travelled all the way from England to state the obvious.'

'It seems that I have. Since the laws of Venice rigidly forbid all private intercourse between any member of the government and the ambassador of a foreign power, you are debarred by your office from steps possible only to an individual visiting Venice in an ostensibly private capacity.'

Sir Richard made a gesture of impatience. 'My dear sir, there are ways of doing these things.'

'If there are, they are ways that do not commend themselves to Mr Pitt.'

Mr Melville accounted that he had been standing long enough. He pulled up a chair, and sat down facing the ambassador across his Louis XV writing-table, which was of a piece with the handsome furnishings, the gildings and brocades of that lofty room.

Sir Richard glared, but kept to the subject.

'Yet those ways are so manifest, that I fail, as I have said – utterly fail – to perceive the necessity for the intervention of a…a secret agent.' His tone was contemptuous. 'That I suppose is how you are to be described.'

'Unless you would prefer to call me a spy,' said Mr Melville humbly.

Suspecting sarcasm, Sir Richard ignored the interpolation. 'I fail to see what good can come of it. In fact, at this juncture, I can conceive that harm might follow; great harm; incalculable harm.'

'Considering what has happened at Lodi, I should have thought that the representations I am charged to make have become of a singular urgency.'

'I do not admit, sir, your qualifications to judge. I do not admit them at all. You must allow me to know better, sir.' His ruffled vanity was stiffening him in obstinacy. 'The importance of what happened at Lodi may easily be exaggerated by the uninformed; by those who do not know, as I know, the resources of the Empire. I have sure information that within three months Austria will have a hundred thousand men in Italy. That should abundantly suffice to sweep this French rabble out of the country. There is the answer for timid alarmists who take fright at these lucky successes of the French.'

Mr Melville lost patience. 'And if in the meanwhile Venice should be drawn into alliance with France?'

Sir Richard laughed unpleasantly. 'That, sir, is fantastic, unimaginable.'

'Even if France should tempt the Serenissima with offers of alliance?'

'That, too, is unimaginable.'

'You are sure of that?'

'As sure as that I sit here, sir.'

Mr Melville fetched a sigh of weariness, produced his snuffbox and proceeded to shatter that complacency.

'You relieve me. I desired to test your opinions by that question. I find, as I supposed, that I cannot trust myself to be guided by them.'

'By God, sir! You are impudent.'

Mr Melville snapped his snuffbox. With a pinch of snuff held between thumb and forefinger, he tapped the writing-table with his second finger. 'The proposals of alliance which you so complacently assert to be unimaginable have already been put forward.'

The ambassador's countenance momentarily reflected his dismayed astonishment. 'But... But... How could you possibly know that?'

'You may accept my assurance that the French Ambassador here has received instructions from Bonaparte to propose an alliance to the Serenissima.'

Sir Richard announced his recovery by a fleering laugh.

'Only an utter ignorance of procedure could permit you so easily to be deceived. My good sir, it is not for Bonaparte to make such proposals. He has no such powers. These are matters for governments, not for soldiers.'

'I am as aware as you are, Sir Richard, of the irregularity. But it does not affect the fact. That Bonaparte has done this I know; and the presumption is that he has grounds for believing that his government will support him. Generals who achieve what Bonaparte has achieved do not want for influence with their governments.'

Before Mr Melville's impressiveness, Sir Richard was driven from irony to sullenness.

'You say that you know positively. But how can you know?'

Mr Melville took time to answer him.

'Just now, Sir Richard, you described me as a secret agent. You need not have boggled at the word "spy". It would not have offended me. I am a spy in a cause that dignifies the calling; and it happens that I am a good spy.'

Sir Richard's expression suggested the presence of an offensive smell. But he said nothing. Mr Melville's revelation left him with a sense of defeat. Still, obstinately, like a stupid man, he struggled against reason.

'Even if all this were so, I still fail to perceive what you can hope to accomplish.'

'Are we not wasting time? Does it really matter that you should perceive it? You have Mr Pitt's orders, as I have. It only remains that acting upon yours, you should enable me to act upon mine.'

The mildness of the tone employed could not rob the rebuke of its asperity. Sir Richard, deeply affronted, coloured from chin to brow.

'By God, sir, I find you singularly bold.'

Mr Melville smiled into the fierce greenish eyes. 'I should not otherwise be here, sir.'

For a long moment the scowling ambassador considered. Irritably, at last, he spoke, tapping the letter before him.

'I am asked here to lend you support and assistance. I am asked to do this in a letter brought to me by a man whom I do not know. There is the question of your identity. You will have papers; a passport, and the like.'

'I have not, Sir Richard.' He did not attempt to explain how this happened. There was only his word for it, and this man would certainly affront him by refusing to accept it. 'That letter should be my sufficient passport. Mr Pitt, you observe, has taken the precaution of adding a description of me at the foot. However, if that does not suffice, I can produce persons of eminence, integrity, and repute in Venice who are personally acquainted with me.'

Mr Melville read in his glance the man's mean satisfaction at being at last able to gratify the rancour aroused in him by the appointment of this envoy-extraordinary and nourished by the defeat he had suffered in argument.

'Until you produce them, sir, and until I am satisfied that they are as you describe them, you will not wonder that I decline to act as your sponsor.' He touched a bell on the table as he spoke. 'That, I am sure, is what Mr Pitt would expect and desire of me. I must be very sure of my ground, sir, before I can take the responsibility of answering for you to His Serenity the Doge.'

The door was opened by the usher. There was no invitation to dinner from the British Ambassador.

'I have the honour, sir, to wish you a very good day.'

If Mr Melville departed in any perturbation, it was only to see England represented in Venice at such a time by such a man. When he came to contrast the shrewd smoothness of Lallemant – one who had won to his position by the proofs of ability he had afforded – with the stiff-necked stupidity of Sir Richard Worthington – who no doubt owed his appointment to birth and influence – he began to ask himself whether, after all, there might not be grounds for the republican doctrines which had found application in France and which everywhere in Europe were now in the air; whether the caste to which he belonged was not indeed already an effete anachronism, to be shovelled by men of sense out of the path of civilization and progress.

These misgivings, however, did not sink so far as to imperil the championship of the cause of aristocracy to which he was pledged. After all, he belonged to that caste; the recovery of his estates of Saulx depended upon the restoration of the monarchy in France, and this restoration could not take place until the anarchs were brought to their knees and broken. Personal profit apart, however, the cause was one to which by birth he owed his loyalty, and loyally he would spend himself in its service, right or wrong.

From the austere English lady, his mother, he had inherited a lofty and even troublesome sense of duty, which his education had further ingrained.

An instance of this is afforded by the order in which he handled the matters concerned with his presence in Venice. That affair of his own primarily responsible for the journey – and one which might well have justified impatience – was yet to be approached. His approach of it now may have gathered eagerness because Sir Richard Worthington's cavalier treatment of him rendered it politically as necessary as previously it had been personally desirable.

When, on the death of his father, Marc-Antoine had undertaken at the call of duty to his house and caste that hazardous and all but fatal journey into France, Count Francesco Pizzamano was, and had been for two years, Venetian Minister in London. His son Domenico, an officer in the service of the Most Serene Republic, was an attaché, at the Legation, and between him and Marc-Antoine a friendship had grown which had presently embraced their respective families. Gradually Marc-Antoine's interest in Domenico had become less than his interest in Domenico's sister, the Isotta Pizzamano, whom Romney painted, and whose beauty and grace are extolled in so many memoirs of the day.

The events – first Marc Antoine's excursion into France and then the recall of Count Pizzamano – had interrupted those relations. It was his ardent desire to resume them, now that the way was clear, which had dictated his journey to Venice.

A thousand times in the last month he had in fancy embraced Domenico, gripped the hand of the Count and pressed his lips upon the fingers of the Countess, and more lingeringly upon the fingers of Isotta. Always she was last in that recurring day-dream. But at the same time infinitely more vivid than the others. Always he saw her clearly, tall and slender with a quality of queenliness, of saintliness, in which your true lover's worshipping eyes will ever array his mistress. Yet always in that fond vision she melted from her virginal austerity: the vivid, generous lips in that otherwise nunlike face smiled a welcome that was not only kindly but glad.

This dream he was speeding now to realize, in an anticipation almost shot with apprehension, as all things too eagerly anticipated ever must be.

Chapter 6

Casa Pizzamano

His gondola brought him to the marble steps of the Casa Pizzamano on the Rio di San Daniele, by the Arsenal, as the summer dusk was deepening into night.

He came in a shimmer of black satin with silver lace, a silver-hilted sword worn through the pocket. A jewel glowed in the fine old Valenciennes at his throat, and paste buckles sparkled on his lacquered shoes.

He stepped into a wide hall whose walls were inlaid with marble, where the red-liveried porter was lighting the lamp set in a great gilded lantern that once had crowned the poop of a Venetian galley. By a wide marble staircase he was conducted to an anteroom on the mezzanine, whilst a lackey to whom he gave the name of Mr Melville went in quest of Captain Domenico Pizzamano, for whom the visitor had asked.

Some moments only was he kept waiting, with quickening pulses. Then the door opened, to admit a young man who, in his tall slimness and proud, darkly handsome face, was so reminiscent of his sister that Mr Melville momentarily seemed to see her in him.

The young captain stood at gaze upon the threshold, his expression almost scared, his hand trembling on the cut-glass door knob.

Marc-Antoine advanced briskly, smiling. 'Domenico!'

The lips, so red against the pallor which had slowly overspread the Venetian's face, parted now. But his voice was husky as it ejaculated in French: 'Marc! Is it really you? Marc!'

Marc-Antoine opened wide his arms. 'Here to my heart, Domenico, and assure yourself that it is really I, in bone and blood and sinew.'

Domenico flung forward to embrace him. Thereafter he held him at arm's length, and scanned his face. 'Then you were not guillotined?'

'My neck is witness that I was not.' Nevertheless he became grave. 'But have you believed it all this while?'

'It was the last news we had of you before we left London. For your poor mother, who so bitterly upbraided herself for having sent you, it was the end of the world. We did what we could.'

'Oh, yes. I know how good you all were. It strengthens my love of you. But my letters, then? I wrote twice. Ah, but letters in these days are like shots fired into the dark. We don't know where they'll go. The more reason why I should come to render my accounts in person.'

Domenico was very solemnly considering him. 'That is why you've come? You have journeyed all the way to Venice, to come to us?'

'That is the cause. If I happen to be charged with other matters that is a mere effect.'

The solemnity of the young Venetian's eyes increased. His glance searched almost uneasily the flushed and smiling face of his friend. He faltered a little in answering. 'You make us very proud.' And he went on to mention the joy to his parents of this visit and the miracle of Marc-Antoine's survival.

'And Isotta? She is well, I trust.'

'Oh, yes. Isotta is well. She, too, will be glad to see you.'

Marc-Antoine detected a vague embarrassment. Did the rogue suspect what particular member of the House of Pizzamano had drawn him across Europe? His smile broadened at the thought, and he was very gay and exalted in mood when he came to the salon where the family was assembled.

It was a vast room that ran the entire depth of the palace, from the Gothic windows of the balcony above the Canal of San Daniele to the fluted pillars of the loggia overlooking the garden. It was a room made rich by treasures which the Pizzamani had assembled down the ages, for their patrician house went back to a time before the closure of the Grand Council and the establishment of the oligarchy in the fourteenth century.

A Pizzamano had been at the sack of Constantinople, and some of the enduring spoils he had brought home were here displayed. Another had fought at Lepanto, and his portrait painted by Veronese, against a background of red galleys, faced the entrance. There was a portrait by Giovanni Bellini of Caterina Pizzamano who had reigned as a Dogaressa in Bellini's day, and another by Titian of a Pizzamano who had been Governor of Cyprus, and yet another noteworthy one from an unknown brush of that Giacomo Pizzamano who had been created a Count of the Empire two hundred years ago, and so had brought the title to these patricians of a state that bestowed no titles.

The coffered ceiling bore frescoes by Tiepolo in frames that were nobly carved and gilded, the floor was of rich wood mosaics, with here and there a glowing rug that evoked memories of the Serenissima's Levantine traffic.

It was a room which for splendour of art, of wealth, and of historical significance could be found in no country of Europe but Italy, and in no city of Italy but Venice.

Its glories were only vaguely revealed to Marc-Antoine in the soft glow of candlelight from clusters of tapers in great golden branches fantastically chiselled, their bases set with stones of price. They had been the gift of a Pope to a long dead Pizzamano, together with the Golden Rose, and it was believed that Cellini's hands had wrought them.

But it was not to the treasures of the room that Marc-Antoine turned his eager eyes. He sought its inhabitants.

They had been seated in the loggia: the Count, very tall and spare and gaunt with age, a little old-fashioned in his dress, from his red-heeled shoes to his powdered wig, but of an aquiline countenance full of energy and vigour; the Countess, still comparatively young, gracious and noble, and bearing about her something as elusively fine and delicate as the point de Venise of her fichu; and Isotta, her tall, straight slenderness stressed by the sheathing indoor gown, of a material so dark as to seem almost black in the half-light.

It was upon her that his eyes came to rest as he stood to face them where they had risen, startled by Domenico's announcement. She was framed, with the fading turquoise of the evening sky for background, between two slender columns of the loggia, columns of marble which had been weathered to the tone of ivory, and as pale as was now that face which held for Marc-Antoine the sum of all nobility and loveliness. Her very lips seemed pale, and her dark eyes, the normal softness of whose glance tempered the austerity of her features, were dilated as she stared at him.

She had ripened, he observed, in the three years and more that were gone since he had last beheld her in London, on the night before he left for France. But it was a ripening that was no more than the rich fulfilment of the promise of her nineteenth year. It had not then seemed that she could be more desirable; yet more desirable he found her now; a woman to cherish, to worship, to serve; who in return would be a source of inspiration and a fount of honour to a man. For this is what love meant to Marc-Antoine.

So rapt was he in this material contemplation of her whom the eyes of his soul had so steadily contemplated through all the trials and tribulations of the last three years that he scarcely heard the ejaculations, first of amazement, then of joy, with which the Count and Countess greeted him. It needed the hearty embrace of the Count to awaken him, and to send him forward to kiss the trembling hands which the Countess so readily extended.

Then he stood close before Isotta. She gave him her hand; her lips quivered into a smile; her eyes were wistful. He took the hand, and whilst it lay ice-cold in his, there followed a pause. He waited for some word from her. None coming, he bowed his dark glossy head, and kissed her fingers very reverently. At that touch of his lips he felt her tremble and he heard at last her voice, that gentle voice which he had known so melodious and laughter-laden, now strained and hushed.

'You said that you might one day come to Venice, Marc.'

He thrilled with joy at this evidence that she had remembered what were almost his last words. 'I said that I *would* come if I lived. And I am here.'

'Yes. You are here.' Her tone was lifeless. It turned him cold. Still more lifeless, and therefore invested for him with peculiar significance was what she added: 'You have delayed your visit.'

It was, he thought, as if she said to him: 'You have come too late, you fool. Why, then, have you come at all?'

Uneasy, he half-turned, to discover concern and even alarm in the eyes of her parents. Domenico stood aloof, his glance upon the ground, a frown knitting his brows.

Then the Countess spoke, gently, easily, her voice level.

'Do you find Isotta changed? She has aged, of course.' And before he could proclaim the enhancement he discovered in her beauty, the words had been added that made all this constraint clear, resolved his doubts into a conviction of despair. 'She is to be married very soon.'

In the stillness that followed, an observant, anxious stillness, he felt much as he had felt that day three years ago when Camille Lebel, presiding over the Revolutionary Tribunal of Tours, had sentenced him to death. And at once, now as then, his sense of doom was suffused by the recollection that he was Marc-Antoine Villiers de Melleville, Vicomte de Saulx and peer of France, and that he owed it to his birth and blood to hold up his head, to admit no tremor from his lips, no faltering to his glance.

He was bowing to Isotta.

'I felicitate that enviable, that most fortunate of men. It is my prayer that he may prove worthy of so great a blessing as he receives in you, my dear Isotta.'

It was well done, he thought. His manner had been correct; his words well chosen. Why then should she look as if she would weep?

He turned to the Count. 'Isotta has said that I have delayed my coming. Not my inclination, but the events delayed it.'

Shortly he related how he had bribed his way out of prison at Tours; how he had returned thereafter to England, where he was claimed by duty to the cause of the émigrés; how he had been in the disastrous affair of Quiberon, and, later, in that other disaster at Savenay, where he had been wounded; how thereafter he had continued in the Vendée with the army of Charette until its final rout by Hoche a couple of months ago, when he was so fortunate as to escape alive from France for the second time. He had returned to England; and defeat having at last relieved him of all duty, he had turned his mind to the gratification of his personal aspirations, whereupon duties had once more been imposed upon him, but duties fortunately no longer at war with his own dispositions.

He had for the purposes of the service he had undertaken anglicized his name to Melville, and he begged them to remember that to all in Venice he was Mr Melville, an English gentleman of leisure seeing the world.

Mechanically he rehearsed these matters, in a tone that was listless, in a manner that was flat. His mind was elsewhere. He had come too late. Within Isotta's gift lay all that it imported him to have of life, and it had not occurred to him, poor fool, that what he found so divinely desirable would be coveted by others. What was this silly talk he made of a mission, of service to the monarchist cause, of opposition to the forces of anarchy that were loose in the world? What was the world to him, or monarchies or anarchies? What had he to do in all this, since for him the light had gone from the world?

Nevertheless, even if the manner of his narrative had been dull, the matter of it was lively enough in itself. It was an Odyssey that moved his listeners to wonder and sympathy, and deepened the esteem and love in which they already held him.

At the end of the tale the Count got to his feet in the intensity of his feelings on the subject of Marc-Antoine's mission to the Serenissima.

'God prosper you in that,' he cried passionately. 'The effort is needed if we are not to be extinguished and the glory of Venice, already so sadly tarnished, become as if it had never been.'

His long, lean face was flushed.

'You will find your path beset by obstacles: sloth, pusillanimity, avarice, and this canker of Jacobinism which is corroding the foundations of the State. We are impoverished. Our impoverishment has been gradual now for two hundred years, and accelerated of late by incompetent government. Our frontiers, once so wide and far-flung, are sadly shrunken; our might that in its day evoked the League of Cambrai against us, so that we stood to face a world in arms, has largely withered. But we are Venice still, and if we hold fast we may yet again become a power with which the world must reckon. Here we stand at the crisis of our fate. Whether we are to go down in ruin or maintain ourselves to rise again in glory, and be the proud and worthy bridegroom of the sea that once we were, will depend upon the courage we display and the will for sacrifice in those who still have something to lay upon the country's altar. Stout hearts there are still amongst us: men who advocate the armed neutrality that must compel respect for our frontiers. But so far they have been overborne in the Council by those who in their secret hearts are francophile, by those who prefer supinely to think that this is the Empire's affair, and by those who – God forgive them! – fearing the cost, cling like soulless misers to their sequins.

'The Doge himself is of these, for all his enormous wealth. Heaven forgive me that I should speak ill of our prince; but the truth must prevail. Lodovico Manin was not the Doge for us in such an hour. We needed a Morosino, a Dandolo, an Alviani, not this Friulian, who lacks the fervent patriotism that only a true Venetian could supply.

Still, your messages from England, and the evidences of French intentions with which it has pleased Heaven so opportunely to supply you, may have their effect.'

He sat down again, shaken almost to the point of exhaustion by the passion surging in him: the contempt, despair, and anger that sprang from a patriotism nothing short of fanatical.

The Countess rose, and went to soothe and pacify him. Isotta looked on with an odd solemnity, like a person entranced, whilst Marc-Antoine, observing her with eyes from which he manfully withheld the pain that gnawed him, was beset by the notion that these matters about which Count Pizzamano waxed so phrenetic were less than nothing.

Domenico's voice aroused him. 'If there is any help you need, you know that you may count upon us.'

'To my last breath and my last sequin,' the Count confirmed his son.

Marc-Antoine wrenched his mind back to this political business. 'There is a service that I require at once. Fortunately, it will not greatly tax you. I need a sponsor: someone in authority to give me the necessary credentials to His Serenity.'

He felt that he should explain how this came about. But he was too weary to go into it unless they should press him. And of this they had no thought.

'I will take you myself to the Doge tomorrow,' Count Pizzamano assured him. 'My knowledge of you is not of yesterday. Come to me at noon, and we'll go when we have dined. I'll send word to His Serenity, so that he may expect us.'

'You will remember that to him as to all without exception I remain Mr Melville. If by any indiscretion my true identity were to reach the ears of Lallemant, there would be a sharp end to my activities.' And even as he said it he was conscious of how little it really had come to matter.

After this they sat and talked of other things, of Marc-Antoine's mother, of common friends in England, but most of all of Bonaparte, this portent unknown three months ago, suddenly arisen to focus the attention of the world.

Isotta, in the background with folded hands and vacant eyes, played no more than a listener's part, if, indeed, she listened. Thus until an interruption was created by the arrival of Leonardo Vendramin.

Chapter 7

Leonardo Vendramin

Marc-Antoine beheld a tall, floridly handsome man, past his first youth, but still graceful of shape and carriage, very easy of manner, with a ready laugh, and debonair to the point of effusiveness: one, obviously, whose main desire was to stand well with all the world. That he stood well with the Count and Donna Leocadia, the Countess, was instantly plain. With Domenico he seemed less successful, and Isotta, whilst graciously receiving his marked, almost proprietary greeting, yet appeared to shrink a little as he bowed over her hand.

Presented as his future son-in-law by the Count to Mr Melville, Ser Leonardo smothered the supposed Englishman in voluble congratulations upon his nationality and swept into fulsomeness on the score of England. It had never yet been his felicity to see that marvellous country which by her dominion of the seas had assumed in the world the place that Venice once had held; but he knew enough of her great institutions, had seen enough of her noble people, to realize how fine a thing it was, how enviable, to have been born an Englishman.

Persuaded that he would have said precisely the same to a Frenchman or a Spaniard, Marc-Antoine acknowledged the compliments with cool civility, wondering the while why this man's name should seem familiar to him.

Thereafter and during supper, to which Marc-Antoine was retained, he was intermittently subjected to a bombardment of questions as to when he had arrived, where he was lodged, how long he proposed to stay, and what was the object of his visit. French – which in Venice then was the common language of the polite world – was being spoken by Vendramin out of regard for a stranger whom he could not suppose to be fluent in Italian.

He set his questions with such an air of friendly good-nature that their probing quality might have been overlooked. To the last of them Marc-Antoine returned the answer that his objects were to amuse and instruct himself, and to resume relation with his good friends the Pizzamani.

'Ah! You are old friends, then? But that is charming.' He looked about him, nodding, smiling, at once possessive and ingratiatory. But his vividly blue eyes, thought Marc-Antoine, were oddly watchful. They came to rest upon Isotta. As if challenged by them, she supplied the information he appeared to seek.

'Mr Melville has been very dear to us all from our London days, and he is too old a friend for you to pursue with your inquisitiveness.'

'Inquisitiveness! Just Heaven!' Ser Leonardo uplifted his eyes in mock distress. 'Ah, but Mr Melville, I am sure, does not mistake for inquisitiveness the deep interest he arouses in me. And if he is an old friend of yours, why, that should make another bond of sympathy between us.'

Mr Melville was entirely formal. 'You are too gracious, sir. I am deeply honoured.'

'But what impeccable French you speak for an Englishman, Monsieur Melville! There is no disparagement of your fellow-countrymen in that,' he made haste to explain. 'It is only that it is unusual to hear so pure a fluency from one who was not born a Frenchman.'

'I have enjoyed exceptional opportunities,' was the answer. 'I spent much of my youth in France.'

'Ah, but tell me of that. It is so interesting, so unusual to meet a man…'

'Who asks so many questions,' Domenico completed for him.

The gentleman, whose speech had thus been cropped, stared his displeasure; but only for a moment. At once he recovered his bonhomie. 'I am rebuked.' He laughed airily, waving a hand that was smothered in a cloud of lace. 'Oh, but justly rebuked. I have allowed my interest in this charming Mr Melville to outrun my manners. Bear me no rancour, my dear sir, and count me at your service – oh, but very much at your service – while you are in Venice.'

'Reveal to him the beauties of the district of San Barnabó,' suggested Domenico with sarcasm. 'That should entertain and instruct him.'

And then at last Marc-Antoine knew where he had heard the name and in what connection. Lallemant had mentioned Leonardo Vendramin as a barnabotto, a member of that great class of impecunious and decayed patricians, called barnabotti from the district of San Barnabó in which they herded. Because of their patrician birth, they must not degrade themselves by toil, nor yet could they be suffered to starve. And so they lived as parasites upon the State, imbued with all the faults and vices found where poverty and vanity are in alliance. They were maintained partly by an official dole from the government, partly, and in the case of those who possessed wealthy relatives, by the doles they levied in the euphuistic guise of loans. Because of their patrician birth they possessed the right to vote in the Grand Council and could exercise upon the fortunes of the State a control denied to worthy citizens whom the accident of birth had not so favoured. Occasionally, as a result, a barnabotto who was able and spirited could by the votes of his brethren in exalted mendicancy procure election to one of the great offices of State with its rich emoluments.

Marc-Antoine recalled now what Lallemant had said of this Vendramin, but he was more concerned to speculate how it happened that a member of that poverty-stricken class could display the extravagant richness of apparel that distinguished this man. He was also asking himself how it came to pass that Isotta, daughter of one of the greatest families of senatorial rank, who would have graced and honoured any house into which she had married, should be bestowed by her stiff-necked aristocratic father upon a barnabotto.

Meanwhile Vendramin, choosing to perceive a pleasantry in the insult from his prospective brother-in-law, replied by a pleasantry of his own at the expense of the esurience of his barnabotto brethren. Then, swiftly and skilfully he shifted the talk to the safer ground of politics and the latest rumours from Milan concerning the French and this campaign. He indulged the optimism that obviously was fundamental to his nature. This little Corsican would presently receive a sound whipping from the Emperor.

'I pray God you may be right,' said the Count with fervour. 'But until the events so prove you, we can relax no effort in our preparations for the worst.'

Ser Leonardo became solemn. 'You are right, Lord Count. I do not spare myself in what is to do, and I am making progress. Oh, but great progress. I have no anxieties, no doubt that soon now I shall have brought my fellows into line. But we will talk of this again.'

When at long last Marc-Antoine rose to depart, he thought that at least he could take credit for having so dissembled his hurt that none had even suspected it.

It was not quite so, however.

Gravely Isotta's gentle glance searched his face when he stood before her to take his leave. Its pallor and the lassitude and sadness which he could not exclude from his eyes as they considered her, told her what the lips withheld.

Then she realized that he was gone, and Ser Leonardo effusive to the end had insisted upon going with him, upon carrying him off in his gondola to deposit him at his inn.

Domenico, darkly thoughtful, had retired abruptly, and his mother had followed.

Isotta lingered in the loggia whither she had now returned, looking out into the garden over which the moon had risen. Her father, thoughtful, too, his countenance troubled, approached her and set a hand affectionately upon her shoulder. His voice was very gentle.

'Isotta, my child. The night has turned chilly.'

It was a suggestion that she should come indoors. But she chose to take him literally.

'Chilly, indeed, my father.'

She felt the increased pressure of his hand upon her shoulder, in expression of understanding and sympathy. There was silence awhile between them. Then he sighed, and uttered his thought aloud.

'Better that he had not come.'

'Since he lives, his coming was inevitable. It was a pledge he made me in London on the night before he set out for Tours. It was a pledge of more than a journey. I understood, and I was glad. He came now to fulfil and to claim fulfilment.'

'I understand.' His voice was low and sad. 'Life can be very cruel.'

'Must it be cruel to him and me? Must it, father?'

'My dear child!' Again he pressed her shoulder.

'I am twenty-two. There is perhaps a long life before me. Believing Marc dead, it was easy to resign myself. Now...' She spread her hands and helplessly broke off.

'I know, child. I know.'

The sympathy and sorrow in his voice lent her courage. Abruptly she spoke, in a passion of rebellion.

'Must this thing be? Must it go on?'

'Your marriage with Leonardo.' He fetched a sigh. The clear-cut old patrician face looked as if carved of marble. 'What else is possible in honour?'

'Is honour all?'

'No.' His voice rose. 'There is Venice too.'

'What has Venice done for me, what will Venice ever do for me, that I should be sacrificed to Venice?'

He was very gentle again. 'I can answer you only that it is my creed, and so it should be yours since you are my child, that we owe all that we possess to the State whence we derived it all. You ask, my dear, what Venice has done for you. The lustre of the name you bear, the honours of your house, the wealth with which we are endowed are the great gifts we have received from Venice. We lie under the debt of these, my dear. And in the hour of our country's need, only if we are ignoble will we shrink from honouring that debt. All that I possess is at the service of the State. You see that it must be so.'

'But I, father? I?'

'Your part is plain. A very noble part. Too noble to be set aside for personal considerations, however dear or deep. Ponder the situation here today. You heard what Marc has learnt of the intentions towards us of the French. Even if he can stir the Doge with that tomorrow, what can His Serenity achieve against a Council in which men, fearful of sacrifice, considering only personal interest, prefer to stand inert and hoard their gold? Wilfully they refuse to perceive the danger, because to avert it would be costly, and because they believe that even if the danger to the State is realized there will be no danger to their own substance.

'The barnabotti remain. They can muster some three hundred voices in the Council. With nothing to lose themselves, they may be brought before it is too late to vote for the costly policy that will save Venice; and if they do, they will establish a preponderance. At present, because they have nothing to lose, they imagine there may be something to gain from an upheaval. It is ever so with the needy and the worthless. And their ranks are rotten with Jacobinism; so that even without an invasion of French arms, the Serenissima may yet succumb to an invasion of French anarchical ideas.

'Leonardo is one of them. A man of gifts, of force and of eloquence. His influence with them is notorious and is increasing. Soon he will have them in the hollow of his hand. He will control their votes; which means, in short, that the fate of Venice may come to lie at the mercy of his will.' He paused a moment, and then added slowly: 'You are the price we pay for his conservatism.'

'Can you trust the patriotism of a man who sells it?'

'Sells it? That is not just. When he aspired to you, I saw the chance to bind him to us. But already he leaned our way and his patriotism was stout and pure, or else I should never have received him. He was seeking guidance. He brought me doubts and I resolved them. The rest was accomplished by his love for you. So that now he is wholly on the side of those who set the State above any personal interest. He would have come to it in the end without us, I am persuaded. But if we were to reject him now, we should be in danger of arousing a despair and a vindictiveness which would drive him with all his barnabotto following into the camp of the Jacobins. And that we dare not contemplate.'

To this she had no answer. It left her with a sense of being trapped.

She hung her head in misery and confusion.

He set an arm about her, and drew her close. 'My child! In this cause I am prepared to sacrifice all. I ask of you and of Domenico no more than the same preparedness.'

But now he seemed to step beyond the unanswerable bounds.

'Ah, but this!' she cried. 'This that is asked of me! To marry, to give myself to a man I do not love, to bear him children, to... Oh, God! You talk of readiness to sacrifice. What have you to sacrifice that will compare with this? If you gave the last sequin of your wealth and the last drop of your blood, you will still have given nothing by comparison with what you bid me give.'

'It may be as you say. But I who am not twenty-two take leave to doubt it. Be honest with yourself and me, Isotta. If you faced a choice between death and marriage with Leonardo, which would you choose?'

'Death without hesitation.' She was almost fierce.

'I urged you to be honest,' he reproached her softly, drawing her against him. 'I said if you faced the choice. But the choice has always been before you, and yet you have not taken what you tell me is the easier road. You see, my dear, how a surge of emotion may deceive us. And tonight you are the victim of it, and overwrought. Presently your views will readjust themselves. When all is said, Leonardo cannot be repugnant to you, or you would have recoiled before now from the prospect of this marriage. He has great qualities, for which you will come to esteem him. And to sustain you, you will have the proud, exultant thought of a high duty selflessly performed.'

He kissed her tenderly. 'My dear, you may have tears to shed. Believe me, child, they will not be half so salt as those which I shall shed on the grave of your personal hopes. Courage, my Isotta. It needs courage to live worthily.'

'Sometimes it needs courage to live at all,' she answered, choking on the words.

But she was conquered, as she had known from the outset that she would be. If his fanaticism had been of the kind that is thundered forth in uncompromising behests, open rebellion would have met him. But he was so gentle and sincere, he reasoned so patiently, pleaded so mildly that he persuaded where he did not convince and shamed opposition into silence.

Chapter 8

The Lady in the Mask

Marc-Antoine in a blue-and-gold bedgown sipped his chocolate on the following morning in his pleasant salon at the Inn of the Swords. He sat before windows set wide to the shallow balcony and the sunshine of a perfect May morning. From the canal below came intermittently the swish of the long oar, the gurgle of water under the swanlike prow of a passing gondola, the inarticulate sounding cry of gondolier giving warning as he swung round the corner from the Grand Canal, and, mellowed by distance, a sound of church bells from Santa Maria della Salute.

It was a morning to make a man glad that he was alive. But Marc-Antoine found little gladness in it. A beacon which for three years had glowed steadily to guide him had suddenly gone out. He was in darkness and without orientation.

Presently there were sounds of a gondola that did not pass. A hoarse hail from a gondolier before the portals of the inn: 'Ehi! Di casa!'

Some moments later the landlord, thrusting a bald head round Marc-Antoine's door, announced that a lady was asking for Mr Melville; a lady in a mask, he added, with a suggestion of humour about the set of his lips.

Marc-Antoine was on his feet at once. A lady in a mask was no portent in Venice, where the habit of going masked abroad was so common among gentlefolk that the unique city may have gathered from it something of its romantic reputation for mystery and intrigue. The portent lay in the fact that a lady should be seeking him. It was inconceivable that the only lady instantly occurring to him should be his visitor. Yet so it proved when presently the landlord had left her with Marc-Antoine behind closed doors.

She had masked herself with the completeness Venetian habit sanctioned. Under the little three-cornered gold-laced hat, a black silk bauta, that little mantilla edged in lace, covered her head and fell to the shoulders of the black satin cloak that concealed every line of the figure.

When she removed the white silk vizor, Marc-Antoine sprang to her with a cry that was of concern rather than of joy; for the face she showed him framed in the black lines of the bauta was more nunlike than ever in its pallor. Her dark eyes were wistful pools through which a soul looked out in sorrow and some fear. The heave of her breast told of her quickened nervous breathing. She pressed upon it her left hand which was closed about a white fan, the golden frame of which was set with jewels.

'I surprise you, Marc. Oh, I do a surprising thing. But I shall know no peace until it is done. Perhaps not much peace even then.'

It was more surprising even than Marc-Antoine suspected. Gone might be the days when, perhaps from her close relations with the East, Venice imposed so claustral a seclusion upon her women that only a courtesan would show herself freely in public places. The march of progress had gradually mitigated this, and of late those new ideas from beyond the Alps had introduced a measure of licence. But for patrician women this licence was still far indeed from the point at which a reputation could survive such a step as Isotta was now taking.

'I have to talk to you,' she said, her tone implying that nothing in the world could equal this in consequence. 'And I could not wait for opportunity, which might be indefinitely delayed.'

Troubled for her, he pressed her gloved hand to his lips, and strove to keep his voice level as he said: 'I exist to serve you.'

'Must we be formal?' She twisted her lips into a wistful smile. 'God knows the situation does not warrant it. There is nothing formal in what I do.'

'Sometimes we take refuge in formal words to express a meaning that is deep and sincere.'

He conducted her to a chair, and, with the fine consideration that distinguished him, placed her with her back to the light. Thus he thought she might find herself at some slight advantage. He remained standing before her, waiting.

'I hardly know where to begin,' she said. Her hands lay in her lap clutching her fan, and her eyes were lowered to them. Abruptly she asked him: 'Why did you come to Venice?'

'Why? But did I leave anything unexplained last night? I am here on a mission of state.'

'And nothing else? Nothing else? In pity's name be frank with me. Do not let anything that you find impose restraint. I desire to know.'

He hesitated. He had turned pale, as she might have seen had she looked up.

'Could the knowledge profit you?'

She seized upon that. 'Ah! Then there is something more to know! Tell me. Give me the help I need.'

'I do not perceive how it will help. But you shall have the truth since you demand it, Isotta. The mission of state followed upon the resolve I had taken to come to Venice. That, I think, you gathered from what I said last night. But the real motive of my visit… Your heart must tell you what it was.'

'I desire to hear it from you.'

'It was the love I bear you, Isotta. Though God knows why in all the circumstances you should compel me to say what I had never meant to say.'

She looked up at him at last. 'I had to hear it for my pride's sake; lest I should despise myself for a vain fool who had attached to words more meaning than they held. I had to hear it before I could tell you how clearly I had understood those words – I mean the words you spoke to me on the night before you left London to go to

Tours. That, as they were a pledge from you, so my silent acceptance of them made up a pledge from me. If you lived, you said, you would follow me to Venice. You remember?'

'Could I forget?'

'I loved you, Marc. You knew that, didn't you?'

'I hoped it. As we hope for salvation.'

'Ah, but I want you to know it. To know it. To be sure of it. I was nineteen; but no vain, empty maid to take as a trophy what was a pledge of a man's love. And I want you to know that I have been steadfast in my love. That I love you now, Marc, and that my heart, I think, is broken.'

He was on his knees beside her. 'Child, child! You must not say these things to me.'

She set a gloved hand upon his head. Her other wrought the while upon the fan as if she would crush it. 'Listen, my dear. It broke, I think – nay, I know – when word came that you were dead. Guillotined. My father and mother knew; yes, and Domenico. And because they, too, loved you, they were very tender and compassionate with me; and they helped me back to calm and to a measure of peace. The peace of resignation. The superficial peace we carry over memories that are stirred to life a hundred times a day to bleed the heart in secret. You were gone. You had taken with you all of pure joy and gladness that life could ever bring me. Oh, I am a bold maid to be so frank with you. But it is helping me, I think. You were gone. But my life had still to be lived; and helped as I was by my dear ones, I brought to it such courage as I could.'

She paused a moment, and then continued in that level, lifeless recital. 'Then Leonardo Vendramin came. He loved me. In any time but this, his position in life would have made a barrier that he would not even have attempted to surmount. But he knew what an endowment he gathered from his influence with men in his own sorry case; he knew how this must be viewed by a man of my father's burning patriotism. He knew how to present it, too, so that it should profoundly impress my father. You understand. They put it to me that I could do a great service to the tottering State, by enlisting on the side of all our ancient sacred institutions a man of enough influence to sway the issue if it came to a struggle between parties. At first I withstood them, repelled. I belonged to you. I had sustained myself with the thought that life is not all; that existence on earth is little more than a school, a novitiate for the real life that is to follow; and that out there, when this novitiate was over, I should find you, and say: "My dear, though you could not come to me on earth, I have kept myself your bride until I should come to you now." Do you understand, my dear, the strength of resignation which I gathered from that dream?'

She did not give him time to answer before resuming. 'But they would not leave me even that. It was shattered for me like the rest. It bent and finally broke under their persistent pleading, under the argument – oh, very gently urged, but not to be misunderstood – that I should devote to a worthy and sacred cause a life which was otherwise in danger of remaining empty. That was specious, wasn't it? And so, my dear, I yielded. Not lightly, believe me. Not without more tears in secret, I think, than I shed even at the news of your death. For now it was my soul and my soul's hope of you that was being slain.'

She fell silent, and left him silent. For one thing he could find no words for the emotions dazing him; for another he felt that she had not yet reached the end; that there was something more to come. She did not keep him waiting long.

'Last night, after you had gone, I sought my father. I asked if this thing still must be. He was very gentle with me, because he loves me, Marc. But he loves Venice more. Nor can I resent it. Since I know that he loves Venice better than himself, it is reasonable that he should love Venice better than his daughter. He made me see that withdrawal now would be a worse disaster than if at first I had refused; that if I drew back now, it might drive Leonardo in rancour to march his forces into the opposite camp.

'Do you conceive how I am torn, and yet how helpless I am? Perhaps if I were really brave, Marc, negligent of pledges, of honour and of all else, I should say to you: my dear, take me if you will have me, and let betide what will. But I have not the courage to break my father's heart, to be false to a pledge that is given in which he is concerned. Conscience would never let me rest thereafter, and its reproaches would poison our lives – yours and mine, Marc. Do you understand?'

Kneeling ever, his arm round her, he had drawn her close. She sank her head to his shoulder. 'Tell me that you understand,' she implored him.

'Too well, my dear,' he answered miserably. 'So well, indeed, that you need hardly have given yourself the pain of coming here to tell me this.'

'There is no pain in that. No added pain; but rather a relief. If you do not see this, then you do not yet understand. If I cannot give you myself, my dear, at least I can offer all I have to give of my mind and soul, by letting you know what you are to me, what you have been since that veiled pledge was passed between us. There is a solace to me in knowing that you know; that between us all is clear; that there can be no doubtings, no searchings of spirit. Somehow it absolves me of what I have done. Somehow it revives my hopes in that future when all this is over. For whereas, before, the knowledge was buried in myself, now you share it: the knowledge that whatever they may do with the rest of me, the spiritual part of me is and always will be yours, the eternal Me that wears for a while this body like a garment, and suffers all that wearing it imposes.' She let the fan which she had been bending and twisting fall into her lap, and she turned to take his face in both her hands. 'Surely, my Marc, you believe with me that this life on earth is not all that there is to us? If I have hurt you, as God knows I have hurt myself, by the course to which I am committed, will you not find solace where I find it?'

'If I must, Isotta,' he answered. 'But all is not yet done. We have not come yet to the end of the journey.'

Still holding his face, her eyes abrim with tears, she shook her head.

'Torture neither yourself nor me with any such hopes.'

'Hope is not torture,' he answered her. 'It is the anodyne of life.'

'And when it fails? What of the pain then? The agony?'

'Ay, when it fails; if it fails. But until then I'll bear it in my heart. I need it. I need courage. And you have brought it to me, Isotta, with a nobility to have been looked for in none but you.'

'Courage I desired to bring you, and to take from you for my own needs. But not the courage of a hope that leads to cruellest disillusion. Content you, dear. I pray you.'

'Yes, I'll content me.' His tone rang clear. 'I'll content me whilst I wait upon events. It is not my way to order a requiem while the patient lives.' He rose, and drew her up with him, so that her breast was against his breast, his hands gripping her arms. From her lap her fan and her mask fell to the floor.

There was a tap upon the door, and before Marc-Antoine could speak, it opened.

Facing it, as he stood with Isotta in his arms, Marc-Antoine beheld the landlord framed for a moment in the doorway, his countenance startled at realizing his intrusion. Over his shoulder, in that moment, he had a glimpse of another face, fair and florid. Then, as abruptly as it had been opened, the door was closed again by the hurriedly retreating landlord. But a deep, rich laugh from beyond it came to add to the confusion of Isotta, conscious of that momentary detection.

They fell apart, and Marc-Antoine stooped to pick up fan and mask. In her panic she almost snatched the white vizor, and hurriedly with fumbling fingers readjusted it.

'Someone is there,' she whispered. 'Waiting at the door. How am I to go?'

'Whoever it is will not venture to hinder you,' he promised her, and stepping to the door he flung it wide. On the threshold the landlord waited, Vendramin beside him.

'Here is a lord who will not be denied, sir,' Battista explained himself. 'He says he is your friend, and expected.'

Vendramin was broadly smiling as if with infinite, unpleasant understanding.

'Ah, but, morbleu, the fool, did not say that you had a lady with you. God forgive me that I should be a marplot, that I should come between a man and his delights.'

Marc-Antoine stood stiff and straight, admirably masking his deep irritation.

'It is no matter. Madame is on the point of going.'

Isotta, responsive to his glance, was already moving towards the door. But Vendramin made no shift to give her passage. He continued to fill the doorway, observing her approach with his slyly humorous eyes.

'Do not let me be the cause of that, I pray you.' He employed an oily gallantry. 'I was never one to drive out beauty, madame. Will you not unmask again, and let me make amends for my intrusion?'

'The best amends you could make, sir, would be to suffer the lady to pass.'

'Suffer is indeed the word,' he sighed, and stood aside. She swept past him, and out, leaving no more behind her than a faint perfume, for the Venetian to inhale.

When the landlord had departed in her wake, Vendramin closed the door, and came breezily to clap Marc-Antoine on the shoulder.

'Oh, my Englishman! You lose no time, faith. Scarce twenty-four hours in Venice, and already you show a knowledge of its ways that is not usually acquired in weeks. Morbleu, there's more of the Frenchman about you than the accent.'

And Marc-Antoine, to cover that retreat, to avoid the birth of the least suspicion of the truth, must feed the obvious foulness of this rakehell's mind by pretending the levity with which it credited him. He laughed, and waved a careless hand.

'It is lonely for a man in a foreign country. We must do what we can.'

Vendramin thrust playfully at his ribs. 'A coy piece, on my life! And she looked neat. Let her be never so muffled, I have eyes, my friend, that can strip a nun.'

Marc-Antoine thought it time to turn the talk. 'You told the landlord that you were expected?'

'You'll not pretend to have forgotten it? You'll not break my heart by saying that you had forgotten it, indeed? The last thing I said to you last night, when you landed here, was that I would come and take you to Florian's this morning. And you are not yet dressed. This négligé… Ah, yes, of course, the lady…'

Marc-Antoine turned away, dissembling disgust. 'I have but to don a coat and my walking-shoes. I will be with you at once.'

He yielded without argument so as to have a moment to himself, a moment in which to master the emotions Isotta had left in him, and those produced by this most inopportune intrusion. And so, he left the salon to pass into his bedroom beyond.

Messer Vendramin, smiling and nodding at the picture his imagination conjured of the doings he had interrupted, sauntered slowly towards the balcony. Something grated under his foot. He stooped and picked up an object that in size and shape was like the half of a large pea. The sunlight struck a dull glow from it as it lay in his palm. He looked over his shoulder. The door to the bedroom was closed. He continued his walk to the balcony. There he stood contemplating the little jewel. A malicious smile took shape on his full lips, as he realized that he held a clue. It would be amusing if chance were to lead him one day to find the indiscreet owner. The smile broadened as he dropped the cabochon sapphire into his waistcoat pocket.

Chapter 9

His Serenity

Past the majestic portal of Santa Maria della Salute and across the Basin of Saint Mark they were borne in Vendramin's gondola, with the funereal exterior trappings which the old sumptuary laws ordained, but enriched within the felza – the little cabin amidships – by delicate carvings, little painted escutcheons and wide cushions covered in leather that was wrought with scroll-work in gold and ultramarine and red. Whilst of no startling extravagance, yet for a pauper patrician it seemed to Marc-Antoine too much.

Ser Leonardo presented something of a problem to him. But, for that matter, so did all Venice as he saw it that morning. Everywhere life seemed inspired and suffused by the bright sunshine in which it was lived. In the crowds moving along the Riva dei Schiavoni, idling in the Piazzetta, or sauntering in the greater square, all was gay, careless vivacity. The mood of the Venetians, populace, burghers, and patricians, seemed as serene as the blue dome of heaven overhead, without apparent care or even thought for the mutterings of a storm that might at any moment overwhelm them.

It was little more than a week since on Ascension Thursday the Doge, aboard the great red-and-gold bucentaur of forty oars, with splendours as great as those displayed by the Serenissima at her zenith, had gone to the Port of Lido for the annual ceremony of the espousal of the sea.

Today, before the wondering eyes of Marc-Antoine, the sparkling human stream poured along the Schiavoni, past the gloomy prison and the unfortunate wretches who showed themselves grimacing behind the massive bars or thrust forth claws for alms, to be commiserated by some, but to move the derision of more. Westwards, past the Gothic marble-encrusted loveliness of the Ducal Palace, linked with the prison by that marble gem, the Bridge of Sighs, the human current flowed on, to lose its impulse in the spaces of the Piazzetta, to pause there or eddy about the Zecca and the columns of Eastern granite, one of them surmounted by Saint Theodore and the dragon, the other by the Lion and the Book, the emblems of Saint Mark.

Marc-Antoine stood on the pavement of trachyte and marble, spread like a carpet before the Byzantine glories of Saint Mark's. He caught his breath at the vision of the vast, arcaded square with that miracle of grace, the Campanile, thrusting, like a gigantic spear, its point into the blue.

This was the heart of the great city and here the pulsations of its vivid life were strongest.

By the rich bronze pedestals of the three great flagstaffs a quacksalver, in a fantastic hat with a panache that was a rainbow of dyed cocks' feathers, hoarsely called his unguents, perfumes, and cosmetics. By San Geminiano an itinerant little puppet-show was holding a crowd from which laughter intermittently exploded to startle the pigeons circling overhead.

They came to a table at Florian's on the shady side of the Piazza.

Here among the fashionable loungers of both sexes circled itinerant merchants, hawking pictures, Eastern rugs, trinkets of gold and silver, little gems of Murano glass and the like.

Of the poverty which in her decadence was consuming ever more swiftly the entrails of the State, there was no sign upon the glittering surface here displayed. The apparel of the men and women about these little tables was nowhere in Europe exceeded in extravagance, and their gay, inconsequent, leisurely air gave no hint of gloomy preoccupations.

If, thought Marc-Antoine, the Serenissima was, indeed, as some had diagnosed, upon her death-bed, she would die as she had lived, in luxury and laughter. Thus, we are told, had the Greek republics perished.

He sipped his coffee, listened indifferently to the chatter of the amiable Ser Leonardo and gave his real attention to the pattern woven before his eyes by the shifting loungers. Sauntering gallants and ladies in silks and satins, an occasional masked face amongst them; more soberly clad merchants; here the black of a cleric, there the violet of a canon, or the coarse brown of a friar, hurrying by with his eyes upon his sandals; occasionally the scarlet toga of a senator proceeding importantly to Pregadi, or the white coat and cockaded hat of a swaggering officer; groups of kilted Albanians or Montenegrins, sashed and jacketed in red or green, soldiers these from the Serenissima's Dalmatian provinces.

From time to time Ser Leonardo would point out a person of distinction in their environment. But there was only one who arrested Marc-Antoine's rather dazed attention: a sturdy, swarthy little man of middle age, in a black wig and a rusty coat; a man with observant, questing eyes, and the hint of a sneer about his tight-lipped mouth. Not only did he sit alone, but in a loneliness made conspicuous by the empty tables immediately about him, as if he bore some disease upon him of which others avoided the infection. Upon being informed that he was Cristofero Cristofoli, a well-known agent – confidente was the term employed – of the Council of Ten, Marc-Antoine wondered what was to be discovered by a spy whom everybody knew.

A couple passed, thrusting contemptuously through the crowd, which without resentment gave way at once. The man was short and mean of appearance, very swarthy and ugly in a suit of shabby camlet that an artisan on holiday might have disdained. A fat, untidy woman of fifty hung wobbling on his arm. They were followed by two men in black, each with a golden key upon his breast to proclaim him a chamberlain, and after these rolled a gondolier in a threadbare livery.

'Who is the scarecrow?' Marc-Antoine inquired.

Ser Leonardo's ready laugh rang out. 'Most apt! A scarecrow, indeed; in fact, as well as in appearance. Well might he scare some sense into these silly, strutting crows.' He waved a long supple hand to indicate the people about them. 'He is an itinerant warning to all Italy, and most of all perhaps to Venice. Oh, yes; a scarecrow. He is the Emperor's cousin, Ercole Rinaldo D'Este, Duke of Modena, lately chased from his dominions by the Jacobins, who, uniting Modena with Reggio, have formed the Cispadane Republic. The woman is Chiara Marini, said to be his second morganatic wife. He's a precious instance of how little the Imperial aegis can now shelter a man.'

Marc-Antoine nodded without comment as tightly reticent in this as in other matters, and evasive of the persistent questions with which the Venetian still sought to probe him. He discounted the repugnance which Vendramin inspired in him, lest some of it should result from a jealous resentment which he had not been human and a lover had he not experienced.

So when they parted at last, it was without much progress made on either side in knowledge of the other, but with effusive promises from Vendramin to seek him shortly again.

Marc-Antoine hailed a gondola at the steps of the Piazzetta, and was borne away to San Daniele and Count Pizzamano.

He dined with the Count and Countess and Domenico, Isotta keeping her room on a plea of indisposition. Later in the afternoon the Count carried him off to the Casa Pesaro, where the Doge resided.

Lodovico Manin, apprised of their coming, received them in the richly hung chamber that served him for a work-room.

Marc-Antoine bowed before a man of seventy who inclined towards obesity, whose scarlet gown was caught about his loose bulging loins by a girdle set with gems of price. His head was covered by a black velvet cap worn instead of a wig. His face was large and pallid, with sagging cheeks and very dark, lack-lustre eyes under heavy tufted black brows. The aquiline nose had been thickened by age; the upper of the heavy lips protruded, adding an expression that was almost foolish to the general weariness of his unimpressive countenance.

He received his visitors with a courtesy touched, in the case of Count Pizzamano, by a hint of deference.

Marc-Antoine was presented as Mr Melville, a gentleman charged with a mission from His Britannic Majesty's Government. The Count had known him intimately in London, and was in every way prepared to answer for him.

Evidently no better credentials were required, for Lodovico Manin, turning upon Mr Melville those dark eyes of his in which apprehension seemed to deepen, formally announced himself honoured and entirely at Mr Melville's service.

'It is irregular, perhaps, that I should receive thus in private a gentleman coming to Venice as an envoy-extraordinary. But these sad, anxious times and the persuasion of my friend Count Pizzamano will perhaps justify me. I scarcely know. There is so much nowadays to bewilder us. However, sir, be seated, and let us talk.'

With quiet impressiveness, and making it clear that his words were the words of Mr Pitt, Marc-Antoine spoke of the French menace to all Europe, and of the urgent need in the interests of civilization that all should unite against this common enemy. He touched upon the coalition that had been formed, and deplored the abstentions from it of some whose interests were surely identical with those of England, Austria, and the rest. In the forefront of these he ventured to place the Most Serene Republic, directly menaced now by the presence of the French armies on her very frontiers. If hitherto Venice might have been justified in holding aloof on the reasonable assumption that the allied Piedmontese and Austrian armies more than sufficed to preserve Italy inviolate, that justification had now been extinguished. The Piedmontese army had been shattered and Savoy had been surrendered to France. As a warning of what might ensue, His Serenity had the recent Jacobin revolt, with French assistance, of Modena and Reggio, which had formed themselves into the Cispadane Republic and had set up the anarchical rule of Liberty, Equality, and Fraternity.

His Serenity raised a podgy hand to interrupt him there.

'What has happened in Modena is one thing; what could happen in Venice quite another. That, sir, was a state resentful of government by a foreign despot, and, therefore, ripe for revolt. Venice is ruled by her own patricians, and the people are happy in their government.'

Marc-Antoine made bold to set a question: 'Does Venice consider that the happiness of her people is a sufficient guarantee that her frontiers will not suffer violation?'

'By no means, sir. Our guarantee of that lies in the friendly attitude of the French Directory towards Venice. France makes war upon Austria, not upon Italy. Only last week Monsieur Lallemant, speaking for General Bonaparte, desired the Council of Ten clearly to indicate our line of frontier on the mainland, so that it might be respected. Does it appear from this that we have cause to share the apprehensions which your Mr Pitt does us the honour to entertain on our behalf?' He spoke with the air of one who delivers checkmate.

'It does not appear so because the French are careful of appearances, and until their plans are ripe they will deceive you with false ones.'

This moved the Doge to petulance. 'That is an opinion, sir.'

'Highness, it is a fact of which by great good fortune I have secured and am able to bring you the fullest evidence.'

He produced Barras' letter to Lebel, unfolded it and handed it to the Doge.

The only sound for some moments after that was the heavy breathing of Manin, and the rustle of the document as it shook in his soft white hand. At last, in clear dismay, his expression dull and dazed, he turned the document about. 'It is genuine, this?' he asked, and his voice was husky. But the question was rhetorical and scarcely required the clear assurance that Marc-Antoine afforded.

'But then... ?' The dull eyes stared.

Marc-Antoine was blunt.

'That which three months ago would have been a gracious and generous concession for the Most Serene Republic is today a stark necessity if she is to be saved from annihilation.'

The Doge started to his feet, shuddering. 'My God! Oh, my God! Do not use such words.'

The Count took a hand. 'It is as well to use the words that apply. Then there can be no misconceptions. We see where we stand. It only remains to arm and unite with Austria against the common foe.'

'Arm!' The Doge looked at him in horror. 'Arm? And the cost of arming? Have you counted that?' He seemed at last to have come fully to life. Perhaps the richest man in the Republic, indeed owing his election to his very wealth, he was notoriously a miser.

'The cost of arming?' he stormed on. 'Virgin Mother! How is it to be defrayed?'

Marc-Antoine supplied the answer. 'However defrayed, the cost should prove less than the levy a victorious Bonaparte will exact.'

'Bonaparte! Bonaparte! You talk as if Bonaparte were already here.'

'He is almost at the gate, Highness.'

'And since you know the true French intentions,' growled the Count, 'you cannot suppose that he will stand hat in hand on the doorstep.'

His Serenity almost raged. 'Is there not the Empire? If Beaulieu's army were smashed to atoms, the resources of the Emperor would scarcely be broached. Austria has lost Belgium already. Do you suppose she will let her Italian provinces go the same way?'

'Her loss of Belgium,' said Marc-Antoine, with an exasperating calm, 'was in spite of her resources.'

Impatient, yielding to his fierce patriotism, the Count again cut in.

'And, anyway, are we come so low that we must look to another to fight our battles, whilst we stand idly by? That is an attitude, sir, for women; not for men.'

'It is not yet our battle. It is Austria's.'

This was mere obstinacy, and the Count's impatience flared in his tone. 'But we are to profit by the spending of Austrian blood and treasure, and contribute nothing of our own. Is that the argument? Will the Council tolerate it?'

The Doge turned away in distress and anger. Bowed and trembling, he shambled from them, towards the window.

Marc-Antoine addressed the broad, receding back. 'By Your Serenity's leave, what is of more immediate importance than these abstract considerations is that, whilst you wait for the Empire to develop her resources, Venice may be under the conqueror's heel. Can she, having done nothing for Austria, having done nothing even for herself, look then to Austria to come to her deliverance?'

It was a long moment before Manin turned, and he had come slowly back to them before he spoke. By then he had recovered his lugubrious self-control.

'Sirs, I am obliged to you. Amongst us here we can do no more. This matter is one for the Council. I shall lose no time in convening it.' He drew a hand wearily across a brow that was damp. 'And now, if you will give me leave…' His glance embraced them both. 'I am shaken, deeply shaken by all this, as you may conceive.'

Back in their gondola, the Count was grimly bitter. 'I told you it was an evil day for Venice when she elected a Friulian to Doge. You have seen him. He will pray; he will have masses said; he will burn candles rather than levy men and arm them. Always will he put his trust in alien help: in Austria's or in Heaven's. But we have still some Venetians left, like Francesco Pesaro, who from the outset have demanded that we arm. And the barnabotti shall stiffen them. This is a matter for Vendramin. The time for action has arrived.'

On the whole Marc-Antoine could give himself peace. He might, had he so chosen, account his mission accomplished. But he did not yet choose so to account it. Therefore, the next day saw him waiting once more upon Lallemant.

He had been busy, he announced. In his pretended character of Mr Melville he had seen the British Ambassador, who mistrusted him and therefore would do nothing to assist him.

'That man,' said Lallemant, 'would mistrust his own mother.'

They laughed together, and Marc-Antoine proceeded. He had found, however, in the Senator Count Pizzamano, a member of the Council of Ten, one who believed in him well enough to sponsor him to the Doge. He had seen Manin. Such a man need give them no anxieties.

The ambassador, whilst amazed at the audacity of this Lebel, cordially agreed with him. He was contemptuous of the Venetian Government and Venetian patricians. They lived upon an illusion of greatness from the past, and refused to read the present. Venetian industries were languishing, her trade, crushed by taxation, was moribund. Consequently her finances were desperate.

'As in the case of all nations sweeping to the last stage of decay, she multiplies public offices and takes upon herself the burden of maintaining more and more of her pauper subjects. It is as if a man, finding himself impoverished, hopes to combat it by undertaking to support his needy relatives.'

This brought him naturally to speak of the barnabotti, and of Vendramin, whom he described as a man of great influence in that regiment of paupers.

'That one, at least,' said Marc-Antoine, 'displays no sign of pauperdom.'

Lallemant's broad face broke into creases of amusement. 'Why, no. We see to that.'

Marc-Antoine breathed more quickly. 'He is in your pay?'

'Not yet. But it's only a question of time.' The shrewd eyes were amused. 'He's important to us. If it comes to a struggle in the Council between our aims and those of the Austrophiles, the issue, believe me, will lie with the man who can control the vote of the barnabotti. Vendramin is that man. Therefore I shall buy him.'

'That is well conceived. But if he will not sell?'

'There are ways of compelling such men, and – faith! – I have no compunctions.' His lip curled in scorn. 'These vicious profligates, otherwise useless to humanity, exist only so that they may be used where possible for the furtherance of worthy aims. The Vicomtesse has charge of the affair.'

'The Vicomtesse?' Marc-Antoine's tone was heavy with interrogation.

Lallemant was impatient of his dullness. 'Why, your Vicomtesse, of course. Or, if not yours, Barras'. From his seraglio, I suppose. But as a Vicomtesse she's of your own creation. Shrewd of you to have her pass for an émigrée. A clever little baggage.'

'Oh, that!' said Marc-Antoine, wondering who the devil she was, but daring to ask no questions. 'Oh, yes. Clever enough.'

Chapter 10

Faro

It would be a couple of days later when Leonardo Vendramin came to fulfil a promise to show Mr Melville something of Venetian society, and carried him off to the Casino del Leone under the Procuratie. It was one of those little resorts, some owned privately and some in the nature of clubs, which had sprung up to replace the fashionable Ridotto, abolished by the Council of Ten nearly twenty years ago. But the gaming, which had been the main cause of the existence of those assembly-rooms, and the scandals connected with which had led to their suppression, was the main reason for the existence now of most of these casini.

Mr Melville found himself in an elegant anteroom of brocaded panels, elegant furnishings, crystal chandeliers and Murano mirrors, that was tolerably filled by persons of fashion. The atmosphere, tepid, and oppressive with mingling perfumes, reverberated gently to light, gay chatter and rippling laughter. Ser Leonardo, evidently a familiar figure, appeared to enjoy the acquaintance of all. He presented his companion to one and another, and Mr Melville noted the patrician names of those he met. Here a Moncenigo or a Condulmer, there a lady of the great houses of Gradenigo or Morosini, who eyed him coyly over the edge of a fan, or gave him a more liberal welcome by making room for him to sit awhile beside her.

Lackeys in white stockings, their heads heavily powdered, circulated with trays of cooling drinks and sorbets; somewhere a string band was softly playing an air from Mayr's latest opera, *Lodoiska*, which was then being performed at the Fenice Theatre.

Mr Melville discovered something vaguely unwholesome and repellent in this resort of voluptuaries, this obvious temple of frivolity and inconsequence, so incongruously set up, as it seemed to him, upon the crust of a volcano from which an eruption might shatter it at any moment.

He was rescued by Ser Leonardo from the light persiflage of Donna Leonora Dolfin, and swept away to the faro-room, which Vendramin described as the inner temple. On the threshold their way was blocked by a sturdy, dark-haired young man, pallid of face and with dark, restless eyes, who in extravagance of dress outvied even Vendramin himself.

Ser Leonardo presented him as 'Fortune's most insistent and audacious gallant', a description which the young man, whose name was Rocco Terzi, repudiated with a laugh of some bitterness.

'Present to him Fortune, rather, as the most obdurate and unyielding of all the objects of my wooing.'

'What would you, Rocco? You know the proverb: "Lucky in love…" ' He took him by the arm. 'Come you back, my friend. Men unlucky in themselves will often invite the luck for others. Stand by me for five minutes whilst I punt. You will permit it, Monsieur Melville?'

The five minutes grew to ten without, apparently, Ser Leonardo being aware of it; when they had grown to twenty, he was probably not even aware that he kept a guest waiting. Guest and the world and time were forgotten in the battle he was fighting against persistent losses.

Rocco Terzi yawned wearily. He occupied with Marc-Antoine a rose-brocaded settle where they had a clear view of Ser Leonardo, flushed and desperate, at the faro-table.

'You see the luck I bring him,' growled Messer Rocco. 'I don't function even as a charm. The Goddess not only hates me; she hates my friends.' He stood up, stretching his limbs a little. 'My only compensation for the flaying I have endured this afternoon lies in the pleasure of becoming acquainted with you, Monsieur Melville.'

Marc-Antoine rose, and they shook hands.

'We shall meet again, I hope. I am commonly to be found here. If you will ask for me, it will be an honour. Rocco Terzi, sir, your very humble servant.'

He sauntered out, with a nod here and a word there, his restless, uneasy, deep-set eyes being everywhere at once.

Marc-Antoine sat down again, to wait.

A dozen punters, of whom one half were women, sat about the oval green table; as many spectators stood over them or moved about. The bank had been made by a corpulent man, whose back was turned towards Marc-Antoine. Immovable as an idol, there was no sound from him beyond an occasional hiss or chuckle as the croupier made his announcements and plied his rake.

Vendramin was losing steadily, and in a measure as he lost his methods grew more obstinately reckless.

Not once when he won did Marc-Antoine see him take up his winnings. Each time, in a voice that became gradually more and more husky and aggressive, he would make paroli, and if he won again his 'sept et le va' came like a defiance to Fortune. Once only, winning this, he went to 'quinze et le va', and cursed the luck he had tempted when he saw all his gains swept away.

Marc-Antoine set his losses at between two and three hundred ducats before diminishing stakes implied the approaching end of his resources.

At last, he pushed back his chair, and wearily rose. After a moment, his eyes alighting on Marc-Antoine, he seemed suddenly to grow conscious of a forgotten presence. He came round to him with dragging feet. For once there was no effusive sparkle in his air.

'The worst of my cursed luck is that I must cease to play at a time when by all the laws of chance the tide should turn.'

'There are no laws of chance,' said Marc-Antoine.

They were the idlest words. But Ser Leonardo chose to perceive in them a challenge. 'A heresy! Lend me a hundred ducats, if you have them at hand, and I will prove it.'

It happened that Marc-Antoine had the money. He was abundantly supplied. His London bankers had opened a credit for him at Vivanti's in Venice, and Count Pizzamano had been his sponsor to that great Jewish financier.

Vendramin took the rouleau with a short word of thanks, and in a moment was back at the table punting again.

Within ten minutes, pale now and feverish of eye, he was once more staking his last ten sequins. And once more it proved a losing one, so that the borrowed money was consumed.

But before that final card was turned, a slight wisp of a woman in palest violet, with golden hair piled high and almost innocent of powder, no doubt from pride in its natural bright colour, had come to take her stand behind Vendramin. Marc-Antoine had not observed her entrance; but he observed her now, for she was a woman to take the eye of any man, delicately exquisite as a piece of Dresden porcelain and looking as fragile.

She watched the turn of the card, craning her slender neck a little, her fan moving gently to and fro beneath a countenance quietly composed. She even smiled a little at the muttered oath with which Vendramin greeted his final loss. Then her hand descended suddenly upon his shoulder as if to detain him in his seat.

He looked up and round to meet a reassuring smile. From a little brocaded bag she carried she drew a rouleau which she placed beside him on the green table.

'Of what avail?' he asked. 'My luck is out.'

'O coward,' she laughed. 'Will you own defeat? It is endurance that wins the day.'

He resumed, staking heavily, wildly, losing steadily, until once more all was gone. But even then she would not let him rise. 'I have an order here for two hundred on Vivanti's bank. Countersign it and take the money. You'll repay me from your winnings.'

'My angel! My guardian angel!' he apostrophized her tenderly, and bawled to a lackey for pen and ink, whilst the play went on.

At first he lost. But at last the tide turned. His winnings were piled before him like a rampart, when the obese banker at last announced that he had had enough. At this, Vendramin would have swept up his winnings, and departed; but his temptress stayed him.

'Will you insult Fortune when she smiles so winningly? My friend, for shame! Make a bank with what you have.'

The gamester hesitated only for a moment.

The bank he made ran steadily in favour of the punters. Swiftly the piled rouleaux diminished, and Vendramin, livid, fevered, the urbanity all departed out of him, played anxiously and savagely.

In the lady who had spurred the gamester to this folly, Marc-Antoine had little doubt that he beheld the mysterious Vicomtesse of whom Lallemant had spoken, the lady upon whom, according to Lallemant, Lebel had bestowed a title so as to facilitate her activities as a secret agent. He observed her very closely. Whether because she detected his interest, or whether because moved by an interest of her own, her eyes, blue as myosotis and serene as a summer sky, gave him what consideration she could spare from Messer Vendramin.

Had he not been expected at the Casa Pizzamano and already in danger of being late, he would have lingered if only to make her acquaintance. But the game looked as if it would continue for hours. He rose quietly, and quietly withdrew, his departure unnoticed.

Chapter 11

The Grand Council

Lallemant, curt and surly, handed Marc-Antoine a sealed letter from Barras. It confirmed to Camille Lebel the instructions to preserve friendly relations with the Serenissima, but indicated that presently it might be desirable to allow the Venetians a glimpse of the iron hand within the velvet glove. Barras was proposing to demand the explusion from Venetian territory of the ci-devant Comte de Provence who now called himself Louis XVIII. The hospitality extended to him by the Serenissima might be construed as hostile to France, since from Verona, which he had converted into a second Coblentz, the soi-disant King Louis XVIII was actively intriguing against the French Republic. Barras waited only until his views should be shared by his colleagues, who were still hesitating to ruffle so serene a surface as Venice appeared to present.

Marc-Antoine was distressed. Loyalty to the man whom he must regard as his present sovereign made him grieve to think of this unfortunate gentleman who had been driven from one state of Europe to another – for he was welcome nowhere – being sent again upon his travels.

In silence he folded and pocketed the letter, and only then observed the surliness with which the ambassador, elbows on the table, was observing him.

'There is nothing here for you, Lallemant,' he said, as if to answer that curious glance.

'Ah!' Lallemant stirred. 'Well, it happens that I have something for you.' He seemed at once stern and ill-at-ease. 'It is reported to me that the British Ambassador has been overheard to say that Bonaparte has urged an alliance with Venice.'

The most startling thing to Marc-Antoine in this was the evidence of the thoroughness of Lallemant's organization of espionage.

'You said yourself that the man is a fool.'

'It is not a question of his wits, but of his information. What he is saying happens to be true, as you know. Can you explain how he comes by his knowledge?'

Lallemant's tone had hardened. It flung down a challenge. Marc-Antoine's smiling pause before answering betrayed nothing of his momentarily quickened heart-beats.

'Quite easily. I told him.'

Whatever reply Lallemant had been expecting, it was certainly not this. He was disarmed by the assertion of the very thing that against his will he had been suspecting. Blank astonishment showed on his broad, peasant face. 'You told him?'

'That was the object of my visit to him. Didn't I mention it?'

'You certainly did not.' Lallemant was testy. He was rallying – as his manner showed – the forces of suspicion momentarily scattered. 'Will you tell me with what purpose?'

'Isn't it plain? So that he might repeat it, and thereby lull the Venetians into a sense of false security that will keep them inactive.'

With narrowing eyes Lallemant considered him across the table. Then he delivered, as he believed, checkmate.

'Why, then, since you hold that view, did you so definitely instruct me to suppress Bonaparte's proposal? Answer me that, Lebel.' In a gust of sudden fierceness he repeated: 'Answer!'

'What's this?' Marc-Antoine's agate eyes were at their hardest. 'I suppose I had better answer and kill whatever maggot is stirring in your brain. But – name of God! – the weariness of pointing out the obvious to dullards.' He set his hand on the table, and leaned towards the ambassador. 'Are you really unable to perceive for yourself that it is one thing to make a formal offer, which might conceivably be accepted, and quite another to seek such advantage as may be derived from the circulation of an irresponsible rumour to the same effect? I see that you do perceive it now. I am relieved. I was beginning to despair of you, Lallemant.'

The ambassador's antagonism collapsed. He lowered his eyes in confusion. His voice faltered. 'Yes. I should have seen that, I suppose,' he admitted. 'I make you my excuses, Lebel.'

'For what?' It was a sharply delivered challenge to an avowal that Lallemant dared not make.

'For… For having troubled you with unnecessary questions.'

That night Marc-Antoine wrote a long letter in cipher to Mr Pitt, in the course of which he did not spare Sir Richard Worthington, and next morning he conveyed it in person, together with a letter for his mother, to the captain of an English ship lying off the Port of Lido.

That was by no means the only official letter that he wrote in those days. His correspondence with Barras, steadily maintained, represents one of the most arduous and skilful of all the tasks that he discharged during his sojourn in Venice. It was his practice to write his dispatches currently in his own hand, as if a secretary were employed, appending the signature and flourish of the dead Lebel, which he had rehearsed until he could perfectly reproduce them.

Days followed of observant waiting for the Grand Council which the Doge had promised to convene.

It came at last, and on the evening of that day Marc-Antoine sought, at the Casa Pizzamano, news of what had occurred.

He found Vendramin there, flushed with the triumph he had scored. From the tribune of the vast hall of the Grand Council he had eloquently denounced the Senate's neglect to put the country in a posture of defence. Governors had been appointed: a Proveditor of the Mainland, a Proveditor of the Lagoons, a Proveditor of This and a Proveditor of That; officials had been multiplied, and money had lavishly been spent; but of effective preparation, as they now saw, there had been none.

Passionately he had formulated in detail his demand that troops be raised overseas and brought at once to garrison the cities of the Venetian mainland; that arms be furnished by supply and manufacture; that the Lido forts be properly equipped and manned, and that the same be done by the ships of the Serenissima; in short, that all measures be instantly taken to provide for a state of war to which the Most Serene Republic, despite her ardent and laudable desire for peace, might at any moment find herself constrained.

When he descended from the tribune, a sense of awe pervaded the great patrician multitude assembled under that fabulous ceiling with its gildings of purest gold leaf and its treasures from the brushes of Tintoretto and Paolo Veronese. From their portraits along the frieze the eyes of some seventy doges, who had ruled in Venice since the year eight hundred, looked down upon these their descendants in whose enfeebled hands lay now the destinies of a nation which once had been amongst the most powerful and opulent of the earth.

It was idle to take a vote, for it was known that the applauding barnabotti, of whom there were close upon three hundred present, had been marshalled by Vendramin to support him.

Lodovico Manin, trembling in his ducal chlamys, his countenance grey under the corno – the jewelled gold cap of his princely office – announced briefly and in a lifeless voice which was lost in those vast spaces that the Senate would take steps at once to carry out the wishes of the Grand Council, and for the rest he prayed God and Our Lady to have them in Their Holy Keeping.

The few stout patriots like Count Pizzamano, who placed the glory of the Serenissima above every earthly consideration, could feel at last that their feet were set upon the road of action, which was the road of dignity and honour.

Hence, that night, the Count's caressing manner towards Vendramin; hence the unusual civility towards him of Domenico, who had come from the Fort of Saint' Andrea di Lido to attend the Council; and hence, too, perhaps, the increasing wistfulness which Marc-Antoine detected in Isotta.

After supper, when they sought in the loggia the cool of the summer night, she hung behind, and took her way alone to the harpsichord placed under the window at the long room's other end. The strains of a sweetly melancholy air of Cimarosa's broke forth under her fingers, as if in expression of her mood.

Marc-Antoine, intolerably urged to bear her comfort, quietly rose, and, whilst the others were engrossed in their talk of the day's events and of the things to follow from it, went to join her.

She greeted his approach with a smile at once wan and tender. Her fingers mechanically found the familiar sequence of keys, and Cimarosa's air continued uninterrupted.

Since that morning when so audaciously she had sought him at his lodgings they had not exchanged above a dozen words, and these in the presence of others. But her murmur now was an allusion to his last utterance in that clandestine interview.

'You may order the Requiem, my Marc.'

Facing her across the instrument, he actually smiled.

'Not while the body lives; and it still does. I never trust appearances only.'

'There is more than the appearance here. Leonardo has performed what was required. Soon now he will claim payment.'

'Soon he may not be in a position to claim it.'

Her hands fell idle on the keys a moment. Then, lest the interruption should be observed, she resumed, and with the melody to mask her words, she questioned him.

'What do you mean?'

He had spoken upon impulse, uttering more than he intended. Just as he saw no reason in honour to raise a finger to frustrate Lallemant's scheme for the seduction of the barnabotto leader, so he also felt that he should do nothing to promote it... His part was to stand passively by and wait; to pick up the fruit when another shook the tree. Meanwhile both honour and prudence sealed his lips, even to Isotta.

'Merely that life is uncertain. Too often we forget it, preparing for joys that perish on the way, or trembling at evils that never reach us.'

'Is that all, Marc?' He caught the disappointment in her voice. 'This evil, this… horror, my dear, is already on the threshold.'

Often the mere utterance of a thought will raise its poignancy beyond endurance. So now with Isotta. Having given this expression to her besetting dread, she was forsaken by the little courage that had still upheld her.

Her hands crashed a discordant jangle from the keys, her head sank forward, and Isotta, usually so calmly proud and self-contained, was bowing over the instrument and sobbing like a hurt child.

It lasted no more than a few seconds; but long enough to be perceived by those in the loggia, already startled by the explosive discord from the harpsichord.

Donna Leocadia came hastening down the room in a flutter of maternal concern; and, no doubt, with more than a suspicion of the source of this distress. The others followed.

'What have you said to her?' Vendramin was angrily demanding.

Marc-Antoine raised his eyebrows. 'Said to her? Said to her?'

'I demand to know.'

Domenico thrust between them.

'Are you mad, Leonardo?'

Before this need to be collected, Isotta rose. 'You make me ashamed. It is only that I am not so well. I will go now, mother.'

Vendramin moved towards her in concern.

'Dear child… '

But the Countess gently waved him back. 'Not now,' she begged.

Mother and daughter departed, and the Count, protesting that here was a deal of turmoil because a girl was feeling indisposed, drew Vendramin back to the cool of the loggia, leaving the other two to follow.

But Domenico detained Marc-Antoine. His manner was hesitant.

'Marc, my friend, are you not being imprudent? You don't misunderstand me? You know that if I could change the course of things I would not spare myself.'

Marc-Antoine was short. 'I will study to be prudent, Domenico.'

'You see,' the young soldier continued, 'there is Isotta to consider. Already her fate is hard enough.'

'Ha! You perceive that, do you?'

'Can you suppose that I am blind: that I don't see, that I don't feel – for both of you?'

'Leave me out of account. If you feel so much for Isotta, why do you do nothing?'

'What is there to be done? You see how my father fawns upon him tonight now that he has given proof of his power. That is the expression of my father's love for Venice. Against that selfless passion of patriotism, to which he will sacrifice everything that he possesses, don't you see that it is idle to contend? We must bow, Marc.' He pressed his friend's arm.

'Oh, I am bowing. But whilst I bow, I watch.'

'For what?'

'For a gift from the gods.'

Domenico still detained him. 'They tell me you are a deal together: you and Vendramin.'

'That is by his seeking.'

'As I supposed.' Domenico was scornful. 'To Vendramm all travelling Englishmen are wealthy. Has he borrowed money from you yet?'

'How well you know him,' said Marc-Antoine.

Chapter 12

The Vicomtesse

Battista, the landlord of the Inn of the Swords, had procured a valet for Mr Melville: a Frenchman named Philibert, who was an excellent hairdresser.

This Philibert, a plump, soft-voiced, soft-footed man of forty, had dressed for years the hair of the Duc de Lignières. But the guillotine having taken off the Duke's head, Philibert found himself out of work, and since other aristocratic heads in France seemed equally impermanent, Philibert, following the example of his betters, had emigrated from a republic in which the National Barber left hairdressers without employment.

Marc-Antoine, who was fastidious about the appearance of his glossy black mane, thanked God for it, and took the soft-voiced man into his service.

Philibert was at his duties on the head of his new master; to be particular, he was in the act of shaving him. Upon the intimate operation, Messer Vendramin, very brave in lilac taffeta, intruded. He strolled in familiarly, swinging a gold-headed cane, and found himself a chair by the dressing-table, whence he faced the lathered Mr Melville.

He entertained the supposed Englishman with small talk and little anecdotes, mostly scandalous and sometimes salacious, of which invariably he was the hero. The presence of Philibert set no restraints upon him. Ser Leonardo made it appear that in Venice reticence was little practised. Besides, he was of those for whom kissing would lose half its delights if there were no telling.

Mr Melville, wishing him at the devil, let him chatter, and grew somnolent.

'I shall take you today,' Vendramin announced, 'to one of the most elegant and exclusive casinos in Venice: that of the exquisite Isabella Teotochi. You'll have heard of her?'

Mr Melville had not. The Venetian prattled on.

'I take you there at the request of a very entrancing lady who has remarked you, and desires your acquaintance: a very dear and charming friend of mine, the Vicomtesse de Saulx.'

Razor in hand, Philibert leapt back with a cry of dismay. 'Ah, Dieu de Dieu!' His voice was soft no longer. 'Not in twenty years has such a thing happened to me. Never shall I forgive myself, monsieur. Never!'

A crimson stain suffusing the lather on Mr Melville's cheek explained the valet's anguish.

Vendramin was pouring abuse upon the luckless Frenchman. 'Clumsy, maladroit lout! You should be caned for that, by God! What the devil are you? A valet or a butcher?'

Mr Melville was languid, yet with a hint of sternness. He waved Ser Leonardo into silence.

'If you please, sir! If you please.' He took a corner of the towel, and dabbed the gash. 'It's not a question of whether you can forgive yourself, Philibert; but whether you can forgive me for having spoilt the record of your twenty years. The fault was mine, my friend. I was drowsing, and I started under your hand.'

'Oh, monsieur! Oh, monsieur!' Philibert's tone expressed the inexpressible.

Vendramin was sneering. 'I vow to Heaven you English are incomprehensible.'

Philibert was bustling feverishly; finding a fresh towel; mixing something in a basin. 'I have water here that will staunch a cut almost at once, monsieur. By the time I have dressed your hair the bleeding will have ceased.'

He approached to minister. 'You are very good, sir,' he said, and the gratitude in his tone was touching.

Mr Melville's next words announced that the subject was closed.

'You were speaking, Ser Leonardo, of a lady, I think; of a lady to whom you are to present me. You named her; did you not?'

'Ah, yes. The Vicomtesse de Saulx. You will be glad to meet her.'

'I can think of no one who would interest me more,' said Mr Melville in a tone that sharpened Vendramin's glance.

'You will have heard of her?'

'The name is extraordinarily familiar.'

'She is an émigrée. The widow of the Vicomte de Saulx who was guillotined in the Terror.'

So that was it! Beyond a doubt this would be the Vicomtesse described by Lallemant as of Lebel's creation. That, in itself, went far to explain the title Lebel had chosen for her. Considering that dead scoundrel's connection with Saulx, it would, of course, be the first to occur to him. Of the danger attached to meeting her in his present circumstances, Marc-Antoine could only judge when he had met her. And since, in any case, it would be his duty to denounce her for a spy, she would not remain a danger to him long.

They came to the casino of Isabella Teotochi, the famous and beautiful Greek précieuse, who, separated from her first husband, Carlo Marin, was now being ardently wooed by the patrician Albrizzi. This private casino, conducted for her by a French director, bore no resemblance to the Casino del Leone. There was no gaming here. Its rooms were devoted to intellectual reunions. It was a temple of arts and letters, in which La Teotochi was the high priestess; in which the compositions of the day supplied the topics of conversation; and in which the advanced ideas of life imported from France were given a free flight. So much was this the case that already the British and Russian ambassadors, looking upon these assemblies as hotbeds of Jacobinism, were urging the inquisitors of state to give attention to them.

In Marc-Antoine the lovely Teotochi could discern no claim to her lofty interest. She gave him a languid, careless welcome. She was absorbed and entranced at the moment by a youth with a lean, pale, Semitic face and ardent eyes, who, leaning over her where she reclined, talked volubly and vehemently.

If he made a pause when Vendramin presented his Englishman, it was merely to glare his impatience at the interruption. He acknowledged by a curt, contemptuously absent-minded nod the expansive greeting which Vendramin addressed to him.

'A mannerless Greek cub,' Ser Leonardo condemned him as they withdrew.

Later Marc-Antoine was to learn that he was Ugo Foscolo, a young student from Zara turned dramatist, who already at the age of eighteen was startling Italy by his precocious genius. But at the moment his attention was elsewhere.

He had discovered the porcelain lady of the Casino del Leone enthroned on a settee, receiving the courtship of a little group of lively gallants, amongst whom he recognized Rocco Terzi of the uneasy eyes. Observing her he reflected that it is rarely given to a man to enjoy the advantage of contemplating his own widow.

Her quickening glance apprised him that she was aware of his approach. Then, he was bowing before her, and she was telling him archly that he arrived in time to check the scandalous tongues of those about her to whom no character was sacred.

'That is too severe,' Terzi protested. 'We leave sacred things alone. Madame Bonaparte is hardly sacred even when hailed by the mob as a divinity.'

He alluded to the accounts which had just reached Venice of the worship of Madame Josephine since the arrival in Paris of the captured Austrian standards sent home by Bonaparte, and to the title of 'Our Lady of Victor', by which she was hailed whenever she showed herself in public.

Presently Marc-Antoine found the opportunity he sought.

'We have acquaintances in common, I believe, madame. In England I know another Vicomtesse de Saulx.'

The blue eyes flickered. But the movement of the slowly waving fan was never checked or troubled. 'Ah!' she drawled. 'That will be the dowager Vicomtesse. My late husband's mother. He was guillotined in '93.'

'So I had heard. And then there are others.' His dreamy-looking eyes watched her closely. 'There is Camille Lebel, for instance.'

'Lebel?' She frowned in thought, and slowly shook her head. 'I do not number anyone of that name among my friends.'

'I could not suggest that. But you will have heard of him. Lebel was at one time the Vicomte de Saulx's steward.'

'Ah, yes,' she said vaguely. 'I think I remember that. But I never met the man to my knowledge.'

'That is strange; for I seem to recollect that he spoke of you and told me that you were in Italy.' He sighed, and then, to complete the test, abruptly flung his bombshell.

'Poor fellow! He died a week or two ago.'

There was a little pause before she answered him.

'We need not trouble about him, then. Talk to me of the living. Sit here beside me, Mr Melville, and tell me of yourself.'

This utter lack of interest in Lebel's fate reassured Marc-Antoine. The steward of Saulx must, he assumed, have been personally unknown to her. His connection with her had gone no further than the indication to Barras of the title she might conveniently assume.

Her interest in Marc-Antoine had dispersed her audience. Only Terzi and Vendramin remained, and Terzi was stifling a yawn. Ser Leonardo took him by the arm.

'Do not let us restrain these confidences, Rocco. Let us go and annoy the Levantine Foscolo by praising Gozzi to him.'

Alone with the lady who claimed to be his widow, Marc-Antoine found himself subjected to a rapid fire of questions. Above all she desired to know why he was in Venice and what the nature of his relations with the Pizzamani. She was a little arch on this. But he did not choose to notice it.

He answered that he had known the Pizzamani in London when the Count was Venetian Minister there, and they had become friends of his.

'One of them in particular, no doubt.' She watched him slyly over the edge of her fan.

'Oh, yes. Domenico.'

'You disappoint me. Leonardo, then, troubles himself in vain?'

'Ser Leonardo troubles himself? On my account?'

'You know, of course, that he is to marry Isotta Pizzamano. He senses a rival in you.'

'And he has left us together so that you may ascertain for him whether he has cause to do so?'

She was shocked. 'You are blunt, you English. Mon Dieu, how blunt! It is what renders you adorable. And how sternly you can look upon a woman! With those eyes upon me I could never lie to you. Not that I should ever want to. Can you keep faith?'

'Put me to the test if you doubt it.'

'You've guessed the truth. An easy guess to one who knew Leonardo better. Unless he had ends to serve, he would not so readily have left us alone together.'

'Let me hope that he will often have ends to serve. Is it possible that I could have the honour of making him uneasy on your account as well?'

'Are you so ungallant as to be surprised?'

'It is the plurality of his jealousies that confuses me. Are there in Venice any ladies with whom I may be friends without going in peril of assassination by Monsieur Vendramin?'

'Now you want to laugh, and I am serious. Oh, but very serious. He is as jealous as a Spaniard, and as dangerous in his jealousy. Am I to reassure him on the score of Monna Isotta?'

'If I interest you sufficiently that you should not desire my death.'

'Far from it. I desire to see more of you.'

'In spite of the Spanish jealousy of this jealous Venetian?'

'Since you are so brave as to make a jest of it, come and see me soon. I am lodged at the Casa Gazzola, near the Rialto. Your gondolier will know it. Will you come?'

'In imagination I am there already.'

She smiled. A sweet, alluring smile, he accounted it; but he observed how it deepened the creases about her vivid eyes, betraying an age more advanced than was at first to be supposed in her.

'For an Englishman,' she said, 'you do not seem to lack enterprise. But, then, you'll have learnt it with your excellent French.'

Vendramin and Terzi were returning. Marc-Antoine stood up, and bowed over her hand.

'I shall expect you,' she said. 'Remember!'

'Superfluous injunction,' protested Marc-Antoine.

Terzi bore him away to make him known to others present and to give him refreshment. As he sipped a glass of malvoisie and listened to a heated argument upon the sonnet between two dilettanti, he saw Vendramin in the place he had vacated beside the little spurious Vicomtesse, very deeply and earnestly in talk.

The precise extent of Vendramin's entanglement with this woman was only half – and the less important half – of the problem that confronted Marc-Antoine. Knowing her for an active French secret agent, charged at this very moment with the corruption of a man as valuable to the anti-Jacobin cause as Vendramin, it was his duty at once to denounce her. A man so engaged he would destroy without compunction. But she was a woman, and very delicate and frail, and the vision of that slender white neck in the strangler's cord was a vision of pure horror. Chivalry, then, made duty's course repellent. The reflection that Vendramin's corruption if accomplished would open a door of escape for Isotta must – even had there been in that no profit to himself – make the course impossible. Duty, however, demanded imperiously that he should follow it.

In this conflict of aims personal and political he postponed solution of his problem until he could see ahead more clearly. He could keep this charming widow of his under closest observation, and he would watch no less closely the measures taken for the seduction of Vendramin.

This took him a few days later to the legation, at a time when Venice was agog with the news that the Austrians, pleading the necessities of war, had occupied the fortress of Peschiera.

He found Lallemant rubbing his hands over the news.

'After this,' said the French Ambassador, 'it seems to me that we do as we please. Having tolerated the violation of her frontiers by the Austrians, Venice can hardly complain if we do the same. Unarmed neutralities have no rights that I can discern.'

Marc-Antoine was caustic. 'If it will remove the necessity for your reckless waste of the nation's money, that will be something to the good.'

Lallemant looked up from his dispatches. 'What flea is biting you now? Of what reckless waste am I guilty?'

'I was thinking of Vendramin, on whose corruption you have spent so much so vainly.'

'So vainly? Ah, that! You are well informed.'

'Well enough. I see a scurry of warlike activity where hitherto all has been peaceful indifference, and I know where the reason is to be found: in Vendramin's eloquence at the last meeting of the Council, when he was supported by the entire barnabotto rabble. Having spent so much gold and pains upon his corruption, you might have completed it in time to avoid that.'

'Bah!' Lallemant stretched his hand across the table palm upwards, the fingers and thumb clawing inwards. 'I have him there whenever I want him.'

'Then why let him go bleating of defences and armaments? How much longer will you leave him to do the work of the Austrophiles?'

'All in my own good time, citizen-representative. The further he is led into this quagmire, the more difficult will it be for him to extricate himself.' He turned aside to take up two packages from his table. 'Here are letters for you.'

One of these was from Barras. The Director wrote on various matters, and particularly stressed the need for harmonious co-operation with Bonaparte, who must be given every assistance. Marc-Antoine observed here a change of tone reflecting the growing influence of the commander-in-chief of the Army of Italy.

The other letter was from Bonaparte himself. It was cold, curt, peremptory, and remarkable for bad spelling. It informed the Representative Lebel that General Bonaparte required soundings taken of the canals by which the city of Venice was to be approached. He added that he was writing to Lallemant in the same sense, and he commanded rather than requested the representative to co-operate diligently with the ambassador.

Since thus the matter was already in Lallemant's knowledge, Marc-Antoine at once took it up with him as if he were giving him news.

'Yes, yes,' he was interrupted. 'I have a letter from the General, too, on that. He's behind the fair. These soldiers think they alone can discern the obvious. We've been at work on it here for some weeks already.'

Marc-Antoine displayed a proper interest.

'Who is at work on it?'

'Our invaluable Vicomtesse.'

'You are not telling me that she is taking soundings, are you?'

'Don't be a fool. She has charge of the matter. She has corrupted a rascal named Rocco Terzi – another starveling barnabotto – and he is employing three or four scoundrels of his own. They work for him by night and bring him daily their results from which he is preparing charts. Considering what I have done, I propose, myself, to inform the General in detail.'

Marc-Antoine shrugged indifferently. 'You will save me the trouble.'

He repressed his excitement until he was closeted with Count Pizzamano.

The Count was in exasperation at the hedonistic apathy into which he observed the Government and the people alike to be relapsing. In particular he was disgusted with the Doge. Along the canals and through the narrow streets of the city was to be heard a new song:

> El Doge Manin
> Dal cuor picenin
> L'é streto de man
> L'é nato furlan.

But not even this lampoon directed at the meanness of His Serenity's contribution to the defence fund, in which his Friulian birth was mockingly urged as the reason for his little heart and tight hand, could sting him into an energy of patriotism.

'I am, then, the more opportune,' said Marc-Antoine. 'I bring you something that must make Lodovico Manin realize the seriousness of the French menace.' And he disclosed the matter of the soundings.

He did not know whether the Count was more appalled than uplifted. But he was certainly in a simmer of excitement when he carried Marc-Antoine off to the Casa Pesaro and the Doge.

Two barges stood at the palace steps and an encumbrance of chests and cases filled the vestibule, heralding the imminent departure of Manin for his country seat at Passeriano.

The Prince consented to receive them. But his greeting was peevish. He was dressed for travelling, and they were delaying a departure already belated if he were to reach Mestre before nightfall. He hoped that their news was of an importance to justify this.

'Your Serenity shall judge,' said the Count grimly. 'Tell him, Marc.'

When he had heard the story, the Doge wrung his hands in distress. And yet he was disposed to discount its importance. It had an ugly look. Oh, yes. He would admit that much. But, after all, so had the preparations the Serenissima was making. Most probably the French were, like themselves, merely disposing for a remote eventuality. He was the more persuaded that it was remote in view of the assurances he had received that peace between France and the Empire would not now be long delayed. That would put an end to all these troublesome questions.

'But until the peace is signed,' ventured Marc, with a daring hardness of voice, 'these troublesome questions will exist, and answers to them must be found.'

'Must be found!' The Doge stared at him, deeply offended that a stranger, one who was not even a Venetian, should take this tone with the Prince of Venice.

'Your Highness will remember that I speak with the voice of the British Government. It is as if Mr Pitt himself were speaking to you. Myself, I am of no account. Remembering this, perhaps Your Serenity will pardon a frankness which duty seems to impose upon me.'

The Doge shambled ill-humouredly about the room. 'At so inconvenient a moment,' he was muttering. 'As you see, Francesco, I am on the point of leaving. My health demands it. I am too fat to endure the heat here. I am going to Passeriano. I shall be ill if I remain in Venice.'

'Venice may be ill if you depart,' said the Count.

'You, too! Always am I addressed in the language of exaggeration, except about my own personal concerns. My God! You would make me think that you suppose a Doge not to be a man any more; not to be flesh and blood. There are limits to his endurance as to another's. And I am not well, I tell you. Notwithstanding, I am to remain here in this stifling heat to investigate every rumour that you and others choose to bring me!'

'This is no rumour, Highness,' said Marc-Antoine. 'It is a fact, and one from which the gravest inferences may be drawn.'

The Doge checked in his aimless, peevish wanderings. He squared himself before his visitors, his hands on his broad hips.

'After all, how do I know that it is a fact? Where is the evidence of this incredible story? For it is incredible. Utterly incredible. Every known circumstance contradicts it. After all, Venice is not concerned in this war. It lies between France and the Empire. The action here of the French is simply a wide outflanking movement to relieve the pressure against their armies on the Rhine. If men would remember that, there would be less of this alarmist nonsense, less of this frenzy of arming. This is what may bring us trouble. It may be interpreted as provocative, and so bring upon us the very calamity which fools pretend that it will avoid.'

There is no arguing with an obstinacy so ingrained that it finds in all things its confirmation. Marc-Antoine kept narrowly to the matter.

'Just now Your Serenity asked for evidence. The evidence will be found at the house of Rocco Terzi.'

He merely provoked a deeper impatience.

'So that what you bring me, really, is a denunciation! Really, Francesco, you should know better than to trouble me with this. Denunciations are for the inquisitors of state. It is to them you should address yourselves. Time enough to trouble me when they have found evidence to support this incredible story. Go then to the inquisitors, Francesco. Lose no time.'

Thus he got rid of them, which appeared to be his main concern so that he might be free, himself, to set out for Mestre.

The Count, his soul laden with contempt, carried Marc-Antoine to the Piazzetta and the Ducal Palace. They found the secretary of the inquisitors in his office there; and to him, at Marc-Antoine's request – since he desired to appear in these matters no more than he must – the Count formulated the denunciation of Rocco Terzi.

In the dead of that night Messer Grande, as the Captain of Justice was called, attended by a dozen of his men descended upon Rocco Terzi in the house at San Moisé where he lived in a luxury that in itself should have betrayed him. Cristofoli, the alert confidente of the secret tribunal, went carefully through the prisoner's effects and papers, and amongst them found the charts that were in course of being completed.

A brother of Terzi's, hearing of the arrest, presented himself two days later before the inquisitors of state, to offer with brotherly solicitude to procure anything lacking for the prisoner's comfort.

He received from the secretary the smooth sibylline reply that nothing whatever was then necessary to the prisoner.

It was the literal truth, for Rocco Terzi, of the uneasy eyes, convicted of high treason, had been quietly strangled in the Piombi.

Chapter 13

The Ultimatum

Marc-Antoine sent up his name to the Vicomtesse de Saulx. He was kept waiting. The Vicomtesse was in a state of distraction, which at first prompted her to deny herself. On second thoughts she decided to receive him.

Dressed with the care and elegance demanded by a visit of gallantry, the visitor was ushered into a dainty boudoir that was hung and tapestried in faded golds to make a background for delicate ebony furniture with ivory inlays. The Vicomtesse had made no effort to compose herself. The signs of distraction were plainly upon her. Thus she could come more directly to her very object in admitting him.

'My friend, you arrive in a sad moment. You behold me inconsolable.'

He bowed over her slim white hand. 'Nevertheless, give me leave to essay consolation.'

'You will have heard the news?'

'That Austrian troops are pouring down from the Tyrol to the relief of Mantua?'

'I mean about poor Rocco. Rocco Terzi. He has disappeared, and the rumour is that he has been arrested. What do they say in the Piazza?'

'Oh, yes. Of course. Rocco Terzi. A friend of Vendramin's. That is the rumour: that the inquisitors have arrested him.'

'But why? Have you heard?'

'It is said, I think, that he is suspected of holding communications with General Bonaparte.'

'Preposterous! My poor Rocco! A butterfly; a joyous creature concerned in life only with its gay aspects. And so amusing. Do they say what it was that he communicated?'

'I don't think it is known. The inquisitors work very secretly.'

She shuddered. 'That is what frightens one.'

'You! But of what should you be frightened?'

'That harm may come to this poor, foolish Rocco.'

'So much concern! He is enviable a little, this Messer Rocco.'

Vendramin was announced and ushered in at the same time. Marc-Antoine observed that here was one who did not wait to discover if he would be received.

He came in airily with that swaying, jaunty step of his, and frowned upon beholding Marc-Antoine. His greeting was tart.

'Sir, I protest, you begin to have the gift of ubiquity.'

'A little, yes.' Marc-Antoine smiled amiably. 'I develop it. I do what I can.' Then he turned the subject. 'This is sad news I hear of your friend Terzi.'

'No friend of mine, by God, sir. The treacherous rogue. I pick my friends with care.'

'Fi donc, Leonardo!' cried the Vicomtesse. 'To deny him at such a time. That is not nice.'

'Time to deny him. High time. Do you know of what they accuse him?'

'Of what? Tell me.'

Her eagerness faded into disappointment when it was discovered that he merely repeated what was known already.

'I sicken to think that such a man moved freely amongst us,' he protested.

'Yet,' Marc-Antoine objected, 'all that you know at present is that he has been arrested. The remainder is rumour.'

'I want no friends about whom such rumours are possible.'

'How is rumour ever to be suppressed? It builds on the flimsiest grounds. Rocco Terzi, for instance, is said to have lived in luxury, and yet he is known to have been without any proper source of means. Is it not usual in such cases for rumour to suggest an improper source? Might not the suspicion born of this be the sole reason for his arrest?'

Vendramin had entirely lost his genial look. His eyes were almost malevolent at this reminder that Rocco Terzi's case in that respect was very much his own.

He came to it with the Vicomtesse as soon as Marc-Antoine had gone, which was quite soon thereafter, for Ser Leonardo made him feel that here his room would be more welcome than his company.

'You heard what that damned Englishman said, Anne? That Rocco may have been arrested on suspicion because of the means he displayed. Do you know whence he derived them?'

'How should I?'

He got up from the couch, where he had been sitting beside her, and paced the little room. 'It is cursedly odd. It must be that what is said is true. He was being paid by the French Government. They'll most likely rack him to make him speak.' He shivered. 'The inquisitors stop at nothing.' He stood still and looked at her. 'Suppose now that I...'

He did not dare, nor was it necessary to continue; nor for that matter did she give him time.

'You are starting at shadows, Leonardo.'

'A shadow seems to me to have been all that there was against Rocco; the same sort of shadow they may discover that I am casting. Like Rocco's my resources are beggarly; yet like Rocco I live well and lack for nothing. Suppose they put me on the rack to discover the source of my means. Suppose that I break down, and confess that you... that you...'

'That I have been lending you money. What then? I am not the French Government. They may despise you for living on a woman. But they can't hang you for it.'

The phrase made him uncomfortable. He flushed and looked at her in annoyance. 'You know that the money is only borrowed. I am not living on you, Anne. I shall pay you back every penny.'

'When you make your rich marriage, I suppose.'

'Do you sneer? You are not jealous, Anne? You are never jealous?'

'Why not? You are jealous enough of me. But perhaps you have the exclusive right to jealousy. You certainly behave as if you had, and as if you suppose that others have no feelings.'

'Oh, Anne!' He set a knee on the couch beside her, and put an arm about her shoulders. 'How can you say this to me? You know that I make this marriage because I must. That all my future hangs upon it.'

'Oh, yes, 1 know. I know.' She spoke a trifle wearily. He stooped to kiss her cheek. She suffered it without excitement. And he discovered that he was straying from the point.

'You are not the French Government, you have said. But a good deal of the money has been in drafts on Vivanti's drawn by Lallemant.'

'What then?' She was sharply impatient. 'How many times have I told you that Lallemant is my cousin and has charge of my affairs. When I want money, it is thus he gives it to me.'

'I know, my love. But if this were discovered? You see this misfortune of Rocco's has made me cursed nervous.'

'How could it be discovered? You are being foolish. What does the money matter? Do you suppose I care whether you pay me back or not?'

He slid down onto the couch, and took her in his arms. 'How I love you for your sweet trust.'

But the lady was not thrilled. 'Nevertheless you will marry Madame Isotta.'

'Why will you rally me, my angel? You have said that you will not marry ever again.'

'Certainly not you, Leonardo.'

He frowned annoyance. 'Why not?' he demanded.

Impatiently she thrust him away from her. 'God in Heaven! Was there ever such a vain fribble of a man? You are to love where you please and marry where you please, and those upon whom you place the sacred seal of your kiss are to hold themselves in perpetual fidelity to you! Faith, you are modest in your claims. What woman could deny you? It annoys you that I should not be ready to marry you, given the chance, whilst you would take no chance of marrying me.' She stood up, a slight wisp of lovely, dainty anger. 'Do you know, Leonardo, there are moments when you make me sick. And this is one of them.'

He was in an alarm of penitence. He protested that he was just a poor devil at the mercy of a cruel fate, with a great name to maintain and perpetuate, and able to do it only by a marriage of convenience. Knowing how he loved her, as she must know from the proofs he had given, it was cruel of her to cast his misfortunes in his teeth. He was on the point of tears before she consented to make her peace with him. In the sweetness of that reconciliation he forgot the fate of Rocco Terzi and his own fears, persuaded himself that he had been starting at shadows, as she had declared.

But there were others who had not at hand such delectable means to stifle alarm at the fate of Rocco Terzi. And Lallemant was of these.

Profoundly disturbed and exercised by the event, he welcomed the arrival of Marc-Antoine.

'I have just left the Vicomtesse,' the supposed representative announced. 'I found her distressed by news of the arrest of a friend of hers, one Rocco Terzi.' And then he dropped his voice. 'Was not that the name of the man who was charting the canals?'

'It was,' said Lallemant, with a queer dryness.

He sat at his writing-table in a crouching attitude, watching Marc-Antoine with eyes that were like gimlets in his pallid face. The tone and the look were warning enough for Marc-Antoine. He knew himself in danger.

Meditatively he stroked his chin, his face a mask of glumness.

'This is very serious,' he said.

Again the Frenchman was incisively laconic. 'It is, Lebel.'

Swiftly Marc-Antoine stepped close up to the table. He lowered his voice until it was little more than a whisper, but a whisper sibilant with fury.

'You fool! Have I not warned you against using that name?' His eyes played briskly round to the door, and back to Lallemant's big face. 'With a spy in your household, you talk without the least circumspection. God of God! Do you think I want to end like your Rocco Terzi? How do you know that Casotto is not outside that door at this moment?'

'Because he is not in the house,' said Lallemant.

Marc-Antoine gave visible signs of relief.

'Was he in the house the other day, when you told me about Terzi?'

'Not to my knowledge.'

'Oh! So you don't even know when he comes and goes?' Marc-Antoine was carrying the war into the enemy's territory. 'Anyway, whether he is here or not, I should prefer to talk to you in that inner room. I don't know why you should lately have grown careless.'

'I am not careless, my friend. I know what I do. But have it your own way.' He heaved himself up, and they passed into the farther chamber.

This gave Marc-Antoine time to think. And the need to think had rarely been more imperative. He stood, he realized, on the very edge of discovery. And he most certainly would be hurled over that edge unless he could completely stifle Lallemant's well-founded suspicions. To accomplish it some ultra-Jacobin gesture was necessary at whatever cost.

Before they had come to rest in that inner room the memory of Barras' last letter came to suggest a course. Odious and repellent though it was, yet he must take it if he was to restore and consolidate his shaken credit.

'Do you know,' Lallemant attacked him, 'that I find it more than odd that when a secret matter passes between us here, it should be followed by almost immediate publication. There was that business of Sir Richard Worthington. You explained it. But the explanation seems to me less plausible today than at the time.'

'Why so?' Marc-Antoine was dry and haughty, very much the citizen-representative of their first interview.

'Because of this affair of Rocco Terzi. Until I told you four days ago, not a soul in Venice knew of it but Terzi and myself. And then that very night Rocco is arrested, his papers seized, and by now, if I know their methods at all, he will have been strangled.'

Accusation could hardly have been plainer.

Marc-Antoine stood before him, stiff and cool.

'Not a soul but Terzi and yourself, eh? And the Vicomtesse whom you employed to corrupt Terzi? Does she count for nothing?'

'That is brave! That is clever! You accuse her, do you?'

'I do not. I merely indicate to you the general looseness of your statements.'

'My statements are not loose. The Vicomtesse did not know the purpose for which I employed Terzi. She did not know, do you hear? Do you think I tell all my business to my spies? She did not know.'

'You never doubt, do you? No, you are just the man to make sure of things. How do you know that Terzi did not tell her?'

'That is unthinkable.'

'Why? Because you don't choose to think it. There's stout reasoning, on my soul. And how do you know that one or another of the men working for Terzi did not blab? I must suppose they knew what they were doing?'

Lallemant showed exasperation. 'They were being well paid. Would any of them cut off a supply of money easily earned?'

'One of them may have taken fright. It would not be surprising.'

'Is there anyone else upon whom you can cast suspicion?'

'Upon whom do you prefer to cast it, Lallemant?' Marc-Antoine's voice had grown hard as steel.

Lallemant gulped. His eyes were furious. But he hesitated.

'Well?' quoth Marc-Antoine. 'I am waiting.'

The other took a turn in the room, his double chin in his hand. The aspect of the representative was a little terrifying. Lallemant swayed helplessly between doubts.

'Will you frankly answer me a question?' he asked at last.

'I should welcome a direct one.'

'Will you tell me why you went to the Ducal Palace on Monday evening, with Count Pizzamano, and whom you went to see there?'

'Do you set spies upon me, Lallemant?'

'Answer my question. Then I will answer yours. What were you doing at the Ducal Palace a few hours before Terzi's arrest?'

'I went to see the inquisitors of state.'

As once before the immediate frankness of the admission was like a blow.

Lallemant rallied. 'For what purpose?' he insisted, but already he had lost half his fierce assurance.

'For a purpose which I came here to discuss with you today. Sit down, Lallemant.' All at once he was peremptory, the hectoring official in authority. 'Sit down,' he repeated, more harshly, and Lallemant, almost mechanically, obeyed him.

'If you kept your wits about you, and addressed yourself to the real interests of the Nation instead of frittering away your energies and resources on trivialities, what I have now had to do would have been done long ago. You will have known in your time, Lallemant – you must have done, for they are to be met everywhere – chicken-witted men of law, who run cackling after the small grains of detail so diligently that they lose sight of the main issues. You are like those, Lallemant. You sit here so intent upon the little foolish webs of intrigue that you are spinning with such self-complacency that you have no eyes for the things that matter.'

'For instance?' growled Lallemant, whose face was turning purple.

'I am coming to the instance. In Verona there is a fat slug of a man, the ci-devant Comte de Provence, who calls himself Louis XVIII, keeps a court that in itself is an insult to the French Republic, and is actively in correspondence with all the despots in Europe, weaving every kind of intrigue to sap our credit. That man is a menace to us.

Yet for months he has been suffered to continue unmolested in the enjoyment of Venetian hospitality, abusing it to our constant detriment. Have you really been blind to the harm that he is doing us? It seems you must have been, since it has been necessary for me to take in hand the work you should have done.'

His level gaze was steadily, almost hypnotically, upon the ambassador, whom he had now cast into bewilderment.

'Here was the chance to serve two purposes at once: on the one hand, to put an end to an intolerable interference; on the other, to establish a sound grievance against the Serenissima; to create a pretext for the measures which our arms may presently find desirable. Thoroughly to establish this a written ultimatum would not serve. That is to follow. It shall go from here today. It was necessary – or I judged it so – that I should first attend before the inquisitors and test the extent of their awareness of the monarchist activities of this so-called Louis XVIII.'

Lallemant interrupted him. 'Do you mean that you went in your own person? As the Representative Lebel?'

'Since I am here and alive, you may be sure that I did not. I went in the character of a friendly mediator, who had been informed by you of what was proposed, and requested by you to see the inquisitors first, so as to mitigate the blow. That is why I enlisted the assistance of Count Pizzamano. You understand?'

'No. That is – not yet. Not quite. But continue.'

'The inquisitors met me with the assertion that the gentleman to whom they had given shelter in Verona was known to them only as the Comte de Lille. I pointed out as politely as I could that a change of name does not imply a change of identity. I pointed out to them, speaking as a friendly onlooker holding certain commissions from the British Government, that by his intrigues this unfortunate exile had put them in an extremely false position. I informed them that it was within my knowledge that an ultimatum from France on the subject would reach them almost at once. I urged them in their own interest to conciliate France by an immediate compliance with the terms of this ultimatum when it came.'

He paused. There was a scornful curl to his lip as he pondered Lallemant's dazed agitation.

'Now that you know what I went to do at the Ducal Palace, you will perhaps realize that it is something you should have done months ago.'

Indignation surmounted the ambassador's bewilderment. 'How could I take a step of such gravity without express orders from Paris?'

Marc-Antoine was sententious. 'A fully accredited ambassador requires no special orders to perform that which is so obviously in the interests of his government.'

'I do not admit that it is so obviously in our interests. I cannot see that it is in our interests at all. We shall certainly provoke resentment; bitter resentment. The Venetian Government cannot comply with our demand without covering itself with opprobrium.'

'What have we to do with that?'

'We shall have something to do with it if they are driven into resistance. Where shall we stand then?'

'The whole purpose of that preliminary step of mine was to ascertain the chances of active resistance. I have no cause to suppose that it will be offered. And, anyway, my mind is made up. The ultimatum must go at once. Today.'

Lallemant got up in agitation. His broad peasant face was purple. He no longer had a thought for the suspicions which had originally been urging him. He was already far, indeed, from those, more than persuaded of their utter idleness. This man Lebel showed himself to be an extremist, a revolutionary of the intransigent school which had passed away with Robespierre. To suspect the republican zeal of a man capable of conceiving such an ultimatum was utterly fantastic. He might not yet perfectly understand Lebel's explanation of his visit to the inquisitors. But he was no longer even concerned to understand it, in view of the fruits of it with which he was presented. These were quite enough for his digestion.

'Are you asking me to send this ultimatum?' he demanded.

'Haven't I been clear?'

The rather corpulent figure stood squarely before Marc-Antoine.

'My regrets, citizen. I cannot take your orders.'

Marc-Antoine was very cold and dignified. 'You are aware of the powers vested in me by the Directory.'

'I am perfectly aware of them. But I cannot do such violence to my judgment. I regard this ultimatum as rash and provocative, and opposed to my instructions which are to keep the peace with the Serenissima. It demands of the Venetian Government an unnecessary humiliation. Without express orders from the Directory itself, I cannot take the responsibility of putting my signature to such a document.'

Marc-Antoine looked him squarely between the eyes for a moment. Then he shrugged. 'Very well. I will do no violence to your feelings. I must take upon myself the responsibility that you shirk.' He began to draw off his gloves. 'Be good enough to call Jacob.'

It was Lallemant's turn to stare. He had understood the intention.

'That, of course, will be your own affair,' he said, at length. 'But I tell you frankly that if I had the power to oppose you, I should exercise it.'

'The Directory will be thankful that you have not. Jacob, if you please.'

To the swarthy little secretary when he came, Marc-Antoine dictated the curt terms of his communication, whilst Lallemant paced up and down the room simmering with suppressed indignation.

It was addressed to the Doge and Senate of the Most Serene Republic of Venice, and couched as follows:

I have the honour to inform you that the French Directory views with the gravest misgivings the shelter afforded in Verona to the so-called Comte de Lille, ci-devant Comte de Provence, and the facilities for conspiring and for intriguing against the French Republic, One and Indivisible, which the said ci-devant has there enjoyed. As evidence of this we hold and are prepared to submit to Your Serenities letters of the said ci-devant Comte de Provence to the Empress of Russia, which were intercepted by us as lately as last week. In consideration of these activities we must regard the said ci-devant's sojourn in Verona as a breach of the amity existing between our two republics, and we are under the necessity of demanding the immediate expulsion of the ci-devant Comte de Provence from the territory of the Most Serene Republic of Venice.

When Jacob had completed it, Marc-Antoine took the quill from him, and signed the document: 'Camille Lebel, Representative of the Directory of France.'

'Let it be delivered at the Ducal Palace without the least delay,' he ordered. 'You understand, Lallemant?'

'Oh, but of course,' was the ill-humoured answer. And again he repeated: 'The responsibility is yours.'

Chapter 14

Justification

If Marc-Antoine went home that day in the well-founded conviction that he had extinguished in Lallemant's mind all suspicion of double-dealing on the part of so intransigent a republican as he had proved himself, nevertheless, his heart was heavy.

His explanation of his visit to the Ducal Palace would not for a moment have been believed had he not backed it by that cruel ultimatum which must bring a measure of persecution to his unfortunate prince. Not even to save himself from the destruction that had faced him could he have taken that odious step had he not been persuaded by the tone of Barras' last letter that it could be only a matter of days before orders for that very measure would come from the Directory.

Even so, he wished that some lesser sacrifice might have served his ends. This ultimatum was a very ugly business.

And a very ugly business the Serenissima accounted it when it reached her.

In the course of inveighing against it, Count Pizzamano startled Marc-Antoine by informing him that it was known to the inquisitors of state that the Deputy Camille Lebel was in Venice. This, because in the ultimatum, which bore his signature, an event of the previous week was given as the immediate cause of it. Since there could not have been time to communicate with Paris on that matter, it became clear, not only that this Lebel was in Venice, but further that he was acting upon his own initiative. His ultimatum was regarded as a gesture of officious malice on the part of an extreme Jacobin.

This exposition made Marc-Antoine aware of a blunder committed in mentioning the intercepted letter to the Empress of Russia. He was not, however, disposed to attach importance to it.

The Serenissima bent in servile humility her once proud head. She ate dust, complied with the French ultimatum, and Louis XVIII departed from Verona on his travels.

He did not depart without some characteristic expressions of petulance, utterly beneath the dignity of a prince. His case is an illustration of how the conferring of benefits can appear to establish a liability to continue them. Instead of gratitude for the hospitality enjoyed, he displayed only resentment that it should be discontinued, and that Venice should be unwilling to defy on his behalf the guns of Bonaparte. He demanded that the name of Bourbon should be erased from the Golden Book of the Serenissima, and that a suit of armour presented to Venice by his ancestor Henri IV should be restored to him. They were childish demands, and they were so treated. Nevertheless, they served to increase the Senate's sense of shame and humiliation.

Within a week Marc-Antoine was relieved by the definite orders to present just such an ultimatum which reached Lallemant from the Directory; so that to the ambassador's impressions of Lebel's ardent Jacobinism was now added an increased respect for his acumen and foresight.

It was also of some relief to Marc-Antoine that the problem presented by the Vicomtesse was resolved for him by the events. In the first place to denounce her now must, in view of the suspicions that had attached to him in the matter of Terzi, be in the last degree imprudent; in the second place, it became desirable to leave her at liberty because her activities, being observed by him, supplied a channel of information.

As the summer advanced, the disregard of Venetian rights by both belligerents became more marked. Yet Manin curbed the impatience of public opinion with the news that a fresh Austrain army under General Wurmser was about to descend into Italy. It came at the end of July; and pouring down the slopes of Monte Baldo, inflicted a rout upon the French. There was joy in Venice, and its faith in the Empire was maintained thereafter even when by the middle of August Wurmser, defeated, was in full retreat towards the Tyrol. The procrastinators could still point to Austrian victories on the Rhine, and to the fact that Mantua still held, insisting, not without truth, that as long as Mantua held, Bonaparte was comparatively immobilized.

Thus, save for transient alarms and transient upliftings, life in hedonistic Venice flowed much as usual, and Marc-Antoine found in it little more than the part of the English idler he had assumed.

In those months his only activity on behalf of the cause he served was concerned with another denunciation. He had gleaned from Lallemant that a successor to Terzi had been found, and that soundings were once more being charted. When he inquired into the identity of this successor, Lallemant shook his head.

'Let me keep that to myself. If there should be an accident, I cannot again commit the folly of suspecting you of indiscretion.'

The accident followed. The inquisitors of state, on information supplied through Count Pizzamano by Marc-Antoine, employed the Signori di Notte, as the night-police of Venice was termed, to keep a sharp lookout for any boats that might be fishing in unlikely waters between Venice and the mainland, and to track them carefully down. After weeks of patient vigilance, the Signors of the Night were at last able to report such a boat. After operations which could have no legitimate object, this vessel was wont to repair to a house in the Giudecca. The person with whom the boatmen communicated there was a gentleman in poor circumstances named Sartoni.

This time not only was Sartoni taken by order of the inquisitors, and upon conviction suppressed as Terzi had been, but the two boatmen were also caught and sent to share his fate.

To Lallemant the distressing event supplied confirmation of the rashness of his earlier suspicions of Lebel.

Chapter 15

The Choice

Marc-Antoine beguiled his abundant enforced leisures in amusements, which even in those days were never far to seek in Venice. He was to be seen at theatres and casinos, often accompanied by Vendramin, who continued freely to borrow money from him whilst keeping him under observation.

He was being a source of definite anxiety to Vendramin, who could not rid himself of the feeling that between Marc-Antoine and Isotta some intelligence existed. Marc-Antoine was too constantly at the Casa Pizzamano for the peace of mind of Vendramin, who knew nothing of his political activities. There were water-parties to Malamocco, and occasional visits to Domenico at the Fort Sant' Andrea, in which Marc-Antoine was invariably included, whilst once in September, when some British ships of war stood off the Port of Lido, Marc-Antoine took Isotta and her mother with him to visit the captain of one of them who was a friend of his.

He was also frequently met by Vendramin at the lodgings of the Vicomtesse de Saulx in the Casa Gazzola. This, too, was becoming disquieting, if only because Marc-Antoine, fully aware by now of Vendramin's liaison with the Vicomtesse, might be moved to carry the tale of them to Isotta. And Vendramin had good cause to dread its effect upon the mind of a patrician Venetian maid, who had been so cloistered and guarded from knowledge of the world's impurities.

So far he had played his cards shrewdly with Isotta. He had affected an austerity which should make him stand well in her virginal mind. And he had taken care that the Pizzamani had never even heard the name of the Vicomtesse de Saulx, an easy matter considering how different were the social worlds in which they moved. Isotta's was a very restricted circle, and she had never seen the inside of a casino. Nor for that matter had her parents, whilst for the last few months Domenico had been chiefly absent on the duties of his command.

But the possibility of betrayal by a man whose rivalry he sensed so clearly set him brooding upon measures for bringing matters to an issue.

He was in this obsession when he went one afternoon of late September to the Casa Pizzamano, to be informed by the porter that his excellency the Count was above stairs, and that Madonna Isotta was in the garden. As a matter of natural instinct the lover chose the garden.

There he found not only Isotta, but Marc-Antoine, walking with her.

Jealousy has the faculty of taking every attendant circumstance for its confirmation. Because the sky was grey and there was an edge to the wind of that autumnal day, it must seem to Vendramin unnatural that these two should choose to saunter in the open; he must see in it evidence of an overwhelming desire to be alone together, to escape the restraining surveillance indoors; and at once, disregarding the intimate standing of Marc-Antoine with the Pizzamani, he must perceive here an impropriety.

In a less degree some consciousness of this may have been upon the straitly-reared Isotta herself. She had gone out to cut a few roses that still lingered within the shelter of a trim, tall, boxwood enclosure. Marc-Antoine, espying her from above, had slipped away, leaving the Count and Countess in talk with Domenico who happened that day to be on leave from the fort.

She had greeted him with a glance so timid as to be almost apprehensive. With constraint they had talked of roses, of the garden, of the fragrance of the vervain that was everywhere, of the summer that was dying, and of other things as remote from what was in the mind of each. Then, with her little sheaf of roses red and white in the hand coarsely gloved for her task, she turned to re-enter.

'What haste, Isotta,' he reproached her.

She met his eyes with that serenity in which she had been schooled, and which she had by now recovered.

'It is kindly meant, Marc.'

'Kind? To avoid me? When I so rarely, so very rarely have a moment with you?'

'How else shall we save unnecessary heartache? See! You make me say things that I should not say. We have the knowledge of them to place among our memories. But there is no strength to be gathered from adding to it.'

'If you would only hope a little,' he sighed.

'So that I may heighten my ultimate despair?' She smiled as she spoke.

He attacked on a new line. 'Why do you suppose that I linger in Venice? What I came to do is done so far as I can do it. Which is to say that I have accomplished nothing, and that nothing is to be accomplished. I have no illusions on that score. Whether Venice stands or falls depends today no longer upon those entrusted with her government, but upon whether the French or the Austrians prevail in this struggle. Therefore, it must seem to me that Vendramin can have little claim to be rewarded for services he will never be called upon to render.'

Sadly she shook her head. 'A sophism, Marc. He will still claim fulfilment of a promise, a fulfilment not to be withheld in honour.'

'But the promise was in the nature of a bargain. Domenico perceives this, 1 know. If Vendramin is given no opportunity to perform his part, the bargain fails. So at least I see it, and therefore I remain in Venice, and I wait. I keep my hopes alive. You are so pale and wan these days, Isotta.' His voice assumed an ineffable tenderness that tortured her. 'There is not yet the need for this despair, my dear. I have been looking for a chance to tell you this; to tell you, too, that I am not entirely idle; that I not merely wait and watch. It is not only in the cause of monarchism that I am a secret agent here in Venice.'

This hint of action stirred her sharply. Her hand closed suddenly over his. 'What is it that you do? What is it that you can do? Tell me.'

Did he catch in her voice the tremor of that hope which she insisted was dead? His hand turned in the clasp of hers, to clasp in its turn.

'I cannot tell you more than that just yet, my dear. But I do implore you fervently not to count lost a battle that has not yet been fought.'

And then Vendramin was upon them, and found them thus: with hands clasped, looking intently into each other's eyes, the cold and stately Isotta in a flushed agitation such as he, certainly, had never succeeded in arousing in her.

He controlled his feelings. He had the sense to know that he could not rant here as in the salon of the Vicomtesse. Isotta, of whom he went a little in dread and must so continue until he married her, was not the person to tolerate either sarcasm or innuendo. So he swallowed rage and fears, and arrayed himself in his usual effusiveness.

'In the garden braving these autumn winds! But is it prudent? For our good friend Marc this may have no dangers. The chilly climate of his native land will have toughened him. But for you, my dear Isotta! Of what is your mother thinking that she permits it?'

With such solicitous reproaches he hustled them indoors, very gay and friendly on the surface, but tormented in the depths of him. What if the mischief he feared should have been done already? What if this sneaking Englishman should have told her of his relations with that Frenchwoman? His anxious eyes scanned her closely as he talked, and found her more than usually aloof and chill.

He took his resolve. There must be an end to this indefinite state.

And so for once he outstayed Marc-Antoine and that evening requested a word alone with the Count. The Count conducted him to a little room in which he kept his archives and transacted business, and beckoned Domenico to go with them. Vendramin would have preferred to be entirely private with the Count, and reminded him that this had been his request.

But the Count had laughed: 'What? And put me to the trouble of repeating whatever it may be to Domenico? Nonsense! I have no secrets from the boy, either family or political. Come along.'

Father and son sat behind closed doors in that rather musty little room, the elder Pizzamano gaunt and masterful, yet amiably disposed, the younger very elegant in his well-fitting blue coat with yellow facings, and stiff military stock. His air was alert, yet invested with that chill dignity that to Vendramin was so damnably reminiscent of his sister.

Although he had considered his opening, Vendramin was ill-at-ease.

He had accepted the proffered chair and had sat down at the Count's bidding. But as he began to speak he got up again, and continued after that to pace the room, his glance chiefly upon the wood-blocks that made a pattern on the floor.

He alluded to his fervent patriotism and in great detail to the energy he had displayed in swaying opinion among the recalcitrant barnabotti until he had them in his control and had been able to direct them into conservative channels with such signal effect as had been seen at the last momentous meeting of the Grand Council. He assumed that these claims of his would be conceded.

'My dear boy,' the Count soothed him, for as he proceeded his assertions had become vehement, 'what need to protest with so much heat that which we know already? Surely we have never stinted praise of your efforts, or admiration for your patriotic energy and skill.'

'No. That is not my complaint,' said Vendramin.

'Ah! He has a complaint.' It was a dry interjection from Domenico.

The Count repressed his son by a glance. 'But let us hear it, Leonardo.'

'The praise and the admiration, my lord, are but words. Oh, I nothing doubt their sincerity. But words they remain, and words profit a man little. I have, as you well know, certain aspirations, which you have encouraged; certain very dear hopes for the fulfilment of which... in short, it would be a poor compliment if I were not naturally impatient.'

The Count, reclining easily in his chair, his legs crossed, smiled gently. Perhaps had Vendramin left the matter there, he would better have served his aims. But he must be talking. His recent political labours had rendered him aware of a gift of rhetoric.

'After all,' he pursued, 'I must and do recognize that a marriage is in the nature of a contract to which each party must bring something. I am a poor man, my lord, as you well know; so that I could not approach Isotta with the ordinary endowments. But I am rich at least in power to serve my country; rich enough in this to have deserved your opinion that it abundantly compensates for what I may otherwise lack. If evidence of this, as it were, abstract wealth of mine lay in protestations, I should not have the temerity to...to come before you now with...with my impatience.' He fumbled and faltered a little here. Then went forcefully on. 'But it has been established by my activities, the fruits of which have already been placed upon the altar of our country.'

He struck an attitude, his blond head thrown back, his hand on his heart.

Domenico smiled sourly. But the Count continued benign.

'Yes, yes. You preach to the converted. And then?'

This easy surrender seemed almost to cut the ground from under Ser Leonardo's feet. To make himself really effective he needed some opposition against which he could lean. The lack of it left him with a sense of anti-climax.

'Then,' he said, 'since it is seen, and since you, my lord, so generously admit that my part of the contract is fulfilled, you will not – you cannot, I am sure – resist my demand that you should now fulfil yours.'

Domenico startled both his father and Ser Leonardo by the question he fired into that pause.

'Did you say "demand", sir?'

Vendramin's challenging attitude lost something of its noble poise. But, resentful, he was not to be put down.

'Demand. Yes. Natural, impatient demand.' Having thus defended his dignity, he could afford to make a concession. 'The word may not be of the happiest, of the best chosen to express what is in my heart. But then…'

'Oh, the word is excellently chosen,' said Domenico. 'It is most appropriate.'

The Count turned his head to look at him. He was a little puzzled. Domenico explained himself.

'You have very truly said yourself, Leonardo, that your betrothal to my sister is in the nature of a contract. Therefore, when one party to a contract has fulfilled his obligation under it, he is within his rights to *demand* a like fulfilment from the other party. So that we need not quibble over words which so exactly express the situation.' Vendramin sensed something ominous under this silky surface. And it came at once. Domenico turned to the Count. 'What you have rather to consider, father, are the facts themselves; whether Leonardo may properly be judged yet to have done as much as he claims.'

The Count in his benignity raised his brows and smiled tolerant at his son.

'But is it to be doubted, Domenico?'

'I am by no means sure that it is not. It is for you, my lord, to judge. You see, Leonardo himself has very properly classified this betrothal as a bargain, and…'

He was indignantly interrupted by Vendramin. 'Bargain, sir! I mentioned no such odious word. I spoke of a contract. A very proper term.'

'But does not a contract imply a bargain? Is not a contract the record of a bargain?'

'You twist words, sir. My meaning…'

'Your meaning was clear when you demanded the fulfilment of our part, as due upon the fulfilment of your own.'

Vendramin looked at his prospective brother-in-law without love. He tried to smother the poison of his answer in a laugh.

'On my soul, Domenico, you should have been a lawyer.'

The Count uncrossed his legs, and sat forward, interposing. 'But what is all this bother about words? What difference does it make?'

Resolutely Domenico stood his ground, in this battle he was fighting for his sister. 'Have you considered, my lord, what would happen if Leonardo were to turn slothful in marriage, and should neglect to maintain his influence upon his fellow-barnabotti?'

'This, sir, is too much,' Vendramin protested. 'You have no right to insult me by such an assumption.'

'Why perceive insult? We are dealing with a bargain struck. A bargain in which your part cannot be accounted fulfilled until we have reached the end of this sad struggle.'

Vendramin smiled sourly upon Domenico. 'I thank God, sir, that your father does not share your narrow and offensive views.'

This moved the Count to defend his son.

'They are not offensive, Leonardo. You are to consider that, all else apart, patriotism justifies a demand for the very fullest guarantees. If it were a question only of our own personal interests, I could be lenient. But the interests of Venice are concerned, and these impose that we should see your services fully rendered before we reward them.'

Anger betrayed Vendramin into sheer folly.

'You want guarantees? Why should I not demand guarantees from you? Guarantees that it is not in vain that I am holding barnabotto opinion in conservative channels?'

Sitting forward, elbow on knee, the Count looked up sideways at the tall, imposing figure of Vendramin.

'But,' he said, 'you are not suggesting that you could possibly do otherwise?'

Too quickly Vendramin answered out of his irritation. 'Could I not? I could let it run its natural Jacobin course. And why should I not if I have no guarantees that faith will be kept with me?'

Domenico rose, a twisted smile on his lips. 'Is this your patriotism? Is this all that Venice matters to you – to you, who resented just now the word bargain? Is this the man you are, Vendramin?'

Vendramin had the sense of being trapped, and now, like a trapped creature, twisted and turned in his efforts to extricate himself.

'You misunderstand me again. Wilfully. Oh, my God! How is it possible to weigh my words, Domenico, when you drive me frantic by your opposition?'

'It is the words that are not weighed that are the most revealing.'

'But those did not represent my mind.'

'I pray God they did not,' said the Count, as cold and stern now as hitherto he had been conciliatory.

'They did not, my lord. They did not. How could they? I was so goaded that I spoke without considering the implications of what I said. I vow to God that I would be flayed for Venice as Brigadin was flayed at Famagosta. I have been taunted into hasty words that do not express my mind. It was never my intention to do more, sir, than plead with you; than beg you to consider whether what I have already done is not proof enough of my zeal; enough to entitle me to enter upon the great happiness, the great blessing to which you know that I aspire.'

Domenico would have answered him, but that he was stayed by his father. The Count spoke quietly, gently, but with a definite coldness.

'Had you confined yourself to pleading, Leonardo, I must have found it difficult to withstand you. But the expressions that you have used…'

'I have said, sir, that they do not represent my mind. I swear that they do not.'

'If I did not believe you, I should deny you my house after tonight. But words have been uttered which shake my faith in you, and something must remain of them. Enough to make me perceive that your marriage with Isotta should await the end of this sad struggle in which we are engaged. I owe this as much to Venice as to myself.'

Vendramin had cause to rage that his own folly and the astuteness of Domenico, by whom he knew himself to be disliked, should have encompassed his defeat. But at least he was in no worse case than he had been before making this attempt. It remained only to retire in good order. He bowed his head.

'I have deserved it, of course, and I must accept your decision, Lord Count. I shall study to make amends for tonight's impatience by my resignation to this postponement. I shall hope to deserve some credit in your eyes for that.'

The Count stepped up to him, and let his hand rest on his shoulder for a moment. 'We will forget all this, Leonardo. I think I understand. We will forget it.'

But from what followed when Vendramin had departed, Count Pizzamano did not look at all as if he had forgotten. In the chair which he had resumed he sat wrapped in gloomy thought whilst for a little spell Domenico silently observed him. At last the soldier spoke.

'You realize now, sir, I hope, to what manner of rascal you are marrying your daughter.'

The tone of the Count's answer was laden with weariness. 'I have counter-balanced all the shortcomings of which I have been aware in him by his ardent patriotism. But you surprised him into expressions which reveal this patriotism to be a sham, a posture assumed for profit by a man without loyalty and without conscience. Oh, yes, Domenico, I realize. But, as I told him, I must forget it. He has threatened us. His retraction counts for nothing. I am not a fool. He has shown me that, if I were to break off his engagement to Isotta, he would go over with his pestilent barnabotti to the already swollen ranks of the obstructionists, the Francophiles, the Jacobins. And I know, as you know, Domenico, that if this happened, with such a weakling as Lodovico Manin in the ducal seat, the doom of the Most

Serene Republic would be written. Even if Bonaparte were defeated or were to spare us, we should still go the way of Reggio and Modena. Our traditions would be torn up, our dignity bespattered, and all that has made Venice glorious would be extinguished. A democratic government would follow, and the Tree of Liberty would be planted in Saint Mark's Square. That is the alternative which this scoundrel offers us. And it is an alternative which we cannot face.'

Chapter 16

The Dragon's Eye

It was a subdued Vendramin who was to be seen at the Casa Pizzamano in the days that followed; a Vendramin in sackcloth and ashes seeking by humility to be taken back into the full favour he had earlier enjoyed. It helped him that Domenico was kept absent by his military duties. Francesco Pizzamano was by nature of that philosophical turn of mind which endeavours hopefully to colour the inevitable. In his manner there was never an echo of that painful scene. But at the same time there was now a chill upon the courtesy he extended to Vendramin. Sensing it, Vendramin was not quite happy. But it was the least of his worries. Financial difficulties which he had hoped to relieve by an early marriage grew daily more oppressive. The Vicomtesse, hitherto so liberal, displayed an increasing reluctance to untie her purse-strings. The dangers never absent from delay were magnified in Vendramin's mind by his abiding dread of the rivalry of Marc-Antoine. And then, quite suddenly, he was afforded evidence, not merely of the reality of this rivalry, but that it went to depths which he could never have suspected.

It happened one evening that whilst at her father's request Isotta was playing for them an air by Paisiello, Ser Leonardo wandered down the room to the harpsichord, to do her the little service of turning the sheet from which she was reading.

Standing close behind and immediately over her, Vendramin fell appreciatively to considering the rich mass of her dark hair. A faint elusive fragrance that arose from it had the effect of quickening his perception of her other charms. With the eye of an experienced dilettante, he passed on to appraise the lovely column of the neck and the smooth shoulders, whiter than the foam of lace from which they emerged. He became aware of advantages other than those of wealth and position to be derived from making her his wife. By contrast with a beauty so regal, the porcelain daintiness of the Vicomtesse de Saulx became trivial and commonplace.

His day-dream was disturbed when Isotta paused, waiting for him to turn the sheet of music. Leaning forward to do so, his eyes strayed to the fan which she had placed on top of the harpsichord. He had seen it many times in her hand, or hanging from her girdle; but he had never before had this opportunity of considering the beauty of its workmanship. Its shafts were of gold in the lower half and very delicately carved, presumably by Chinese hands, into the semblance of a dragon. There were little emeralds in the tail and little rubies in the nostrils. But the dragon's eye was missing; the disproportionately large eye-socket was empty.

Idly he picked up the fan, and turned it over in his hand. The design on the other side was the same and identically jewelled; but here the eye was present, a grotesquely bulging cabochon sapphire.

He turned the fan over again, and perspiration broke out in his palm.

He had a sudden vision of a lady surprised in Mr Melville's arms, and then of that same lady scurrying masked from Mr Melville's lodging. The vision was conjured by the dragon's missing eye. Just such a cabochon sapphire was in his malicious possession, and at need, to convict her, he could fit it to this empty socket.

Whilst her skilled, graceful fingers drew Paisiello's melodies from the harpsichord, he stood immediately behind her with hell raging in his soul. The eyes that so lately had grown soft and tender as he regarded her burned now with hate. In this delicately fashioned lady, so cold and virginal and aloof, they contemplated a consummate hypocrite, a wanton. And he, poor fool, for all his vaunted experience of her sex, had been so easily deluded by her false, prudish airs.

He was the more enraged because he perceived at once, despite the disturbance in his mind, that he could not call her to account for her wantonness without irrevocably wrecking all those worldly prospects which were already in jeopardy. He was being grossly abused and swindled. She would accept him for her husband so that his support might be given to the cause the Pizzamano had at heart. But the false jade, with her airs of dignity and her nunlike reserves, cheated him in advance by taking a lover.

Small wonder that he had sensed the existence of intelligences between Mr Melville and this wanton, this cold piece who could never suffer to be left alone for a moment with her future husband lest the proprieties should be outraged. He saw this imposture, and must submit to it, pretending not to see it. It was an intolerable situation to a man of feeling.

But if he dared not denounce it, at least he could in part avenge it upon Mr Melville. That would be something towards restoring his self-respect. And not only would it set a term to the dishonour he was suffering, it would remove that other danger he had been apprehending. In this perception he so far recovered his equanimity as to be able to dissemble his black thoughts.

He found his opportunity two days later at the Casino del Leone, where, as if to supply him with yet another grievance, he came upon Mr Melville in the company of the Vicomtesse.

Vendramin came accompanied by a young gentleman named Nani – a nephew of the Proveditor of the Lagoons – and he thrust his way without ceremony into the little group of which Marc-Antoine formed part. From this group one or two fell away immediately on his approach. Vendramin's was not a company that was ardently sought by all Venetian gentlemen. Young Balbi and Major Andrea Sanfermo, between whom and Marc-Antoine a certain friendliness, if not actual friendship, had been growing in these last few months, remained, but with assumptions of aloofness.

Vendramin flung a hearty greeting to them all, and stooped to kiss the hand of the seated Vicomtesse.

As he straightened himself, his smiling eyes met those of Marc-Antoine.

'Ah, Monsieur l'Anglais! You, too, are here. Still lingering in Venice. You threaten to become permanently domiciled.'

'The enchantment of Venice is an abundant justification. But I don't like "threaten". I am not a menace, Ser Leonardo.'

'Not a serious one. No,' said Vendramin, in a tone that set them staring. 'And I can understand that these our enchantments should lay a potent spell upon one accustomed to a barbarous northern country.'

There was a stir at this. But Marc-Antoine, whilst mystified, continued easily to smile.

'Alas, yes! We are barbarians up there. So we come to Venice to improve our manners; to study the elegancies of deportment, the courtesies of phrase.'

Major Sanfermo laughed outright at the sly hit, and some laughed with him, hoping to end the matter thus.

'You come then to achieve the impossible; to grow figs on thistles.'

Marc-Antoine could no longer be in doubt of Vendramin's purpose, however little he might understand the reason for it. But, unruffled, he avoided Sanfermo's uneasy, warning glance.

'You judge us harshly, Ser Leonardo. Possibly you will not have known many Englishmen.'

'As many as desirable. I have known you.'

'I see. And so with you it is ex uno omnes.' No tone or manner could have been more amiable. 'But it is bad reasoning to assume that the shortcomings discerned in one poor Englishman are common to all his fellow-countrymen. Even if you had been the only Venetian I had ever met, I should still hesitate to believe that all Venetians are crude and mannerless, stupid and vulgar.'

There was a sudden hush about them. Vendramin was looking white and ugly. Roughly he shook off the clutch of the Vicomtesse, who had risen in alarm.

'That will suffice, I think. None could expect me to suffer quite so much. My friend here, Messer Nani, will have the honour to wait upon you at your lodging.'

Marc-Antoine looked innocent surprise. 'To what end?'

There was a hubbub about them, for by now most of the occupants of the anteroom had been attracted to the spot. The Vicomtesse was begging Sanfermo to intervene, imploring Nani not to heed his friend.

Then Vendramin, thrusting back those who pressed about him, made himself heard. 'Do you ask me to what end? You'll know something, I suppose, even in England, of satisfaction between gentlemen.'

'I see. I see,' said Marc-Antoine, with the air of one penetrated at last by understanding. 'Forgive my dullness. It arises from our different codes. I do not know what I may have done to invite this provocation. But I do know that there are certain circumstances which it seemed to me must make impossible in honour a meeting between us. It would certainly be impossible in barbarian England. And even now I can hardly believe that this is how you pay your debts in Venice.'

'Pay our debts? What the devil do you mean?'

'Oh, but is it possible that I am obscure?'

He was still the essence of urbanity, and still supremely at ease. Carelessly he flicked a speck from his laces as he spoke. But under this serenity a wickedness was stirring. There had been so many reasons why he could not himself have taken the easy road of provoking Vendramin. But since the fool delivered himself so into Marc-Antoine's hands, he should have full measure. Marc-Antoine would spare him nothing. He would humble him to the dust, strip the fine coat from this detestable fellow's shoulders and reveal the ulcers it covered.

'I must be plainer, then. In the last three months, Vendramin, you have borrowed from me various sums amounting in all to about a thousand ducats. It does not suit me that you should cancel the debt by killing me. Nor does it suit me to lose my money by killing you.

No man of honour would compel me to put the matter quite so plainly.'

Vendramin's face was the colour of lead. Here was a foul, cowardly blow that he had not expected.

He strove with Nani and the Vicomtesse, who were holding him, and then suddenly he fell still to hear Major Sanfermo's vibrant exclamation.

'You are right, by God! no man of honour would.'

'My affair just now is with this Englishman, Major Sanfermo; this coward who shelters himself behind his ducats.'

But Marc-Antoine was concerned to shelter himself no longer. His wicked purpose had been served. For Vendramin there were now only scornful eyes and hostile mutterings.

'Oh! If you call my courage in question, that is entirely another matter, ducats or no ducats.' He bowed to Nani. 'I shall have the honour of expecting you, sir.'

Even as the gleam of satisfaction leapt to Vendramin's eyes, it was quenched by Nani's unexpected answer.

'I carry no messages for Messer Vendramin.'

'Nor will any other Venetian gentleman,' added Major Sanfermo.

Vendramin looked about him, bewildered, furious, everywhere to meet eyes of condemnation. He understood now to the full how Melville had dealt with him. For an instant he was shaken. Then he rallied his wits and his courage.

'You are very quick to conclude, and very quick to condemn. As rash, indeed, as Mr Melville. It does not occur to you, any more than it occurred to him, that a man of honour would liquidate his debts before meeting his creditor. You make it necessary that I should tell you that Mr Melville shall be paid to the last ducat before we meet.'

'You will be putting the meeting off indefinitely,' sneered Balbi.

Vendramin turned on him sharply. 'Your irony is wasted, Balbi. I count upon meeting Mr Melville tomorrow, or the next day at the latest. And I shall not want for a gentleman to carry my message, without troubling any of you.'

He swung on his heel, and went out, swaying more than ever from the hips in his walk.

Marc-Antoine laughed softly. 'He had the last word, after all.'

They were closing in upon him, men and women, volubly condemning Vendramin, whilst scarcely a man amongst them, in his eagerness to vindicate the Venetian character, did not offer his service to Mr Melville in what might follow.

The Vicomtesse in an obvious agitation hung on the skirts of the little crowd. At first she had made shift to follow Vendramin when he had left. Thinking better of it, she had turned again; and in her eyes Marc-Antoine could read now the anxiety with which she waited for a word with him.

When presently he was departing, she made the opportunity by requesting his escort to her gondola which waited at the Piazzetta steps.

As they came out under the arcades of the square, she hung heavily on his arm. She was wearing mask and bauta, for they were in October now, from when until the following Lent the mask was worn so commonly in Venice that scarcely a lady of quality would show her uncovered face abroad.

'What have you done, monsieur?' she wailed. 'What have you done?'

'I could answer you better if I knew for whom you are concerned; for me or for him.'

'I am concerned for you both.'

'Be reassured, then. We shall not both die.'

'Oh, in God's name, do not jest about it. There must be no meeting between you.'

'You will prevail upon him to apologize?'

'If necessary, I will endeavour.'

'There's a more certain way,' said Marc-Antoine. They were crossing the square in the dusk. Lights gleamed from shops under the procuratie. The stained-glass windows of Saint Mark's ahead of them glowed like colossal jewels, and the rhythmic pealing of bells was in the air, for this was Saint Theodore's Eve. 'There's the condition attaching to this meeting. He is first to pay me a matter of a thousand ducats. If when he comes to borrow the money from you, you deny him, that will settle the matter.'

Amazement robbed her of breath for a moment. 'Why...why should you suppose that he would come to me for the money?'

'The answer is a simple one. Because he has nowhere else to go. No one else – forgive me – would be so foolish as to lend it to him.'

She reflected. 'You are quick. Quick and shrewd.' Her little nervous laugh was an admission. 'Do you promise me that unless he pays you the money you will not meet him?'

'I swear it.'

She seemed to breathe more freely. She swore in her turn that Vendramin should not have a sequin from her.

And upon that oath she acted when, on arrival home, she found Vendramin awaiting her.

Her refusal left him stricken. Her assertion that she could not procure the money, or even half that sum, threw him into a passion. He pointed to the string of pearls about her neck, to the brilliants flashing in her solitaire. Did she hold these baubles dearer than his honour?

This roused on her side a royally responsive anger. Was she to strip herself naked so that he might be clothed? How much money had he had from her in these last six months? Did she know that it amounted to more than five thousand ducats? If he denied or doubted it, she could bring him the drafts which Vivanti's Bank had honoured, all bearing his signature in proof that he had received the money.

He looked at her with dull eyes. 'If you won't help me, Anne, in God's name, what am I to do?'

He sprawled dejectedly on her brocade couch. She stood over him, white-faced, almost contemptuous.

'What need had you to vent your spleen against him? Why did you not think of this, you fool, before you deliberately put this quarrel on him?

133

He could not tell her how deeply he had been provoked. For it could not suit him to pillory the lady he was to marry; and in any case the plea was not one that would win favour with a mistress.

'Could I suppose, could any gentleman suppose, that he would take refuge behind a debt? It's only an Englishman could behave so basely. My God, Anne, I shall kill that man.' He got up, trembling with passion. He looked at her keenly, then caught her wrist, and pulled her roughly to him. 'Does he matter to you, that you are afraid of that? Is that why you won't lend me the money? Because you want to protect this dog?'

She wrenched herself away from him. 'Oh, you are mad. God knows why I suffer you.'

He advanced upon her again. He caught her in his arms this time, and crushed her to him. 'You suffer me because you love me, Anne. As I love you, dear Anne. Dear Anne! Help me this once. I am ruined, shamed, dishonoured, unless you come to the rescue. You could not let that happen to the man who worships you, who lives for you. I have given you such proofs of my love, Anne.'

'You have certainly taken almost all that I possess,' she conceded. 'That is why you find me now at the end of my resources.'

'But there is your cousin, the ambassador.'

'Lallemant!' She laughed without mirth. 'If you knew the scenes he has made me of late because of my extravagance. My extravagance! If he knew the truth… Oh, but there! I cannot wring another ducat from Lallemant.'

He returned to the subject of her jewels, and whined to her that she should let him raise money on those. He protested that he would soon be married now; and then he could redeem the trinkets and restore them together with all that he had borrowed.

But she was not to be moved by his entreaties, not even when the tears sprang from his eyes. So that in the end, he flung out of her lodgings, cursing her for a hard-hearted Jezebel who had never known the meaning of love.

It certainly seemed as if Fate were against the affair. For just as this solid obstacle stood in the way of Vendramin, so another, no less solid, came to be placed in the way of Marc-Antoine.

This happened on the following evening, which was that of the feast of Saint Theodore, a public holiday in Venice, where Saint Theodore was held in a veneration second only to that of Saint Mark. Marc-Antoine sat in his lodging at the Swords, writing letters, when, to his surprise, Domenico suddenly stood before him.

The little affair at the Casino del Leone had created, naturally enough, gossip, and some of this had actually been borne to the Fort of Sant' Andrea by one of Domenico's brother-officers. It was responsible for Domenico's presence, as he now announced.

'It's a sweet mark of friendship,' said Marc-Antoine. 'But you have little occasion for concern.'

'You speak, Marc, as if the issue could be in no doubt. It is not your way to boast.'

Marc-Antoine shrugged. 'When a man engages in undertakings such as that which has brought me to Venice, and when he knows that his life may hang at any moment upon his use of his weapons, he's a fool unless he studies them closely. Do you account me a fool, Domenico?'

Domenico set a hand on his shoulder. 'I hope this quarrel was not of your provoking. I have had an account of it, but... '

'I give you my word that it was deliberately sought by Vendramin. And to my astonishment, he publicly insulted me.'

'That is how I heard the tale. What are you going to do?'

'I cannot suppose that the meeting will take place. I so handled Vendramin as to make it impossible until he pays me a matter of a thousand ducats that he owes me. It seems equally impossible that he should find such a sum.'

'I hope you may be right. I hope it devoutly.' Domenico explained himself. 'In my heart, Marc, I could wish that you should kill him. But if that happened, my father would never forgive you. You would be dead to us, Marc. It would be held against you that you had killed the only chance remaining to our cause, such is the power in certain quarters exercised by this worthless scoundrel. There have been things… Oh, but what use to talk of them? I do not think my father has many illusions left on the score of Vendramin. Nevertheless, for the sake of what Vendramin can do for Venice there is no sacrifice that my father will not make for him.'

'Including Isotta,' said Marc-Antoine in a dull voice. 'His daughter and your sister! Can fanaticism go further?'

'I have sought to combat it. But it is idle. My father put me in the wrong. He shamed me with my lack of patriotism.'

'And yet, Domenico, I tell you – and I have cause to know it – the chances are that in the end this dog will fail you. So if you love Isotta, play for time. Postpone and postpone the irrevocable until we reach the end.'

Domenico took him by the arm. 'You know something against him?'

'I know nothing in his favour. Nor does anyone else.'

'It will need more than that to save Isotta.'

'I shall hope to provide it. But I need time. That is all that I can say now.'

Domenico tightened his grip of his friend's arm. 'Count upon all the time that I can make for you. For Isotta's sake'

'Oh, and for mine,' said Marc-Antoine, with his wistful smile.

Chapter 17

The Meeting

Marc-Antoine's confidence that it must prove impossible for Vendramin to find the money was abruptly shattered on the morrow.

He was waited upon at an early hour by Colonel Androvitch, a middle-aged officer of the Slavonian regiment stationed at San Giorgio Maggiore. The colonel, a short, spare man, but as tough of body as of manner, placed two heavy bags upon the table. Having done so, he clicked his heels together, bowed from the waist, stiffly, and announced that the bags contained gold to the value of nine hundred and fifty ducats due from Messer Leonardo Vendramin.

He passed on to state that as Ser Leonardo's friend he would be happy to hear from Messer Melville when it would suit his convenience to afford Ser Leonardo the satisfaction due between them.

Remembering Domenico's warning, Mr Melville preserved with difficulty a calm deportment. He assumed, of course, that the woman who called herself the Vicomtesse de Saulx had, after all, allowed herself to be persuaded, reluctantly or otherwise, to provide the money.

And just as Vendramin had found this, so he had found a Slavonian officer to carry the message which Andrea Sanfermo had said that no gentleman would carry for him.

For Mr Melville, however reluctant he now might be, there was no retreat.

He could only accept the assurance of Colonel Androvitch that the piece of ground behind the riding-school on the Giudecca would in the early hours be a suitable place for the transaction of their business. When he had agreed to attend there at seven o'clock on the following morning, accompanied by a friend, the colonel clicked his heels once more.

'Most fortunate to have had the honour.' He bowed. 'Your very obedient servant, Monsieur Melville.' And he creaked out in his long military boots.

Later in the day the uneasy Marc-Antoine sought Major Sanfermo, and found him in the gaming-room of the Casino del Leone. He drew him aside.

'Vendramin has paid me his debt.'

'I wonder whom he has robbed.'

'And we meet tomorrow morning. May I count upon your services, Sanfermo?'

Sanfermo bowed formally. 'Deeply honoured.' His dark eyes -were grave. 'This Vendramin, like all rascals who live more or less on their wits, has a reputation as a swordsman.'

'I trust I shall not help him to maintain it,' said Marc-Antoine. That night he wrote a letter to Domenico Pizzamano: 'I am meeting Vendramin tomorrow morning. You are not to suppose from this that I am breaking faith with you. He has paid the money, and I cannot help myself. I shall do what I can; but if there should be an accident, save Isotta from this scoundrel.'

He also wrote letters to his mother and to Isotta, which he left, with definite instructions, in the hands of Philibert.

For what occurred on the morrow Vendramin blamed the dullness of the light and the slipperiness of the ground; for it was a grey morning, and it had rained a little in the night. These, however, were excuses urged to save his face. The light was not merely abundant, it was excellent because there were no reflections. And the turf on that strip of ground with its single rather melancholy sycamore, behind the long, low, brick building of the riding-school, whilst damp was certainly not slippery.

Vendramin came to the engagement with the confidence of acknowledged mastery, and the first few engages with which the adversaries tested each other revealed him for a graceful and accomplished, if academic fencer.

Marc-Antoine's play displayed a greater flexibility; but neither Sanfermo nor Androvitch, who stood watchfully at hand, and both of whom had been trained in the Italian school, could approve his methods. Sanfermo was fearful and Androvitch confident of the issue. Neither of them had a high regard for the French school. This may have been because neither of them had ever seen an exponent of it who was in the first class. The straight Italian arm, with its consequent extremely close parries and ever-menacing point, seemed to them infinitely superior, because entailing infinitely less exertion, than the bent arm of the French method which kept the elbow close to the body. And to Marc-Antoine, who had never yet opposed an Italian swordsman, that extended reach and steady point were at first so disconcerting he could not do himself full justice. He could do himself justice enough, however, successfully to deflect every attempt to pass his guard. Presently growing accustomed to the opposing method, and settling down more to his own, he gave a demonstration which surprised them of the advantages of the French school. Its greater flexibility permitted of double feints; and their lightning speed was impossible to the Italian rigidity, which confined a swordsman to single time, wherein parry and riposte were almost one. With a succession of attacks following upon these whirling double feints, Marc-Antoine presently drove Vendramin before him in such a manner as to make the seconds reconsider their opinion.

The Venetian was irritated by what at first he accounted a buffoonery of the French academies as practised by an Englishman. This was not fencing as he understood it. In his irritation he swore to himself that he would not be made to go dancing off like this before these charging thrusts. He would stop the next one with a time lunge that should put an end to the comedy. But his time lunge when it came was eluded by a demi-volte, followed by a riposte delivered from the flank. Vendramin twisted precipitately to parry. At a disadvantage the movement was an awkward and ungainly one. He succeeded in deflecting the thrust, but so narrowly that the sweat started from his brow in panic. Then he leapt back again out of reach, in spite of his resolve to give no more ground. Only thus could he regain his poise, mental and physical.

His surprise was shared by the seconds. But with a difference. There had been an instant in Marc-Antoine's execution of that movement when his opponent was entirely uncovered to him. But in that instant he had seemed to hesitate; and in this hesitation his chance had been lost.

Had Marc-Antoine been untrammelled in this duel, had his aim been merely to wound without recking whether he slayed, there would have been no hesitation; the mechanics of his manoeuvre would have been completed, and his blade would have gone through his adversary's flank before Vendramin could effect his clumsy recovery. But even as Marc-Antoine checked the completing thrust, he perceived how and where it should be delivered so as to serve his purpose. Because this was unforeseen, there was that hesitation which had saved his opponent.

Marc-Antoine, however, was now instructed. He saw his way. Confidence surged up in him. He was this man's master. What had been done once could be done again. Nor did it even prove necessary to be strategic so as to create the occasion. Vendramin himself created it, made rash by anger.

His poise recovered, he bounded forward to attack relentlessly, to make an end. Before his fury, it was Marc-Antoine who now fell back, lightly, nimbly, just eluding that hard-driven vicious point, and so making his opponent feel that his reach was never quite long enough, so luring him to extend himself again in a lunge that should end the business. And at last it came. Again it was eluded by that treacherous demi-volte. But now there was no hesitation to give leisure for recovery. This time Marc-Antoine riposted with the speed of lightning and Vendramin's weapon fell from suddenly numbed fingers. His opponent's sword had skewered the muscles of his sword-arm.

He uttered an 'Ai!' of pain as the blade was withdrawn; then he reeled away, his nether lip in his teeth, to come to rest against Androvitch who had sprung to his aid.

It was not only pain that turned his face drawn and livid. There was the discomfiture, the shame of this defeat to a man of his mastery. And then he heard Sanfermo addressing his principal in a buoyant tone.

'The most magnanimous thing I have ever witnessed, sir. I am proud to have been out with you.'

It needed only this: that it should be bruited through Venice that he owed his life to the magnanimity of his adversary. He steadied himself. Sanfermo, who had kept his principal's coat over his left arm, was now holding it for Marc-Antoine.

'What are they supposing?' Vendramin asked Androvitch. 'This is not over yet. This is no first-blood affair. I fence as well with my left arm as my right. Tell them that it is my intention to continue.'

'Continue? You are in no case to continue. You are bleeding horribly.'

'What then? Can't you patch me up? Can't you make a bandage? Tear up my shirt, man.'

But here Sanfermo intervened. 'We do not continue, Colonel Androvitch. My friend came out solely to prove a courage which had been called in question. If Messer Vendramin is not lying dead at this moment, that is due entirely to Messer Melville's clemency, as you yourself have seen.'

'You lie, Sanfermo,' shouted Vendramin. 'And if you have the audacity to repeat it, I'll prove it on your body.'

Sanfermo made a little bow to Androvitch. 'Let me suggest that you restrain your friend. He is in no case to provoke resentments, and I am not disposed to take notice of him. But there are decencies to be observed. And, anyway, I am taking my friend off the ground. This matter is at an end.'

It was indeed at an end as became suddenly plain to Vendramin's swimming senses. He was faint from loss of blood and in need of immediate attention.

Sanfermo's enthusiasm for his principal's conduct led to Mr Melville's finding himself that same afternoon at the Casino del Leone in a celebrity which he was far indeed from desiring.

But in one quarter he found himself the object of reproaches. Momentarily alone with the Vicomtesse, he confronted an unusual hardness in her glance.

'So, you broke faith with me,' she said. 'And I thought you a man whom one might trust.'

'That was the reproach I had for you,' he answered.

'What?' He thought there was more than surprise in her face. 'Are you telling me that he paid you? A thousand ducats?'

'I should not have met him else. And are you telling me that you did not give him the money?'

'I certainly did not.'

They looked at each other in mutual unbelief.

Chapter 18

The Bridge of San Moisé

At a stormy meeting of the Grand Council on the last Monday in October, Leonardo Vendramin signally proved once more that, although nothing in himself, and contemptible in the eyes of almost every patrician of account, yet, by a queer irony which the oligarchic system made possible, he wielded a power which might well give him control of the destinies of the State.

The proceedings were opened by Francesco Pesaro, a leading member of the Senate, who from the outset had vigorously striven for armed neutrality. He came sternly to indict the policy of drift pursued in spite of undertakings wrung from the Doge at their last assembly. He pointed to the fruits of this in the contempt with which the French armies overran the Venetian provinces, trampling with impunity on their every right. Thence he came to a passionate plea that even at this late hour they should take up arms so that they could bring to account those who presumed to violate the neutrality Venice had assumed.

He was answered with well-worn financial arguments; with the old assertion that this war was not in any sense the quarrel of Venice; and with pleas that it was better to bear with resignation the ills resulting from their provinces having become the cockpit of this campaign, rather than sow the seed of greater distress in the future by a reckless squandering of the shrunken substance of the State.

To those who urged these arguments of pusillanimity and avarice came Vendramin to answer. Pale from the blood he had lost, and refined by his pallor to an air of asceticism, his injured arm so craftily slung under his patrician toga that its condition was not to be perceived, he stood in the tribune tall and dominant before his brother-oligarchs. He began by a slow, emphatic announcement of the fatal error of assuming that the independence of Venice was not menaced. It was well within the knowledge of some, and he had reason to believe that His Serenity the Doge was amongst this number, that if the French should emerge victorious from their contest with the Empire, the independence of Venice might well be placed in jeopardy. Having dwelt at length upon the intransigence of Bonaparte, he asked them whether they could really suppose that if that man were ultimately victorious in Italy he would withhold his brigand's hands from the treasures of the Most Serene Republic.

With that, protesting that already more words had been used in that hall than the occasion justified, he demanded that the vote be taken upon the motion presented to them by the Senator Francesco Pesaro.

The barnabotti, of whom there was a full muster present, voted solidly as their leader indicated. It is possible even that Vendramin's advocacy swayed some of the more solid patricians who were hesitating, for when the votes were counted it was discovered that, in spite of a hundred abstentions, there was a majority of over one hundred in favour of the motion. By this the Senate was required to proceed with the utmost dispatch to increase the armaments so that the Serenissima should be in a position to declare that, in view of the abuses committed upon her territories and her subjects, she was constrained to pass from an unarmed to an armed neutrality, and to demand the evacuation of her provinces by the belligerent forces.

The meeting dispersed with the feeling that only at its peril could the Senate neglect to carry out a recommendation so strongly supported.

Once more Vendramin had given proof of his capacity, through his worthless barnabotti following, to sway decisions.

From this he derived a sense of consequence marred only by the memory of his defeat at the hands of Mr Melville. Upon this, however, measures were being taken. Vendramin thanked God that he did not lack for friends, even if his associates in the Casino del Leone and other similar meeting-places were looking a little askance at him these days.

These good friends had the matter in hand.

On the Thursday of that week Marc-Antoine attended, with Sanfermo, Balbi, and another of his recent Venetian friends, a performance of Panzieri's ballet *Odervik* at the Fenice Theatre. The theatre was gaily filled, which was the rule at all theatres in Venice that winter; for the pleasure-loving Venetians did not suffer anxieties begotten by the political situation to deprive them of their gaieties.

The Vicomtesse occupied a box, and Vendramin in lilac and silver, his arm in a lilac sling, was with her, besides two other men, one of whom Balbi recognized for a barnabotto named Ottolino. He was known to practise as a fencing-master, one of the very few occupations which a patrician might pursue without loss of caste, and he was held in sinister repute as a bully swordsman.

At the end of the performance, the night although cold being fine, the four friends, ignoring the press of gondolas in the little basin before the main entrance, left the theatre on foot. In the vestibule they had passed the Vicomtesse, who smiled a greeting to them, undeterred by the scowl of her cavalier. Even as he was bowing to her, Marc-Antoine had seen Vendramin turn his head to speak to Ottolino, under cover of a three-cornered hat held across his face.

The four friends crossed the Bridge of La Fenice and walked together as far as Santa Maria Zobenigo. Here they were greeted by the strains of music from the Casino of La Beata, where a ball was in progress. Sanfermo halted them before the door, which was hung with coloured lanterns and festooned with ramage and artificial flowers. He urged that they should join those revellers for an hour or two. The other two Venetians were eager. But Marc-Antoine excused himself. He was a little tired, and he would go straight back to his lodgings.

So they parted company there, and Marc-Antoine went on alone in the direction of San Moisé. Even as he was bidding them good-night and good enjoyment, he caught a glimpse of two dark figures that were coming very slowly down the street from the direction of La Fenice. As he looked, they crossed the light issuing from the open doorway of a malvasia, and in one of them he recognized Ottolino. This evoked a vision of Vendramin, half-covering his face with his hat, as he spoke to him over his shoulder.

For a moment Marc-Antoine hesitated on a thought of following his late companions into La Beata. Then, annoyed with himself for having even thought of being driven by a suspicion into amusements for which he had no inclination, he went briskly forward. He had not, however, gone a dozen paces before he was aware that those saunterers were sauntering no longer. They, too, had suddenly lengthened their stride to match his own. He could not doubt that he was being followed, or that mischief was intended. He was nearing the Bridge of San Moisé, and had still some way to go to reach the Piazza, where he would be rendered safe by the people still astir. But here he was virtually alone with these two who tracked him. He unwound the cloak in which he had been tight-wrapped against the chilly night, and let it hang entirely loose upon his shoulders. Similarly, he loosened in its scabbard the small-sword that he was fortunately wearing. This without checking or shortening his stride. Behind him the rapid steps of his followers rang briskly upon the pavement of the narrow street. They were steadily gaining. And yet, if his suspicions were correct, why did they not attack at once? For what were they waiting? He guessed the answer when he reached the opening at the foot of the Bridge of San Moisé, and when at last the short, swift rush took place. They preferred to set upon him at a spot where a canal would enable them instantly to dispose of his remains.

With delicate precision he calculated the moment at which to turn and face them. He chose to do it standing on the lowest step of the bridge, a position which would give him a slight command of them when they charged. As he span round, he drew his sword with one hand whilst with the other he swept the cloak from his shoulders. He knew exactly what he was going to do. They should find that a gentleman who had been through all the hazards that had lain for him between Quiberon and Savenay did not fall an easy prey to a couple of bully swordsmen.

In the street itself the shadows had been dense. But here at the opening by the bridge the light of a moon in the last quarter, aided perhaps by its reflection from the water, made things dimly visible.

As he turned to meet the charge, one of his assailants, a full yard ahead of his fellow, was within striking distance on his left, and Marc-Antoine caught the livid gleam of his sword levelled for the stroke. Onto that level blade Marc-Antoine flung his cloak, to bear it down. As it sank under the weight, and uncovered the man, Marc-Antoine doubled him, winded, by a kick in the stomach, and almost simultaneously parried the thrust of the second assassin, who was Ottolino. Before he could riposte, the parried blade had disengaged. Ottolino had sprung nimbly to the right, so as to take his man in flank, trusting to the gloom to mask his movement.

But Marc-Antoine was whirling his blade to cover himself at all points. It caught the sidelong thrust, enveloped it in a circular parry, and drove home a counter-thrust that sank through his assailant's body.

Without a pause, he swung to the left again, to meet the renewed attack of the other bully, who had by now recovered. In his haste Marc-Antoine had not even waited to see what happened to Ottolino. Already his blade was engaged again when a loud splash informed him of where the led-captain fell. It may also have been the other assassin's first intimation of disaster to his fellow. And it may have been due to this that he suddenly sprang back well out of reach. Craning forward, Marc-Antoine could just make him out crouching there in the gloom three or four yards away. He did not crouch to spring, but to guard himself as he retreated. Farther and farther back he went thus, until, judging that the distance made it safe, he suddenly straightened himself, turned and ran. Marc-Antoine let him go, sheathed his sword, and recovered his cloak. He went up the steps of the little bridge, and, pausing on the summit, leaned on the parapet to recover breath and survey the canal. Moonbeams danced upon the diminishing ripples of Messer Ottolino's plunge. They were the only signs of his presence somewhere under that oily-looking surface.

The warning cry of a gondolier broke the silence, and a lantern suddenly showing told of a gondola swinging round the corner ahead. Marc-Antoine sauntered off, and went home without further adventure.

Chapter 19

The Shield

On the following afternoon, wandering into the Café Bertazzi, that patrician resort at the head of the Piazza, where nowadays Marc-Antoine was known and welcomed, he found there the lively Major Sanfermo, who, to make him regret having parted company so early on the previous night, entertained him with an account of their lively doings at La Beata. They had danced until daylight, and then on their way home a further entertainment was supplied them. By the Bridge of San Moisé they had come upon the Signors of the Night with the body of a man they had just fished out of the canal under the bridge.

'And who do you think it was?' Sanfermo asked him.

'That bully swordsman we saw in the box at La Fenice with Leonardo Vendramin. I think you said his name was Ottolino.'

Sanfermo's mouth fell open in ludicrous surprise.

'How the devil should you know that?'

'For the best of reasons. I put him there.'

Sanfermo was dumbfounded by the cool announcement. Then a light of angry understanding flashed in his eyes. 'By the Host! Do you mean that you were attacked?'

Marc-Antoine rendered a brief account. 'I came here looking for you; to tell you about it. And to ask you what I should do now.'

'Do? Faith, it seems to me you've done all that matters.'

'But the Signors of the Night will be looking for a murderer.'

'They're more likely to be concerned with the fact that they've found one. This is the common end of such rascals as Ottolino. Men who live by the sword... You know.'

'Don't forget that one of them got away.'

'I see. And you expect him to testify, do you?' Sanfermo smiled.

'Then there is also Vendramin. He will know whose hand killed Ottolino.'

'And of course he will go and inform the Signors of the Night, explaining to them, when they ask him, that he knows because he sent Ottolino and another rogue to murder you. My dear Melville, you plague yourself without need. That matter is ended for you, and well ended. What isn't ended is Vendramin's murderous intention.' The Major was serious. 'That remorseless villain will not leave the matter where it is. Let me think of something. But in the meantime, take your precautions, especially at night.'

'You may depend upon it,' said Marc-Antoine.

With just that intention, Marc-Antoine took himself off to the French Legation, and, breaking in upon ambassadorial labours, drove Jacob out of the room.

'What the devil is the matter now?' grumbled Lallemant.

'The devil is the matter. My life is threatened.'

Lallemant was startled. 'Peste...' Then a grin broke on his broad face. 'We shall be wanting a pretext for hostilities presently. It would be a fine one if the Representative Camille Lebel were murdered here in Venice.'

'Much obliged to you, Lallemant. When Bonaparte wants that pretext I should prefer to be alive to provide it. Meanwhile, I am curious to know how much longer you propose to postpone the coercion of Leonardo Vendramin into your service.'

Lallemant conceived a reproof in this. He thrust out a deprecatory lip.

'You are supposing that it's time we gagged him; that he is working mischief against us by his stormy advocacy of armed neutrality. You see I keep myself informed of what happens in the Grand Council. But you're mistaken. The time is past when a state of armed neutrality could distress us. Very soon now we shall require a pretext for definite aggression, and in a state of armed neutrality it should not be difficult to find one.'

His shrewd eyes challenged Marc-Antoine to contradict him. As no contradiction came from that solemnly attentive gentleman, the ambassador continued.

'There are letters here from Bonaparte which you should read. Mantua can't hold out much longer. Once it capitulates, we shall be in a very different position.'

Marc-Antoine ran his eye over the letters. They were brief and definite, like all General Bonaparte's dispatches.

'And this new Austrian army under Alvinzy?' he asked.

'You see what he says. Alvinzy's strength has been exaggerated here in Venice. He will be broken as easily as Wurmser before him and Beaulieu before Wurmser. The only mischief we have to dread is that Venice, arming to her full capacity, should ally herself with Austria. That is the English dream. But there's no danger of it as long as the spineless Manin is Doge of Venice. So by all means let Vendramin advocate armed neutrality. I shall pray that the Senate listens to him.'

To Marc-Antoine there was a dismaying irony in the reflection that the efforts which were establishing Vendramin in the eyes of Count Pizzamano as the champion and saviour of his country had now become the very efforts welcomed by the enemies of Venice because rendering her vulnerable to their designs.

Lallemant interrupted the stream of his thoughts.

'But what's this you were saying about your life being threatened?'

'I am glad it has some interest for you.' He told Lallemant of his duel with Vendramin and of last night's sequel to it.

The ambassador was flushed with indignation. Nor was his wrath merely official. Ever since the Terzi affair his relations with the supposed Lebel had steadily increased in warmth.

'What do you want me to do? What can I do to protect you?' he demanded.

'Nothing, since policy won't allow you to do what I require. I shall have to anticipate you, and do it for myself.' Answering the question in the other's eyes, he added: 'I propose to borrow the means you possess to fetter Vendramin.'

Lallemant understood at once. 'Ah, that name of name! But it may be awkward.'

'Not so awkward to me as my assassination. Display a little common humanity, Lallemant.'

'My dear friend! Oh, my dear friend!' Lallemant was on his feet in a fervour of concern. 'To suppose me callous!' So great indeed and apparently genuine was his alarm for this good Lebel that he ended by wondering whether it was really necessary for him to continue in Venice.

Marc-Antoine was indignant. Did Lallemant really suppose that he was the man to run away from danger? And as for his utility in Venice, his work there had not really yet begun. That would come when the crisis was reached.

'And, anyway, how can I leave until I am recalled?' He picked up his three-cornered hat from Lallemant's table. 'There's only one course. And I am going to take it.'

His gondola bore him to the district of San Felice, to a palace on the canal of that name in which Vendramin was lodged. Not for him any of the houses of San Barnabó, placed by the State at the disposal of impoverished patricians. Here on the second floor of this fine palace he dwelt in a comparative luxury that was in the nature of a problem to those who were aware of his actual resources.

An elderly manservant in a plain livery opened to Marc-Antoine's knock, and peered at him suspiciously.

'Ser Leonardo Vendramin?' he asked.

'He lives here. Yes,' the man replied in dialect. 'What do you want with him?'

'The pleasure of a little chat.'

Still guarding the entrance, the man half-turned and called.

'Ser Leonardo, xé un moossoo che gha domanda.'

A door opened within. A tall man in a brocaded dressing-gown of crimson, his feet in slippers, his head swathed in a kerchief, made his appearance. The right sleeve of his dressing-gown hung empty.

He advanced, craning, to see who asked for him. Upon perceiving Marc-Antoine, his face flushed scarlet.

His voice came harsh with anger. 'What do you want? Who told you to come here?'

Marc-Antoine advanced into the narrow opening. So as to prevent the door from being slammed in his face he carefully set his foot against the edge of it.

'I have to talk to you, Vendramin. It is urgent, and it is very serious – for you.' He took the tone of a gentleman speaking to an undutiful lackey, and the look on his face matched the tone.

'You can talk to me elsewhere. I do not receive... '

'No. I can understand it.' Marc-Antoine's hard, light eyes played over the servant at his elbow, whose attitude was almost menacing. 'But you will receive me.'

A moment still Vendramin stood glaring at him. Then abruptly he surrendered.

'Come in, then, since you insist. Let him pass, Luca. Let him pass.'

Marc-Antoine advanced into the passage. Vendramin flung out his left arm towards the doorway from which he had emerged. 'In there, if you please,' he said.

They went into a fair-sized salon which if without splendours was also without meanness in its furnishings; indeed, it gathered a certain pretentiousness from a spread of tapestry covering one of its walls and the gildings on some of the movables.

Vendramin remained with his back to the closed door. Marc-Antoine turned, one gloved hand holding his hat in the crook of his left arm, the other leaning lightly upon his gold-headed cane.

'I don't think you are pleased to see me,' he said, with ironic affability.

'What do you want with me, Monsieur l'Anglais?'

'I want to tell you that it might have had the most serious consequences for you if I had not been able, as a result of any arrangements you had made for me, to have paid you this little visit. You will have heard, of course, that a friend of yours was fished out of the Canal of San Moisé in the early hours of the morning. You will have surmised how he got there. I hope you have some sense of your responsibility for that poor fellow's untimely end.'

'I don't know what you mean.'

'I mean, my dear Messer Leonardo, that at your next attempt upon my life, you had better send at least four of your bullies to the job. Two are hardly enough.'

Vendramin smiled balefully. 'That, my dear Monsieur Melville, is my intention.'

'I see that we shall understand each other.'

'Will you take a piece of advice from me? Leave Venice while you are able to do so. The air here is not very healthy for meddling foreigners.'

'Your concern touches me. But my health, I assure you, is excellent.'

'It may not so continue.'

'I am content to take the risk. But does your own health give you no concern? Have you reflected how short might be your shrift if the inquisitors of state were to discover that in the past six months you have received five or six thousand ducats from the French Legation?'

Vendramin went white to the lips. He took a step forward. 'What do you mean by that lie? It's a foul lie, do you hear?'

'Of course if it's a lie, it should give you no anxiety.'

'I have not had a farthing; not a farthing from the French Legation.'

'Strictly speaking, perhaps you have not. But there are drafts in existence for that amount, issued by the Legation, endorsed by you, and cashed at Vivanti's Bank. How would you satisfy the inquisitors of state that you have innocently acquired all this French money? How would you persuade them that you had not received it for the purposes which they must naturally assume?'

Vendramin glared at him, speechless and trembling. Marc-Antoine continued pleasantly.

'You would go the way of Rocco Terzi, whom it would be remembered was your friend; who, as impecunious as yourself, was as unable as you might be to explain upon what resources he lived in surroundings similar to these. Unless you want this to happen to you, you will meddle no more with me. When you realize that this is what I came to tell you, perhaps you will not resent my visit quite so much. It does not suit me to leave Venice just at present. It does not suit me to lie under a perpetual menace of assassination. And it does not suit me to move about with a bodyguard to protect me from your bully swordsmen. Therefore, I have taken my precautions; and they are such that I should advise you to do all in your power to promote my good health and my well-being.' He had been smiling. But he hardened now his tone. 'I have provided that at any accident to me, of whatsoever nature, and even if not fatal, information will immediately be lodged with the inquisitors of state which will lead them to ask you some awkward questions. You understand, I hope?'

Vendramin showed his strong teeth in a rigid grin.

'Do you think you can frighten me so easily? Where are the proofs?'

'You don't suppose that the drafts have been destroyed. They could be produced under inquisitorial insistence.'

'By whom? By whom?'

'I will leave you to find the answer to that question. You are warned, Vendramin. I will detain you no longer.'

Mechanically Vendramin wiped the beads of sweat from his upper lip. 'You miserable coward, to shelter yourself behind this lie! Is this how men of honour protect themselves in England? I swear to God that not a penny of this money is in payment for any treasonable service.'

'But will the inquisitors believe you? You will have to reckon with what they suppose. And that is easily imagined.'

'My God! I believe you know the truth. And yet, you scoundrel, you can hold this menace over me! My God, it's unbelievable.'

'Of course, I could adopt your methods, and hire ruffians to assassinate you. But I prefer to do things in my own way. And now, if you will let me pass, I will be wishing you good-day.'

Violently Vendramin threw the door open.

'Go, sir! Go!'

Marc-Antoine went out without haste.

Chapter 20

The Galled Jade

Messer Vendramin descended in wrath upon the Vicomtesse de Saulx that afternoon. He found her holding a reception in the dainty black-and-gold salon that was so admirable a setting to her own delicate elegance.

The queenly Isabella Teotochi, with the dissipated-looking little Albrizzi in passionate attendance, was the dominant figure in that fashionable gathering.

The barnabotto leader found here the cool reception which was everywhere being vouchsafed him nowadays. He fortified himself in a scorn of them, which was genuine enough. Simpering, affected, presumptuously critical and self-assertive, they made up a noisy group to be found in every age and in every society.

There was a great deal of talk of Liberty, the Age of Reason and the Rights of Man; and a great deal of ill-digested matter from the encyclopaedists was being tossed about by these pseudo-intellectuals, over ices and coffee and malvoisie. There was also some scandal. But even this was dressed-up in intellectual rags, implying on the part of those who mongered it a breadth of outlook as startling as it would have been indefensible by any reasonable canons.

He was fretted by impatience until the last of them had departed.

Then the Vicomtesse reproached him with the disgruntled air and manner he had paraded among her friends.

'Friends?' he said. He was very bitter. 'Faith, if you find your friends among these posturing pimps and these silly spirituelle baggages I can believe anything of you. Nothing surprises me any more. Not even that you should stoop to betraying me.'

She accommodated herself of her black-and-gold settee, and spread on either side of her the blue panniers of her gown. 'Oh, I see. Your ill-humour is rooted in jealousy again.' She sighed. 'You grow intolerably tiresome, Leonardo.'

'I have, of course, no cause. Your loyalty renders my suspicions shameful. They emanate from the intemperance of my own mind. That is what you would say, is it not?'

'Something of the kind.'

'You would be wise to leave flippancy. I am not in the humour for it. And you had better not provoke me more than you have done already.'

But the dainty little lady laughed at him. 'You are not threatening me, by any chance?'

He looked down upon her malevolently. 'My God! Are you quite shameless?'

'It must be that I follow your example, Leonardo, although with less cause for shame.'

'What I ask myself is whether a woman ever had cause for more.'

'Your mother, perhaps, Leonardo.'

He stooped and seized her wrist viciously. 'Will you curb that pert tongue of yours before I do you a mischief? I will not have my mother's name on your lips, you jade.'

She rose, suddenly white and fierce, a galled jade, indeed, under his insult. She wrenched her wrist from his grasp.

'I think you had better go. Out of my house!' And as he stood sneering at her, she stamped her daintily shod foot. 'Out of my house! Do you hear me?' She twisted away, to reach the bell-rope. But he interposed himself.

'You shall hear me first. You shall render me an account of your betrayal.'

'You fool, I owe you no account. If we are to talk of accounts, you had better think of how you stand in my debt.'

'I have occasion to think of it since you have published it.'

'Published it?' Some of the vixenish anger fell from her in surprise. 'Published it, do you say?'

'Yes, published it, madame. Published it to your paramour, to this damned Englishman from whom you have no secrets. I could forgive your infidelity. After all, I can make allowances for your wanton kind. But I cannot forgive you for betraying that. Do you know what you have done? You have placed me in this man's power. But that, I suppose, is what you intended.'

Her clear blue eyes were fixed upon him now in distress rather than in anger. She passed a slim white hand across her brow, disarranging the golden tendrils that curled on either temple.

'My God, this is Greek to me. You are raving, Leonardo. It is all false, this. I have never said a word to Melville or to anyone of the money you have had from me. That I swear to you. As for the rest... ' She curled her lip, and shrugged. 'That Melville is not my lover matters little compared with this.'

'That you should have told him this proves him your lover even if I had no other evidence. For you are lying to me. Why is he always here? Why does he always hover about you when you meet elsewhere?'

'Leave that!' she cried impatiently. 'Keep to the main point. Keep to what is really important. This matter of the money. I swear to you again that I have never so much as whispered it.'

'Oh, yes, you'll swear and swear. Perjury has never mattered to women of your kind.' And fiercely, interlarding his narratives with opprobrium, he told her, with reservations, of his interview that morning with Mr Melville.

'Now,' he asked at the end, 'will you still think it worth your while to deny your infamy?'

She was too startled even to show resentment of his insults. Her smooth white brow was knit. She pushed him away, and under the force of her will rather than of her hand he fell back and let her pass. She went to resume her seat on the couch, set her elbows on her knees, and took her chin in her hands. Doubting, he watched her and waited.

'This is much more serious than you realize, Leonardo. I can understand your anger. You would suppose it justified. But that is nothing. There is something else here. You have exaggerated nothing, I suppose, in what you have told me? Oh, but what matter if you have? The main fact is there. Melville's knowledge. His incredible knowledge. What is to discover is how he comes by it.'

'Can there be more ways than the one I perceive?' he asked, and there was still a sneer in his tone.

'I beg you to be serious; for it seems to me we face a real danger. I solemnly assure you, Leonardo, that the only other person who knows anything from me is my cousin Lallemant from whom the supplies came. Melville could have discovered it only from him.'

'From Lallemant! Do you pretend that the French Ambassador is in relations – and in such intimate relations – with this man, with this Englishman?' Almost idly, he added: 'If he is, indeed, an Englishman.' But even as the rhetorical sentence left his lips, he caught his breath on it, and he repeated on quite another tone: 'If he is, indeed, an Englishman.'

His chin sank to his neck-cloth, and very slowly, very deeply in thought, he moved to stand before her again. But he was not looking at her. His eyes were fixed upon the ground. If this golden-headed little trull were indeed speaking the truth, then only one conclusion seemed possible.

'If what you say is true, Anne, and this man's relations with the ambassador of the French Republic are as intimate as this would prove them, then there is only one inference to be drawn; that he's a damned spy.'

It was not merely, as he supposed, his suspicion that brought the startled look to her face. It was the fact that this suspicion was the very one that she had just reached independently. Having reached it, her duty to the service in which she was at work made her regret that she should so incautiously have supplied the clue to that conclusion.

'Oh, but that is utterly impossible!' she cried.

He was smiling wickedly. 'It's a matter, anyway, for investigation. The inquisitors of state have a short, quiet way with spies just now in Venice. And he had the temerity to threaten me with them!'

She sprang up. 'You are not going to denounce him on this paltry assumption! You dare not, Leonardo.'

'Ah, that alarms you, does it?'

'Of course it does. For you. Without hurting him, if you should be mistaken, you will destroy yourself. Don't you see? What did you say was his threat? That at any accident to him, of whatsoever nature, information touching those drafts on Vivanti's will be lodged with the inquisitors of state. That is what you have told me. And if he should really be a spy, isn't this just one of the precautions he will have taken?'

This quenched his rising exultation. He took his chin in his sound left hand. 'God! How that infernal scoundrel has hobbled me!'

She came to him whilst in that dismayed mood and set a hand upon his arm. 'Leave me to act,' she urged him. 'Let me sound Lallemant, and see what I can discover. There may be some explanation quite other from what you are assuming. That surely can't be right. Leave this with me, Leonardo.'

He looked down upon her gloomily. He put that sound left arm of his about her shoulder, and pulled her to him. 'I suppose, you lovely little white devil, you are not just fooling me? This is not just a trick of yours to put me off the scent, to cover up your own lying tracks?'

She disengaged herself from his arm. 'You're a coarse beast. Sometimes I wonder why I tolerate you here at all. God knows I've never taken joy in a fool before.'

It was the tone that brought him whimpering to heel. He abased himself in excuses for his roughness, pleaded the cursed jealousy that tormented him, and passionately reminded her that jealousy was the first-born of love.

It was a scene they had often played before, and usually it led to kisses at the curtain. But this evening she remained cold and disdainful. It was not easy even in the service of her ends to submit to the caresses of a man who had uttered that deadly insult: 'I will not have my mother's name on your lips, you jade.'

She had never liked him; she had never carried anything but contempt in her heart for this worthless man whom she had been set to trap. But tonight she loathed him so much that she could scarcely conceal it.

'I have had to forgive your boorishness too often,' she answered him. 'It will take me some time to forget what you've said to me tonight. You had better wash your mouth and mend your manners before you approach me again, or you'll approach me for the last time. Now go.'

Whilst his eyes glared at her, his lips shaped a foolish grin.

'You are not really sending me away?'

She gave him a look that was like a blow. She had reached the bell-cord, and she pulled it.

'I doubt if you will ever understand the decencies of life,' she said.

And he just stared at her until the door was opened by her French lackey.

'Messer Vendramin is leaving, Paul.' she said.

Chapter 21

The Diplomats

The Vicomtesse de Saulx paid the Citizen Lallemant a visit, with two definite objects.

Settling herself in a gilded armchair, she loosened the costly furs in which she was swathed, partly for adornment and partly for protection against the rigorous weather which had now set in. Encased in a little fur bonnet that was fastened under her chin by a ribbon of palest blue satin, her delicately featured, delicately tinted face looked a miracle of allurement.

Lallemant, at his table, considered her with an appreciative smile on his broad peasant face, and desired to be informed how he could serve her.

'I want to know,' she said, 'how much longer I am to keep this fellow Vendramin on the chain.'

'My dear child, until I need him, of course.'

'Will you be good to me, and let that happen soon? I am growing very tired of him.'

Lallemant sighed. 'God help me! You have the capriciousness, the inconstancy that goes with ardent temperaments. You should, nevertheless, remember that I am not concerned with your amusements, but with your official duty.'

'My official duties are a little too personal to be entirely at the mercy of official requirements.'

'You are doing very well out of it. You are being very handsomely paid. You should remember that.'

'Oh, I remember it. But we are reaching a point where not all the gold in the Bank of France, if there is any gold there, will compensate me for what I have to endure. This imbecile makes me sick. It is not only that he is absurdly exacting. But he threatens to become violent.'

'The Italian temperament, my dear. We must reckon with it.'

'Thank you, Lallemant. But I happen to have a temperament, too. And I have feelings. This rascal outrages them. I have never liked him. A vain, strutting, self-complacent peacock. But now I have grown to detest and fear him. I have to submit to quite enough in this service, without being asked to risk my life as well. That is why I want to know how much longer I am to endure him. How soon do you propose to take him off my hands?'

Lallemant had ceased to smile. He considered. 'At the moment it suits me too well to have him where he is. Without suspecting it, he is giving us just the service that we require. So you must have a little more patience, my dear. It will not be for long. I promise you it will not be for a moment longer than it must be.'

She was mutinous. He got up, and wandered round to her. He patted her shoulder, he coaxed her, he praised the work she had done, fanned the embers of her patriotism, and so conducted her into a state of resignation.

'Very well,' she consented at last. 'For a little while longer, I'll do my best. But now that you know what I am enduring, I'll depend upon you not to try my patience too far.' Then, stroking the fur of the enormous sable muff in her lap, she said casually: 'But I wish you would use more frankness with me, Lallemant. To keep me in the dark about things as you do might even have serious consequences. How long has Mr Melville been in the French service?' She looked up at him suddenly as she asked the question.

Lallemant raised his brows. 'That is an extraordinary question.' Then he laughed at her. 'And such a feminine method of investigating a suspicion. But isn't the suspicion a little wild for such shrewd wits as yours? Mr Melville is a very good friend of mine. That is all, my child. Disabuse your mind of anything else.'

'I am to believe that the French Ambassador in Venice is the very good friend of an Englishman in such times as these? Such a good friend, in fact, that embassy secrets are communicated to him?'

'Embassy secrets? What embassy secrets?' Lallemant was suddenly very stern. Inwardly he was a little alarmed. Like the prudent man he was, he never allowed one secret agent to know of another unless the knowledge were rendered absolutely necessary. In the case of Lebel there were more than ordinary reasons for his identity to remain closely veiled.

Her answer partly allayed his apprehensions. For she was entirely frank with him on the subject of what last night had been communicated to her by Vendramin.

Lallemant's tone and manner made light of it. 'Oh, that! But that is not an embassy secret. In what I disclosed to Melville there was no betrayal of our intentions concerning your barnabotto. Melville happened to inform me that his life had been attempted, and that he went in danger of assassination by this rascal Vendramin.'

'What's that?' Her tone was like the edge of a knife, and the dainty little face looked suddenly pinched and vicious. 'Vendramin never told me that. All he told me was that Melville acted on a suspicion of intentions. But is it really true, this?'

'True enough. He sent a couple of bully swordsmen after Melville some nights ago. Melville disposed of those. But he perceived that there would presently be others. He told me what had happened. It lay in my power to present him with a very effective shield. That's all. But you are oddly moved, my dear.'

'Why should you be concerned to employ that secret so as to shield an Englishman who has no official connection with you?'

'I am on my defence, it seems. Well, well. I am helpless in your hands. Shall I tell you a secret? Although Melville has no official connection with me at present, I have cultivated him because I have a notion that I may be able to make use of him one of these days.

There are all sorts of ways of using a man without directly employing him.'

Here at last was a reasonable explanation. Her knowledge of Lallemant's methods made it convincing. But her scorn was oddly aroused. 'Do you know that sometimes you disgust me, Lallemant; you and this vile service of yours? You sit here in this office weaving webs like some fat obscene spider. Why must you want to enmesh a decent man like Mr Melville in your slime?'

Lallemant laughed without a trace of irritation. 'What an interest, my dear, in this Mr Melville! A moment ago you looked as if you could murder Vendramin. And now you look as if you could murder me. And all this fury because you conceive that we might injure the little Englishman. Take care, Anne! Beware the ardent temperament!'

'Don't be a beast, Lallemant.'

He merely laughed again, and sauntered back to his table. But the laugh wounded her,

'Don't be a beast, I say, and jump at the beastly conclusion that Mr Melville is my lover. That's what you are hinting, I suppose.'

'But why beastly? Mr Melville is entirely to be envied. God knows if I were ten years younger, my dear...'

'It would make no difference to you if you were twenty years younger. Let that assurance reconcile you to your age. You're a slug, Lallemant, a nasty-minded slug. And you're wasting time if you think that you will ever get Mr Melville into your toils. You don't know the man.'

'You certainly seem to have the advantage of me there, spider and slug that I am.' His mockery so infuriated her that it brought her to her feet.

'Yes, I have. I know him for a man of honour; courteous, kind, considerate, and brave. I take pride in numbering him among my friends. And God knows I haven't many. He's not like the others, who pursue me because I am a woman, who turn my stomach with their gallantries and nauseate me with their calculated flattery. Because I pass for a widow without a man to protect me, they regard me as something to be hunted and trapped by their sickly seductive arts.

Mr Melville is the one man in Venice who has sought my society and at the same time deserved my respect; because he has refrained from making love to me.'

'Thereby, as I perceive, exciting your interest all the more violently. It's the subtler method.'

She looked at him without affection. 'Your mind is a cesspool, Lallemant. I am wasting my time on you. I talk of things you can't understand.'

'At least be grateful to me for the service I have done your Galahad.'

'I'll be grateful when you complete it by ridding me of this pig Vendramin.'

He abandoned his gross jocularity. 'That will follow soon, child. A little more patience. It shall be well rewarded. You know that. You've never found us stingy.'

But she was still angry with him when she departed.

Chapter 22

Arcola and Rivoli

Warned by Marc-Antoine of the present French attitude towards armed neutrality and of the pretext it might provide for a declaration of war, Count Pizzamano bestirred himself with the energy of despair. As a result there was an assembly a week later in Lodovico Manin's study in the Casa Pesaro. Seven alarmed gentlemen came there to consider with the Doge the situation in which the Serenissima found herself and the measures to be taken. There was Francesco Pesaro, the leading advocate of action; Giovanni Balbo and Marco Barbaro, members of the Council of Ten, the State Inquisitor Catarin Corner, and Giacomo Nani, the Proveditor of the Lagoons. To these, who were to form his deputation, the Count had added Leonardo Vendramin, as the leader of the Barnabotti.

These were bad days for Vendramin. He moved precariously, and haunted by dangers; the danger of losing Isotta and the great fortune that went with her; the danger of losing his very life on a false charge at the hands of the inquisitors of state.

The scoundrel Melville held poised over his head a sword from which he was helpless to guard himself. The rage engendered by his bitter sense of wrong was held in check by fear alone.

Meanwhile, he did what he could for himself by displaying to Count Pizzamano more than ever his patriotic zeal, and he came to this meeting at Manin's house to give the Count's demand a passionate support.

This demand was for an offensive and defensive alliance with Austria.

Whatever the Doge had been bracing himself to hear, he had certainly been very far from expecting this. Pale and agitated, he rose to denounce the proposal as sheer madness.

Francesco Pesaro, however, that gravely courteous gentleman, who was perhaps the strongest man in Venice in those disastrous days, constrained the irresolute Doge to hear the facts.

In the Tyrol and on the Piave the Austrian troops were massing. Soon Alvinzy would oppose an army of some forty thousand men to a similar number under Bonaparte. Although the French were under the handicap of having Mantua strongly held against them, yet the scales were somewhat too evenly balanced for assurance of Austrian victory, in which today it must be admitted lay Venice's only hope of security.

Manin would have interrupted him here. But Pesaro ploughed steadily on.

He pointed out with irresistible force that for the present state of things in Italy the blame must rest upon the irresoluteness shown by Venetian statesmen. If from the outset, generously responding to the appeal for help, Venice had ranged herself on the side of the allies with the army of forty or fifty thousand men which they could have put into the field, Bonaparte's invasion of Italy would have been definitely frustrated, Savoy would never have passed into the possession of the French, and not a French soldier would ever have reached Lombardy. But with a parsimony and an egotism that were contemptible – the time for mincing terms was overpast, and he must speak frankly – Venice had excused herself on the ground that the quarrel was not her affair.

After Beaulieu's defeat, the Emperor had sent down a second army under Wurmser. The alliance with Austria which earlier would have been a matter of generosity had then become a matter of expediency. The recent events throughout the violated Venetian provinces were an eloquent proof of how wrong was their shameful aloofness. The abuses committed by the French troops were daily accumulating. The Serenissima was being treated with the contempt which her irresoluteness had earned. Plunder travestied as requisition was everywhere being suffered; arson, rape, and murder ravaged their mainland provinces, and if their governors or emissaries ventured to protest, they were insulted, maltreated, and threatened.

Were Venetians prepared to see this state of things continue until worse ensued, until their fair lands were appropriated by France, as Savoy had been appropriated, as Lombardy had been appropriated?

They knew from what Count Pizzamano had just told them that already the French were seeking pretexts for conquest, and that, today, they would actually welcome the armed neutrality which earlier might so effectively have hindered them.

Yet, even now, by the mercy of God, Venice was for the third time offered the chance which twice before she had neglected. Well might it be the last chance that would be vouchsafed her by a Providence weary of her pusillanimity. Strategically they were well placed to co-operate with Alvinzy. Whilst he made his frontal attack, they could assail the French on the flank. Could anyone doubt the issue of such overwhelming co-operation? Thus would Italy be delivered from the French; Venetian honour would be vindicated and her prestige restored.

Before the Doge, shaken and distressed, could find words, Vendramin had taken up the argument at the point where Pesaro left it. Since the last meeting of the Grand Council, troops had been recruited; ships had been fitted and conditioned; they had been working day and night at the arsenal, so that they were now in a position to put an equipped army of thirty thousand men in the field within a week, and these numbers might be increased by further levies from the Dalmatian provinces. This army, intended for the tardy defence of Venetian property, could with equal effect be rendered definitely hostile by an alliance with the Austrian forces.

When the trembling Doge cried out to know upon what grounds they could declare war on France, Pizzamano answered him sharply that grounds for hostilities, which were never difficult to create, existed in abundance in the ravages Venetian provinces had suffered. He reminded the Doge that His Serenity was the keeper of Venetian honour, and that posterity would hold him up to execration if he neglected what was perhaps the last opportunity of defending it.

At this Manin broke down before them. He sank his elbows into his knees, and took his big head in his hands. Sobs shook him whilst he inveighed against the day when the ducal dignity and the ducal corno had been thrust upon him.

'These were not honours that I desired. They were honours that I sought, as you all know, to avoid.'

'But having assumed them,' said Pizzamano gently, 'you cannot evade the responsibility they carry.'

'Do I seek to evade them? Am I an autocrat? Is there not a Grand Council, a Senate, a College, a Council of Ten, to rule the destinies of this Republic? You, who are the representatives of these bodies, know that for one voice preaching what you preach, there are three that preach neutrality as the only course of duty. You come to me as if I alone were opposing you. It is unjust. It is unconscionable.'

They reminded him that in the executive bodies there were many who wavered undecided, looking to the Doge to lead them.

'And must I assume the responsibility of leading them along a course which I am not myself satisfied is the prudent one?'

Vendramin threw in an audacious phrase.

'Prudence from being a virtue may become a crime in a situation in which energy and courage are required.'

'Is not the reverse also true? This warlike spirit with which you strive to inspire me rests, after all, upon a scrap of rumour; that the French are seeking pretexts.'

He swung to his old arguments. Why should the French seek pretexts? This was not an Italian war. It was a vast flanking movement in a great campaign, the chief theatre of which was on the Rhine. If the French had committed abuses in Venetian territory, these had not been acts of deliberate hostility, but merely the expressions of the brutality from which armies were never free; and

171

they should perceive that if France had violated Venetian territory at all, it was under the necessity of war dictated by the fact that this violation had first been committed by the Austrians when they occupied Peschiera.

'An occupation,' said Pesaro, 'that could never have taken place if we had been in the state of armed neutrality for which you and those who share your easy views refused to perceive the necessity.'

'That was not to have been foreseen!' the Doge exclaimed.

'It must have been,' answered Pesaro. 'For I foresaw it.'

And then Catarin Corner, the inquisitor, interpolated yet another argument. He spoke with quiet incisiveness, his clear-cut, ascetic face as calm as his tone. He denounced the error of assuming friendliness on the part of the French. He pointed to the fanaticism with which the French were spreading their religion of Jacobinism. He alluded to the Cispadane Republic, established in Italy under the auspices of French Jacobinism and lately swollen by embracing Bologna and Ferrara. He dwelt upon the subterranean work of proselytizing that was going on here in Venice, and of the dangerous extent to which this was sapping the foundations of the oligarchy. From his office as one of the inquisitors he derived authority for what he said. Their spies were diligently at work, observing and at need pursuing the ubiquitous French agents, not all of whom were French. There had been, he informed them in his quiet, level voice, more secret arrests than perhaps they suspected, and, after convictions of correspondence with the French, not a few secret executions. Vendramin was conscious of a chill down his spine as he listened to this.

But although the argument was protracted for some hours, they could not tear the weak, vacillating old Doge from the errors to which he clung so obstinately.

The matter ended, as all matters ended with which he had to deal, in compromise. The Proveditor of the Lagoons should continue his activities of preparation, and further recruiting should be set on foot at once, so that they might be in a state of preparedness for whatever course the events should prove desirable. In the meanwhile he promised that he would keep in mind and further consider all that the deputation had urged, and that he would pray for guidance.

He was still considering when in the early days of November Alvinzy's army began to march. And then, suddenly, Venice rang with news of Austrian successes. Masséna had been beaten on the Brenta; Augereau, heavily defeated at Bassano, was retreating upon Verona.

Stimulated by this, Pizzamano and his resolute associates returned to the assault. This was the moment. Whilst the French were staggering, let Venice strike the blow that must put a definite end to the menace of Bonaparte. They were still urging this when, by the end of the month, the French situation had grown so desperate that every temporizer, from Lodovico Manin down to the most neutral senator, now accounted his policy justified by the events. By inaction, whilst the war rolled forward, by economy of blood and treasure, they had conserved unimpaired the strength of the Most Serene Republic.

Such firebrands as Pesaro and Pizzamano were convicted of a rashness, which if it had prevailed must have impoverished Venice and left the Lion of Saint Mark to lick his wounds.

Against this there were no arguments. The men contemned could only look on in silence, and pray, like the loyal patriots they were, that those who contemned them might be right.

It certainly seemed so now.

Bonaparte's hopeless situation finds expression in the cry contained in his dispatch of the thirteenth of that month of November to the Directory: 'The army of Italy reduced to a handful of men is exhausted... We are abandoned in the interior of Italy. The brave men remaining regard death as inevitable amid chances so continual and with forces so inferior in number.'

And then, when all seemed ended, when the loud jubilation in Venice bore witness to relief from the anxieties that had been simmering under her ever-frivolous surface, the genius of the Corsican blazed forth more terribly than ever. Four days after writing that dispatch, he heavily defeated Alvinzy's army on the bloody field of Arcola, and drove its wreckage before him.

But the consequent dismay was not long to endure. Soon it was realized that the French had snatched victory from the ashes of defeat at a cost they could not afford. They had gained a breathing space; no more. Heavy reinforcements were being hurried to Alvinzy. Mantua held firmly against Serrurier's blockade. Arcola, in the Venetian view, had merely postponed a conclusion which it could not avert. The French were face to face with ruin.

In vain did the advocates of intervention denounce this crass optimism which would not learn from past experiences. God and the Austrians, they were confidently answered, would settle matters very soon. So why should the Government of Venice shoulder this burden?

Marc-Antoine himself was encouraged to agree with the optimists by the pessimism which he now discovered at the French Legation. There was more than the exhausted state of the Army of Italy to trouble France at that moment. Her armies on the Rhine were also doing badly, and it looked, indeed, as if at last Europe were to be rid of the French nightmare.

Effectively to maintain the role of Lebel, Marc-Antoine wrote strongly to Barras, as Lebel would have written, urging Bonaparte's need of reinforcements if all that had been won were not to be thrown away. He had no qualms in writing thus. His representations, he knew, could add nothing to those which Bonaparte himself was making; and it was clear that if the Directory had not found it possible to respond adequately to similar demands in the past, the events on the Rhine would render it even less possible now.

His letters, however, produced one unexpected result, communicated to him by Lallemant, whom he found one day more than ordinarily perturbed.

'I am wondering,' said the ambassador, 'whether, after all, there is anything to justify your lingering here. I have sure information that the police are hunting Venice for you at this moment.'

'For me?'

'For the Citizen-Representative Lebel. They are assured of his presence. They have, of course, been more or less aware of it ever since that ultimatum of yours on the subject of the ci-devant Comte de Provence.' He sighed a little wearily. 'These Venetians are rousing themselves to audacity now that they think our claws have been cut. My last courier was held up by General Salimbeni at Padua. He was eventually allowed to proceed with my dispatches to the Directory. But I learn that a letter of yours to Barras was detained on the ground that it was a personal, and not an official, communication. It is now in the hands of the inquisitors of state, and Messer Grande has received orders to discover and arrest you.'

As once before, the only thing in all this that really impressed Marc-Antoine was the efficiency it revealed of the secret service which Lallemant had organized.

'It is not possible that they should identify me with Lebel,' he said.

'I am of the same opinion. But if they should, it would go very hard with the man whom they regard as having placed them under the shame of expelling the soi-disant Louis XVIII from Venetian territory. And I should be given no chance of intervening on your behalf. The inquisitors move very secretly, and they leave no traces. Only this week I have lost one of my most valuable agents: a Venetian. By no means the first. He has simply disappeared, and I have no doubt at all that he has been quietly strangled after a secret trial. As he was not a French subject, I cannot even lodge an inquiry about him.'

'I thank Heaven that I am at least a French subject, and...'

'You forget,' Lallemant interrupted him, 'that you pass for an English one. I can't claim you without admitting the fraud. That wouldn't improve your chances.' He paused there, to repeat a second later: 'I really think you would be wise to leave.'

But Marc-Antoine dismissed the suggestion.

'Not while the service of the Nation may create a need for my presence.'

That same evening he received confirmation of the news from Count Pizzamano. The Count accepted the interception of Lebel's letters as a sign that at long last the Serenissima was asserting her rights. The presence in Venice of Barras' cat's-paw Lebel was one

175

more evidence of the evil intentions of the French, and it would go very ill with this secret envoy when he were found.

This did not trouble Marc-Antoine at all. Messer Grande – as the Venetian Captain of Justice was called – would hunt in vain for Camille Lebel. What troubled him was that the prospect of French defeat, instead of uplifting him, was actually and disloyally dejecting him because of its dangers for Isotta.

Meanwhile, if Vendramin's hatred of Marc-Antoine, by whom he accounted himself so outrageously wronged, abated nothing, at least he was able to dissemble it on those comparatively rare occasions when they met at the Casa Pizzamano.

In this stagnation, Christmas came and went. It was celebrated in Venice with gaieties as unrestrained as usual, or, if restrained at all, restrained merely by the intense cold of a winter that brought the rare spectacle of snow on the house-tops and ice-floes in the canals of Fusina and Marghera. The result was to drive the people to seek indoor amusements. The theatres were never more crowded; the cafés did a roaring trade; and the casinos were thronged with those who went to gamble, to dance, or merely to flirt and gossip.

With the new year the city disposed itself for the licences of carnival, as if these were no serious matters to preoccupy it.

Marc-Antoine killed time as best he could. With a party of friends he attended the first performance of Ugo Foscole's *Tieste*, and supped, as was the carnival custom, in the box which they had rented. He allowed himself to be taken to masked balls given at the Filarmonici and the Orfei, which presented scenes of light-hearted merriment the like of which he had never witnessed. The numerous attendance at these functions of Venetian officers who flocked into the city from their quarters on Malamocco and elsewhere, far from reminding the merrymakers of the clouds of war that still hung upon the horizon, merely served to contribute to the general gaiety.

Whilst life flowed so carefree now in Venice, the Austrians marched to relieve Mantua, and to deliver the decisive blow that should end this campaign. Their defeat on the snow-clad field of Rivoli, with the capture of Provera's division of seven thousand men and thirty guns, gave pause for a moment to the carnival gaieties in Venice. But even now the alarm was far from being either as deep or as general as the circumstances warranted. With the aim of overriding panic, the Government deliberately circulated the assurance that it would provide for whatever might be necessary. In that assurance amusement was resumed.

Along the Riva dei Schiavoni and in the Piazza, as the weather became milder with the advent of February, there were constant throngs of idlers and revellers, and little crowds congregating about the itinerant shows set up for their amusement: the marionettes, the tumblers, the quacksalvers, the story-singers, the astrologers, the fortune-telling canaries, the Furlana dancers, or the circus in the Piazza. Patrician men and women, in mask and bauta, their quality proclaimed by their silks and velvets and gold-laced hats, mingled freely with the noisy populace, sharing their greed of laughter, and as reckless of the doom which was advancing so relentlessly upon the Serenissima.

For now the pace of events was quickening. The fall of Mantua followed upon Alvinzy's defeat. Rendered mobile thereby, Bonaparte went off to Rome and constrained the Pope to the Treaty of Tolentino. As one result of it three great convoys, including bullock carts laden with bronzes, pictures, and treasures of art of every description plundered from the Vatican, took the road to France.

Yet Venice, unable, it seemed, to tolerate any protraction of depression, was uplifted within a few days of the fall of Mantua by definite news that the Archduke Charles was coming with reinforcements from the Rhine to take command of the remains of Alvinzy's army.

Those in authority and those with real vision or real knowledge saw little ground for confidence in this fourth Austrian attempt against Bonaparte. For Bonaparte, too, had received at last, and unstintedly, the reinforcements for which he had so long been clamouring. With an army of sixty thousand men at his back, more than well-found in artillery upon which he placed so much reliance, and rid at last of the Mantua incubus, he was incalculably more formidable than ever before in this campaign.

So formidable, indeed, that the Doge and his councillors, in insisting more passionately than ever upon inaction, completely reversed their former arguments. Hitherto it had been that the Austrian strength more than sufficed to shield them. Now it was that the strength of the French must render futile anything that Venice could do.

The city itself and the surrounding islands swarmed with the troops that had been levied. There were four thousand men at Chioggia; three Dalmatian regiments on Malamocco, one at the Certosa, and a battalion on the Giudecca. There was a Slavonian regiment at San Giorgio Maggiore, and a battalion of Italians under Domenico Pizzamano at Sant' Andrea. Sixteen companies were quartered at Murano; the Croatian company of Colonel Radnich was at Fusina; and there were further troops quartered at San Francesco della Vigna and at San Giorgio in Alga. The total came to some sixteen thousand men, without taking into account a further ten thousand in garrisons on the mainland. In addition, there were seven naval divisions, stationed at Fusina, Burano, in the Canal of the Marani, and elsewhere. Nevertheless, it was deemed, even by minds as intrepid as that of Count Pizzamano, that these forces were inadequate now for an offensive alliance.

Manin was constrained to admit, at least in private and almost in tears, the error of having missed the moment for action which had presented itself just before Rivoli. To take such action now would be in the nature of a gambler's throw. And if the dice fell against them, the independence of the Serenissima would be the forfeit.

Austria having failed them, Manin perceived their only hope to lie now in the favour of Heaven. By his orders there were special prayers, services, and processions, and the unveiling of a miraculous image in Saint Mark's. The only result of this was to alarm the people and lead to demonstrations hostile to the Signory for not having taken timely measures.

Chapter 23

The Citizen Villetard

Marc-Antoine was roused on the morning of the first Sunday in Lent by a peremptory summons from Lallemant.

Masks and mummeries had disappeared from the streets and canals of Venice, and the church bells were summoning a sobered population to devotion. The sun shone with a hard brightness, and already there was a feeling of spring in the air.

Closeted with Lallemant, Marc-Antoine found a young-old man of middle height, whose pallid, foxy countenance, lean, dry, and lined, seemed too old for his lithe, active body. His spare, sinewy legs were encased in white buckskins and black knee-boots with reversed yellow tops. He wore a long riding-coat of rough brown cloth with silver buttons and very wide lapels. And on the conical brown hat which he retained he had plastered a tricolour cockade. He was without visible weapons.

Lallemant, who did not appear to be in the best of humours, presented him as the Citizen Villetard, an envoy from General Bonaparte.

The keen glance of the man's small, sunken eyes played searchingly over Marc-Antoine. His nod was curt, his voice, harsh and rasping.

'I have heard of you, Citizen Lebel. You have been some months in Venice. But you do not appear to have accomplished very much.'

Marc-Antoine met aggressiveness with aggressiveness.

'I render my accounts to the Directors, from whom I take my orders.'

'General Bonaparte finds it necessary to supplement them. That is why I am here. The Little Corporal is tired of temporizings. The hour for action has arrived.'

'So long,' said Marc-Antoine, 'as his wishes coincide with those of the Directory, we shall do our best to realize them for him. Since he has thought it worth while to send you to Venice, I trust that you bring some useful suggestion.'

Villetard was visibly taken aback by an arrogance that seemed to wrest from him his authority. Lallemant, who had just been hectored by this envoy, permitted himself the ghost of a smile.

Villetard frowned. 'You do not seem to understand, Citizen Lebel, that I have been sent here to co-operate with you. With you and the citizen-ambassador.'

'That is different. Your tone led me to suppose that you came here to give orders. That, you must understand, is inadmissible until the Directory relieves me of my responsibility.'

'My dear Citizen Lebel...' the other was beginning to protest, when he was interrupted by the peremptory hand which Marc-Antoine raised.

'Here in Venice, Citizen Villetard, I am known as Mr Melville, an English idler.'

'Ah, bah!' Villetard was jocularly contemptuous. 'We can afford to throw off our masks now that we are about to prick this oligarchic bubble.'

'I shall prefer that you wait until the bubble has been pricked. Shall we come to business?'

It transpired that Villetard's first business was to obtain and forward at once to Bonaparte the charts of the soundings taken in the canals approaching Venice from the mainland. Lallemant had to confess that they were incomplete. After the arrest and suppression of Terzi and Sartoni, he had abandoned the matter as too obviously dangerous.

Villetard was sarcastic. 'I suppose you have been assuming that Bonaparte would invade Venice with an army of ducks.'

Coldly Marc-Antoine asserted himself again. 'Would not consideration of the means to employ be more profitable than offensive pleasantries? It will save time. And you have said yourself, Citizen Villetard, that there is no time to lose.'

'What I have said is that too much time has been lost,' was the truculent answer. 'But certainly let us consider what means are now available. Do you dispose of anyone capable of undertaking the work? After all, it does not entail a great deal of intelligence.'

'No,' said Lallemant. 'But it entails a great deal of risk. It is certain death to the man who is detected.'

'Therefore, the man to be employed should be one who is not otherwise valuable,' was the cynical answer.

'Of course. I would, naturally, not employ a Frenchman. And, as it fortunately happens, I have under my hand a Venetian whom I think we can coerce.'

He mentioned Vendramin and the nature of the coercion. Marc-Antoine was conscious of excitement.

'Vendramin?' said Villetard. 'Oh, yes, I've heard of him. One of the preachers of francophobia.' He appeared to be very fully informed. 'It would be poetically humorous to constrain him to perform this service. If you are really able to do it, let it be done without loss of time. Where is this barnabotto to be found?'

They found him that same Sunday evening at the lodging of the Vicomtesse de Saulx. And they found him there because Lallemant so contrived it, by instructing the Vicomtesse to ask Vendramin to supper. Accompanied by Villetard, the ambassador presented himself at the Casa Gazzola at nine o'clock, by when he judged that supper would be over.

It was. But Vendramin and the Vicomtesse were still at table. Vendramin had accepted the invitation with alacrity as a mark of favour of which lately the marks had been few. This to his distress, because he was becoming more and more urgently in need of favour. His hopes ran high that the Vicomtesse would prove more generous than she had been of late; and he was in the very act of moving her compassion for his needs when, to his annoyance, Lallemant was announced.

The ambassador was of a disarming urbanity when the Vicomtesse presented Ser Leonardo. He had heard of Monsieur Vendramin, of course, from his cousin Anne, and had long desired the felicity of meeting him. Villetard's acknowledgments of the presentation might have been considered equally flattering but for the contemptuous smile on his grey, wolfish face.

'Monsieur Vendramin's name is well known to me, too, although I am new to Venice: well known as that of a patrician of great prominence in the councils of the Most Serene Republic. Not exactly francophile, perhaps. But I am of those who can admire energy even in an enemy.'

Vendramin, flushed with annoyance and discomfort, mumbled empty amiabilities. Beautifully dressed himself, for the occasion, in a shimmering satin coat that was striped in two shades of blue, he eyed with disgust the unceremonious redingote and buckskins and loosely knotted neckcloth in which this very obvious Jacobin presumed to intrude upon a lady of quality.

Lallemant made himself at home. He even did the honours, setting a chair for his companion, providing him with a glass and placing a decanter of malvoisie before him. Then he drew up a chair for himself, and sat down at the table.

'Do you know, cousin François, you arrive very opportunely,' said the Vicomtesse, with her sweetest smile.

'You mean, I suppose,' said the portly ambassador, 'that you will be wanting something. The day is long past when a lovely lady accounted me opportune on any other grounds.'

'My friend, you do yourself injustice.'

'So does everybody else. But what is it that you are requiring?'

'Do you think that you could advance me two or three hundred ducats?'

Vendramin felt a pleasant warmth rising in his veins. After all, his annoyance at this visit had been premature.

The ambassador blew out his red cheeks, and raised his brows. 'God of God, Anne! You say two or three hundred, as if there were no difference between the one figure and the other.'

'What is the difference, after all?' She set a hand, long, slim, and of a dazzling whiteness upon the ambassador's black satin arm. 'Come, François. Be a good child, and let me have two hundred and fifty.'

Lallemant looked at her gravely. 'You don't seem to realize how large a sum it is. What can you want it for?'

'Need that matter to you?'

'Very much; you do not dispose of such a sum; and if I am to advance it, I have some sort of right to know how it is going to be spent. After all, I am in a sense responsible for you.' He looked across at Vendramin, and his eyes usually kindly had become a little hard. 'If, for instance, you are proposing to add this, or any part of this, to the money that this gentleman already owes you…'

'Monsieur!' exclaimed Vendramin. His face flamed scarlet. He made as if to rise, then sank together again on his chair, as the Vicomtesse exclaimed: 'Francois! How can you? This is to betray my confidence.'

Villetard quietly sipped his wine like one who seeks to efface himself.

'Betray your confidence, my dear! What will you say next? Can Monsieur Vendramin suppose that in a few months I would advance you sums, amounting in all to some six or seven thousand ducats, without informing myself of what was becoming of the money? I should be an odd guardian if I had done that, should I not, Monsieur Vendramin?'

From flushed that it had been Vendramin's face had turned pale. He was breathing hard.

'Really!' he ejaculated. 'I had no notion of this. A transaction of so very private a nature…' He swung in dark annoyance to the Vicomtesse. 'You never told me, Anne, that…'

'My dear Leonardo,' she interrupted him, a pleading little smile on her distressed face, 'where was the need to trouble you? And, after

183

all, what does it matter?' She swung again to the ambassador. 'You have made my poor Leonardo uncomfortable, and this before Monsieur Villetard, too. It is not nice. You'll do penance by letting me have that two hundred and fifty tomorrow morning.'

For all his annoyance, Vendramin watched the ambassador from under his brows. Lallemant shook his big head slowly. Slowly he turned his glance upon the Venetian.

'You realize, sir, that the sum you are owing the Vicomtesse is a very heavy one. I should not be doing my duty to her if I allowed her to increase the debt without some clear assurance of how and when this money is to be repaid.'

The Vicomtesse flashed in with vexation in her voice. 'Why do you plague him with such remarks? I have told you already that Monsieur Vendramin is to make a rich marriage.'

Lallemant affected to recollect. 'Ah, yes. I remember now.' He smiled deprecatingly. 'But marriages sometimes miscarry. What would happen, for instance, if, after all, Monsieur Vendramin were not to make this rich marriage? You would lose your money. Well, as your cousin, and in some sort your guardian, I do not want to see you lose such a sum as that. It is very much more than you can afford to lose. I wish you to understand that, Monsieur Vendramin.' His manner had become stern.

And now, to increase Vendramin's almost intolerable and speechless discomfort, Lallemant's saturnine companion thrust himself into the matter.

'There is no reason why the citoyenne should not be repaid at once.'

'Ah?' Lallemant slewed round on his chair to gaze interrogatively at the speaker.

'Transfer the debt from the citoyenne to the French Republic, as moneys paid to this Venetian gentleman out of the secret service funds, on account of services to be rendered.'

'That is an idea,' said Lallemant, and in the deathly stillness that followed, his dark eyes questioned Vendramin.

The Venetian stared blankly. 'I do not think I understand.'

Villetard again intruded. 'God of God! It's plain enough, isn't it? You have received from the French secret service funds an advance of six thousand ducats, or some such sum, on account of services to be rendered. The time has come to render them.'

'To render them?' said Vendramin. 'What services?'

Villetard leaned forward to answer him. 'The nature of the services doesn't matter. You'll receive full instructions about that. May we take it that you will adopt this method of discharging your debt?'

'You may take nothing of the kind,' was the furious answer. 'Is this a trap, sirs? Anne!' he appealed wildly to the Vicomtesse. 'Is this a trap?'

'If it is,' said the rasping voice of Villetard, 'it is a trap of your own making.'

Vendramin pushed back his chair and rose. 'Sirs,' he announced, with a sudden access of dignity, 'I have the honour to wish you a very good-night.'

'It will be a very bad night for you if you do,' sneered Villetard. 'Sit down, man.'

Tall, straight, and disdainful Vendramin looked down at the Frenchman beyond the table.

'As for you, sir, who have had the effrontery to impugn my honour with such a proposal, I should be glad to know where a friend of mine can find you.'

Villetard leaned back and looked up at him through half-closed eyes, a tight-lipped smile on his lean, ashen face. 'You bleat of honour, do you? You prey upon a woman, and borrow from her large sums of money which you are unable to repay unless, as a result of a prospective marriage, you commit an act that is even more flagrantly dishonest. Yet you boast an honour that may be impugned. Do you not even suspect that you are ridiculous?'

With a foul oath Vendramin snatched up a decanter from the table. He was baulked of his murderous intention by the Vicomtesse. Suddenly on her feet, she clutched his arm. A glass was swept to the floor and shivered there. Almost like an echo of the sound came the rasping voice of Villetard, who had not moved.

'Sit down!'

Vendramin, however, remained standing; panting and swaying. The Vicomtesse, still clinging to him, was murmuring 'Leonardo! Leonardo!' the music of her voice cracked by agitation. She took the decanter from his hand, and replaced it on the table. His spasm of passion spent, he let her have her way.

Villetard, still sitting back and slightly tilting his chair, still looking at him with that expression of contempt, spoke again.

'Sit down, you fool, and listen. And in God's name, let us be calm. In heat nothing was ever accomplished. Just survey your position. You have had these sums from the French secret service funds. They have been paid to you in drafts on Vivanti's issued by the French Legation, and these drafts have been countersigned by you in acknowledgment of the money. Do you suppose that you will be allowed to swindle the French Government by refusing now to do the work for which you have been paid?'

'That is infamous!' cried the livid Venetian. 'Infamous! Did you say swindle? It is you who are attempting a swindle. A gross, impudent swindle. But you are dealing with the wrong man, let me tell you. You may take your treacherous proposals to the devil. Where I am concerned you may do your worst. My answer to you is no. No, and be damned to you.'

'Very fine and heroic,' said Villetard. 'But I don't happen to be the man to take "no" for an answer. You say that we may do our worst. Have you reflected what that would be? Have you even considered how you would allay the natural assumptions of the inquisitors of state as to the purpose for which you received this money from the French Embassy?'

Vendramin stood there with the feeling that the blood was draining from his heart. The defiant spirit that had been sustaining him a moment ago was slowly perishing. Gradually sheer terror came to stare out of his prominent blue eyes.

'Oh, my God!' he said. 'My God!' He swallowed, and made an effort to brace himself. 'You mean that you would do that? That you would use this lying blackmail against me?'

'You happen to be necessary to us,' said Lallemant quietly. 'Just as this money was necessary to you. You did not scruple to take it from my cousin. You did not trouble to inquire whence it came or whether she could spare it. Why should we be less unscrupulous with you?'

'You try to make a case against me, so as to justify the vileness of what you do. You are just a pair of scoundrels; low, Jacobin scoundrels; and this woman has... been your decoy. Mother of God! What company have I been keeping?'

'Very profitable company,' said Villetard. 'And now we call the reckoning.'

'And insult will not help you,' added Lallemant. 'After all, Venice will not suffer more than she must by what you do. If you should persist in refusing, someone else will be found for the service we require. It is only that we do not waste the money of the Nation. You are paid in advance.'

Villetard shifted impatiently. 'Haven't we had words enough? Our proposal is before Monsieur Vendramin. If he is such a fool as to prefer the Prison of the Leads and the garrotter, let him say so, and have done.'

Vendramin leaned heavily upon the back of a chair. In his heart he cursed the day when he had first seen the Vicomtesse, cursed every ducat that he had ever borrowed from her. That scoundrel Melville had been able to blackmail him with this threat into foregoing a just vengeance; and now the thing was being used again to force him into this treachery. His mind remained clear; in fact, it was rendered more than ordinarily clear by the peril in which he stood. The suspicion concerning Melville, which this little Delilah had quieted, was now stronger than ever. It was too much of a coincidence that both he and these admitted French agents should adopt exactly the same method of imposing their wills upon him.

And from this suddenly sprang a thought which proved the determining factor in his agony of vacillation.

He looked at them with eyes that narrowed suddenly.

'If I were to listen to you… If I were to agree to do what you want, what guarantee should I have that you would keep faith with me?'

'Guarantee?' said Villetard, raising his brows.

'How should I know that you would not still betray me?'

'There would be our word,' Lallemant assured him.

But Vendramin, still stinging where he could, shook his head. 'I should need something more in so grave a matter.'

'I am afraid that is all that we can give you.'

'You can give me the drafts that you hold as proof of what you call my debt to you.'

On the point of answering, Lallemant suddenly checked. He sat silent and thoughtful, his eyes on the wine-glass which he was twirling by its delicate stem. Thus, until Villetard broke in impatiently: 'But why not? He has a sort of right to them once the debt is paid.'

'Once it is paid, yes,' the ambassador slowly agreed. Then, taking his resolve, he became more brisk. 'Come to me at the embassy tomorrow in the forenoon, and we will settle the terms with you.'

'You mean that you agree?' Vendramin was eager.

'I mean that I will let you know tomorrow morning.'

'I will serve you on no other terms,' Vendramin defied him.

'Well, well. We will talk of it tomorrow.'

After the Venetian had departed, Villetard expressed impatience of a procrastination for which he could discover no reason. But Lallemant postponed explanation until the two men were in their gondola, on the way back to the Madonna dell' Orto. Then, at last, he satisfied Bonaparte's envoy.

'I have my reasons, of course. Naturally I could not state them in the presence of this Venetian. Just as naturally I preferred not to state them after he had departed.'

'But why not, since Madame la Vicomtease… '

Lallemant interrupted him, adopting the tone of the master towards the dilettante.

'My dear Villetard, the experience gathered in controlling as I do a considerable secret service has taught me never, unless there are very good reasons for it, to allow one secret agent to be aware of another. In the case of Lebel there are more than ordinary reasons why none of my people should be allowed to guess his real identity. It would have been impossible to have discussed this matter before the Vicomtesse without disclosing it. That is why I preferred to wait until we should be by ourselves.'

'I don't myself see what there is to discuss. This miserable barnabotto was ready to come to terms, and...'

Again he was interrupted. 'If you will have a little patience, my dear Villetard, you shall learn what there is to discuss.' And he disclosed how, to shield himself from the danger of assassination, Lebel employed those drafts on Vivanti's which Vendramin now asked them to surrender. 'Now, if harm should befall Lebel through my having neglected any precautions, that would be a very serious thing. I do not care about the responsibility.'

Villetard was impatient. 'If the Little Corporal doesn't get what he wants, the consequences may be still more serious. I don't care for the responsibility of that. Lebel must take his chances. He seems a man well able to take care of himself.'

'But I must consult him before accepting Vendramin's condition?'

'Why?' Villetard was vehement. 'Suppose that he opposes it? What then? Is General Bonaparte... Is France to forego advantages because of risks to the Citizen Lebel?' And he quoted: ' "Salus populi suprema lex." '

'Yes, yes. But if Vendramin won't hear reason, I might find another man to do the work?'

'When?' barked Villetard.

'Oh, soon. I should have to look round.'

'And is the Army of Italy to wait while you look round? Name of a name! I begin to think it is fortunate I was sent to Venice. There is one thing only to be done. Duty points it out quite clearly.' His tone hardened. 'Tomorrow, you will agree to Vendramin's terms. And you will conveniently forget to mention the matter to Lebel, or to anyone else. I hope that is clear.'

'It is clear,' said Lallemant, stifling his resentment of that hectoring tone. 'But let it be also clear to you that I shall not do it until I have exhausted every attempt to constrain Vendramin without going quite so far.'

'That is legitimate,' Villetard admitted. 'But it is the utmost that I will permit.'

Chapter 24

Emancipation

Firmly on the morrow Lallemant went as far as Villetard gave him leave. And Villetard himself was present to see that he went no further. For the rest Villetard loyally supported him in the assertion that they must retain the drafts in their possession, and that Vendramin must rest content with their assurance that they would not be employed to his detriment unless he himself provoked it.

Vendramin on his side was no less firm. A night's reflection had hardened him in his purpose. Unless by this act of treachery to Venice he could break the intolerable fetters in which Melville held him, he would not undertake it.

What he said to Lallemant was that without a definite guarantee he would not act; and that no guarantee would serve him short of delivery to him of the actual drafts upon his fulfilment of what was required of him.

Upon this he was actually on the point of taking his leave when Villetard intimated surrender.

'Since he sets such store by it, Lallemant, let him have his way.'

And Lallemant, venting his reluctance in a sigh, had felt constrained to yield.

When, later that day, Marc-Antoine called at the embassy to inquire whether Vendramin had been enlisted, the uncomfortable Lallemant disingenuously brushed the matter aside.

'I have no doubt,' he said, 'that he will come to it,' and he changed the subject.

The ambassador had been able to simplify the task ahead of Vendramin by putting him in communication with a survivor of the associates of Sartoni. This man procured two others who were willing to work with him. But since the fate of their predecessors went to show with what terrible risks the task was fraught, these scoundrels required very substantial emoluments.

Vendramin found the embassy accommodatingly liberal. Lallemant did not stint supplies. Not only did he furnish the necessary funds for those wages of treachery, but he made no difficulty about adding fifty ducats, as a douceur to relieve the temporary embarrassment which Vendramin had not hesitated to confess to him.

As a result, and also because driven by anxiety to obtain possession of those incriminating drafts, Vendramin went to work with zealous and assiduous diligence.

Each morning when Zanetto – the chief of the men employed – brought him a rough note of the night's labours, he would spend some hours in carefully recording the figures on the chart he had prepared to receive them.

This, however, did not prevent him from making simultaneously a fuller parade than ever of his patriotic zeal at the Palazzo Pizzamano, where he was an almost daily visitor. There was, however, little to be done just then. Hope was encouraged by the persistent rumour that although Bonaparte was now in great strength, and although the Archduke Charles at Udine was not relaxing his warlike preparations, negotiations for peace were actively on foot.

Vendramin displayed a shrewdness, which he thought that future events might well come to establish, by refusing to share this optimism. He declared that the perceptible underground activities of the French contradicted these rumours. Venice, he reminded them, was full of French agents and French propagandists, working incalculable mischief.

One day, meeting Catarin Corner at the Casa Pizzamano, he actually expressed himself with some bitterness on the subject of the comparative inertia of the inquisitors.

'The danger,' he declared, 'is perhaps more to be feared than the guns of Bonaparte. It is an invasion of ideas, creeping insidiously into the foundations of the State. It is the hope of the apostles of Liberty, Equality and Fraternity, that if the Venetian oligarchy is not to be destroyed by force of arms, it shall nevertheless succumb to Jacobin intrigue.'

Corner assured him that the inquisitors were by no means either indifferent or inert. Idleness on the part of the inquisitors was not to be assumed from the absence of signs of their activities. It was not the way of the Three to leave footprints. If those responsible for military measures had been one half as active, the Republic today would stand delivered of every menace.

Vendramin deplored so much secrecy at such a time. A parade of the functioning of the inquisitors must prove a salutary deterrent to enemy agents.

Pizzamano listened and approved him, and in this way Ser Leonardo improved his credit with the Count, and at the same time increased the despair of Isotta.

She moved wan and listless in those days, and Vendramin's attitude towards her was not calculated to lighten her burden. Whilst outwardly the perfect courtier, yet his courtship held now an indefinable undercurrent of irony, which, whilst so slight and elusive that it was impossible to seize upon it, was nevertheless perceptible to her keen senses.

Sometimes, when Marc-Antoine was with them, she would detect on Vendramin's lip a faint curl that was not merely the secret mockery of one in whom he perceived a defeated rival; and in his glance at moments she would surprise a malevolence that made her almost afraid. Of the meeting between the two men she knew nothing, and of the open enmity between them they had tacitly agreed to allow nothing to transpire here. The fact that they had no love for each other was beyond dissembling: but at least they used towards each other a cold and distant civility.

Sometimes, when Vendramin leaned over her with words of flattery, there was a smile on his lips that made her soul shudder. He had a trick of alluding to her innocence of the world's evil and to the purity of her inexperience in terms so exaggerated that it was impossible not to suspect their sarcasm, far though she might be from understanding it. She could not guess the bitterness festering in his soul, the hatred which at times surged up in him for this woman whom he was to marry, but by whom he accounted himself so basely cheated. He would make her his wife so that he might win an established position and escape from the life of makeshifts which had hitherto been his. But he could never forgive that, whilst she might gratify his ambition, she cheated him of all else to which he was entitled, cheated him even of the satisfaction of telling her that he knew her stately calm, her cold, virginal austerity for the brazen masks with which she covered her impurity. One day that satisfaction might yet be his; and nearer at hand lay that other satisfaction of striking at her through her paramour, and thus at one blow avenging himself upon both. There should be, he thought, a measure of solace for him there.

To this end he worked so diligently that, within a fortnight of having set his hand to the task, he was able secretly to repair to the French Legation one night and lay before Lallemant the chart which he had completed.

The two Frenchmen examined it carefully. Lallemant still had in his possession some of the details supplied to him by Rocco Terzi before he was taken. By these he checked as far as possible the work of Vendramin, and found it accurate.

They behaved generously. From a strong-box Lallemant took the drafts that had been cashed at Vivanti's and surrendered them. After that he counted out a hundred ducats in gold, which he had promised the Venetian as a further gratuity when the task should be accomplished.

Vendramin pocketed first the heavy bag of gold, and then, when he had carefully examined them, the incriminating drafts.

Villetard, who had looked on with his habitual cynical smile, spoke at last.

'Now that you know where good money is to be earned, you may find it suits you to continue in our service.'

Vendramin looked at him in resentment of both tone and words.

'I shall not again find myself at your mercy.'

The cynicism of Villetard's smile deepened. 'You are not the first escroc I've met who could be lofty in words. It's part of your stock-in-trade, my lad, and we're not deceived. You'll remember my offer.'

Vendramin went out, secretly fuming at the insolence of such assumptions. But the feeling did not last. It was outweighed by the exhilaration of possessing those drafts on Vivanti's Bank. He was like a man whose fetters have been knocked off. He was emancipated; free at last to settle accounts with Mr Melville without dread of consequences. At last – as he expressed it to himself – he was in a position to repair his honour.

He lost no time in setting about it. With a definite purpose he made his way to Saint Mark's.

Payment of his debts would consume all of the hundred ducats in his pocket. But Vendramin was not thinking of paying his debts. He was not even thinking of wooing fortune with this money at the Casino del Leone, which is probably how he would have employed it, his creditors notwithstanding, but that he knew of a still sweeter use for it.

He strolled the length of the Procuratie, scanning the occupants of the tables at Florian's, greeted here with a nod and there with a wave of the hand. Those who hailed him were chiefly fellow-barnabotti taking the spring air, and a little wine at somebody's expense. For some time he did not find what he sought. Having come to the end, he passed round again to the middle of the Piazza, and so retraced his steps towards Saint Mark's. It was only as he was returning that his glance met that of a middle-aged, vigorous man in a rusty suit with tarnished lace, who walked with his hands behind him, a cane swinging from them, and a sword worn through the pocket of his coat.

Ser Leonardo halted in this man's path. They greeted each other, and Vendramin, turning, fell into step beside him.

'There's a service I am needing, Contarini,' he said. 'If you can render it there are fifty ducats for you, and another thirty to be shared between any two likely lads you may know who will lend a hand.'

The expression on Contarini's sallow, hungry-looking face scarcely changed.

'Does it need three of us?' he asked.

'I am making certain. I want no accidents. And there will be four of us. For I shall be of the party.'

Chapter 25

The Warning

Isotta occupied a high-backed settee, near the glass doors leading to the loggia at the garden end of the salon. A servant had placed it for her so that she immediately faced the light with the piece of needlework upon which she was engaged. She worked mechanically, her mind overclouded by the melancholy of a hopeless waiting. It was late afternoon, and as the March daylight began to fade, she relinquished her work, and reclined with closed eyes. Eye-strain had induced a drowsiness to which she yielded.

Suddenly she was aware of voices at the other end of the room. From this and the deepening twilight, she realized that she had been asleep. The voice that had aroused her was her father's, loud and vehement; and now it was answered by the smooth, level tones of Catarin Corner's. She moved to rise and disclose herself, when the red inquisitor's words thrust her back again, breathless.

'That Camille Lebel and your friend Messer Melville are one and the same person there is, I assure you, no possible doubt. He will be arrested tonight, and a thorough search will be made of the effects at his lodgings. But whether that discloses anything or not, there is quite enough before the inquisitors already to determine his doom.'

'And I assure you that this is sheer lunacy.' The Count was excited. 'My acquaintance with him is not of yesterday. And the British Ambassador here can speak for him very definitely.'

'Unfortunately for him, our spies can speak more definitely still. This man has covered his traces very cleverly, taking advantage of, no doubt, laudable antecedents so as to establish his credit. Whoever he may really be, the French Legation knows him for Camille Lebel, and the activities of this elusive Camille Lebel, whom we had almost despaired of discovering, make up a heavy account against him.'

'But it is preposterous, Catarin. His comings and goings at the French Legation prove nothing. If he had not been in relations with Lallemant, passing himself off as a francophile agent, he would never have obtained the valuable information which from time to time he has passed on to us. I will tell you this, and you may obtain confirmation of it from Sir Richard Worthington: Melville came to Venice primarily on a mission from Pitt, and his labours here have been unremittingly anti-Jacobin.'

'If you had ever held my office, my dear Francesco, you would know that there never was a secret agent of any value who did not pretend to serve both sides. It is the only way in which he can really render service.'

'But then! Knowing this, and remembering what he has done for us, isn't that a sufficient answer to those silly suspicions?'

'They are not suspicions, Francesco. They are facts very well established. That he is Lebel we know definitely upon the evidence of Casotto.'

'Even so… '

'There is no even so to that. No, no. The little services with which this Lebel has so craftily flung dust in your eyes are as nothing to the disservices the Republic has suffered at his hands. There is that letter of his which we intercepted in which he informed Barras of our situation.'

'Information of no value whatsoever,' the Count interjected.

'Not in itself, perhaps. But the terms of the letter prove a regular correspondence. All the information he sent would not be of as little value as this.'

'How can you assert that?'

'From what we know of his true character. Have you forgotten that the infamous ultimatum by which Venice was put to the shame and indignity of defiling her hospitality, of expelling the King of France from Verona, bore this man's signature?'

Isotta, huddled, trembling and horror-stricken, in her corner of the settle, heard her father's gasp of dismay.

Corner went on, a warmth of indignation creeping into a voice that normally was so suave and level. 'There was evidence, you will remember, in the ultimatum itself that this fellow Lebel was acting in the matter upon his own responsibility; that he was not even executing orders from the Directory. Had this been the case, the ultimatum would have come to us from Lallemant. There was in that action a depth of ill-will towards us which nothing can condone. The intention must have been to discredit us in the eyes of the world, as a measure of preparation for whatever the French were brewing. For that, if there were nothing else against him, it has always been our intention to deal with this spy, when discovered and caught, as spies are always dealt with.' He paused, and there was a moment's silence before he continued: 'You see, Francesco. Knowing your interest in this young man...'

'It is more than interest,' the Count interrupted him miserably. 'Marc is a very dear friend.' In angry protest he exclaimed: 'I utterly refuse to believe this nonsense.'

'I can understand,' said Corner gently. 'If you desire it, I will have you summoned as a witness at his trial, so that you may urge anything in his favour. But probably you realize that no intervention will avail him.'

'I am very far from realizing it.' The Count spoke with a renewed access of confidence. 'Whatever he may have done, I am quite certain that the man who fought at Quiberon and Savenay, and who incurred the perils Marc has incurred in the service of his Prince, could never have been the author of that ultimatum. Instead of incriminating him, it definitely proves to me that he is not Lebel. If you want another proof, you'll find it in his real identity. His name is

199

not Melville, but Melleville; and he is the Vicomte de Saulx. That should prick this bubble.'

'The Vicomte de Saulx, did you say?' There was profound amazement in Corner's voice. 'But the Vicomte de Saulx was guillotined in France two or three years ago.'

'That is what is generally supposed. But it was not so.'

'Are you quite sure?'

'My dear Catarin, I knew him and his mother in England before the journey to France in the course of which he was reported guillotined.'

'And you say that this is the same man?'

'What else am I saying? You see, Catarin. The disclosure of that fact alone blows all your assumptions into dust.'

'On the contrary,' he was slowly answered. 'It supplies one more and very significant piece of incriminating evidence against him. Have you never heard of the Vicomtesse de Saulx?'

'His mother. I know her well.'

'No. Not his mother. A lady of fashion here in Venice, commonly to be met in the more modish casinos.'

'I do not frequent casinos,' said the Count, with a touch of scorn.

The inquisitor continued: 'She is said to be a cousin of Lallemant, she is known to us for a spy, but is shielded by her relationship – real or pretended – with the ambassador. She also pretends to be a widow; the widow of the Vicomte de Saulx, who was guillotined, but whom you now tell me was not guillotined. You perceive the implications?'

'I perceive a mare's nest. Are you telling me that he has a wife; a wife here in Venice?'

'I am telling you that there is a lady here who claims to be the widow of the guillotined Vicomte Saulx. You are as capable as I am, Francesco, of drawing an inference.'

'She must be an impostor! You have said that she is known to the inquisitors for a spy.'

'If she is an impostor, your Vicomte de Saulx is singularly tolerant. He sees a good deal of the lady. Considering what she is known to be, do you really think the revelation of his true identity will assist this unfortunate young man?'

'My God! You bewilder me. All this is fantastic. Opposed to everything I know about Marc. I must see him.'

'You will hardly now have an opportunity of doing that.' There was the scraping of a chair. 'I must be going, Francesco. I am awaited at home. It has been a shock to me to find my own convictions respecting this young man shattered by Casotto's revelations. Consider tonight whether you desire to attend his trial in the morning. Send me word if you do, and I will contrive it.'

'But of course I will.'

They were moving towards the door. 'Well, well. Give it thought. Consider all that I have said.'

They went out, and the door closed upon them.

Isotta continued huddled in panic. This was as terrible as it was preposterous. Not for one moment, not under any arguments urged by Corner had her confidence in Marc-Antoine known the least wavering. That matter of the existence of a Vicomtesse de Saulx, imperfectly understood by her, she dismissed as the mare's nest her father had denounced it. Scorn of wits that could leap at such rash conclusions mingled with her terror on Marc-Antoine's behalf. In their rashness, in their present state of nerves on the subject of French agents, the two black inquisitors might easily share Corner's conviction of Marc's guilt, and in that case she knew how swiftly execution would follow.

By this time tomorrow, unless something were meanwhile done, it might be too late to do anything. With a sense of suffocation she realized the urgency of action. From the way Corner had spoken it might already be too late even to warn him. And what else was there that she could do?

She was suddenly on her feet. Her limbs were stiff and cold, her teeth chattered. She pressed a hand to her brow as if to constrain thought. Then, having made her determination as swiftly as the case demanded, she rustled from the room, and sought her own chamber.

Her maid, awaiting her in her room, cried out in concern at the deathly pallor of her face.

'It is nothing. Nothing,' said Isotta impatiently.

In a breath she ordered the girl to summon Renzo, her brother's valet, who in Domenico's absence made himself generally useful.

Whilst the maid was about that errand, she scrawled a hurried note with fingers scarcely able to hold a pen.

This note hastily sealed, she delivered to the young man ushered presently by Tessa. Her instructions, if breathlessly delivered, were yet precise.

'Listen, Renzo. You will take a gondola; two oars, so as to make the better speed; and you will go straight to the Inn of the Swords on the Rio delle Beccherie. You will ask to see Messer Melville, and you will deliver this note to him in person. In person, you understand?'

'Perfectly, madonna.'

'Listen still. If by any chance he should not be there, endeavour to discover where he is. He has a valet, a Frenchman. See him. Question him. Tell him that the matter is of great urgency, and have him help you, if he can, to find his master, so that you may deliver the note at the very earliest moment. It is very, very important, Renzo, do you understand? And I depend upon you to do all in your power to reach Mr Melville with it without losing a moment.'

'I understand, madonna. If I am wanted here…'

'Never mind that,' she interrupted him. 'Tell no one where you are going, or even that you are going. I will answer for you if you are missed. Now go, boy; I pray God you may make good speed. And bring me word the moment you are back.' She gave him a handful of silver and so dismissed him.

Deriving some relief from the sense of having at least done something, Isotta sank down on the stool before her dressing-table and viewed her ghostly face in its long Murano mirror.

It would be an hour after the Angelus had sounded, and night had already closed in when Renzo reached the Inn of the Swords to be met by the landlord with the information that Messer Melville was absent. Since the landlord could add nothing to this information,

Renzo asked to see Messer Melville's valet. He was conducted by the landlord above-stairs.

The keen-faced Philibert desired to know what the young man wanted with his master. Renzo told him frankly, whence he came and what his errand.

'Morbleu,' said Philibert, 'it seems, then, that all Venice is hunting Monsieur Melville this evening. Half-an-hour ago it was Monsieur Vendramin, just as eager to find him. It's fortunate I overheard him ordering his gondolier, or you would both be disappointed. He left here to go to the Casa Gazzola, if you know where that is.'

'By the Rialto. I know.' The breathless Renzo would have departed, but that Philibert caught him by the arm.

'Not so much haste, my lad. You have a proverb in Italy that he goes safely who goes slowly. Remember it. When you come to the Casa Gazzola, ask for Madame la Vicomtesse de Saulx. Madame la Vicomtesse de Saulx,' he repeated. 'That's where you'll find him.'

Renzo flung down the stairs and back to the waiting gondola. Within ten minutes he was at the Casa Gazzola.

The Vicomtesse was from home, the porter informed him. She had gone out nearly an hour ago.

'It is not the Vicomtesse I was seeking, but a gentleman I was told I should find here with her. A Messer Melville. Do you know him? Is he here?'

'He left with madama. If your business is urgent, you may find him at the French Legation. At least, that's where they were going when they left here. Do you know where it is? In the Corte del Cavallo, Fondamenta of the Madonna del' Orto. Palazzo della Vecchia. Anyone there will point it out to you.'

Renzo re-embarked, and the black boat glided away and swung presently from the broad waters of the Grand Canal, aglitter with the lights of the Rialto Bridge, into the darkness of a narrow rio to the north. It was a long way to the Madonna del' Orto, and Renzo prayed that he was not making the journey merely again to be sent on somewhere else.

Chapter 26

The Pursuers

Marc-Antoine had been visited at his lodging that morning by the secretary Jacob, who brought him a letter addressed to Camille Lebel which had arrived at the French Legation two days ago. It was accompanied by a note from Lallemant inviting him to supper at the Palazzo della Vecchia that evening, and asking him to act as an escort to the Vicomtesse de Saulx, who was also expected.

Now that he had actually parted with the drafts to Vendramin, Lallemant was not entirely without uneasiness on Marc-Antoine's behalf. Anyway, the job being done and Villetard in possession of his charts, there was nothing to prevent the ambassador from discharging what he regarded as a duty to Lebel by informing him of what had taken place. If he did this in the presence of the Vicomtesse, that should avoid him the recriminations which he had cause to fear. So he asked them both to supper.

Marc-Antoine sent word back by Jacob that he would be glad to come, and then opened the letter. It was from Barras, and it proved perhaps the most startling communication that the Directors had yet addressed to their plenipotentiary Lebel.

Writing in the name of the Directory, Barras began by contrasting the strength of the Army of Italy with that of the imperialists under the Archduke. In view of the greatly superior French forces, the Austrian defeat was considered inevitable. When it occurred, if the situation were properly handled, it should be possible to end, not merely the campaign, but the war itself. Austria, if properly approached, should be more than ready to make peace. To ensure this, the plan of the Directors was that Austria should be offered the Venetian provinces both in Italy, Istria, and Dalmatia as compensation for the loss of Lombardy. In the view of the Directors there was little doubt that the Austrians would count themselves fortunate in being able to make peace on such terms.

Barras went on to state that instructions to this end were being sent to General Bonaparte; and Lebel was desired to co-operate as might be necessary, and empowered to take all measures that he accounted desirable for the promotion of the end now in view. He was particularly desired to see that an adequate pretext for hostilities was supplied by Venice. Hitherto the Serenissima had yielded supinely to every demand, however rigorous. If she persisted in this, she might rob France of all justification for employing the strong hand. Lebel on the spot would see where provocation might be given of a kind to draw Venice into an act of hostility that should open the door for a declaration of war.

Marc-Antoine sat with his elbows on his writing-table, his head in his hands and that letter before him. In these months in Venice he had tasted more than once the bitterness of failure; but never so completely as now. This was definitely the end. The doom of the ancient, great and glorious Republic of Venice was written. The Serenissima was to pay with her independence for the spinelessness of her Doge and the meanness of spirit of the preponderance of her governing patricians.

It seemed to him, too, that it must prove the end of those personal hopes in which he had come to Venice, and which so far he had been able to sustain in spite of what he found there.

That sense of failure paralyzed his wits, and in this despairing acceptance of defeat he remained all day. In the mechanical pursuit of the processes of existence, he was suffering Philibert to dress him that evening, when suddenly he perceived that this was not yet necessarily the end. Sometimes those whom an excessive caution has brought to the point of ruin will, when face to face with it, adventure all upon a gambler's throw.

The indolent, irresolute Doge had hitherto leaned ever upon the conviction that Venice would be saved by other hands than her own. This plan of the Directory should bring him at last to face the fact that, if Venice was now to be saved at all, she could be saved only by her own effort. In an eleventh-hour alliance with Austria there was no longer the assurance of victory that there would have been before Rivoli; but in anything short of that alliance there was only the assurance of extinction. Perhaps, when this was perceived, that supreme and tardy effort would be made.

It was too late for action tonight. But early tomorrow he would bear to Count Pizzamano the news of this daring French plan to end the war, and leave it to the Count to arouse the Serenissima to the needs of the hour.

Uplifted a little from his earlier despondency, he went off in the dusk to the Casa Gazzola, so that he might escort thence the lady to whom in his thoughts he always alluded derisively as his widow.

She received him with reproaches. 'It is two weeks and more since you came last to see me. Fi donc! Is that the way to treat a friend?'

He made excuses that were condemned as too vague to be sincere.

But in the gondola her mood completely melted, and abruptly she manifested a solicitude that startled him.

'I want you to be on your guard, Marc, with Lallemant, and particularly with a friend of his named Villetard whom you will probably meet tonight. I don't know how far you may have been imprudent to have become so friendly with the French Ambassador at such a time. But, in Heaven's name, tread carefully. I don't want you enmeshed in any of his schemes.'

Marc-Antoine laughed gently, and thereby earned her reproof.

'This is not a matter for laughter. I beg you to take care, Marc.' She pressed his arm affectionately as she spoke.

It was not the first time that the little baggage had issued one of these little caressing invitations to a greater intimacy, and each time he had been conscious of a certain distress. It gave him a feeling of treachery towards her, remembering that she was at liberty only by his favour, and that in certain circumstances he might find himself constrained to speak the word that should lead to her arrest.

He spoke lightly. 'You are afraid that he will enrol me in his regiment of spies. Few things are less likely.'

'I hope so, indeed. But I am sometimes afraid that he may have been seeking something that would give him a hold upon you. He is quite unscrupulous in his recruiting methods, Marc. I have meant to warn you before.'

'You place me in your debt by this concern.'

She nestled a little nearer to him, and his nostrils were assailed by essences as of roses that came to him from her pelisse. 'It is a very genuine concern, Marc.'

He parried the half-avowal by a flippancy. 'I thank Heaven that Vendramin can't overhear you, or I should expect to find my throat cut by morning.'

'Vendramin! Oh, that!' She spoke in contempt, as if something unpleasant had been mentioned. 'I am delivered of him at last, thank Heaven. That nightmare is over.'

To Marc-Antoine, knowing what he knew, this could only mean that Lallemant had taken the Venetian off her hands. But it was not a matter upon which he could question her.

He sighed. 'The loveliest dreams will turn to nightmares sometimes. It is saddening to hear that it has been so with you.'

There was a silence, at the end of which she turned to him. In the rays of the lantern he could dimly make out her delicate little face. 'You imagine that it was ever a lovely dream for me?' She asked the question on a note of bitterness. And then, abruptly, she was pleading. 'Marc! Don't despise me more than you must, my dear. If you knew all... If you knew all about me, and all that has gone to make me what I am, you would find excuses for me. Your mind is

generous, Marc. If I had known a man like you earlier in my life…'
She broke off as if her voice failed her.

He sat quite still, deeply troubled, wishing himself anywhere but
in the close propinquity to which the felza compelled him. For a
moment he asked himself was she acting, and then dismissed the
suspicion as ungenerous. She was speaking again, more steadily, but
in a voice gone suddenly dull.

'I don't want to sail under false colours with you, Marc. For you
have been so frank and open with me. Shall I tell you about myself?
Shall I tell you how I know that Lallemant may have those intentions
concerning you?'

'My dear Anne,' he said quietly, in dread, 'I was not made to be
father confessor to penitent beauty.'

'Marc, don't jest. I am very serious. Very serious and very sad. I
must take you for my confessor, dreadful though you may account
my confession. But it is less dreadful to me that you should know the
real truth than that you should suppose that I could be moved to
love for such a man as Vendramin. Listen, then, my dear, and listen
compassionately. Let me begin at the beginning.'

'Neither at the beginning, nor at the end,' he cried. 'A gondola is
not a confessional box; nor is this the hour; nor yet will I permit you
to yield to a passing emotion.' He seized on this as on an inspiration,
with which to stop the avowal that he knew was coming. 'Tomorrow
you might regret this surrender to sentiment.'

'Not tomorrow, or ever.'

'For my sake, then, let it wait. Let it wait until you have coldly
considered. If tomorrow you should regret that I have silenced you
tonight, why, tomorrow you will still be in time to speak if you must.'

'But why for your sake?'

It was not easy to answer her, but he contrived it after a second's
thought. 'Lest afterwards you should hate me for the knowledge you
will have given me of yourself.'

'Never that. I want you to know. Perhaps it is you who will hate
me when you have the knowledge. But at least I shall have been

honest with you. That is what I most desire. To be honest with you, Marc.'

He no more doubted her sincerity than he doubted what it was that she desired to tell him. Compassion for her surged in him, and a bitter awareness that there was something of the Judas in his attitude towards her. He was the betrayer who held his hand for just as long as it suited his purposes. Meanwhile, he had acted the friend in such a manner as to urge her to be honest with him to the point of self-betrayal. He realized again, as he had realized when for his own safety's sake it had been necessary for him to fling Louis XVIII to the lions, that to be an effective secret agent it was necessary to approach too closely the border-line between honour and dishonour.

'My dear,' he said quietly, 'you owe me no avowals detrimental to yourself. And whatever avowals are in your mind, let them wait until you have considered further.'

'You do not help me,' she complained.

'Perhaps I do,' he said. 'You will know tomorrow.'

She yielded to his will in the matter, and by that very yielding showed him for how much his wishes counted with her.

Lallemant received them in his workroom, and gave them a very cordial greeting. Madame Lallemant, too, would rejoice, he assured Marc-Antoine. It offended her sense of hospitality that Mr Melville should have dined with them only once in all the months he had been in Venice. It made her doubt the skill with which she strove to furnish her table.

And then Madame Lallemant arrived to speak for herself, and to carry off the Vicomtesse, leaving in her place Villetard, who had accompanied his hostess.

The three men were no sooner alone than Marc-Antoine was asking the question uppermost in his mind.

'Lallemant, you never informed me of what happened in the matter of Vendramin.'

'Oh, that.' The ambassador, suddenly uncomfortable, affected indifference. 'That is all over and finished. At the pistol-point he did what was required, and so expeditiously that Villetard is already in possession of his chart.'

Marc-Antoine frowned first upon one and then upon the other of them. 'Why was I not informed?'

The ambassador turned to Bonaparte's envoy. 'That's your affair, Villetard. You had better tell him.'

Villetard, with a sneer for Lallemant's cowardice, related coldly, briefly, and exactly what had taken place.

Marc-Antoine's manner betrayed his annoyance. 'And you surrendered to him these drafts!'

For months he had been waiting patiently to see that scoundrel drawn into a situation in which he could be dealt with for what he was. And now that he learnt of it, he learnt at the same time that the fellow had been allowed, not only to escape from the net, but to take with him the only evidence upon which he could have been incriminated.

'Why do you suppose that I am here?' he asked them, suddenly white with fury. 'You leave me marvelling at your temerity in ignoring me in such a matter.'

Villetard took it upon himself to answer. He imagined, of course, that regard for his own skin was at the bottom of the representative's annoyance. And whilst he could excuse it, he was not disposed to bow to it.

'What the devil could you have done? Was there any alternative? The fellow would act only upon certain terms. Should you have withheld them?'

Lallemant came to the rescue, more conciliatory. 'Name of a name,' he exclaimed, as if in sudden realization. 'I am reminded that you held that rogue in check by a threat of those drafts. On my soul, I am sorry.'

'That is no matter,' said Marc-Antoine, which was the truth, although neither of them believed him. 'I am not thinking of that, but of your presuming to act upon a matter of this importance without so much as informing me.'

'I must take the blame for that,' said Villetard, with insolent indifference.

'Is that so? Then let me inform you that the next time you expose yourself to similar blame, the consequences will be serious. I'll say no more about it now. But if we are to work in harmony, Citizen Villetard, you will keep it present in your mind that here I am the plenipotentiary representative of the Directory, that steps of any political significance are not to be taken behind my back, but only after consultation with me.'

There was a faint stir of colour in Villetard's lean, grey cheeks. But Marc-Antoine gave him no time to express resentment. Determined at least to make what capital he could out of this situation in which he had lost so much, he swept on. 'And that brings me to another matter; a matter of far graver significance, in which I may require your co-operation, and in which I shall certainly expect it to be given to me loyally and unstintedly.' He drew Barras' letter from his pocket. 'If you will both read this, it will inform you exactly. I shall leave it here with you, Lallemant, that you may file it with my other documents.'

Lallemant took the sheet, and Villetard, silenced by Marc-Antoine's manner and spurred by curiosity, came to stand by the ambassador so as to read at the same time.

The terms in which Barras wrote were an emphatic and timely reminder to the overbearing envoy from Bonaparte that in the plenipotentiary Lebel he was to recognize his superior. He was a little awed even by the words in which Barras empowered Lebel 'to take all measures that he accounted desirable for the promotion of the end now in view.'

Having read them, he went as far as it lay in his arrogant nature to offer an expression of regret, which, however, Marc-Antoine not ungraciously cut short.

But a sense of their offence against the plenipotentiary burdened both Lallemant and Villetard throughout dinner, whilst Marc-Antoine himself, dejected by the thought that Vendramin should

211

have escaped him so completely, contributed as little as they did to the liveliness of the repast. It was left for the spy Casotto, who was also of the party, to exert himself to entertain the ravishing little Vicomtesse de Saulx, whose presence at this dinner would be mentioned tomorrow in his bulletin to the inquisitors of state.

Scarcely was the meal ended than Marc-Antoine, on a plea – perfectly understood by the ambassador and Villetard – of letters to be written, took leave of his hostess. Upon that, the Vicomtesse begged to be allowed to take advantage of Monsieur Melville's escort for her return to the Casa Gazzola, and so they prepared to depart together, as they had come.

It would be at just about the time that they were rising from table that the valet Renzo reached the Corte del Cavallo, and he made his way swiftly to the Palazzo della Vecchia.

But he was not the only one who was speeding thither that night in quest of Messer Melville.

Shortly after Renzo's call at the Inn of the Swords, Philibert was claimed yet again to render an account of the movements of his master, and this time it was by an imposing gentleman in a red surcoat, in whom Philibert recognized at once the Captain of Justice, known to all Venetians as Messer Grande. He brought at his heels two archers, and a stiffly built, sly-faced man in civilian clothes. An alarmed landlord hovered in the background.

'Monsieur Melville is not here,' said Philibert, in mild alarm.

The captain turned. He addressed his civilian attendant. 'Come along, Cristofoli. You, at least, can set about your task.'

Cristofoli became brisk. 'Stand aside, my lad. I am coming in.'

Philibert stood aside. Not for him to argue with the law.

'Now, then, my man,' Messer Grande was questioning him. 'Do you happen to know where Messer Melville is to be found?'

Twice already that evening Philibert had answered this question truthfully. This time, however, it seemed to him that the truth might not be in the best interests of his master.

'Oh, yes. I think so,' he said. 'He told me he was going to San Daniele, to the Palazzo Pizzamano.'

'The Palazzo Pizzamano, eh?' Messer Grande swung on his heel. 'Come on,' he barked to his men, and they marched off in his wake, leaving Cristofoli to his work.

Philibert saw them off the premises. Bareheaded, he stood on the steps of the inn watching the lantern of Messer Grande's great barge until it had swung round the corner to turn eastwards. Then he hailed a passing gondola, and desired to be conveyed westward to the Casa Gazzola. He urged the gondolier to exert himself, for he desired to make the most of the advantage gained by sending Messer Grande in the wrong direction.

Chapter 27

Honour Vindicated

Renzo stood in the wide stone vestibule of the Palazzo della Vecchia inquiring breathlessly for Messer Melville. The burly French porter emerging from his lodge ended the lad's anxieties with the answer that Monsieur Melville was above-stairs, and he sent up his wife to inform the gentleman of this messenger who begged for a word with him. Discreetly Renzo withheld all mention either of a letter or of its sender.

The woman returned with the information that the gentleman was about to descend, and presently Mr Melville, accompanied by a lady who was cloaked and hooded, stood before Renzo, and recognized him by the light from the great gilded lantern overhead.

By that same light Mr Melville read Isotta's hurried, trembling scrawl.

'You are in great danger. The inquisitors of state believe they have proof that you are someone who has been calling himself Labelle, or some such name, and that you are a spy, and they intend to arrest you tonight. I shall die of terror if you fall into their dreadful clutches. Heed this warning, my dear, if you love me; and leave Venice the moment it reaches your hands. Do not lose a moment. I am praying God and the Virgin that I may still be in time. Renzo, who bears this, is to be trusted. Use him in your need. God keep you, my dear. Send me a word by Renzo if you can, to reassure me. Isotta.'

The loving terror of that letter, whilst moving him to tenderness, yet exalted him. Here there was no thought or care for what he might have done; no doubt of him; no concern of whether he might or might not be one with this 'Labelle' who was a spy. These hurried lines breathed only a love that was sharpened by fear. Very tenderly his lips smiled as he read it for the second time. Then, folding it, he placed it in an inner pocket in the breast of his coat.

He had been prepared for this, and he was not perturbed. It would be an easy matter for him, with the aid of Count Pizzamano and Sir Richard Worthington – who had long since been severely admonished by Mr Pitt for his attitude towards Mr Melville – to establish his real identity, and the mission which had brought him to Venice. The circumstances of his having assumed the identity of Lebel, and the apparent betrayals which he had been constrained to commit in the character of that representative, would then be clear and credible.

He stepped into the porter's lodge, calling for pen and ink, with which he wrote three lines: 'Your thought for me is to my soul as a draught of wine to my body. Dismiss your sweet alarms. Arrest would have no perils for me. I am quite safe, and I shall come in person to assure you of this tomorrow.'

'That is to your mistress, Renzo, and this for your pains.' He pressed a gold sequin into the lad's hand, and so dismissed him.

When Mr Melville came forth with the Vicomtesse on his arm, Renzo, vaguely discernible in the clear night, was vanishing into the narrow passage that led from the Corte del Cavallo to the fondamenta where the gondola waited.

The Vicomtesse, following his shadowy figure with her glance, saw at that moment another shadowy figure detach itself from the deeper shadows of a building at the mouth of the alley, hover a moment as Renzo approached, then melt back again into the gloom. But she saw without observing, her mind preoccupied.

'You were a long time below with Lallemant and Villetard,' she said probingly. 'And, at dinner, you were strangely silent and thoughtful. Something is troubling you. I hope you remembered my warning, Marc. But that man Villetard fills me with dread. He is horrible.'

'Have no concern,' he answered. 'But you are right to suppose that something is troubling me.' He was wondering in his mind whether, being so obviously well-disposed towards him, she might assist him when she learnt of how he was uncovered to Vendramin by Lallemant's action. 'We will talk of it at the Casa Gazzola. I may need your help.'

He felt her weight increase upon his arm. 'I would give it you so gladly,' she assured him.

They entered the narrow passage leading to the fondamenta. At the far end of it they could perceive the livid gleam of water.

'It would be a happiness...' she was beginning, and there she suddenly checked, looking sharply over her shoulder, to cry out suddenly in loud alarm: 'What's here?'

Steps were pattering quickly after them. Two figures were approaching at a run from the Corte del Cavallo, and momentarily there was from one of them the glitter as of a naked blade. Their design was not to be left in doubt.

A piercing scream for help rang out from the Vicomtesse before the two were upon them.

Marc-Antoine's first assumption was that he had to deal with the poursuivants of the inquisitors. But the sinister silence of this attack put the assumption in such doubt that he whipped out his blade. And only just in time. At the scream of the Vicomtesse, one of the twain, leaping in advance of his fellow, thrust at her savagely, whilst at the same moment the one who followed hurled at her an obscene epithet such as was not to be cast at the most abject street-walker. A white vizor covered his face. Whether from this or by intention, his voice was thick and muffled.

In the very last second of time Marc-Antoine's blade leapt forth to deflect the murderous thrust at the Vicomtesse. That parry took the assassin by surprise, as did the riposte that came in one movement with it to tear through the muscles at the base of his neck. He reeled back with a cry, accounting himself a dead man, and staggered into his companion who was close on his heels in that narrow passage.

From the other's muttered oath, and accompanying exclamation, 'Get out of my way, you fool,' it was easy to guess how he was hampered. Darting forward, and crouching so as to see as much as possible in that darkness, Marc-Antoine could just discern the group they made. The man he had pinked had collapsed with his back against the breast of his advancing fellow, who was heaving to cast him aside. Over the shoulder of the wounded man Marc-Antoine thrust instantly, heard another oath, and saw the group sag down into a black heap.

He waited for no more. He groped for the arm of the Vicomtesse; clutched it in the dark, and, dragging her with him, turned again in the direction of the fondamenta. 'Come,' he said, but, even as they started, he caught his breath to find himself confronted by yet another couple who were advancing to meet them.

This was too much. Marc-Antoine became really angry. He could not hope for the same luck a second time. Whilst he hung there, hesitating, instinctively he wrapped his cloak round his left arm. Then the Vicomtesse was tugging at the skirts of his coat. 'In here!' she cried breathlessly. 'Take shelter in here.' She had discerned a cavern of a doorway on her left, the deep porch of a warehouse, and so made him aware of it.

He thrust her in, followed, and in that shelter, stood to meet these newcomers, whilst the Vicomtesse rent the night again with her cries for help.

Swords came licking like long tongues of steel into the gloom by which Marc-Antoine was so effectively surrounded. Invisible to his assailants he could see enough of them to hold them at bay with his darting point. And then, to his disgust and dismay, he heard the same muffled voice that he had heard before, the voice of the man in the white vizor urging them on, and he realized that the blades opposing him had been increased to three. In his haste and in the dark he had done his work badly on that fellow, and had merely scratched him.

From behind the white vizor came a fierce, rapid mutter. 'We shall have the whole quarter about our ears in a moment. If you can't get the man, for God's sake, stop the screeching of that hell-cat.'

In his urgency to end things, the speaker came forward rather recklessly. Marc-Antoine in whom anger had stifled prudence succumbed to the lure of this. Taking the thrusting blade on his own, he enveloped it in a circular parry, and in delivering the counter leaned forward too boldly. One of the newcomers, a burly fellow, who, wary and experienced, had hitherto been more watchful than active, was quick to take the chance this offered, and from Marc-Antoine's uncovered flank passed his sword through his body. 'That settles it. I think,' he grunted.

The weapon dropped from the stricken man's extended hand. For a moment he emerged there into full view, swaying forward erect and rigid on that threshold. Then he crumpled and collapsed forward into the alley, whilst the scream that rang out behind him from the Vicomtesse was on a different note from any that had preceded it.

As Marc-Antoine lay prone and still, the bully who had brought him down touched him with his foot. 'Ay, that's the end of him,' he croaked.

The leader in the white vizor stooped forward. 'Is he dead?'

'As dead as Judas, after what I put through him. Come, man. We must look to ourselves.'

He glanced swiftly to right and left, as he spoke. The cries of the Vicomtesse had not been wasted. Lights were moving in the Corte del Cavallo, and with them footsteps and a sound of voices, whilst from the side of the fondamenta three dark figures were approaching, one of them brandishing an oar.

The assassins were caught between two groups. But the bully who had accounted for Marc-Antoine was Contarini, a man of ripe experience. He was prompt to take charge. 'Here, to me!' he ordered his immediate neighbour. Instead of obeying him, the man in the white vizor turned aside and plunged towards the doorway. His foot was on the threshold, and his blade was already probing the shadows when Contarini's heavy hand fell on his shoulder, and wrenched him back.

'Damn you for a fool!' he was angrily cursed.

'Save your breath for running, my master,' growled Contarini, and dragged him on. 'So. Shoulder to shoulder.' He croaked an instruction to the two behind him. 'Follow close, you others.'

They charged down the alley towards the water, thrusting aside the three who faced them. Before their threatening blades even the man with the oar, who was the only one who had a weapon of any description, fell impotently back.

Thus they reached the quay, and the man in the mask almost tumbled into the gondola that awaited them, sick and faint from a wound which he had ignored until the business was over. As the gondola sped away, he lay on the cushions in the felza, plucked off the vizor and then tore open the breast of his coat, disclosing in the lantern-light linen that was dark with blood.

The burly ruffian, standing over him, swore softly at the sight. 'Saint Mark! Did he get you, Vendramin?' He knelt to lay bare the wound, whilst, behind him, one of his companions was attending to the hurt of the other, who was also very near the end of his endurance.

'It's nothing,' said Vendramin. 'I've lost some blood. That's all. But take a look at it.'

'On my soul,' said Contarini, 'that fellow should have followed my trade. He'd have made a great success of it. It makes me feel like a murderer to have killed a man who could pink two assailants out of four.'

If Vendramin nursed a regret that he had not fulfilled his intentions by serving that false Delilah in the same way, that regret did not suffice to mar the satisfaction in his half-swooning senses. He had settled the account of that damned Englishman and removed all peril of his further interference. He had the exalted sense of honour vindicated.

Chapter 28

Questions

The three who came so ineffectually, but with such good intentions, to the rescue from the side of the fondamenta, were Renzo and his gondolier, and Philibert, the valet, who, re-directed from the Casa Gazzola, was arriving on his errand of warning.

They reached the spot a moment ahead of the party with a lantern, coming down the alley from the other side, a party composed of the porter and his son from the embassy, and the secretary Jacob. The porter carried a blunderbuss, and Jacob brandished an ugly-looking sabre.

On her knees in the mud of the alley the Vicomtesse was whimpering piteously over the body of Marc-Antoine, imploring him in accents of distraction to speak to her. She did not become conscious of the presence of Jacob until he was down on one knee on the other side of the body, with Jacques, the porter's son, holding the lantern for him.

Then she felt hands upon her shoulder and her arms, strong hands that attempted to raise her, and Coupri, the porter from the embassy, was gently remonstrating with her.

'Madame! Madame! Madame la Vicomtesse!'

'Leave me, leave me,' was her answer, impatiently sobbed out. All her attention the while strained upon the intent face of Jacob, whose hands were quietly busy with the body.

He turned Marc-Antoine gently over where he lay, disclosing a pool of blood. As she realized the nature of that dark patch gleaming in the light of the lantern, a long-drawn cry of horror escaped her.

Jacob's face was close to Marc-Antoine's; his hand felt for the heart, his eyes scanned the lips.

In a hushed voice she asked him presently: 'Is he… Is he… ?' she dared not complete the question.

'He is not dead, citoyenne,' said the grave young man.

There was no sound from her in answer. Her whimpering ceased, but it was as if she dared express no thankfulness for something that might yet hold no grounds for it.

Jacob stood up, and gave his orders quietly.

They spread Marc-Antoine's cloak, and placed him upon it. Then Coupri and his son, Philibert and Renzo took each a corner. Thus they bore the wounded man gently up the alley, across the Corte del Cavallo, and so back to the embassy, the Vicomtesse following with dragging feet, supported by Jacob.

When they had laid Marc-Antoine in the porter's lodge, Renzo and his gondolier departed, enjoined by Jacob not to talk of what had happened. The young Jew kept his wits about him and remembered that silence is the best provision for all circumstances.

Renzo, however, did not account his mistress included in that injunction. Introduced to her by her maid, he delivered Marc-Antoine's note, and, when she had read it, he told her what had happened. She stood tense and straight before him, making no outcry, but her eyes were like dark, shining pools in her marble face. Before the tragedy of that countenance, Renzo made haste to assert not only that Messer Melville lived, but that no doubt he would recover.

Swaying a little, she steadied herself against a table, and so remained until a besetting sense of faintness passed. Then she commanded herself. They were a rough-fibred race these Pizzamani, and Isotta, for all her delicate fashioning, had inherited her portion of that toughness. Dry-eyed and in a voice of startling calm she questioned Renzo, but could draw from him no clue to the identity of Marc-Antoine's assailants. It had been so dark in that accursed alley.

High though her courage might be, it was not equal to the suspense that must lie in inaction. On a resolve that overrode every possible restraining consideration, she bade her maid bring her a cloak and hood. Without recking that she might be sought and missed by her mother, who had not yet retired, she slipped from the house, with Renzo for escort. They went by the garden, so that the porter should not see her leave. The garden-gate, which they left unbolted, opened upon a diminutive square. Beyond this, by a bridge over a little watercourse, they came to an open space bordering the wide Canal of Saint George. Thence in a hired gondola they made their way to the Madonna dell' Orto.

To Lallemant, whom this visit profoundly surprised, she was admitted without a moment's hesitation. In the salon that was his workroom, he advanced to meet her, his air deferential.

He was not alone. By the writing-table, in the background, two men remained standing with whom he had been in talk when she was admitted.

One of these was Villetard, whose tired eyes quickened a little to observe the grace and beauty of this woman; the other was a stocky, middle-aged man in formally cut clothes of black, with a face that was at once strong and kindly.

'Monsieur Melville?' she faltered to Lallemant. Then she steadied herself, and became coherent. 'I have just heard what has happened to him. He is a friend of ours. A great friend...'

'I am aware of it, mademoiselle.' Kindly, he sought to spare her explanations. 'I have this very moment learnt how great is your friendship for him.' He stepped to the table and took thence a scrap of paper. 'Doctor Delacoste here has just brought me this. It came from you, I think.'

He held out to her the note she had that evening written to Marc-Antoine. Realizing the nature of the red-brown stain that blurred it, she momentarily closed her eyes.

'Unfortunately,' said Lallemant, with a sigh, 'he did not sufficiently heed the warning.'

'How... How is it with him?' she asked, and waited in terror for the reply.

The ambassador turned. 'Will you tell her, doctor?'

The stocky man came slowly forward, speaking as he approached her.

'His condition is grave, but gives no cause to despair. No cause to despair at all. Almost he makes me believe in miracles. The sword must have been guided through him by his guardian angel. His worst danger is from his terrible loss of blood. But I trust he has not lost more than he can renew.'

Her eyes searched that grave, kindly face, and some of the lifelessness passed from her countenance.

Then Lallemant was speaking. 'We shall take good care of him, and we shall keep him here where he will be safe from any further attempts upon him.'

'Who did this? Is it known?' she asked.

Villetard's harsh voice cut in quickly to answer her. 'Your letter of warning tells us that, I think.' He sauntered forward to join the group.

She took his meaning at once. 'The inquisitors? Oh, no.' But Villetard was insistent. 'Isn't it just how they would deal with one whom it might be inconvenient to arrest?'

'I don't think so, ever. And, anyway, I know positively that only Monsieur Melville's arrest was intended. I know it from Messer Corner, who is one of the inquisitors. Besides, monsieur, the inquisitors are not assassins.'

'I shall cling to my opinion,' said Villetard.

'Oh, but I know that you are wrong. The Inquisitor Corner came to see my father this evening, not merely to tell him that this arrest would be made, but to invite him to be present at Mr Melville's examination tomorrow, so that he might urge what he knows in Monsieur Melville's favour.'

'You see,' said Lallemant to Villetard. 'It isn't even as if he had resisted arrest; for we know that there was no attempt to arrest him. I come back to my first conclusion: that this is the work of that barnabotto scoundrel Vendramm. The dog has lost no time.'

'Whom did you name?'

She asked the question in so sharp and startled a tone, that Lallemant stared a moment before answering: 'Vendramin. Leonardo Vendramin. You know him, perhaps?'

Incredulity swept across her white face. 'Oh, no. That is as impossible as the other.'

'Ah!' Villetard was suddenly eager. 'And so say I. Vendramin would never have dared.'

'He dared it once before.'

'Yes, but the altered circumstances…'

'It is just the altered circumstances would make him dare again,' said the shrewd Lallemant.

'What are you saying?' she asked. And now she learnt from Lallemant, not only of that earlier attempt at assassination, but also of the duel in which Vendramin had been disabled.

Intentionally or otherwise, Lallemant was vague upon the grounds of the quarrel, but quite clear and definite that it was of Vendramin's provoking.

'Considering that this barnabotto owed Monsieur Melville a matter of a thousand ducats which he had borrowed, I can't dismiss the suspicion that he sought to liquidate the debt by a sword-thrust. You'll gather, mademoiselle, that I have no great opinion of Monsieur Vendramin.'

Isotta stood before them, stricken of countenance, mechanically wringing her gloves between her hands; that gesture of hers when troubled which once had played such havoc with her fan.

At last: 'Could I… Could I see him?' she asked. 'Is it possible?'

Lallemant looked at Delacoste, and Delacoste made a lip of ponderous doubt. 'I should prefer that you did not…' he was beginning, when the expression of her countenance moved him to compassion. 'I do not want him disturbed, mademoiselle. But if you will promise to stay no more than a moment, and not to talk...'

'Oh, I promise.' She was fervent in her eagerness.

Delacoste opened the door for her, and they went out.

'That woman,' said Villetard, with the appreciation of a connoisseur, 'explains Lebel's friendship with the Pizzamani much more completely than the duties of his office. Her concern for him makes one suspect that like his master, Barras, he understands the art of combining business with pleasure.'

Lallemant ignored the assumption. 'What is to be done about Vendramin?' he asked.

But Villetard was cynical in all things. 'It will be more convenient to assume your suspicions groundless, at least until we have some evidence that they are not.'

'We may be called to a very stern account for this if Lebel should die.'

'Don't I perceive it?' Villetard was in a state of exasperation. 'But what the devil was I to do when Bonaparte had to be served? We should both be wiser to cling to the belief that this is the work of the inquisitors. It's the explanation that clears us of responsibility. God knows why you must have talked so freely to the Pizzamano. I did my best to check you.'

Above-stairs Delacoste was introducing his companion to a lofty chamber, dimly lighted by a single shaded candle placed on a table below the foot of the canopied bed.

The doctor closed the door and soundlessly drew her forward to the bedside.

At the sight of the face upon the pillow she could scarcely repress an outcry, for it seemed to lie in the livid repose of death. The eyes were closed and deep shadows filled the hollows of cheeks and temples. The black hair was tumbled about a brow that gleamed with moisture. In terror she looked from that face to the doctor's. Delacoste answered her with a little smile of reassurance and a nod.

From beyond the bed there was a rustle, and suddenly Isotta became conscious of another person in the room. A woman had risen, and was standing there, staring across at them.

At the sound she made in rising, the wounded man's eyelids fluttered, and then Isotta found him staring up at her. Into the dull vacancy of those eyes came consciousness like the glow of an ember that is fanned. But for the swift, anticipatory action of Delacoste he would have raised himself.

'Isotta!' Marc-Antoine uttered her name in wonder. 'Isotta!' His voice sank as he spoke. 'I have your letter… your warning… But all is well. All is very well.' His speech became blurred. 'I'll take care. I'll…' His lips continued to move, but sound no longer came from them. As she bent nearer, his eyes slowly closed as if under the weight of an unconquerable lassitude.

The doctor put an arm about her, and drew her gently away.

Outside the room he was stilling her alarm, reassuring her again.

'He is very weak. That is natural. The great loss of blood. But he has much natural vigour. With God's help we shall make him well. Meanwhile, he is safe here and in devoted hands.'

Isotta saw again that slight, sweet-faced, golden-headed woman rising at the bedside.

'Who is that lady?' she asked.

'Madame la Vicomtesse de Saulx.'

'The Vicomtesse de Saulx, did you say?' and the doctor wondered why the question should hold such a depth of incredulity.

'The Vicomtesse de Saulx,' he repeated, and added: 'She will remain with him tonight, to watch him and tend him.'

Only then did Isotta recall that part of the overheard conversation between her father and Corner in which that name had been mentioned. She had never supposed other than that the inquisitor repeated some false rumour. But now it seemed that such a woman did, indeed, exist. It was bewildering. As she tried to recall the exact words that had passed, she heard again her father's confident assertion that the Vicomtesse de Saulx must be an impostor. And yet she found this woman installed here at the wounded man's bedside.

It was disquieting, inexplicable. It still clouded her mind when Lallemant had escorted her to the vestibule where her servant waited. He was assuring her, not only that her friend Melville would be well cared for, but also that he would be safe.

'Here in the embassy, at least, the warrant of the inquisitors does not run. So that even though they may know of his presence, they are powerless to trouble him.'

Yet, when at last she spoke, it was not of this.

'The lady with him is the Vicomtesse de Saulx,' she said.

'Yes. Her interest in him is perhaps natural. She was with him when the attack was made on him. They had both dined here.'

She hesitated over the form of her next question, and uttered at last the best that she could find.

'The Vicomte de Saulx? Is he in Venice?'

Lallemant smiled gently. 'Oh, no. Let us hope that he is in heaven, mademoiselle. The Vicomte de Saulx was guillotined in ninety-three. The Vicomtesse is a widow.'

'I see,' said Isotta slowly, and it seemed to Lallemant as if a cloud had lifted from her.

Chapter 29

Storm-Clouds

For some six days Marc-Antoine's life hung on a slender, but gradually strengthening thread. After another three, there came a morning when Delacoste, seated beside his patient, announced to him that for the present he had fooled the devil.

'But I'll confess to you now that he all but had you. My skill would never have defeated him without that angel who remained at your bedside to beat him back. She has not spared herself. For a whole week she hardly slept. A little more, my friend, and she would have saved your life at the expense of her own.' Pensively the doctor sighed. 'We make too light of women, my friend. There is no self-sacrifice equal to that of which a good woman is capable; just as there are no limits to the sacrifices demanded by a bad one. When we have been the object of such devotion as you have known, that is something that we should go on our knees to acknowledge.'

He got up and called Philibert, who was hovering near the window. He instructed him about a cordial which he had brought, and so departed.

In the last two or three days, ever since his mind had recovered a full clarity, Marc-Antoine had been tormented by thoughts of the vital information he had been about to communicate to Count Pizzamano when he was stricken. It troubled him that the situation must have been rendered much more acute by this delay; but at last the absence of the Vicomtesse from his bedside gave him the chance to repair the matter.

'Prop me up, Philibert,' he commanded.

Philibert was scandalized.

'You'll exhaust me more by argument than compliance,' Marc-Antoine insisted. 'Do as I bid you. It is important.'

'Your recovery is much more important, monsieur.'

'You are wrong. It is not. Don't waste time.'

'But, monsieur, if the doctor should find that I have done this…'

'He won't. I promise you. If you keep faith with me, I'll keep faith with you. Lock the door, and get me pen, ink, and paper.'

His senses swam at first, and he was compelled to waste some moments in waiting for them to steady. Then, as quickly as they would permit him, he scrawled the following lines:

'Bonaparte is in such strength that the defeat of the Archduke seems inevitable. If it happens, it is expected that Austria will be disposed to make peace. To ensure this the settled French plan is to seize the Venetian States and trade them to Austria in exchange for Lombardy. You are warned. Venice must decide whether by joining hands with the Empire, at this eleventh hour, she will make a supreme effort to preserve an independence which otherwise will be lost to her.'

He read the note over, folded it, and handed it to Philibert. 'Hide this carefully somewhere about you. Now take away these things, and let me down again. Then unlock the door.'

At full length once more, Marc-Antoine lay silent for some moments, exhausted by his effort. But the reproachful eyes of the valet drew presently a smile from him.

'Never look so black at me, Philibert. It had to be done. Now listen. Conceal that letter carefully. It is dangerous. When you go out today, go to the Casa Pizzamano at San Daniele. Ask for the Count. See him in person, and deliver that note to him. To him, and to no one else. Should he be absent, wait for him. Is that clear?'

'Quite clear, monsieur.'

'You will inform him fully of my condition, and you may freely answer any questions he may ask you.'

The diligent Philibert delivered his letter that same afternoon, and it was read at once, not only by the Count, but also by Domenico, who was with him at the time.

Captain Pizzamano had come over from the fort at the first opportunity in response to a summons sent him two days ago by his sister. At the time, Isotta, who through Renzo kept herself daily informed of the progress made by Marc-Antoine, had felt the burden to be more than she could bear alone. Today, when at last Domenico had arrived, and she could take counsel with him, the anxiety had already been lessened by the better news that Renzo had brought her. Marc-Antoine was definitely out of all danger.

But her indignation remained and it informed the tale that she told her brother. Appalled, Domenico hesitated to believe, for all his dislike of Vendramin, that the man would stoop to murder. Perhaps that very dislike made him honourably cautious in his assumptions.

Isotta enlightened him. 'They quarrelled before, in October last; and I have learnt that a duel was fought in which Leonardo was wounded. You remember that he was ill then, and kept the house for a couple of weeks. That was the occasion.'

'I know of the duel,' said Domenico. 'But it is a far cry from a duel to an assassination. Though I can see how the one could create a suspicion of the other. But something more is necessary before we can be persuaded.'

'I think I have something more. This attempt on Marc took place on the night of Monday of last week. Since then we have not seen Leonardo, and it is not his way to let a whole week pass without coming to San Daniele, especially such a week as this in which the news has daily made my father fret and wonder at his absence.'

'Ah!' Domenico was now alert. 'But why...'

She cut through his interpolation to continue what she had to say. 'Of the four who attacked Marc, he wounded two, and one of these was the leader, I am told. If it should be discovered that Leonardo has a wound – a wound in the left shoulder – will not that complete the proof?'

'I think it would.'

'That is why I have sent for you, Domenico. Will you seek out Leonardo, and discover this?'

'I will do more. There are to me things I require to know about this duel last October. Amongst others, the real grounds...' He broke off, looking at her keenly. 'Have you no suspicion of what they might have been?'

'Sometimes I have thought...' She broke off with a little gesture of helplessness. 'No, no, I have nothing definite. Nothing, Domenico.'

'But something indefinite,' he said gently, with understanding. 'Well, well.' He rose. 'I will see what I can find out about it all.'

There were other things in his mind, but he thought he could postpone their utterance until the present question was resolved. So he passed out of her boudoir where the interview had taken place and went below for a word with his father before departing.

He found the Count in the library with Philibert. The valet's narrative added nothing to what the captain had learnt from his sister; whilst the letter, which he read after Philibert's departure, came to deepen the grave trouble already agitating every loyal Venetian mind. For whilst Marc-Antoine had lain helpless at the French Embassy portentous happenings had shaken Venice and aroused at last even the most nonchalant to perception of the storm-clouds in the political heavens.

The impotent negligence of the Serenissima to give due protection to her mainland provinces had borne, at last, alarming fruits in Bergamo. The unrepressed Jacobins, under French encouragement, had laid hands upon the neglected helm of government. The city had revolted from Venice, had declared for Jacobinism, had raised a Tree of Liberty, and had established an independent municipal government of her own.

News of this gesture of contemptuous repudiation had reached Venice six days ago, and had created consternation in every mind from that of the Doge to that of the meanest beggar at a traghetto.

Before Domenico could even begin to discuss with his profoundly troubled father this latest evidence of French perfidy, in Marc-Antoine's letter, Messer Catarin Corner was announced.

He came with calamity written upon his finely featured face and in every line of his slight, elegant figure. He brought the evil tidings that another city had gone the way of Bergamo.

The Podestá of Brescia, in flight to save his life and disguised as a peasant, had just reached Venice and sought the Doge with the miserable tale that Brescia, like Bergamo, had now declared her independence, and had set up a Tree of Liberty, at the foot of which in mockery of Venice crouched a Lion of Saint Mark in chains.

'We have begun to pay the terrible price of Manin's weakness,' Corner concluded. 'The Republic is disintegrating.'

The Count sat appalled, staring into space, whilst the inquisitor strained his weak voice in vehement exposition. Order must be taken without delay, before this Jacobin contagion spread to other subject cities. If the Senate itself should not suffice to deal with such a matter, the Grand Council must be convened, and the responsibility shouldered by the entire patriciate.

Then at last the Count roused himself. He spoke in angry pain. 'After the errors we have committed, the chances we have missed, the consistent meanness and selfishness of the policy pursued, can we hope now for heroism? Unless we can, nothing remains but to resign ourselves to the disruption of this Republic which has so proudly endured for a thousand years. Look at this.'

He handed to Corner the letter he had received from Marc-Antoine.

When the inquisitor had read it, his voice trembled as he asked whence it came.

'From a sure source. From Melville.' He smiled sadly. 'You were very quick to assume that he had fled when he heard that he was to be arrested, and for a moment I was so weak as to suppose that you might be right. But now we have the truth. There was an attempt to assassinate him on the very night that you sent to arrest him; it was an attempt that all but succeeded. Since then he has hung between life and death. His first action when he can summon sufficient strength for the effort is to send me this precious piece of information; something done at the greatest peril to himself. I trust this will persuade you in whose interest he works. But let that pass for the moment. The information must be communicated to the Doge. This supreme effort, which the case demands, must be made or we are irrevocably lost, doomed to become an Austrian province, living under the rule apportioned to a conquered people.'

Corner permitted himself an unusual bitterness of expression. 'Will that woman Manin ever make it? Or will he bow to this in the same spirit in which he has allowed our provinces to be trampled under the feet of a ruffianly foreign soldiery?'

Pizzamano rose. 'The Grand Council must compel him; it must sweep the Senate into definite and immediate action. There must be no more mere promises of preparation for contingencies; promises which in the past have led to nothing. Vendramin must marshal his barnabotti for this final battle against the forces of inertia.' Emotion mastering him, he became almost theatrical in his intensity and in the sweep of his gesture. 'If perish we must, at least let us perish like men, the descendants of those who made this Venice glorious, and not like the feeble, yielding women Manin has all but made of us.'

Chapter 30

Constraint

Blood recklessly lost by Vendramin in his murderous adventure in the Corte del Cavallo had so weakened him that for ten days thereafter he, too, was compelled to keep the house. If prudent considerations of health dictated that he should keep it longer, no less considerations of appearances dictated, in the light of the political events, that he should go forth.

So on that same day which had seen Marc-Antoine penning his warning to Count Pizzamano, Vendramin ventured abroad, in defiance of his weakness and his imperfectly healed wound.

The weather was mild and genial, and the sunshine quickened the colours of the houses mirrored in the deep blue of the waters. By these he was borne, reclining on the cushions in the felza from which the leather curtains were drawn back. He was arrayed with care in the lilac and silver suit which he knew became him so well, and his shining golden hair had been carefully dressed and clubbed. Regard for his wound, which was at the junction of neck and shoulder, dictated a sling for his left arm. But regard for the necessity to conceal that he had been wounded, dictated that he carry the limb before him with the thumb hooked into an opening of his waistcoat. He hoped that this would not seem unnatural or attract attention.

His gondola swung westwards down the Grand Canal past the sunlit dome of the Salute and on until it turned into the canal of San

Daniele. In these narrower waters it passed another gondola, hard driven by two gondoliers, in which Messer Corner was departing from the Casa Pizzamano.

Vendramin came so opportunely now as only just to prevent the Count from sending for him.

Pizzamano was expressing this intention when, from below, the lapping of waters under a prow and the melancholy hailing cry of an approaching gondolier attracted Domenico's attention. The long windows to the balcony by which he was standing were open. He stepped out to look over the parapet.

'You are saved the trouble,' he announced. 'Vendramin is here.'

The Count's face brightened a little. In mentioning the timeliness of this arrival, he referred again to the oddness of the fact that Vendramin should not have been seen for over a week.

'Not, in fact, since the attempt on Marc's life,' said Domenico.

So dry was his tone that his father looked at him sharply. 'You are not suggesting a connection?'

'It might exist. Anyway, it would be wise, perhaps, not to let Vendramin suspect the source of your information about this French plan.'

'What are you hinting?'

'Marc has been put to bed at the French Legation. It might be very dangerous for him if this news were to leak out while he is there. It would be best to say no more than that you have the best of reasons for believing this to be the French intention. If you mention that Messer Corner has just been here, you will leave Leonardo to suppose that Messer Corner was the bearer of the news.'

The Count nodded gravely. 'Very well.'

Messer Vendramin came in with a jauntiness that cost him a considerable effort. He was conscious that the eyes of Domenico, in whom he had always sensed an enemy, were searching him from head to foot, observing his pallor, and the dark stains under his eyes, and resting long upon the arm which he strove to carry naturally before him.

He answered the Count's inquiry into his absence by asserting that he had been ill. Pleading that he was still weak, he begged leave to sit, and found himself a chair. The Count and his son remained standing; the captain by the window, with his back to the light, facing their visitor; the Count pacing the small room, whilst he expounded the situation disclosed by Marc-Antoine's letter.

Next he dwelt upon the defection of Bergamo, of which Vendramin was already informed, and upon that of Brescia, of which he had just received news.

'You realize,' said Pizzamano, 'what is to be done, and done at once, if the Republic is to survive. Can you depend, now as before, upon your barnabotti?'

'To the last man. They will stand solidly behind me.'

Vendramin spoke without hesitation. Nor had he any misgivings on the score of his position now that in some degree he had accepted the French service imposed upon him. That had been a limited and specific service. There had been no suggestion of curtailing his activities or constraining his loyalty in other directions.

The Count was standing squarely before him.

'And I can count upon you absolutely, can I not?'

Pizzamano, pleading with voice and eyes, betraying how anxiously he hung upon the answer, revealed to Vendramin the increased advantage which this situation gave him. Never had he been so necessary to Pizzamano. This time not even Domenico's hostility should prevail against him.

'Absolutely,' he said.

In visible relief the Count resumed his pacing. 'In that case, perhaps we need not even lose time in summoning the Grand Council. Between us we may be able to force Manin immediately into the action which the vote of the Grand Council must demand.'

'I am ready to go to him whenever you bid me,' said Vendramin. 'You may depend upon me not to spare myself now, who have never spared myself.'

'I am sure of it, and I bless you for it,' said Pizzamano.

'You bless me for it?' Vendramin spoke slowly, looking up at the Count. 'Would you bless me, I wonder, in something more than words? Would you bless me, my lord, with the proof of confidence I so desire, in return for all the proofs of zeal that I have given?'

The Count checked in his pacing, and looked at him, his brows knit. Vendramin's meaning was plain enough to both father and son. From Domenico he was expecting immediate opposition. But Domenico said nothing.

After a pause Vendramin continued. 'The moment is most apt. If it should come to another struggle in the Council, as your son-in-law, Lord Count, I should command an increase of weight, and so I should be able to sweep many a waverer into our following.'

Still they said nothing, so he brought his plea to a conclusion. 'I confess that I am urging this as much from personal motives as from patriotic ones.'

If the Count was under no delusion that here was an opportunist taking full advantage of the situation, at the same time, with the detached tolerance that he could bring to the judgment of all things outside of his fanatical patriotism, he could not blame Vendramin.

He spoke quietly. 'You have in mind an early marriage.'

Vendramin answered him as quietly.

'You will admit, my lord, that not to be impatient would be a poor compliment to Isotta, and that already I have been tried in curbing it.'

The Count's chin was buried in the lace at his throat.

'It is very abrupt,' he complained.

'So is the situation that advocates it.'

'And, of course, we are in Lent.'

'Naturally I must wait for Easter. That is a month hence. A most propitious season.'

Pizzamano turned to his son. The captain's silence seemed unnatural.

'What do you say, Domenico?'

'That Isotta is the person to whom you should address that question.'

'Oh, yes. Decision, of course, must rest with her. But provided that she is willing to be married so soon, at Easter be it, then.'

As he spoke, the door opened, and Isotta paused on the threshold.

'Are you private, or may I come in?' she asked.

'Come in, child, come in,' her father answered. 'There is a matter you can settle.'

Vendramin sprang up, and turned to greet her.

She came forward, wrapped in calm, and smoothly, with the grace that was in all her movements.

'Ah, Leonardo!' she said. 'I was told that you were here. We have missed you these days.'

He bowed over her hand. 'Then I am compensated for having been none so well.'

'We have been wondering what had become of you; of you and also of Marc. You both disappeared at the same time.'

He looked at her sharply. But her face was entirely candid; she even smiled a little. From this he judged it impossible that she should have heard that Melville was dead.

And then Domenico drew his attention. 'I commented upon the oddness of that coincidence a few moments before Leonardo arrived,' he said. But the captain's face was as bland as his sister's.

Vendramin sighed. 'I am afraid we must resign ourselves to continue to miss him.' He spoke gravely. 'Calling at the Inn of Swords on my way here, I am told that he had disappeared, and I am asking myself whether he has been arrested, or whether he has fled from Venice to avoid it.'

'I can tell you that he has not been arrested,' said the Count.

What Domenico added was less expected. 'And I can tell you that he has not fled.'

Isotta followed her brother with something less expected still. 'And I can tell you that he is not even dead, as you are really supposing.'

The Count looked in surprise from one to the other of his children. He perceived something astir under the surface of things, something which he did not understand. So, at last, did Vendramin. The assertion that Melville lived was as dismaying a shock to him as the terms in which the assertion was made. But until he discovered what else lay behind it he would not flinch. Therefore, he asked the question for which that assertion called.

'But why should I suppose that?'

'Is it not what you supposed when you and your bullies left him in the Corte del Cavallo on the night of Tuesday of last week?'

He was startled as his round eyes showed. But no more than would be natural to anyone under such an accusation. No more, in fact, than the Count appeared to be at hearing it made.

'My dear Isotta! What tale has been carried to you? I am under no necessity to endanger myself by such expedients. I am well able to take care of my honour, as is, I think, well known.'

He alluded to the reputation as a swordsman which he enjoyed. But Isotta was not impressed. She raised her eyebrows.

"Yet you do not seem to have been able to take such care of it – or, at least, of your person – on a former occasion when you met Mr Melville.'

Domenico chose this moment to display a sudden unusual solicitude on behalf of their guest. 'I protest,' he cried, 'that you are keeping this poor Leonardo standing, regardless of his weakness.' He sprang forward as he spoke, and in his haste to set a chair for Vendramin, he hurtled clumsily against him. Off his guard, Vendramin cried out sharply, and his right hand went instinctively to the seat of pain in his left shoulder.

Domenico's face was within a foot of his own, and Domenico was looking straight into his eyes, and smiling apologetically.

'Ah! Your wound, of course. Forgive me. I should have used more care.'

'Oh, I have a wound? On my soul, you give me news upon news of myself, today.' But the effort cost him a good deal. He sank into the chair, and brought forth a handkerchief to mop a brow which was coldly moist.

The Count spoke at last out of his bewilderment. 'What is all this, Domenico? Will you tell me plainly?'

'Let me do that, sir,' cried Vendramin. 'Because some months ago I fought a duel with Messer Melville...'

'Oh! You admit that, at least,' Domenico interrupted. 'But, of course, denial would hardly be worth while.'

'Why should I deny it? We had a difference which admitted of adjustment in no other way.'

'And the subject of it?' the Count asked him.

Vendramin hesitated before answering. 'The subject, Lord Count, was entirely personal.'

But Count Pizzamano's stiff, old-fashioned notions of honour made him insistent.

'It cannot have been so personal that I must be excluded from knowledge of it. The honour of one of the parties must have been impugned. Considering the relationship with me to which you aspire, I have, I think, the right to learn the circumstances.'

Vendramin appeared troubled. 'I admit the right. But it would be impossible for me to disclose the grounds of my quarrel with Melville without causing distress where I should least wish to cause it. If you will allow Isotta, sir, to be your deputy, I will frankly tell her all. Since it is on her behalf that you desire this knowledge, it should serve if I impart it directly to her.'

Count Pizzamano considered. He thought he understood. On the subject of the feeling that existed between his daughter and Marc-Antoine, Isotta had once been very frank with him. For the repression which he was persuaded that both had practised, he had only respect and praise. But he realized that in a man in Vendramin's position a detection of the sentiment might lead to an explosion of jealousy, and that this might well have been at the root of the quarrel. All things considered, it might be best to let Vendramin have his way. An explanation now between him and Isotta might clear the air and facilitate what was to follow.

He bowed his head. 'Be it so. Come, Domenico, let us leave Leonardo to explain himself to Isotta. If she is satisfied, there is no reason why I should not be.'

Domenico departed without protest with his father. But once outside the room he had a word to say to him.

'There is something of greater consequence than the duel that Leonardo should be asked to explain. You observed, sir, that he is suffering from a hurt in the left shoulder. You observed his movement, you heard his exclamation when I jostled him, intentionally?'

'I observed,' said the Count, and surprised his son by the readiness and the gloom of that answer.

'You are forgetting, then, the particulars we heard from the valet. There were four assailants. Two of them were wounded; one of these in the shoulder, and this was the leader of the party. It's a coincidence. Do you draw no inference from it?'

Tall and spare, but less straight than his wont, the Count stood before his son. And Domenico became suddenly aware that his father seemed lately to have aged. The dark eyes flanking that high-bridged nose had none of their old pride of glance. He sighed.

'Domenico, I desire to draw no inference. He has chosen to state the matter of his quarrel with Melville to Isotta. I presume that he will state it all. She will see to that. Let it be hers to judge, since it will be hers to bear the consequences.'

The captain understood that for the first time in his life his father was shirking an issue. It was too much for him. He spoke indignantly.

'And if Isotta, as I warn you, sir, that well she may, should not be satisfied by his explanation? What then?'

The Count laid his hand on his son's shoulder. 'Have I not said, Domenico, that it is for her to judge? I mean it with all that this implies. I merely pray, considering how much is involved – which must be as plain to you as it is to me – that she may judge mercifully. Even more fervently I pray that she may have no cause to judge harshly.'

Domenico bowed his head. 'I beg you to pardon my presumption, sir,' he said.

But within the library Isotta was being afforded little opportunity to pass judgment. The explanations which Vendramin offered her were an accusation rather than a defence.

'Will you sit, Isotta, to justify my remaining seated?' he had begged her. 'I am still weak.'

'From your wound,' she said, as composedly she sat down to face him.

'Oh, from my wound, yes.' He was faintly contemptuous in the admission. 'But it is of my duel with Messer Melville that I am to speak. When I shall have told you of that, I hardly think that you will desire to pursue the matter of our quarrel further. It is quite true that I sought to kill him, loyally, in single combat. And never was a man better justified. For I had discovered that this scoundrel had dishonoured me. Do I need to tell you how?'

'Do you expect me to guess it?'

He looked at her intently, in silence, incensed by her calm. He was very near to hating her for this air of frosty, virginal purity which hung about her like the aureole about the Lion of Saint Mark, and which he knew to be the travesty of a wanton. He marvelled that she should dare to confront him in this half-scornful self-possession, carrying what she carried in her heart. He must see what he could do to shake it.

'I had discovered,' he said, 'that your Messer Melville was the seducer of the lady whom I hoped to make my wife.'

She sat stiff and straight, a slow flush mounting to her brow.

'You cannot be speaking of me,' she said.

He rose, forgetting wound and weakness in the intensity of his emotion. 'Must I advance the proof before you will cease to nauseate me with your hypocrisy? Must I tell you that I know you for the masked lady who fled so precipitately before me from Mr Melville's lodging one morning months ago? Must I tell you how I know it? Shall I tell you what evidence I hold with which to convince others. Shall I...'

'Stop!' she cried, and she too was on her feet confronting him. 'How dare you soil me with your vile assumptions? It is quite true that I was that lady. Can you suppose that I would ever deny anything that I had ever done? But between what I went to do there, and what you so infamously conclude, because your mind is foul, there is the difference that lies between snow and mud.' No longer could he complain that she was a cold, insensible piece, incapable of emotion. Here was emotion and to spare, a withering, scorching emotion of anger before which he found himself flinching.

'Oh, my mind is foul? Test it against any other mind in Venice. Test it, if you dare, against your own father's mind. Ask him what inference he would draw if he found a lady of quality so closeted in a man's lodging; if he had seen her actually in that man's arms. If you want to break a father's heart with shame, ask him that.'

This was to her anger as water is to fire. But perception of the truth of what he asserted did no more than restore her to her normal calm.

Almost composedly she sat down again, and repressing emotion spoke in a quiet, level voice. If there was pleading in what she said, it was in her actual words, not in their tone.

'Listen, Leonardo.' Quietly she told him the circumstances and purpose of that visit of hers to Marc-Antoine. She made of it a long narrative, and weakness drove him to sit again whilst the tale was telling. If it convinced him, he showed no sign of it. On the contrary, his answering comment touched upon its main improbability.

'And for this renunciation, as you call it, no other occasion would serve? Although this man was a constant visitor here and your opportunities of speaking to him were frequent, you preferred a course from which any Venetian lady who prized her repute must have shrunk in horror?'

She knew that it would be idle to explain this by the urgency of her desire to put herself right in Marc-Antoine's eyes, an urgency that could brook no least delay. This was something that he would never understand. The statement would merely earn her an aggravation of his insulting incredulity.

'That,' she answered simply, but very firmly, 'was what I happened to prefer. I may not have perceived the indiscretion. But there was certainly nothing beyond indiscretion in that visit.'

'Will anyone believe that, Isotta?'

'Don't you?' she challenged him.

He considered before answering. When at last he spoke, his manner had subtly changed. 'I believe you now that you have explained. But I am asking myself whether I believe you merely because for my peace of mind's sake I must. Without this explanation I could believe only what all the world would believe. Because I loved you it was necessary that I should kill the only man who had knowledge of what I believed. By killing him I felt that I should kill at least some of the shame attaching to this. That is my explanation to you of a deed that has earned me your displeasure.'

He waited a moment for her to speak. Then, seeing her silent and thoughtful, he rose again and went to stand beside her and over her. 'Now that we have both confessed, shall we absolve each other?'

'You can be generous, then?' she said, and he did not know whether she spoke in sarcasm.

'Cruel question! Much more than that to you, Isotta.' He lowered his rich voice to a wooing note, a note which he believed that no woman could hear without a thrill. For it was a boast to which possibly his experiences may have entitled him that woman was an instrument upon which he was a virtuoso. 'Let us make peace, my dear. I am on my knees to implore it in the great need which my worship of you arouses in me. I have been speaking of our marriage to your father. He consents that it shall take place when Lent is out, provided that this shall be your wish.'

'My wish?' There was a crooked little smile of pain on her lips. 'It can never be my wish.'

He met the rebuff with plaintiveness. 'You break my heart, Isotta, with your coldness.'

'After all that I have just told you – that you have compelled me to tell you – could you expect me to be other?'

'That I understand. To that I am resigned. Resigned in the confidence that by tenderness I shall know how to conquer it. When all is said, Isotta, patricians of Venice should mate with patricians of Venice. You will not deny that I have been very patient, a servant at your orders, which is what you will always find me. What shall I say to your father?'

She sat quite still, looking silently before her, conscious only of horror. The threatened imminence of this step made her realize poignantly the impossibility of taking it.

Yet, if she refused, she would rightly be accounted a cheat, defrauding Vendramin of the wages at which he had been hired by her father, wages which once, perceiving no other use for herself, she had consented to be.

Guessing perhaps something of the conflict in her spirit, he sought slyly to assist her decision.

'If you consent, then your father will conclude that my explanation to you must have been satisfactory, and no more need be said about the matter. If you don't, I shall be under the odious necessity of explaining to him, in justice to myself; and my explanation must be as full as it has been to you.'

'Oh, that is brave! That is brave!' she cried. 'It is worthy of a man who hires bullies to assassinate a rival. What solid foundations of respect you are laying upon which to build this marriage of ours.'

'So that we build it, I do not care upon what we build. That is how I love you, Isotta. With the recklessness that belongs to real love.'

She pondered the evils that confronted her and of which she must make choice, and choice grew more impossible the more she pondered them.

She could no more brave the anger of her father in his inevitable assumptions, and in the shame which he would account that she had brought upon their house, than she could brave the alternative of taking to husband this man who daily grew more odious, who daily revealed himself more vile.

Decision being impossible, it but remained to obtain postponement.

'When Lent is out, you said?' she half-questioned.

'You consent, then, Isotta?'

'Yes,' she answered, and reddened at her own disingenuousness. 'When Lent is out. You may tell my father that I will appoint the date at Easter.'

But at this he frowned. Then uttered the short laugh of the man who sees the trap, and refuses to be taken in it. 'That will not serve. You will appoint the date now.'

Her trouble of spirit was betrayed only by the old gesture of wringing the slim white hands that lay in her lap. Then she perceived her course. Knowing where his interest lay, she played boldly. She rose to answer him, and never was she more stately.

'Am I to be hectored so even before marriage?' She thrust out her chin. 'I will appoint the date at Easter, or I will never appoint it; at your choice.'

His prominent eyes scanned her face and found it resolute. There was no faltering in the glance that met his own. He inclined his head after a moment, accepting defeat upon the minor point. 'So be it. I will wait until Easter.'

To seal the bargain, to stress perhaps his right, he leaned forward and kissed her cheek.

She suffered it with a statuesque impassivity that maddened him.

Chapter 31

The Quest

Isotta and her brother sat alone once more in her boudoir.

Despair had stripped her of her stateliness. She was in tears.

Domenico sat on a painted coffer, his elbows on his knees, his chin in his hands, misery in his face. He had heard from her all that had passed at her interview with Vendramin, and his present consternation chiefly concerned the indiscretion of her visit to Marc-Antoine.

'That you should have taken so foolish a step is nothing. That Vendramin should have knowledge and proof of it is terrible. It places you in that fellow's power. If he were to publish this thing... Oh, my God!' He got up, and stamped about the room.

'I fear that much less than the alternative of marrying him, a profligate, an escroc, a murderer. That is the husband my father imposes on me out of his loyalty to Venice. God of pity! When I consider that I am the bribe, the decoy to lure this villain into patriotic activity, I ask myself, is that less shameful than to be branded for a wanton? What honour do you suppose that his wife will enjoy? Will it be any higher than the dishonour with which he threatens me if I refuse the marriage?'

Domenico went down on one knee beside her and put his arms about her in a sheltering gesture of compassion.

'My poor Isotta! Poor child! Courage, courage! We are not at the marriage yet, and please God we never shall be. Do you think I want that nasty rogue for a brother-in-law? You were clever to compel postponement of the decision. We have a month. And in a month... What cannot happen in a month?' He kissed her tenderly, and as she clung to him, fondly, gratefully, he pursued his encouragements. 'I'll not be idle in the time. I'll begin by trying to discover something more about his quarrel with Marc, and how it came, after all, to be fought. It may be known. Leave me to investigate. Then perhaps we can decide on something.'

But for all his earnest brotherly intentions, Domenico, like his father, having always held aloof from the more frivolous groups of Venetian society, which both Vendramin and Marc-Antoine had been frequenting at the time of the duel, did not find it easy to penetrate it now. Moreover, his opportunities were curtailed by an increase of military duties. The consternation caused by the revolts of Bergamo and Brescia was not allayed by the news that reached Venice as the month of March wore on.

Bonaparte, having forced the passage of the Tagliamento, had steadily thrust the Austrian army back and back until before the end of the month the Archduke Charles was assembling the broken remnants of it at Klagenfurth, and the Army of Italy stood on enemy territory and the road to Vienna.

Lodovico Manin had not even been constrained to face the agony of a pronouncement in the matter of that eleventh-hour alliance with the Austrians, nor had the Grand Council ever been assembled to debate the matter. By the time that Count Pizzamano had placed before the Doge his information concerning the French plan, the Army of Italy was already advancing. It was too late for any measure beyond that of fortifying the actual city of Venice in a deluded hope of preserving her from violation, whatever happened.

For this the Council of Ten had issued the necessary orders, and it may have occurred to them that, considering the anger of the inhabitants with a government whose ineptitude seemed now completely established, if the troops assembled in the capital could not ultimately be used to protect the city from the French, they could certainly be used in the meantime to protect the government from the city.

Meanwhile, as a further measure of pacification, rumours were diligently being circulated. It was said, untruly, that the Emperor was sending down yet another army of seventy thousand men. Less untruthful – but of a significance not yet realized by the people – was the rumour that peace was about to be made.

The display of activity was not confined to the military. The agents of the inquisitors of state were now of an extraordinary diligence, and arrests upon denunciations of Jacobinism, of espionage, or other forms of treason were taking place on every hand. Disappearances in those days of panic were commonplaces.

It was to a Venice scarcely recognizable that Marc-Antoine at last returned when he emerged from his convalescence at the legation. This did not happen until the early days of April, on the morrow, in fact, of the battle of Judenburg in which the Austrians suffered the final defeat of the campaign.

Although in Venice it was not yet suspected, the war was over, and within a week the suspension of hostilities would be signed.

The Vicomtesse had remained at the legation to tend Marc-Antoine until there was no longer a shadow of an excuse to justify her in neglecting the insidious propagandist work that Lallemant was demanding of her, the careful, gradual preparation of Venetian minds for what was to come. It was a work in which he was employing by now a small army of agents, many of whom were actually Venetian.

Her withdrawal had occurred as soon as Marc-Antoine was permitted to leave his bed and sit for a few hours by his window overlooking the Corte del Cavallo. It was an uninteresting prospect; but he sat in the sun, and this and the invigorating air of early spring helped forward his convalescence.

On the day when first he had sat there, in bedgown and slippers, his thick black hair loosely tied and a rug about his knees, he had expressed to the Vicomtesse his unstinted acknowledgment of a debt which it secretly troubled him to have contracted.

'I should not be alive, Anne, if it had not been for your care of me.'

She smiled upon him with a sad tenderness. She had been unsparing of herself, and the battle she had fought on his behalf with death had left its scars upon her. The winsome little face was pinched, and her true age, which in full state of health she dissembled under an almost childish freshness, was starkly revealed.

'That is too much to say. But if I have helped to preserve your life, that gives me something creditable to set against all the rest.'

'All the rest?'

She turned away, and busied herself in the arrangement of some early violets in a piece of majolica that stood upon the table.

When she spoke again, it was on a little note of subdued fierceness to deplore that it did not lie in her power at the same time to avenge him.

'I have no doubt whom you have to thank for a wound that was meant to be mortal. I suspected it at the time. We have had evidence since. One of the men you wounded was the leader of that band. And Vendramin was kept indoors by a wound for ten days after that affair.'

'That is very interesting,' said Marc-Antoine.

'Interesting?' she had echoed. 'It would be interesting if I could bring that murderer to account. At first, I thought myself responsible. Perhaps I am in part. But only in part. He seems to have had cause for jealousy on another score.' She paused. She had come to stand beside him. She fussed with the pillows that supported him. 'Madonna Isotta Pizzamano's interest in you showed me that. It seems our destiny to be rivals, she and I.'

She said it lightly, and laughed as she said it, as if to cover with an air of jesting an admission of the boldness of which she was conscious.

He did not answer her. That mention of Isotta brought his thoughts sharply and painfully to the hopelessness of the situation as it now stood, a situation that for him meant defeat on every side.

For a time the Vicomtesse was content furtively to watch his absorption. Then she broke in upon it.

'I compassionated the lady who was to marry Vendramin even before I suspected that there were such grounds for my pity. What must I do now?' She paused to come and place a hand upon his shoulder. 'If you love Mademoiselle Isotta, why do you suffer Vendramin to marry her?'

He studied his hands for a time, looking so wasted, so white and translucent. Then he raised his glance and found her eyes upon him very intently.

'If you will tell me how I am to prevent it, you will answer a question to which I can find no answer.'

Her glance fell away from his, her hand from his shoulder. It was as if his reply had rebuffed her. She moved away a little, and fetched a sigh. 'I see,' she said. 'It is as I supposed.' And then, as if suddenly conscious that she had betrayed herself, she swung to him again, and spoke with a vehemence that brought a flush to her cheek. 'But don't think that I begrudge her this. So far am I from begrudging her, that there is nothing I would not do to help you to her. That is how I love you, Marc.'

'My dear!' he cried, and impulsively extended one of those wasted hands.

She held it while she answered him. 'I take no shame in confessing something that you must already know, something to which what you have now told me shows me that there can be no return. Nor need you look so troubled, my dear; for it is something that leaves me no regrets.'

Gently he pressed the hand he held. Whilst inevitably and deeply touched by this declaration from one who had given such generous proof of her devotion, he was yet conscious of its oddness in a woman who by adoption bore his name, a woman who announced herself his widow.

The only words he could find seemed trivial and banal.

'Dear Anne, I shall ever hold very gratefully and tenderly the memory of my great debt to you.'

'I ask no more. If you do that, you will repay me.' Again she hesitated. 'Hereafter you may hear things about me...unflattering

251

things. Something you may already know, or, at least, suspect. Will you try to remember that whatever else I may have been, with you I have always been genuine and sincere?'

'It is the only thing concerning you that I could ever hold in my thoughts,' he promised her.

'Then I am content.' But there was no contentment in her blue eyes. They were sad to the point of tears. 'I am leaving you today, Marc. There is no longer any excuse for my remaining. Philibert can do all that is necessary now. But you will come and see me sometimes, as before, at the Casa Gazzola? And remember that if you can discover any way in which I can help you to your heart's desire, you have only to command me.'

Her voice had choked on the last words. When they were spoken, she stopped abruptly, impulsively to kiss his cheek Then she fled from the room almost before he had realized it.

He sat on where she had left him, gloomily pensive, his mind filled with an odd tenderness for this woman whom at any moment he might have accounted it his duty to denounce. Of all that he had done in these months of wasted endeavour here in Venice, his having spared this pseudo-Vicomtesse was the only thing in the thought of which he could now take satisfaction.

Thereafter the care of him rested with Philibert; and at times with that bright young man, Domenico Casotto, who upon occasion came to relieve the valet. Casotto would sit and entertain Messer Melville with news of the events in Venice. He was more entertaining than he suspected, for Marc-Antoine, aware of Casotto's real functions, derived amusement from the rascal's efforts to lure him into a self-incriminating frankness. He might have been less amused had he known how closely the inquisitors of state were watching him through the ingenuous-looking eyes of this lively lad.

Nothing, however, was further from Marc-Antoine's mind than apprehension of the danger of which Isotta had sent him warning on the night when he was assailed. Though the inquisitors might suspect that Lebel and he were one and the same man, proof was not lacking of his devotion to the side that was ranged against Jacobinism or of the services which through Count Pizzamano he had rendered the Most Serene Republic, culminating in the warning which from his sick-bed he had sent the Count.

Hence, when at last in the first week of April he found himself sufficiently recovered to go forth again, he did not hesitate to decide to return to his old quarters at the Inn of the Swords. Confidently he brushed aside the slight misgivings displayed by Lallemant.

'To remain here beyond the time necessary for the healing of my wound would indeed be to invite a suspicion not easily removed. To be of any service I must have complete freedom of movement, and unless I have this, I had better leave Venice at once.'

Villetard was about to set out for Klagenfurth in answer to a summons from Bonaparte. This, as Marc-Antoine surmised, because instructions had reached the General from the Directory similar to those which had been addressed to Lebel.

The campaign was all but over. Lallemant expected news of the end at any moment.

'And then,' he said, 'it will be the turn of these Venetians. But a sound pretext, my friend, is still to seek.'

Marc-Antoine chose to be very much Camille Lebel at that moment.

'What need to be so cursedly fastidious? There's pretext to spare in the shelter given by Venice to the ci-devant Comte de Provence. I established it when I demanded his ejection. I would now present the reckoning if it depended upon me.'

'It doesn't depend upon you,' said Villetard tartly. 'The Directors require something more, as you know.'

'And as you know, too, Villetard,' he was answered, with an asperity serving to remind him that he was not yet forgiven for an interference which had all but cost the supposed Lebel his life. 'What have you done whilst I have been invalided? Here was your opportunity to do some of the fine things you promised us when first you came to Venice. Instead, what have we?' Marc-Antoine looked him over coldly. 'You begin to see perhaps that criticism is easier than performance.'

'Ah, that! Name of a name! It was not in my instructions to act as an agent-provocateur.'

Marc-Antoine's glance was so hard and stern that Villetard's arrogance crumpled before it; the sneer perished on his tight lips.

'Shall I report that speech to the Directors? Shall I tell them how precisely you delimit your service to the instructions you have personally received? They might then remind you that it is in your instructions to do whatever may be necessary for the good of France. However, since it is beneath your dignity to practise acts of provocation...'

Villetard was almost frightened. He interrupted vehemently. 'I never said that. Bear me witness, Lallemant, that I never said that.'

Marc-Antoine went steadily on: 'Since that is beneath your dignity, there is all the more reason why I should go and see what I can do.' He turned to take his leave of Lallemant. 'I will report when there is occasion.'

Chapter 32

The Inquisitors of State

Marc-Antoine landed at the Rialto. He sent Philibert on to the Inn of the Swords to inform Battista, the landlord, that he followed.

His natural promptings were to go at once to the Casa Pizzamano at San Daniele; and yet he was withheld by hesitations. He asked himself in a sort of despair what it was that he could go to do there. All that remained, so far as he could see, was to take his leave of the Count's family and depart whilst he was yet free to do so from this doomed capital of a doomed state where his every endeavour had failed.

He was of those who reflect most lucidly whilst moving; and so it was, in spite of the lingering weakness from his long confinement, that he had chosen to land at the Rialto, and set out to walk as far as Saint Mark's, where he would embark again to complete the journey. He hoped that by the time he reached the Piazza he would have resolved the problem that beset him.

Leaning a little heavily upon his cane, he took his way across the Merceria, where all was life and bustle, where traders bawled their wares in the narrow streets and haggling buyers were scarcely less vociferous, yet all of them jocular and good-humoured under the clear spring sky. He made brisk progress notwithstanding a lingering weakness, an elegant figure that took the eye. But by the time he reached the Piazza he was conscious of fatigue, and his brow was damp under his three-cornered hat.

It was the hour when the great square was most crowded, and today the throng of loungers seemed to him more dense than usual, and also a great deal less joyous than he had ever seen it.

A file of Slavonian soldiers guarded the approaches of the Ducal Palace.

Already there had been one or two demonstrations against the Signory, and in the palace they were fearful of a conflagration in material which from being normally docile now gave signs of having become highly inflammable.

Officers from the various regiments quartered about the city, displaying the blue-and-gold cockade of Venice, were numerous among the saunterers. They mingled freely with the idle men and women, drawn to the open perhaps by the precocious geniality of the weather and the anxiety for news of which this was the great mart. It was a crowd sobered by suspense.

Conscious now of lassitude, and with his problem still unsolved, Marc-Antoine found himself a table at Florian's, in the open, and sat down to remove his hat and mop his heated brow. He ordered himself a bavaroise and he had begun to sip it when he was aware of a presence at his elbow. He looked up to find there a stocky figure in rusty black. A pair of beady eyes regarded him out of the yellow vulturine face of Cristofero Cristofoli, the confidente of the inquisitors of state.

The Venetian, smiling upon him with a certain grimness, greeted him in terms which showed him to be startlingly well-informed. 'I rejoice to see you in health and abroad again. My felicitations. We have been anxious for you. May I sit?' He drew up a chair, and sank to it without waiting for permission. 'Thus we shall be less conspicuous. I suffer from being too well known.'

'At present,' said Marc-Antoine, 'you suffer also from being uninvited. I am flattered by your concern for my health. But I do not think my reputation will profit by your presence.'

Cristofoli sighed. 'That is the common complaint against me. But you do me an injustice. Knowing how little my society is desired, I never inflict it unless I have business.'

Marc-Antoine veiled his annoyance. 'Can it be my misfortune that you have business with me?'

'Do not let us regard it as a misfortune – yet.'

'When I know the business I shall be able to judge.' He sipped his bavaroise.

Cristofoli's beady eyes watched him stolidly. 'You keep to your native drinks even here in Venice,' he observed. 'Habit is hard to repress.'

Marc-Antoine set down his glass. 'You are mistaken. The bavaroise is not an English drink.'

'Oh, I am aware of that. But not that you are English. And that brings me to my business with you.' He leaned across the little table, and lowered his voice, an unnecessary and merely instinctive precaution, for there was no one in their immediate neighbourhood. 'Messer, the inquisitors of state desire to resolve a doubt upon this very question of your nationality.'

Marc-Antoine's annoyance deepened. This was a silly, vexatious waste of time and effort. It was of a piece with everything that he had seen of this Venetian Government, which spent itself in futilities whilst doing nothing to guard against the forces that were sapping the foundations of the State. But he preserved his calm on the surface.

'I shall be happy to assist them whenever they desire it.' The apparitor's smile approved him. 'No time like the present. If you will accompany me, I shall have the honour of conducting you.'

Marc-Antoine looked at him sternly. Cristofoli grinned again.

'There are three of my men over there, and if they were to employ force it would create a scene. I am sure you would wish to avoid that.' He got up. 'Shall we be going, sir?'

Marc-Antoine did not even hesitate. He beckoned the waiter, paid for his bavaroise, and with an impeccably calm demeanour over a raging spirit, sauntered off with the tipstaff.

Past the soldiers guarding the Porta della Carta, they came into the Ducal courtyard, where a half-battalion of Slavonians bivouacked about the great bronze well-heads. They ascended the staircase over which Sansovino's giants presided, and then, by the noble external gallery, came to another staircase at the foot of which there was a guard. They ascended again, and continued to ascend until Marc-Antoine, out of breath, found himself on the top-most floor of the Ducal Palace, where the Prison of the Leads was situated.

Here in a chamber that was something between a guardroom and an office, the confidente at last handed him over to a corpulent official, who desired to know his name, age, quality, nationality, and place of abode.

Cristofoli stood by whilst Marc-Antoine resignedly gave the name of Melville and all the particulars that went with it. His answers were entered in a register. Next, by a couple of archers, acting upon the order of the official, he was searched. But with the exception of his sword, they found upon him nothing of which they accounted it their duty to deprive him.

When this was over, he was conducted by the same archers and preceded by a turnkey to the room assigned to him. It was a fair-sized chamber furnished with a table, a chair, a stool on which stood ewer and basin, and a truckle bed.

He was informed that anything in reason for which he was prepared to pay would be supplied to him, and it was suggested to him by the turnkey that he should order his supper.

After that he was left to reflect as philosophically as he might upon the indubitable fact that he was a prisoner of the inquisitors. This situation, usually accounted terrifying, was to him merely an irritation. Terrors it had none.

He wrote a note to Sir Richard Worthington and another to Count Pizzamano. He claimed the assistance of the first as a right, and begged that of the second as a favour.

He might have spared himself the trouble. For Catarin Corner, whilst more than half-persuaded of his guilt, was yet deeply concerned that he should be afforded every opportunity of establishing his innocence. Therefore, when next morning he was summoned to appear before the dread tribunal of the Three, both the British Ambassador and the Count were in attendance.

It was Cristofoli who came for him, and conducted him below to the second floor of the vast palace. He was led along a wide gallery with windows above the courtyard in which the shadows were retreating before the April sunshine and whence arose the chatter and laughter of soldiers lounging there off duty.

Cristofoli halted his prisoner before a tall, handsome door that was guarded by two archers. In the wall beside this door a lion's head of natural size was carved in stone. The open mouth was the letter-box for secret denunciations.

The door was opened, and Marc-Antoine passed into a splendid lofty antechamber. Two archers in red with short halberts were ranged inside the doorway, and two similar ones guarded another smaller door on the right. A subaltern officer paced slowly to and fro. A blaze of colour from the armorial bearings in a tall window set high at the eastern end of the room was splashed by the sunlight upon the wood mosaics of the floor. Under this window stood two tall figures. They were Sir Richard and the Count.

Turning sharply as Marc-Antoine entered, Francesco Pizzamano, who wore his senatorial toga over his walking-dress, would have come to speak to him, but that he was respectfully restrained by the officer.

This subaltern at once took charge of the prisoner, and, with Cristofoli following him as a guard, ushered him into the presence of the inquisitors.

Marc-Antoine found himself in a chamber, small and intimate, but as rich in frescoes, gildings, and stained glass as was every room in this house of splendours. He was placed at a wooden rail, whence he bowed calmly to the inquisitors. The three occupied wide bucket seats on a shallow dais set against the wall, and there was a writing-pulpit before each of them. Catarin Corner, in red as the representative of the Ducal Council, occupied the middle place, between his two colleagues in black, who were members of the

Council of Ten. For background, covering the wall, they had a tapestry on which the aureoled Lion of Saint Mark stood with one paw supported upon the open evangel.

Beside another writing-pulpit set immediately below the dais stood now a man in a patrician robe, who was the secretary of the tribunal.

The officer withdrew, leaving the prisoner with Cristofoli for only guard.

Then Marc-Antoine, in a tone as easy and confident as his bearing, informed the inquisitors that he had been ill and was still weak, and begged to be allowed to sit.

A stool was provided for him, and the secretary opened the proceedings by reading the lengthy act of accusation. Summarized, it amounted to a charge of espionage and misrepresentation, of conveying to the French Government information detrimental to the Most Serene Republic, information obtained by falsely representing himself as working in the interests of the Serenissima; of passing under the assumed name of Melville and an assumed British nationality, whereas, in fact, he was a subject of the French Republic, a member of the Cinq-Cents, and a secret agent of the Directory, whose real name was Camille Lebel.

The secretary resumed his seat, and Catarin Corner's gentle voice addressed the prisoner.

'You have heard. And no doubt you are aware of the penalties which our laws prescribe for an offence of this gravity. You have leave, sir, to urge any reasons why these penalties should not be imposed upon you.'

Marc-Antoine rose and leaned upon the rail. 'Since these charges rest entirely, or almost entirely, upon the question of my identity, and since my own assertions on this can have little weight, I would respectfully submit that your excellencies hear the British Ambassador and my friend the Senator Count Pizzamano, who are in attendance.'

Angelo Maria Gabriel, the inquisitor on Corner's right, a man of a long, sorrowful countenance, speaking mournfully through his nose, approved the invitation as a very proper one. The other, Agostino Barberigo, a shrunken, trembling, half-palsied old man, nodded a silent, contemptuous concurrence.

Sir Richard was brought in first. He was important and emphatic. He had made a grave mistake once where Mr Melville was concerned, and for this, upon Mr Melville's complaint, he had been severely reprimanded from Whitehall. Until this moment Mr Melville had punished him in Sir Richard's own view – by ignoring him and denying him all opportunity of making amends. But this opportunity being vouchsafed him at last, he meant to rehabilitate himself with his Government by making the most of it.

Hence the vehemence of the oration – it amounted to no less – which he now delivered in Marc-Antoine's defence. When stripped, however, of the imposing rhetoric, which survived even in the French that Sir Richard employed, the ambassador's statements were seen to lack authority. They rested upon letters from Mr Pitt, one of which the Vicomte de Saulx had personally presented and others which had subsequently followed.

Sir Richard was under the necessity of admitting that, having had no acquaintance with the prisoner before their meeting here in Venice, he could not, upon his own personal knowledge, testify to the identity he claimed. He was going on to add that, nevertheless, in view of Mr Pitt's communications, it was impossible to harbour doubt, when the doleful voice of the inquisitor Gabriel – even more nasal and doleful in French than in Italian – cut him short.

'You would not venture, Sir Richard, to exclude the possibility that the prisoner might improperly have obtained the letter he delivered to you. Monsieur Pitt's later communications to you might have been written under a misapprehension created by forgeries committed by the prisoner.'

'I should say,' answered Sir Richard, with heat, 'that such a thing is so extremely improbable as to make the suggestion…fantastic.'

'Thank you, Sir Richard,' droned the tearful voice.

Marc-Antoine knew how far was the suggestion from being fantastic, considering that it expressed precisely what he had done in the character of Lebel.

Messer Corner added graciously his thanks to those which his colleague had expressed, whilst old Barberigo bowed in silent dismissal.

Sir Richard, breathing noisily, but with a lift of the hand and a friendly smile for the prisoner, which he thought must impress the court, was shown out by Cristofoli.

Count Pizzamano followed at once, and with his coming the proceedings became more serious. By virtue of his senatorial rank the Count was offered a seat near the secretary's pulpit, where by a turn of the head he could face at once the inquisitors or the prisoner.

He was clear, and comparatively brief. He had read the act of accusation, and in his mind no doubt existed of the error which the tribunal was committing. The evidence of this was overwhelming.

It was true that the prisoner had assumed a false nationality and had modified his family name to suit that assumption. But he had done it in the monarchist service and to combat the evil of Jacobinism which was the worst evil that had ever confronted the Most Serene Republic. To establish this, the prisoner's real identity and his record before coming to Venice should satisfy any reasonable men. There was, however, a great deal more. There were the real services which he had rendered to the Serenissima during his sojourn amongst them, services rendered at considerable peril to himself.

The Count went on to tell the court that his acquaintance with the prisoner was not of yesterday. That he was Marc-Antoine de Melleville, Vicomte de Saulx, Count Pizzamano could assert from assured knowledge acquired whilst he was Venetian Minister in London. Then he spoke in detail of the Vicomte's record in the Vendée.

'But nothing in that record,' he wound up, 'magnificent as it is, can compare in heroism with the perils he has incurred here in the service of a cause which is the cause of every Venetian to whom his country's welfare is dear.'

Thus his testimony had become an advocacy, and as Marc-Antoine's advocate he now continued and was tolerated out of deference to his senatorial rank. This might be unusual, and yet, as a member of the Council of Ten, he could not, in any case, have been excluded from these proceedings.

Gabriel's lean, red forefinger stroked an equally red and very long nose that jutted from his otherwise pallid face.

'The prisoner,' he whined, 'has assumed so many identities that a man's mind loses its way amongst them. To some he is the Vicomte de Saulx, a French émigré; to others he is Mr Mark Melville, agent of the British Government; and to others still he is the Citizen Camille Lebel, a secret agent of the Directory.'

'If you will review what I have done,' said Marc-Antoine, 'you will realize that I could not otherwise have done it.'

'We are familiar in this tribunal,' said the gentle Corner, 'with the methods of secret agents. We know that to be truly effective in the service of one side, such an agent is commonly under the necessity of pretending to serve the other. In this way we can accept your explanation that it was sometimes necessary for you to pose as Melville and sometimes as Lebel. The real question for us is: in which of these characters – both assumed – were you actually honest?'

'That question, Excellency, should be sufficiently answered by my real identity, upon which you have heard Count Pizzamano. Would the Vicomte de Saulx, who has suffered what the Vicomte de Saulx is known to have suffered at the hands of Jacobins, be likely to imperil his life by promoting the interests of Jacobinism?'

'You are answered, I think,' the Count interjected.

The finely featured, rather whimsical face of Corner was dark with thought. It was old Barberigo who bestirred himself to a rejoinder, a thin streak of sarcasm running through his quavering accents.

'On the surface the answer would seem conclusive. But we are not in a position to say that under the surface no other motive is operating. I can conceive circumstances,' he mumbled on, 'in which the Vicomte de Saulx might find it profitable to serve the Directory. After all, the Directory, we must remember, is not quite the same thing as the Government which dispossessed the Vicomte.'

'To that,' said Marc-Antoine, 'the answer. should lie in the nature of the services I have rendered here. Count Pizzamano can speak to these, if he will.'

The Count spoke at once and with weight. He dwelt upon the valuable information which from time to time the Vicomte de Saulx had brought to him and which he had passed on to His Serenity the Doge. In particular he dwelt upon the denunciations of Rocco Terzi and of Sartoni, matters which had been investigated by this very tribunal. Was more necessary? he asked.

'It would not be,' said the tenaciously malevolent old man, 'if it did not appear that the prisoner's services to the Serenissima as Messer Melville were outweighed by his disservices as the Citizen Lebel.'

This drew from the Count a question that had been troubling him from the outset. 'But is it, then, so clearly established that he and Camille Lebel are one?'

'We have not heard the prisoner deny it,' said Corner. 'Tacitly at least he has admitted it.'

'It is expressly admitted,' said Marc-Antoine at once, and thereby seemed to puzzle the Count. 'It must be clear to your excellencies that I could not have enjoyed the confidence of the French Legation unless I could impose myself there as an accredited agent of the Directory. Let me tell you of the chance that made this possible.'

As briefly as so long a story might be told, he related his adventure with the real Lebel at the White Cross Inn in Turin.

There was a senile cackle from Barberigo. 'A chapter from the Thousand-and-One Nights.'

The melancholy of Gabriel seemed to deepen. 'Do you ask us to believe that you have been able for all these months successfully to impersonate this man at the French Legation?'

'That is what I ask you to believe. Improbable though it may seem to you, I ask it with confidence, since it should be confirmed by the information which from time to time I have conveyed to you.'

It was Corner who took up the argument. 'We do not deny that some of this information has been of real value. But we must beware of persuading ourselves too readily that it might not have been given so as to win our confidence, so as to supply you now with the very contention you are making.'

'Could you reasonably assume that of a denunciation so destructive of French effort as that of Rocco Terzi or of Sartoni?' the prisoner confidently asked.

'Or,' added Count Pizzamano, 'the more recent information of the French plan to declare war on Venice, so as to use her as a pawn in peace negotiations with Austria?'

Old Barberigo wagged a forefinger at him. 'Only the future can establish whether that is true and we are trying the prisoner upon what lies in the past.'

Corner sat back in his chair, his chin in his hand, and addressed the Count. 'Our first difficulty,' he said, 'is that we know, from intercepted letters, that the prisoner has been communicating information of Venetian measures to the Directory.'

Marc-Antoine's answer was immediate and clear. 'You have, yourself, indicated the necessity under which a secret agent lies. To sustain my assumed character of Lebel, it was necessary that I communicate something. I do not know what letters you may have intercepted, but I fearlessly challenge you to produce a single one containing anything which on close examination could be hurtful to the Venetian Republic, or that would not have been a matter of common knowledge by the time my letter could reach Paris.'

Corner nodded silently, as if disposed to accept this explanation. But Gabriel brought his hand down upon his writing-pulpit. 'There is something much graver than that!' he shrilled.

'I am coming to it,' said Corner quietly, almost as if rebuking this vehemence. He sat forward now, and leaned his elbows on his pulpit.

'Some months ago,' he said slowly, 'at a time before the French had crossed our borders, the Senate received an unconscionable, a shameful demand to expel from Venetian territory the unfortunate refugee prince who, under the style of the Comte de Lille, enjoyed our hospitality in Verona. That demand, couched in the terms of an ultimatum, bore the signature of Camille Lebel. Now it has lately come to our knowledge that this demand was not made under any instructions from Paris. It was made entirely upon your own responsibility, and it bore your signature, as Lebel. And this because the French Ambassador deliberately refused to sign at your bidding a document so infamous. If you deny this, I shall place the proof of it before you.'

'I do not deny it, or anything else that is true.'

The answer seemed to take not only the inquisitors by surprise, but Count Pizzamano as well.

'You do not deny it?' said Corner. 'Can you, then, who profess to work in the monarchist and anti-Jacobin interest, explain your motives for an act so malevolent at once to your King and to the Serenissima?'

'Ay, sir!' whined Gabriel. 'How do you reconcile with your professions an ultimatum which inflicted such hardship on your Prince, and compelled the Serenissima to a step which you knew must render her shameful in the eyes of all nations?'

'Answer that,' cackled old Barberigo. 'Answer that, sir. You'll need to stir your invention, fertile though it seems to be. He, he!'

Corner raised one of his delicate hands to repress the malice of his colleague.

Marc-Antoine flashed on the grey old face a glance of contempt, before quietly answering.

'I shall need, I hope, to stir only your excellencies' memories.' He paused under their stern eyes to collect himself, and found in that moment even Count Pizzamano frowning upon him.

'When I admitted that I acted in that without express orders from Paris, I admitted what is true literally; but literally only. Actually the order was foreshadowed by a letter which I had just received from Barras, and, in fact, the order to make that demand arrived a few days after I had made it.'

'But why should you have betrayed such anxiety to perform an act which, if you are what you pretend to be, should be repellent to you?'

'It will be in your excellencies' memory, or, at least, in your records, that this ultimatum came to the Senate within a couple of days of the arrest of Rocco Terzi. That arrest placed me in a position of grave difficulty and danger. I was the only person besides Lallemant – and excepting Terzi's partners in treason – who had knowledge of the work upon which Terzi was engaged. His arrest brought me under the gravest suspicion. If I was to save my life and continue the anti-Jacobin work to which I had devoted myself, it was necessary to restore Lallemant's confidence in me. This was not an easy matter. I accomplished it by an outstanding proof of my Jacobinism. Actually I merely anticipated an order which I was persuaded must reach the embassy at any moment. Even without that I should have been justified. For if I sacrificed my Prince and the dignity of the Serenissima upon the altar of necessity, I sacrificed both so that I might forward the ultimate triumph of both.'

That answer, so frankly delivered, seemed complete. Count Pizzamano, who had listened at first in bewilderment, sank back now with a sigh that expressed relief. The inquisitors hesitated, seeming to question one another with their eyes. Then Corner leaned forward again, quiet and urbane.

'If I understand you correctly, your assertion is that at the French Legation you are believed to be Camille Lebel, and that Monsieur Lallemant does not so much as suspect that you are the Vicomte de Saulx?'

'That is my assertion.'

The fine, ascetic features of the red inquisitor seemed for the first time to lose their gentle expression; the eyes under their fine grey brows grew stern.

'And this,' he said, 'in spite of the fact that Madame, your wife, who passes for a cousin of Monsieur Lallemant, who is constantly in your company, who has remained with you at the French Legation to nurse you through your illness, makes no secret of the fact that she is the Vicomtesse de Saulx.'

To Marc-Antoine the unexpectedness of this was like a blow in the wind. He caught his breath sharply, almost audibly. Messer Corner, after a scarcely perceptible pause, continued: 'Do you really wish us to understand that whilst knowing her – his reputed cousin – for the Vicomtesse de Saulx, Monsieur Lallemant does not know you for the Vicomte? Is that what you ask us to believe?'

Marc-Antoine's hesitation did not last perhaps for more than a couple of seconds. Yet in those seconds his thoughts ranged over a wide field.

He was conscious at once that Count Pizzamano had deliberately slewed round on his stool to face him, perhaps as much taken aback as Marc-Antoine himself by that deadly question.

In certain circumstances the answer would be so easy, and tested by the sequel its veracity must be established. He had but to denounce the so-called Vicomtesse de Saulx for the impostor that she was. He had but to point out that she adopted the title of Saulx on a suggestion from the real Lebel. He could make it clear how, since it was desired to make this woman appear to be an émigrée aristocrat, the title of Saulx was the first that would suggest itself to the man who held the estates of Saulx and who believed that the real Vicomte had been guillotined.

He could have gone on to explain that, when about to denounce her for the Jacobin agent and French spy that he perceived her to be, one of his reasons for pausing was because it would have been imprudent to have let this denunciation follow so closely upon that of Rocco Terzi. Therefore, whilst he had postponed denouncing her, he had entered into relations with her so that he might keep her under surveillance and also so as to use her as a channel of information.

He could not merely have told them all this, he could have indicated how easily the proof of it was to be obtained, and so he could have cleared himself of this last and heaviest suspicion. But he could only so clear himself at the expense of that frail creature, into the lonely wistfulness and perhaps hopelessness of whose soul he had been afforded a glimpse. Denunciation must mean her certain arrest and probable death, secretly at the hands of the garrotter.

He had a swift vision of that horrible instrument of steel, shaped like a horseshoe. It enclosed the back of the neck, whilst across the front of it a silken cord was passed communicating with a winch that was turned and turned. And in the grip of that collar of steel and silk he beheld the slim white neck, and above it the little face, fair and delicate as a child's, with the eyes moist and tender as they had last looked at him, and the lips that had avowed a love that was all service.

To clear himself at that price was to be haunted to the end of his days by this vision, to despise himself with the knowledge of safety purchased at the price of the life of a poor woman to whom at that moment he owed his own existence.

That on the one hand.

On the other there was the thought of Isotta, whose father's stern eyes were turned upon him to question this unaccountable hesitation in him. Though Isotta might be lost to him, yet the thought of what must be her view of him when her father reported this to her was an intolerable anguish.

It was not the first time in his life that a choice of evils had been forced upon him; but never a choice so terrible. He must choose the less, of course, which was the one in which the suffering fell upon himself, for to a heart of any nobility it is easier to bear pain than to inflict it. It was impossible to fling to the lions the poor woman to whom at that moment he owed his life.

And so, at last, all that he answered, very gravely, was: 'That is what I ask you to believe.'

Messer Corner continued for a long moment to regard him sternly without speaking. There was something of astonishment, too, in that glance. It was as if the inquisitor had expected a different answer and were disappointed. At last, with a sigh, he sank back in his seat, and left it to his brethren to pursue the examination.

But Gabriel merely stroked his long nose in contemplative silence, whilst the senile Barberigo yawned and then wiped the tears from his bleary eyes.

Count Pizzamano continued to stare uncomprehending at the prisoner.

Not only was the thing admitted to be true which had seemed to him so fantastic when asserted by Corner, but in tacitly admitting it Marc-Antoine was admitting also his guilt; for the existence of a Vicomtesse de Saulx in the circumstances expounded by the inquisitor seemed a clear proof that Marc-Antoine's true identity must be known to the French Ambassador. And if that were so, one only conclusion was possible. Yet to this conclusion, the Count, unlike the inquisitors, perceived too many obstacles. He was utterly bewildered.

His thoughts swung to his daughter and to his talk with her on the night when Marc-Antoine had first sought them upon his arrival. How deceived the poor child was now proved in her assumption that the journey to Venice had been undertaken by Marc-Antoine primarily on her behalf! What a humiliation was she not spared now by the circumstances of her own betrothal! Also there was the probability that knowledge of this would help to reconcile her to her approaching marriage with Vendramin, a matter which troubled Count Pizzamano more profoundly than he allowed it to appear.

Out of this thought grew the reflection that, all things considered, perhaps it was better so. But was it really so? The more questions he asked himself on this, the fewer answers could he discover.

The gentle voice of Corner came at last to interrupt his speculations. The inquisitor was addressing Cristofoli.

'You will reconduct the prisoner to the room that has been assigned to him. Let him be shown every consideration consistent with his close detention until we make known our pleasure.'

The ominous words struck a chill into Marc-Antoine's heart. He stood up. He grasped the rail before him and hesitated for a moment. Then, realizing that mere protest or assertion would be idle, he bowed to the Three, and in silence suffered himself to be conducted from the room.

When the door had closed upon him, Messer Corner asked Count Pizzamano if he had anything to urge that might assist their deliberations. Wearily Barberigo yawned again.

The Count stood up. 'I would only remind your excellencies that whilst all that you may have against the Vicomte de Saulx is based upon assumptions, that which tells in his favour rests upon solid fact.'

'Be sure that we shall remember it. Our obstacle to a favourable view is his Vicomtesse, as you will understand.'

The Count's chin sank to his neckcloth. 'There I am baffled,' he confessed. 'Chiefly because I can't conceive why he should have concealed his marriage.'

'Is there not a more or less obvious reason? To have acknowledged her would have been to admit his own identity. He could hope, in an emergency, to persuade us that he imposed upon the French Legation by passing there for Camille Lebel. But could he hope to persuade us that his association with the French Government was a pretence if they knew him for the Vicomte de Saulx?'

'As I said before,' Barberigo interposed, 'I could conceive of circumstances in which the Vicomte de Saulx might consider it worth his while to serve the Directory. To me it is plain that we are in the presence of such circumstances. A prospect of restoration to his confiscated estates, for instance, might be a difficult bribe to resist.'

'That, from my knowledge of him, I could never believe,' said the Count stoutly. 'It is but another assumption that you are setting against the known facts of the services he has rendered Venice, every one of which contradicts the conclusion towards which you lean.'

'Be sure,' said Corner, 'that they shall be given due weight.' Then very courteously he inclined his head. 'We are grateful to you, Lord Count, for your assistance.'

Perceiving in this his dismissal, Count Pizzamano bowed gravely to the Three, and passed out, deeply troubled in spirit.

Barberigo shuffled restlessly. 'Need we waste more words on this? The matter is clear, I think.'

Corner turned upon him his gentle, rather whimsical smile. 'I envy you your clarity of vision. My own poor eyes seek to pierce a fog. In what case are you, Messer Gabriel?'

Gabriel shrugged his narrow shoulders. 'Just lost in all the conjectures we have raised.'

'Surely,' grumbled Barberigo, 'it is not in your mind to pursue them further.'

'That would be unprofitable, we should merely travel in a circle.'

'And so say I,' the old man agreed. He cleared his throat shrilly. 'To judgment, then.'

Corner was wistful. 'Would your excellency venture to deliver judgment in a matter so delicately balanced as is this?'

'Would I? Is not that my function? These are not times for hesitations. Beset as we are by spies and enemies, it is our duty to give the State the benefit of any doubt.'

'It is our first duty to be just,' said Corner.

Gabriel turned squarely to the red inquisitor in expostulation. 'But if we are neither to debate the case further nor yet to deliver judgment upon it, what then?'

'Postpone,' said Corner, and tightened his lips. 'The matter being so evenly balanced, as I have said, and as you must agree, it only remains to wait until some fresh discovery disturbs that balance. That is my considered view. If you cannot concur, we shall have to refer the matter to the Council of Ten.'

'You relieve me,' said the doleful Gabriel. 'I concur cordially.'

Together they now looked at Barberigo, and waited. The old man blinked at them with his watery eyes. His head shook more than ever in annoyance.

'I'll not oppose you,' he said at last. 'But this postponement is a waste of time. That young man was of an effrontery that I have always associated with guilt. And I don't want for experience. It would be more merciful not to keep him lingering in suspense, for it is written that he must come to the strangler in the end. Still, since you seem set on it, we will postpone the sentence.'

Chapter 33

Casus Belli

Isotta, my dear, did Marc ever tell you that he was married?'

The Count sat at table with his Countess and their daughter. Supper was at an end, and the servants had left the room.

Isotta looked up with a smile; and smiling was an art that Isotta seemed lately to have lost. 'He must have forgotten to do so,' she said, and her father perceived that she mocked him.

'That is what I supposed.' He was very grave. He, too, had smiled little of late.

The Countess, looking from her husband to her daughter, supposed that a jest was passing which she did not understand. She begged to be enlightened. The Count responded clearly and definitely in a manner startling to both mother and daughter. Isotta, recovering, shook her dark head, and spoke confidently.

'There is an error somewhere in your information.'

Francesco Pizzamano, grave-eyed, denied the possibility of error. He stated whence his information came, and now, at last, Isotta's confidence deserted her.

'Oh! But it is unbelievable!' Her eyes were very round and black in the scared pallor of her face.

'Truth so often is,' said her father. 'Myself at first I could not credit it; not until it was admitted by Marc himself. Since then, considering it, I perceive that he must have had sound reason for his secrecy.'

'What reason could possibly exist?' Her voice shook.

He hunched his shoulders and spread his hands. 'In these times, when a man carries the burdens borne by Marc, reasons are not lacking. The inquisitors have discovered a reason, a very specious reason, that is entirely unfavourable to him. The true reason, whilst putting an entirely different appearance on it, may run it fairly close. What I most find to respect in Marc is that he is a man who will sacrifice everything to the cause he serves.'

'But if the inquisitors...' she began, and then broke off. Abruptly she asked: 'Is he in danger?'

Slowly the Count shook his head. 'My chief hope for him lies in the fact that Catarin is not by any means a fool.'

She questioned him closely, feverishly, upon the precise words that had passed between inquisitors and prisoner. When he had answered her with scrupulous accuracy, she sat as if drugged for a while; then, pleading weariness, she rose from the table, and begged them to excuse her.

When she had gone, Francesco Pizzamano looked gloomily at his Countess.

'Do you judge her to be deeply hurt by this?'

The handsome countess was tragic. 'The poor child looked as if she had taken her death-wound. I'll go to her.' She rose.

'A moment, my dear.'

The Count held out his arm. She came to him. Encircling her waist, he drew her to him where he sat. 'It might be better to leave her. I feared she would take it badly. Though God knows why.'

'I think I know, too.'

The Count slowly nodded. 'All things considered, my dear, it is surely best so. Resignation comes more readily when the thing desired is seen to exist no more.'

She set a hand upon his head. 'You are not hard, Franceschino. I have never found you so. And yet, where your own child is concerned, you consider nothing but expediency. Think of her heart, my dear.'

'I am thinking of it. I do not want it hurt more than it must be. I do not want it to bear more suffering than I have brought upon it. That is why I almost welcome a state of things that imposes resignation.'

'I scarcely understand you, dear.'

'Perhaps that is because you do not credit me with a conscience. I have gambled my daughter. Used her as a stake in a game played for Venice. And the game is lost. I have sacrificed her to no purpose. Just squandered her. I have no more illusions. The Venetian sun has set. Twilight is upon us. Soon, very soon, it will be dark.' His voice was heavy with despair. 'But this I want you to know, my dear: I should never have asked such a sacrifice of my Isotta if both she and I had not believed that Marc was dead. Nor would she have accepted it. The discovery that he lived was tragic. Now that to her he becomes, as it were, dead again, she may resign herself once more to this futile sacrifice to which we are pledged. That is why I say that perhaps it is best so. They loved each other, she and Marc and he was worthy of her.'

'You can say that in the face of this discovery?'

He nodded. 'Because I believe that he has given himself in marriage in some such spirit as that in which I have given her. To serve a cause so great that it commands all that a man may give. When he made answer on this point today, he had the martyred air of one who has immolated himself. If that does not prove true, then I know nothing of human nature.' He rose heavily. 'Go to her now, dear. Tell her that. She may find comfort in it and strength. God help the child! God help us all, my dear!'

But Isotta's burden was heavier than they knew, or than she allowed even her mother to suspect. When at last she could believe this thing, far from bringing her the resignation her father hoped, it robbed her of that to which she had already won. Circumstances might forbid that Marc and she should ever be man and wife; but at least she had taken comfort in the thought of a spiritual bond between them, which should make them one eternally. And now this bond had snapped, leaving her terribly alone, adrift and afraid.

She listened to her father's theory, conveyed to her by her mother. It brought her no conviction. The only explanation that she found was one that loaded her with humiliation. When she had sought him that morning at his lodging, she had done so upon too rash an assumption that it was for her that he had come to Venice. Instead, as it now seemed, he had come solely in the pursuit of his political mission. Not to wound her pride, he had refrained from disillusioning her. And that, too, may have been a reason for his subsequent silence on the subject of his marriage.

The fugitive words of tenderness and hope which he had since uttered she now explained as meaning only that he hoped to deliver her from a betrothal which he perceived to be odious to her. That betrothal lost none of its odiousness as a result of what was now discovered. On the contrary, this wall that had arisen between Marc and herself, in isolating her, robbed her of what little power of endurance remained.

Only if this great spiritual lassitude which beset her should finally conquer her pride would she now submit to marriage with Vendramin.

In those days she began to discover in herself a vocation for a religious life. Nauseated with the world and the meaningless perpetual strife with which man filled it, she conceived a yearning for the peace of the cloister, perceived in it a refuge, a sanctuary which none would venture to deny her. Vendramin might dispute her with man; but he would never dare to dispute her with God.

In the contemplation of this, her courage was restored, and only Domenico restrained her from an immediate declaration of the intention.

He had learnt from his father the little that was known of Marc's marriage, which is to say the little that was disclosed at the trial before the inquisitors. But by an odd chance he learnt it on the evening of a day when he had actually made the acquaintance of the Vicomtesse de Saulx.

In the course of his investigations into the quarrel between Marc and Vendramin, he had sought Major Sanfermo with whom he had formerly been on friendly terms, and by Sanfermo he was taken for the first time in his austere young life to the Casino del Leone, in quest of Androvitch.

He had sought information on the subject of the debt upon the payment of which Marc-Antoine had insisted before he would cross swords with Vendramin, and particularly upon the sources whence Vendramin might have procured such a sum. Major Sanfermo had suggested that conceivably the money had been supplied him by the Vicomtesse de Saulx. Androvitch had definitely denied it. Domenico, however, had scarcely heard the denial.

'Whom did you say?' he asked, like one who conceives that his hearing has deceived him.

'The Vicomtesse de Saulx. She is yonder.' Sanfermo indicated the little lady, who made one of a fashionable, animated group.

The bewildered captain was conducted to her and presented, to be, although he did not suspect it, almost as great an object of interest to the little Frenchwoman as she was to him. When he left her at the end of a half-hour's talk, he was more bewildered than ever, nor did his father subsequently succeed in clearing up the doubts in his mind.

'She maintains the fiction of his death on the guillotine,' the Count explained, 'so as to ensure the concealment of his identity.'

'Does that satisfy you?' quoth Domenico.

'Upon reflection it seems plain.'

What else he had added, on the generous theory he had formed, was now repeated by Domenico to his sister.

'It must be, Isotta, that, like yourself, Marc is a victim of the needs of his country or his party. But you are not yet at the altar. I have discovered something; and I may yet discover more.'

At her brother's bidding, she postponed announcement of the decision that must be her last recourse.

Meanwhile, the days flowed on. Holy Week was reached, it brought darker clouds of despair into her sky, as into the sky of Venice.

The war was over. Of this Venice was now aware, as she was also increasingly aware that this peace, to which for a year she had so eagerly looked forward, did not of necessity mean a cessation of hostilities towards herself. Indeed, what was to follow for the Serenissima was brutally foreshadowed on Holy Saturday.

The revolutions of Bergamo and Brescia had led to the arming of the peasants of the Veneto, so that they might support the militia in the repression of further revolutionary outbreaks. They had also produced throughout the Venetian dominions a violent explosion of feeling against the French who were held responsible for them.

This francophobia had for further stimulant the insolent rapine of which the French had been guilty towards the peasantry, seizing their crops, their cattle, and their women. Everywhere the peasants flocked to the recruiting-stations, and soon there were some thirty thousand of them under arms. They were armed for the repression of revolutionaries. But the only enemy they knew were the French, and wherever small parties of Frenchmen were found, they were made to pay with their lives for the outrages that had been suffered.

To end this state of things Andoche Junot was dispatched to Venice.

Bad manners were the order of the day with the men of the new French régime. Equality, they held, could dispense with courtesies, and was best expressed by an insolent and coarse directness, and by the elimination of all ceremonial. It was strict attention to this which had enabled Marc-Antoine so successfully to play the part of Lebel. The bad manners of Bonaparte were overshadowed by the greatness of the man; his arrogance sprang from consciousness of power in himself rather than in his office. The bad manners of those who surrounded him, each of whom played to other audiences the role of a little Bonaparte, was stark, flagrant, and uncondonably offensive.

To receive this emissary the College assembled in the splendid chamber in which Veronese and Tintoretto had immortalized the power and glory of Venice. Overhead, on the ceiling, depicted in sensuous beauty by Veronese, Venetia was enthroned upon the globe, with Justice and Peace for her supporters. Above the throne of the

Doge glowed the same master's great canvas of the Battle of Lepanto, whilst on the right were ranged Tintoretto's portraits of such great doges as Doná, da Ponte, and Alvise Mocenigo.

Here, arrayed in their patrician robes, the members of the College, with the enthroned Doge presiding, awaited the soldier.

When he faced them from the threshold, booted, spurred, and hat on head, it was as a meeting of the old order and the new: the austere, ceremonious, and gracious with the frankly direct, the boorish, and the graceless.

The Master of Ceremonies, the Knight of the Doge, advanced, wand in hand, to conduct and present the emissary as the etiquette prescribed. But the coarse soldier, thrusting him brutally aside, tramped across the room without uncovering, his sabre clanking after him. Unbidden he mounted the steps of the throne and flung himself into the seat reserved for foreign ambassadors, on the right of the Doge.

The Senators stared askance, stricken dumb by this contemptuous treatment. The sun of Venice had set indeed if an insolent foreign upstart could dare to be so negligent of the deference due to this august assembly. Lodovico Manin, pale and nervous, was so lost to a sense of the dignity of his high office as to offer, nevertheless, the courteous words of welcome that the forms prescribed.

Junot's utter disregard of these was like a blow in the face to every patrician present. He plucked a paper from his belt. It was the letter from Bonaparte. In a voice loud and harsh he read out its contents to them. They were in tune with his conduct. They were inspired by the same brutal, hectoring directness. The commander of the Army of Italy complained of the arming of the peasants and of the murder of French soldiers. On the provocative brigandage by these same French soldiers, the robbery, rape, and murder of subjects of a state which was at peace with France, he was silent.

'You attempt in vain,' Bonaparte wrote, 'to avoid the responsibility of your order. Do you think that I cannot cause the first people of the Universe to be respected?... The Senate of Venice has replied with perfidy to the generosity which we have always shown. My aide-de-camp, who goes to you, will offer you the choice of peace or war. If you do not at once disarm and disperse the hostile peasants and arrest and surrender to us the authors of the murders, war is declared.'

There was more of the same kind.

Having read it to the end, Junot got to his feet as abruptly as he had sat down, and ever with the same coarse disregard of courtesies, he clanked out again.

'Now we see,' said Count Pizzamano, addressing no one in particular, 'how low our policy of drift, our pusillanimity, and our avarice have brought us. From being the first people in Europe, we are become the most abject.'

And abjectly now they sent their apologies to Bonaparte, their expressions of respect and devotion and their promise of immediate compliance with his demands.

With that war-averting answer Junot departed on Easter Monday, and on that same day in Verona to cries of 'Saint Mark!' and 'Death to the French!' the fury of a long-suffering people flamed terribly forth.

The French fled for shelter to the forts, but not before some hundreds of them had been slaughtered. In those forts they were besieged by the Dalmatian troops and the armed peasants who had headed the rising, and Count Francesco Emili was dispatched to Venice to implore the Senate to break with France and to send reinforcements to support the Veronese patriots.

But the Serenissima, which had not broken with France when she might successfully have done so, was horror-stricken at the invitation to break now. Dissociating herself utterly from that rising known to history as the Veronese Easter, she once more asserted her neutrality and her friendship for France, leaving those who had risen in their loyalty to her to prepare for death as their reward.

Meanwhile, Bonaparte dispatched Augier to Verona, and peace was restored there within a few days.

In that massacre of the Veronese Easter was all the pretext that the French required for a declaration of war. But as if it were not enough, there occurred in Venice itself, on the very day that the uprising in Verona was quelled, an act of war of which Domenico Pizzamano was the hero.

On Easter Monday the Council of Ten had published a decree, consonant with Venetian neutrality, excluding from the harbour all foreign warships.

On the following Thursday the French frigate, the *Libérateur d'Italie*, commanded by Jean Baptiste Laugier, and accompanied by two luggers, having taken on board a Chioggia fisherman as a pilot, attempted to enter the Port of Lido.

Domenico Pizzamano, who was in command at the Fort Sant' Andrea, shared the despair and humiliation in which such patriots as his father watched the now inevitable and shameful end of the Most Serene Republic. It may be that he welcomed this opportunity of showing that in Venice there were still embers at least of the great fire that in other days had made her glorious; and in any case his orders from the Council of Ten made his duty clear.

When word was conveyed to him of the approach of those foreign ships, he repaired instantly to the ramparts to survey matters for himself.

The vessels displayed no colours, but they were certainly not Venetian, and whatever might be the case of the two consorts, the *Libérateur*, which was leading, was heavily armed.

Domenico took his decision instantly. He ordered two rounds to be fired across her bows as a warning.

For the luggers this was enough. Without more ado they both went about and stood off. Captain Laugier, however, continued defiantly upon his course, breaking out the French tricolour.

It was now that Domenico may well have given thanks to Heaven that to him, as to those martyrs at Verona, it was vouchsafed to strike a blow for Venetian honour without regard to what might follow. He opened fire in earnest. The *Libérateur* returned it, until crippled by a shot between wind and water she ran aground on a mudbank to save herself from sinking. Domenico went off with two armed launches to take possession of the ship, and was accompanied by a galliot commanded by Captain Viscovich with a company of Slavonian soldiers.

They boarded the French vessel, and after a brief sharp fight, in which Laugier was killed, made themselves master of her as night was falling.

Among her papers, which he seized, Domenico found abundant evidence of intelligence between Laugier and French residents in Venice. These papers he delivered to the Council of Ten, so that action might be taken upon them. But next morning, under the sternest representations from Lallemant, all were surrendered to the ambassador.

On the day after that Domenico was commanded to attend before the Council of Ten. He was received with enthusiasm, officially praised, and encouraged to continue with the same zeal in the discharge of his duty. To the men who had taken part in the affair the Council voted an extra month's pay.

In Domenico's own eyes it was no great thing that he had done. But in the eyes of the Venetians, exasperated by French insolence, he found himself the hero of the hour, and he was saddened by it. It merely showed him how far had Venice been from ever again hoping to hear the roar of the old Lion of Saint Mark that once had been so powerful and so proud.

Chapter 34

Vendramin's Last Card

The week that followed the affair of the Lido was an uneasy one. Venice was full of rumours, and she was being patrolled now day and night by troops. The soldiers originally brought there to defend the State were thus being employed to repress disturbances among the restive citizens. The Lion of Saint Mark had become as a beast that crouches in expectation of the whip.

At the Casa Pizzamano, despite the pride in Domenico for his fearless performance of duty, it was a week of mourning. The Count recognized the moribund condition of the Republic, understood that its hours were numbered.

Perceiving his dark mood, Vendramin hesitated to remind him that Easter had come and gone and that the marriage date remained unappointed. He hesitated the more because the events had robbed him of a good deal of the power of insistence which he had possessed. He no longer had any influence to market. He raged a little at this, and at his own lack of foresight. He should ruthlessly have beaten down all hesitations whilst it was in his power to do so. He had been too foolishly considerate. Perhaps he had been too trusting even. What if this stiff-necked Count and that cold, proud piece, his daughter, should now refuse to honour the debt they had contracted?

Such a thought brought him more than a shiver of apprehension. Never had he been so debt-ridden; never had his credit been so exhausted. He dared not nowadays so much as approach that traitorous Vicomtesse, who formerly, and to his undoing, had kept him so liberally supplied. At the casinos such prestige as he had enjoyed had never recovered from the blow it had received from Mr Melville. There was no one from whom he could today borrow a sequin. In his despair he had even gone the length of offering his services secretly to Lallemant. But Lallemant had shown him the door none too politely. He had pawned or sold most of his jewellery, and now little remained him beyond his fine clothes. His state was parlous. If the Pizzamani should play him false, he did not know what would become of him.

The suspense of this was not to be borne. However the intrusion of so personal a matter might be resented at a time of such national anxiety, Vendramin could not suffer any scruples to deter him.

So he sought Isotta, and found her one afternoon in the loggia that overlooked the garden, where all was green again and fragrant, and where early roses were already budding in the sunshine.

She received him with that cold gentleness which he had always found so exasperating: more exasperating perhaps than an active dislike. With dislike he might have wrestled. But this indifference gave him nothing that he could grasp.

Leaning, tall and graceful, upon the parapet of the loggia, and muting his rich voice to a tone of prayer, he reminded her that a week and more was gone since that Easter for which she had promised him the happiness of the appointment of their wedding-day.

She betrayed no nervousness. She looked at him straightly and candidly with eyes that were full of melancholy.

'If I were to say to you, Leonardo, that it is in my thoughts to take the veil, should you oppose such a desire?'

It took him a moment to realize what she meant. Then he flushed. 'Should I be human if I did not? Are you mad, Isotta?'

'Is it madness to be disillusioned with earthly existence? To perceive the vanity of the world? To centre all hopes upon a future life?'

'In such as you it is no less than madness. Leave that to women who are simple-minded, ugly or decrepit. Let them take that compensation, for the glories of life that are denied them. And, whether it be mad or sane, it is for you to remember that it is not the life to which you are pledged.'

'But if I desire to pledge myself to God, shall not that overrule all pledges made to man?'

He struggled with his rising choler; strove desperately to clutch this thing that he felt was slipping from him. 'Would God accept a pledge that makes you a cheat? Do you suppose they have no sense of honour in Heaven?' Then abruptly he asked yet another question. 'Have you told your father of these crazy notions?'

She frowned at this glimpse of the roughness of which he was capable.

'It was in my mind to tell him today.'

'My God! You are serious, then, in this fraudulent thought; this… this swindle? By the Host! Can you dream that your father will be a party to it? Your father – I thank God – is a man of honour, a man who keeps to his pledged word. Have no illusions about that, Isotta. I have loyally done my part in what was agreed between us, and he will not see me cheated of my…my just reward.'

She looked away from him. 'Should you consider it a reward to take to wife an unwilling maid?'

He had a sense of beating his head against a cold, unyielding wall of fraudulent obstinacy. Fury blinded him. It almost choked him. 'A maid!' he jeered in a thick voice. 'And are you a maid? Are you?'

That drew her eyes to him, and he laughed brutally, hideously into her face. 'Are you even fit to take the veil? To enter upon the mystic nuptials? Have you asked yourself that? Oh, I understand you. You would cheat me now in this, as you cheated me before with lies; persuaded me of the innocence of your visit to that dog's lodging. Will you so easily persuade your father of it?'

'Do you mean to tell him?'

The question suggested to him where his power might yet lie.

'As God's my witness, unless you come to your senses and fulfil your promise.'

That, he thought, should checkmate her. But she looked at him with her unfailing, disconcerting calm.

'So that, soiled as you believe me to be, false, hypocritical, and lying as you tell me that I am, you are still content to take me to wife for the sake of my endowments? That is noble!'

'Sneer all you please. I have earned you, and I will be paid.'

'Even though you dispute me with God?'

'With God or the devil, madame.'

'Will you ring, Leonardo, and bid them ask my father and brother to come here?'

He made no movement to obey. 'What is that for? What are you going to do?'

'If you will ring, you will discover. I shall tell you in my father's presence.'

He glowered upon her. How baffling and obstinate she could be in that accursed repose which he could not shake.

'Remember what I have said. You are warned. Either you fulfil the sacred promise that you made me, or Count Pizzamano shall learn that he has a wanton for his daughter.'

For the first time she showed a flash of resentment. 'You would do well to remember that I have a brother.'

But that veiled threat he met with a fleering laugh. 'To be sure! The heroic Domenico! You will send him to seek satisfaction of me for imputations upon his sister's honour. He may find it a very different matter from emptying guns upon a French warship from a safe distance.' He drew himself up. 'Send this little hero of the Lido to me, by all means. You may have heard that I can take care of myself.'

'When supported by three bullies. Yes, I've heard that. Will you ring? The longer you delay it, the more disgusting I am finding you.

You should judge how this interview has reconciled me to our nuptials.'

'Bah!' he retorted. 'Your hypocrisy nauseates me. You seize on this, so as to buttress your swindling pretences.' As he spoke, he swung round in the loggia to do at last her bidding, only to discover that it was no longer necessary. He had delayed too long. Count Pizzamano and Domenico were in the room beyond.

Seeing them, he grew suddenly afraid. How much had they overheard, and how much must they now be told in explanation?

Vendramin's case was that of every blackmailer. His power endures only so long as the revelation dreaded by his victim is not made. So here. Isotta's fear of the revelation might be a lever to obtain his will. The revelation itself, whilst damaging to her, could nothing profit him.

He stood now a little abashed under the grave, weary eyes of the Count.

The strain of the last few weeks had told heavily upon Count Pizzamano. Much of the man's normal calm urbanity had deserted him.

He advanced, Domenico following a pace behind him; and so they came to the threshold of the loggia. He was very cold and very stern.

'I do not know, Leonardo, when such words as I have overheard from you have been uttered under this roof before. I trust never. Will you tell me the occasion of terms so wanting in respect to my daughter and so threatening to my son?'

'For his threats to me...' Domenico was beginning, when his father's raised hand imposed silence upon him.

Vendramin could see nothing for it but to begin at the point which he had hoped would never have been reached.

'I am sorry that you should have overheard me, Lord Count. But since it has happened, you must be the judge of whether I have cause for heat. After all the patience I have used, after so loyally doing my part, Isotta threatens to evade by fraud her obligation. I appeal to you, sir, to bring your daughter to...to reason.'

'Odd that you should use the word fraud,' said the Count. 'For that is the very subject I was coming to discuss with you. Domenico has been telling me something of the circumstances of your duel with Messer Melville: something that he has lately discovered.'

'My duel with Melville?' Vendramin became impatient. 'What has my duel with Melville to do with this? Let that wait, sir. Let us first settle this fulfilment of a pledge. After that I'll discuss the duel with you to your heart's content.'

'What is this? You take an extraordinary tone, I think.'

But Vendramin was excited, exacerbated, at bay. 'Excuse it, sir, on the score of my anxiety: my anxiety for my rights, which appear to be in danger.'

'Your rights?'

'Are they questioned? That cannot be. As a man of honour, my lord, you cannot hesitate where your word has been given.'

The Count smiled acidly. 'And now we appeal to honour. It is opportune. Well, well! To come to this duel, then...'

'By the Host!' cried the infuriated Vendramin, 'if you must know the causes of that duel, you shall know them.'

But the Count did not suffer him to proceed further. 'Not the causes, sir. That may come after. Or we may not get so far. It is on the circumstances that I desire a word with you.'

'The circumstances?' Vendramin did not understand.

'Tell him, Domenico.'

Domenico was prompt. 'It is common knowledge in the casini you frequent that you owed Messer Melville a thousand ducats, which you had borrowed from him. It is further said that, trusting to your accomplishments as a swordsman, you calculatedly provoked him, hoping thus to liquidate the debt.'

'If you will tell me by whom that abominable lie is being repeated...'

'At the Casino del Leone I found it on the lips of everyone to whom I mentioned the matter.'

'To whom you mentioned the matter? At the Casino del Leone? You mean that you went there to spy upon me?'

'To investigate. Yes. To assure myself that there might be nothing against the honour of the man who proposed to marry my sister. I learnt that you were publicly charged by Messer Melville with the very thing which you denounce as an abominable lie.'

'Does that make it true? The fact is, if you must know, that the coward sheltered himself behind the debt. He paraded it, so that he might excuse himself from meeting me until it was paid. That because he was sure I could not pay.'

'Then, since you met him, it follows that you paid him.'

'Of course. What then?' His manner was blustering, but in his heart he was afraid, suddenly assailed by a premonition of whither this was leading.

Domenico looked at his father with a crooked smile before replying.

'Your duel was fought two days after the feast of Saint Theodore. Was it not?'

'It may have been. Is that important?'

'I think so. Will you tell my father where you obtained so large a sum of money?'

This was the deadly question that Vendramin had been fearing. But he was ready with his answer, and the manner of its delivery was crafty. He folded his arms, to express the self-control that he was exercising. 'I understand,' he said bitterly. 'You think to embarrass me before your sister. To prejudice me with her. So it be. After all, what does it matter? I had the money from a lady; from a lady with whom it follows that I was very friendly. Must I name her? But why not? I borrowed the money from the Vicomtesse de Saulx.'

Domenico's answer came like a blow between the eyes.

'She tells me that you did not.'

In his stupefaction Vendramin unfolded his arms and let them fall to his sides. He stared about him, his lips foolishly parted, at Domenico, at the Count, and at Isotta, all of whom were inscrutably watching him. At last he found his voice.

'She tells you... She tells you that? You questioned her, and she tells you that?' He paused there to add stormily, 'She lies, then.'

'She lies,' said the Count, 'to cancel a debt of a thousand ducats. I never heard a stranger reason for falsehood. However, we must accept your word for it. Tell me this: did this lady know the purpose for which she was lending you the money?'

'I don't know. I don't remember.'

'Then let me help your memory,' said Domenico. 'She must have known, because she was present when Marc made his stipulation that he would not meet you until you had paid your debt. You won't trouble to deny that?'

'No. Why should I?'

The Count answered him. 'If you knew more about the Vicomtesse de Saulx, you would know that for whatever purpose she might have lent you money, she would certainly not have lent it so as to make possible this duel between you and the…between you and Messer Melville.' And then, with an increasing sternness he continued, 'Your falsehood proves what my son's information had led me to suspect.'

'Falsehood, sir! Is that a word to use to me? To my face?'

'I do not know what word to use to you.' The Count's tone now was one of withering contempt. 'Your meeting with Messer Melville took place two days after the feast of Saint Theodore. On Saint Theodore's day you came to me here with a tale that for the purposes of our patriotic campaign you required a thousand ducats. You required it for distribution among some of the more necessitous in your barnabotti following, so as to ensure us their votes at the meeting of the Grand Council that was to follow. What does one say to a man – a patrician of Venice – who can stoop to so loathly a fraud?'

Vendramin clenched his hands. 'By the Sacrament! Wait before you judge. Wait until you learn how I was justified…'

'Nothing can justify a gentleman in stealing and lying,' he was answered. 'I will not hear you now, or ever again. There is the door, sir. I beg you to go.'

But Vendramin had still a card to play; the last card standing between himself and ruin; between himself and destitution and a debtor's prison. For the moment it were bruited abroad that he was not to marry Isotta Pizzamano, his creditors would come down upon him like kites upon a carcase.

He might yet succeed in so bursting the bubble of their silly pride that they would be glad to have him marry the girl, thief and liar though they called him.

But Destiny was to interfere to prevent the playing of that soiled card.

'You think I can be dismissed like that?' he began theatrically.

Domenico cut him short. 'The servants can throw you out if you prefer it.'

And then the door opened, and a lackey entered. He came to announce Major Sanfermo; but to their surprise the Major followed instantly upon the announcement without waiting to be bidden.

He uncovered and bowed respectfully to the Count, who stared frowning uncomprehending displeasure at this intrusion. Then erect in his bright red coat with its steel gorget, the officer formally turned to Domenico and very formally addressed him.

'Captain Pizzamano, I am here to execute an order of the Council of Ten for your arrest.'

Chapter 35

The Hero of the Lido

This order for the arrest of the hero of the Lido, who a few days ago had received the thanks of the Senate for his gallantry, was one of the last submissions that the moribund Republic was called upon to make.

It was consistent with the irresolute conduct of the rulers of Venice that, whilst on the one hand extolling Domenico Pizzamano's patriotic fidelity to duty, on the other they were offering the French General-in-Chief their abject apologies for the deed in which that fidelity had been expressed.

Instructions to placate Bonaparte were sent to the two envoys, who were on their way to the General with the Senate's docile answer to his ultimatum by Junot. Those envoys reached the General at Palmanuova and requested an audience. The request was answered by a letter in which Bonaparte described the death of Laugier as an assassination, and further described it in the inflated language that the revolutionists had made current as 'an event without parallel in the history of modern nations'. In the same language the letter went on to apostrophize them. 'You and your Senate are dripping with French blood.' Finally, it consented to receive them only if they had anything to communicate on the subject of Laugier.

Humbly those two middle-aged representatives of that old patrician order came before the tempestuous young upstart of genius who commanded the Army of Italy.

They beheld a short, lean, tired-looking young man, whose black hair hung dank and ragged across a bulging, pallid brow, whose hazel eyes, large and luminous, stared at them in hostility.

Rudely he interrupted the considered speech in which one of them expressed Venetian friendship. He broke into unmeasured invective against the Most Serene Republic's perfidy. French blood had been shed. The army cried out for vengeance.

He moved restlessly about the room, as he talked in fluent Southern Italian, working himself into a passion real or pretended, and waving his arms in a vigour of gesticulation.

He spoke of the atrocity of Laugier's death, and he demanded the arrest and surrender to him of the officer who had given the order to fire upon the *Libérateur*. From this he went on to demand the immediate release of all those detained in Venetian prisons for political offences, among whom he knew that there were many French. In the ranting theatrical cant of the politicians of his adopted country, he invoked the spirit of his murdered soldiers crying out for vengeance. The climax of his tirade came in the final announcement of his will.

'I will have no more inquisitors. I will have no more Senate. I will be Attila for the State of Venice.'

Such was the report which the envoys brought home.

At the same time Villetard came back with a letter from Bonaparte to Lallemant, in which the French Ambassador was ordered to depart, leaving Villetard as chargé d'affaires.

'French blood flows in Venice,' the General wrote, 'and you are still there. Are you waiting to be driven out? Write a short note appropriate to the circumstances and leave the city immediately.'

The report of the envoys was so terrifying and the conviction so clear of a declaration of war to follow that the Council of Ten wasted no time in complying with the intransigent demands.

The political prisoners in the Leads were restored to liberty, the inquisitors of state were placed under arrest, and it fell to Major Sanfermo's lot to be sent to secure the person of Domenico Pizzamano.

To Count Pizzamano, who had not been in his place in the Council when these measures were decreed, the arrest of his son was the last test of endurance. When Major Sanfermo informed him that he understood that the order resulted from a demand of the French General-in-Chief, the Count could not doubt that Domenico's life was forfeit, that he was to be a scapegoat for the cowardice and weakness of the Government.

He stood stricken, trembling, vaguely conscious that Isotta was at his side, hanging upon his arm. Then, as mastering himself, he looked round, his glance fell upon Vendramin standing there at a loss, momentarily stupefied by the nature of this interruption.

'Why do you wait, sir?' the Count asked him.

And the mortified Vendramin, who was realizing that he had lost all, that he was baulked, by the thunderbolt that had fallen upon this house, of even his last desperate attempt at redemption, slunk out in silent, baffled rage. Deep in his heart he bore the malevolent resolve to return, if only for the satisfaction of flinging his handful of mud at the escutcheon of these proud Pizzamani, who in his own view had so infamously cheated him.

Domenico waited until he had gone, then quietly addressed the officer. 'If you will give me a moment with my father, Major, I shall be at your service.'

But Sanfermo, grim of countenance, surprised them.

'Now that we are alone, I may speak out. I could hardly have done so before Vendramin. My confidence in him is not stout enough for that. I am under orders which I frankly tell you are in the last degree repugnant to me. When I received them, I considered whether I would break my sword and fling it with my service at the feet of the Doge. But... ' He shrugged. 'Others would have taken my place here.' Then, on another tone he proceeded. 'Lord Count, the knell of the Serenissima has sounded. The envoys returning from Bonaparte bring the demand that if war is to be averted, the patrician government must be deposed. He demands the abolition of our oligarchy, and its replacement by a Jacobin democracy. The Lion of Saint Mark is to be flung from his pedestal, and the Tree of Liberty is to be raised in the Piazza. He demands no less than this.'

'Democracy!' It was an ejaculation of pain and scorn from the Count. 'The government of Demos. The government by all that is base in a nation. The ruling of a state by its populace, its lowest elements. The very negation of all that government implies. That is even worse than what I feared for Venice, which was that it might become an Imperial province.'

'That, it seems, is to follow. The democratic government is but a step to it; a sham. The news from Klagenfurt is that the Treaty of Loeben under which peace has been made provides for the cession of the Venetian territories to Austria in exchange for Lombardy. It is clear, my lord, that here there is no more to be done.' He paused, and, instinctively lowering his voice, more directly expressed his mind. 'From Verona we hear that Count Emili and seven others who attempted to vindicate the honour of Venice have been shot by the French. No honest Venetian could suffer that Captain Pizzamano should be added to the roll of martyrs.' He turned to Domenico. 'That is why deliberately I have come alone to effect your arrest. I have brought no men with me. I am easily overpowered. A gondola would take you to San Giorgio in Alga, where the galleys of your friend Admiral Correr are stationed. In one of these you could reach Trieste, and make your way to Vienna.'

When they had recovered from their amazement in the presence of such generosity, there was a cry of relief from the Count, an invocation by him of blessings on the head of this good friend and true Venetian.

But Domenico had yet a word to say.

'Have you thought, sir, of the consequences? Of the consequences to Venice? And perhaps to Major Sanfermo? My arrest becomes a political measure. It is an integral part of the demand of the French Commander, one of the conditions he imposes if he is not to turn his guns on Venice. Is it not also possible that Major Sanfermo may be shot in my place by French vindictiveness, for not having taken proper measures to secure me? Is not that in accordance with French methods?'

'I will take my chance of that,' said Sanfermo, with a stout, careless laugh. 'After all it is a chance. For you, Captain Pizzamano, I tell you frankly there is no chance at all.'

But Domenico shook his head. 'Even if I could profit by your generosity, I must weigh the other consequences that these French brigands would visit upon Venice for my escape.' He unbuckled his sword-belt as he spoke. 'My heart is full of gratitude and wonder. But I cannot take advantage of your generosity. Here is my sword, sir.'

The Count stood grey-faced but grim in the iron self-control which birth and honour imposed upon him. Isotta, trembling, clung to him for strength of body and of spirit.

Domenico came to them. 'If Venice demands of you the sacrifice of a son, at least the sacrifice is one that does us honour. And I may thank God that in his mercy he should have permitted my last action to have been the deliverance of our house from the necessity of making a sacrifice also of its daughter, and a sacrifice that would have been ignoble.'

Not trusting himself to speak, the Count took him in his arms, and pressed him almost convulsively to his breast.

Chapter 36

Deliverance

The inquisitors of state, arrested by order of the Doge and Council, who flung to the lions every victim demanded of them, were conveyed to confinement in San Giorgio Maggiore. The same decree, promulgated in response to the crack of the whip of the French master, opened the prisons of those, amongst others, whose fate until that moment had lain in the hands of the Three.

To many of them it must have been as a sudden transition from darkness into light, leaving them dazzled and uncertain. To none was it more so than to Marc-Antoine.

Descending, with others, the Giant's Staircase in the dusk, given egress by the guards at the Porta della Carta, beyond which he found mounted two pieces of ordnance, he stood in the agitated, curious, vociferating concourse on the Piazzetta, and for a moment did not know whither to turn his steps.

To determine him, orientation was first necessary; he must learn what had been taking place during those weeks of his confinement, shut off from all news of the world. Before his eyes, in the guns at the Porta della Carta and in the double file of soldiers drawn up under arms along the whole length of the Ducal Palace, was the evidence of portents.

After some self-questioning he concluded that the only safe place in which to seek the needed information was the Casa Pizzamano.

He was in an unkempt condition, and he had not been shaved for two days. His linen was soiled and his toilet generally deplorable. But that was no matter, although he was grateful for the dusk that mercifully veiled it. He still had some money in his pocket, remaining over from all out of which his gaoler had swindled him for maintenance.

He pushed his way through the more or less turbulent crowd, and, hailing a gondola at the Piazzetta steps, had himself carried off to San Daniele.

It was some hours after Domenico had departed under arrest, and Marc-Antoine came now to a house of mourning. He sensed it from the moment his foot touched the wide marble steps and entered the noble vestibule, where, although night had completely closed in, the porter was only just kindling a flame in the great gilded ship's lantern by which the place was lighted.

The man looked hard at Marc-Antoine before he recognized him; then he summoned an assistant as lugubrious as himself to conduct his excellency.

Above-stairs lackeys moved silent and soft-footed as if in a house of death.

Amid the splendours of the untenanted salon Marc-Antoine waited, uneasily wondering, until, pallid, sombre, and gaunt, the Count stood before him in the candlelight.

'I am glad to see you at last delivered, Marc. It is a condition for which you are to thank the French.' In bitterness he added: 'The rulers of this Venice for which you have laboured would never have treated you as generously. They have a different way with those who serve them. Domenico has gone to reap the reward of his loyal conduct. They have taken him to Murano. He is a prisoner there in the fortress of San Michele.'

'Domenico!' Marc-Antoine was appalled. 'But why?'

'So that presently he may face a firing-party.'

'I mean on what pretext? What has he done?'

'He had the temerity to carry out the orders of the Government he served, and fired on a French warship that sought to force an entrance to the Port of Lido. The French have asked for his head in expiation, and the brave Manin is tossing it to them.'

Marc-Antoine looked into those weary, blood-injected eyes in speechless sympathy both of sorrow and of anger.

The Count invited him to sit, and, moving past him on dragging feet, flung himself, a man limp and jaded, into a chair. Marc-Antoine, disregarding the invitation, merely wheeled to face him.

'The boy's poor mother is almost out of her mind, and Isotta is not much better. I boasted that I was ready without a tremor to surrender everything to this Republic. Do not suppose that I boasted of more than the event proved me able to perform. To save Venice I would have given son and daughter, life and wealth. But this... This is just waste and wanton immolation that was never in my reckoning.' He sank his head to his hand with a little moan of weariness and pain, and he remained so whilst Marc-Antoine, heavy-hearted, looked on. Thus for a long moment. Then, abruptly rousing himself, he looked up again. 'Forgive me, Marc. I have no right to trouble you with all this.'

'My dear Count! Do you think I do not share your sorrow? Do you forget that I, too, loved Domenico?'

'Thank you, my friend. Now that you are delivered, tell me in what I can serve you, if it is still in my power to serve any man. Now that we have reached the end there will be nothing to keep you in Venice. In fact, it may not even be safe for you to linger.'

Mechanically Marc-Antoine answered him: 'It certainly will not if the French are coming. It will profit nobody that I end my days before a firing-party.'

'I heard this morning that there is an English squadron at Pola,' said the Count. 'Admiral Correr is at San Giorgio in Alga, and at a word from me would send you there in his fastest galley.'

'Ah!' Marc-Antoine's glance brightened with inspiration.

He stood chin in hand, for a thoughtful moment. Then at last he found himself a chair and begged the Count to tell him briefly all that had happened in these last weeks. The Count told him, but not briefly, because Marc-Antoine himself thwarted the brevity he had begged. At every stage he interrupted the Count with questions upon detail.

But at the end of a half-hour the tale was told, and Marc-Antoine stood up again now fully instructed.

'I challenge you,' the Count said, as he rose with him, 'to find me in all history a more lamentable page.' And then, anticipating the question Marc-Antoine most desired to ask, he spoke of Isotta. 'Amid this ruin I can at least thank God that my daughter is spared from marriage with a dishonoured scoundrel.'

Marc-Antoine's eyes were suddenly alight. Yet his only comment, far indeed from expressing the sudden uplift in his soul, was: 'So! You have found him out.' He did not press for details. For the moment the miraculous fact itself contented him. His voice vibrated deeply. 'Then it may yet prove that my journey to Venice has not been entirely wasted.' He swept on without giving the Count time to speak, so that his next question seemed (quite falsely) to supply the explanation. 'It may yet be that the salvation of your son shall follow. I may yet take him with me to those British ships at Pola.'

The Count stared in sudden fierceness. 'Take Domenico? Are you mad?'

'Perhaps. But have you not observed that madmen often prevail in this world?' He held out his hand in leave-taking. 'Unless I fail you, you shall have word of me very soon again.'

'Fail? But what have you in mind?'

Marc-Antoine smiled into those tired eyes. 'Suspend your despair until this time tomorrow, sir. If you have not heard from me by then, you may mourn me together with Domenico. That is all now. It is idle to talk of what may never be accomplished. I go to see what I can do.'

Abruptly he departed.

Half-an-hour later Battista, the landlord of the Swords, was gaping at the ill-kempt, unshaven figure that stood before him asking for Philibert.

'Virgin Most Holy!' ejaculated the paunchy little man. 'But it is our Englishman come back from the dead!'

'Not quite so far, Battista. Where is that rascal of mine, and where is my baggage?'

One and the other were produced. Philibert had remained in the employment of the inn. At the sight of his master he almost fell on his knees in the ardour of thanksgiving. Marc-Antoine, in haste, cut short this ecstasy. He carried off Philibert to his old rooms which were standing vacant.

At the end of an hour he came forth again metamorphosed. Shaved, and his hair carefully dressed, he had arrayed himself as nearly in the livery of Jacobinism as his wardrobe permitted: buckskins and Hessian boots, a long brown riding-coat with silver buttons, a white neckcloth very full and plain, and a conical hat on which, as if to contradict the rest, he had pinned the blue-and-yellow cockade of Venice. For weapons he put a pistol in each of the ample pockets of his full-skirted coat and tucked a cudgel under his arm.

A gondola carried him through the night, wafted by the soft balmy air of early May. By dark oily canals on which flickered reflections of illuminated windows he came to the Madonna dell' Orto, and by the narrow alley in which two months ago he had all but lost his life, to the Corte del Cavallo and the French Legation.

Chapter 37

The Order of Release

The doorkeeper of the Della Vecchia Palace, whom Marc-Antoine's appearance startled, startled the visitor in return with the information that the Citizen Lallemant was no longer at the legation. Nor did Marc-Antoine by any means recover his calm when he heard that the Citizen Villetard was in charge. He had the feeling that in Villetard, who was the creature of Bonaparte, he would meet a sterner opposition than that which Lallemant might have offered.

Because of this when presently under the amazed glances of the chargé d'affaires and the secretary Jacob, who were at work together, he walked hat on head into the room that had been Lallemant's, his air carried all the truculence of the Jacobin in office that he could pack into it.

Villetard sprang to his feet in amazement. 'Lebel! Where the devil have you been these weeks?'

No question could have done more to restore Marc-Antoine's courage. It resolved the one doubt in his mind; assured him that the one danger he might face in coming thus into the lair of the wolf was not present.

Coldly he looked his questioner up and down as if the question were presumptuous. 'Where I was needed, of course,' he answered dryly.

'Where you were needed! Don't you think you were needed here?' He flung open a dispatch-box, and pulled out a sheaf of papers. 'Look at these letters from the Directory for you, all awaiting your attention. Lallemant told me you had not been seen since the day I left for Klagenfurt. He began to fear that you had been murdered.' He dropped the sheaf ill-humouredly on the table within Marc-Antoine's reach. 'Will you explain yourself?'

Marc-Antoine was languidly turning over the letters. There were five, all sealed, and all addressed to the Citizen Representative Camille Lebel. His eyebrows went high above the cold light eyes that fixed Villetard.

'Explain myself? To whom are you speaking, Villetard?'

'And – sacred name of a name! – what are you doing with that cockade in your hat?'

'If in the discharge of my functions I find it necessary to display the Venetian colours – just as I choose to call myself Mr Melville – what affair may that be of yours? Do you know that I find you presumptuous?'

'You give yourself airs, I think.'

'And this being chargé d'affaires here seems to have gone to your head. I asked you just now to whom you suppose that you are speaking. I shall be glad of an answer.'

'A thousand devils! I know to whom I am speaking.'

'I am glad to hear it. I was wondering if I should have to show you my papers, so as to remind you that in Venice I am the plenipotentiary of the Directory of the French Republic.'

Browbeaten, the browbeater changed his tone. He took refuge in remonstrance. 'Name of a name, Lebel, what necessity is there for this?'

'That is what I have been wondering: why it should be necessary for me to remind you that I am here not to take orders, but to give them.'

'To give them?'

'At need. And that is why I have come tonight.' He looked round for a chair, drew one up to the table, sat down and crossed his legs.

'Sit down, Villetard.'

Mechanically Villetard obeyed him.

Marc-Antoine took up one of the letters from the pile, broke the seal, and spread the sheet. When he had read he commented.

'Barras is behind the fair. Here he urges me to do what is done already.'

He opened a second one and scanned it. 'Always the same instructions. Faith! They must be tender in Paris of an adequate pretext for this declaration of war. As I told Lallemant, I provided pretext enough over the matter of the ci-devant Comte de Provence: that is to say, I laid stress on the pretext that existed. But we are becoming as mawkish as if we were under a theatrical régime of aristocrats. We are much too solicitous about the opinion of the despots who still rule in Europe. To hell with all despots, I say. When I die, Villetard, that sentiment will be found engraved on my heart.'

Thus he ranted on whilst he opened the letters, one after the other. Suddenly he found something momentarily to silence him. Then with a snort of contempt he read out the sentence that had riveted his attention.

'General Bonaparte is prone to precipitate and high-handed action. In this matter of a casus belli, you will see that his impatiences are restrained, and you will take care that there is no premature action. All must be done in correct form. To ensure this you must at need exercise the authority in which you are vested.'

Having read it, he folded that letter with the others, and stuffed the bundle into an inner breast-pocket. It was just as well that Villetard should not see that particular letter, for the passage that Marc-Antoine had read aloud had been considerably embellished by improvisations of his own. 'There is nothing in these,' he commented, 'to justify your excitement at the delay in my receiving them. They tell me nothing that I did not know, give me no instructions that I have not already carried out.' He looked across at

Villetard, and smiled sardonically. 'You want to know where I have been, do you?'

Villetard, impressed by what he had heard, even whilst scornful of some of it, made haste to assure him: 'Oh, but as a matter of concern.'

Jacob, all eyes and ears, pretended to busy himself with the papers before him.

Marc-Antoine's manner diminished in arrogance to increase in sarcasm.

'As the plenipotentiary of the Directory I have been doing what you considered beneath the dignity of your office; discharging the functions of an agent-provocateur. To be more precise, I have been with my friend Captain Pizzamano at the Fort of Sant' Andrea. Now perhaps you understand how it happens that one of these milksop Venetians had the temerity to fire upon a French warship.'

Villetard leaned forward, round-eyed. 'My God!' was all that he said.

'Just so. As an agent-provocateur I have every reason to account myself a success.'

The other smote the table with his hand. 'That explains it. When it occurred, I could hardly believe it. It seemed impossible that any of these effete aristocrats should have so much audacity in his bowels. But what a waste when in the Verona business we had all the casus belli that we needed!'

'Yes. But pretexts can hardly be over-multiplied. Besides, news of the Verona affair hadn't reached us in the Fort Sant' Andrea when at last the *Libérateur d'Italie* gave me the chance for which I waited. I pulled the strings and the Pizzamano puppet danced, with the result that a perfectly justifiable state of war now exists.'

'And you did that?' Villetard was lost in wonder.

'I did it. But I want no scapegoat for my action, Villetard.'

'How?'

'I have interrupted other important work to come here tonight to ask you what blockhead is guilty of ordering Pizzamano's arrest.'

'Blockhead!' At last the sneer so habitual to it came back to Villetard's countenance. 'Perhaps you'll choose some other term when I tell you that the order came from General Bonaparte.'

But Marc-Antoine was not impressed. 'A blockhead is a blockhead, whether he commands the Army of Italy or burns charcoal in a forest of the Ardennes. General Bonaparte has proved himself a great soldier; the greatest soldier in Europe today...'

'He will be encouraged by your commendation.'

'I hope so. But I am not encouraged by your sarcasm, and I dislike being interrupted. What was I saying? Oh, yes. General Bonaparte may be a genius in military matters; but this is not a military matter; it is a political one. Politically the arrest of Captain Pizzamano is a blunder of the first magnitude. When I made him a hero, I had no intention that he should in addition be made a martyr. That is not merely unnecessary, but dangerous. Extraordinarily dangerous. It may lead to grave trouble here.'

'Who cares?' said Villetard.

'Every man with the rudiments of intelligence. I happen to be one of them. And I have more than a suspicion that the members of the Directory will care. Care very much. It is foolish to precipitate trouble that can be avoided. Therefore, Villetard, you will oblige me by issuing at once an order for the release of Captain Pizzamano.'

'Release Captain Pizzamano!' Villetard was scandalized. 'Release that butcher of Frenchmen?'

Marc-Antoine waved a hand delicately contemptuous. 'You may leave that cant for the official publications. Between you and me it is not impressive. I require this man's immediate and unconditional release.'

'You require it? Oh, you require it? And Bonaparte has required his arrest. Behold the amusing clash of great wills. You will defy the Little Corporal, will you?'

'As the representative of the Directory, and in doing what I consider the Directory would require me to do, I will defy the devil himself, Villetard, and not be troubled about it.'

The chargé d'affaires stared harder than ever. At last he shrugged his shoulder and uttered a snort of laughter. 'In that case, my faith, you had better issue the order yourself.'

'I would have done so already if my signature would be recognized by the Venetian Government. Unfortunately, I am accredited only here at the legation. We are wasting time, Villetard.'

'We'll continue to waste it as long as you ask anything so preposterous. I daren't issue such an order. I should have to account to Bonaparte for it.'

'If you don't issue it, you will have to account to the Directory for disobedience to their plenipotentiary. And that may be even more serious for you.'

They looked at each other: Marc-Antoine with an air of faint amusement; Villetard sullenly at bay.

Jacob from under his brows watched with interest this duel of wills, carefully concealing his excitement.

At last the chargé d'affaires pushed back his chair and rose.

'It is useless. I will not do it. I tell you I dare not. Bonaparte is capable of having me shot.'

'What? If it were done upon my order? Upon my responsibility? Are you mad?'

'Will your authority, your responsibility, cover me with General Bonaparte?'

'Will you forever cast your General Bonaparte in my teeth?' Marc-Antoine, too, stood up, impatient, angry. 'Do you recognize in me the voice of the French Government, or do you not?'

Out-hectored, Villetard was in despair. He clenched his hands, set his teeth, and at last discovered a way out. 'Give it to me in writing, then!' he cried.

'In writing? The order? Why not? Citizen Jacob, be good enough to write for me.' And he dictated:

'In the name of the Directory of the French Republic, I require Charles Villetard, the French chargé d'affaires in Venice, to issue at once an order to the Doge and Senate of the Most

Serene Republic for the immediate and unconditional release of Captain Domenico Pizzamano, at present detained in the Fortress of San Michele on the Island of Murano.'

He took up a quill from the table. 'Add the date,' he commanded, 'and I will sign it.'

The scratching of Jacob's pen ceased. He rose to place the document before Marc-Antoine. In a hand that much practice had made perfect, Marc-Antoine scrawled at the foot of the sheet the signature and description:

'Camille Lebel, Plenipotentiary Representative of the Directory of the French Republic, One and Indivisible.'

With a touch of scorn he handed the document to Villetard. 'There is your aegis and gorgoneion.'

Villetard scowled over it; he stood hesitant, pulling at his lip; finally he shrugged in ill-humoured resignation.

'So be it,' he said. 'The responsibility is yours. I'll send the order to the Senate in the morning.'

But this did not suit Marc-Antoine. 'You will deliver it to me now, as soon as it is written. I want Captain Pizzamano out of prison before it is even known that he has been put there. You should remember that to the Venetians he is the Hero of the Lido. I want no disturbance such as the news of his arrest might create.'

Villetard flung himself down in his chair, took his pen, and rapidly wrote the order. He signed it and added the seal of the legation. Then, having dusted it with pounce, he handed the completed document to Marc-Antoine.

'I would not be in your shoes for an empire when the Little Corporal hears of this.'

'Ah! And yet, my dear Villetard, they are good solid shoes, of Directoire pattern. I think they will bear my weight if I walk delicately.'

Chapter 38

Discovery

The little lady who called herself Vicomtesse de Saulx was restless and unhappy.

However vexatious to Lallemant might have been the disappearance of Mr Melville and the accumulation at the legation of unclaimed letters addressed to Camille Lebel by the Directory, to her the matter was a source of deepest anxiety. Her besetting fear was that he might again, and this time definitely, have fallen a victim to the vindictiveness of Vendramin. Herself, she could not pursue the matter because Vendramin, in wholesome fear of her after what had happened, now kept his distance. Moreover, his supplies exhausted and without means of renewing them, the man was no longer even to be met in the casinos which formerly he had frequented.

She pestered Lallemant to get on the track of the Venetian. But Lallemant, feeling that he could take no measures without perhaps seriously compromising the supposed Lebel, was doomed to inaction.

It had become her daily habit to visit the legation in quest of news of the missing man. In the pursuit of this habit, she came to Villetard on the morning after Marc-Antoine's visit.

The chargé d'affaires was alone at the time and considerably disgruntled. He was far from easy on the score of this Pizzamano business. Unlike Lebel, he held no mandate from the Government.

He was Bonaparte's creature. And his view of the little Corsican soldier was that he was by no means the most reasonable of men when he was thwarted. Having slept on the matter of that order of release, he was deeply troubled. He balanced desperately between a sense that he had acted unwisely in yielding and a conviction that in view of Lebel's authority he could not have done otherwise. He felt that he was in an unfortunate position in being placed by circumstances between the military and the civil power. It seemed to him inevitable that in any clash between them, he must be crushed unless he moved carefully.

He was poring again over that covering note which Marc-Antoine had left with him and wondering uncomfortably what Bonaparte would have to say about it, when the Vicomtesse entered his room unannounced, and flitted towards him with a mild 'Good-morning, Villetard!'

He was by temperament a man who delighted in the sight of pretty women, and normally the contemplation of the Vicomtesse was a source of pleasure to him. This morning, however, he considered her almost malevolently. In a growling tone he anticipated her daily question.

'You may take satisfaction in the fact that your Monsieur Melville has at last turned up again.'

With flushed cheek and brightened eye she ran round to him. She leaned her arm on his shoulder whilst she questioned him. He answered her gloomily, resenting a gladness he was so very far from sharing. The fellow was well; completely – too completely – recovered. On the subject of his absence Villetard was vague. Lebel's instructions that his identity was to remain veiled were so very definite. Pressed, the chargé d'affaires took refuge in the statement that Monsieur Melville had been in convalescence at the Casa Pizzamano.

This took a little of the joy out of the lady's countenance. Her brow was puckered in thought as she continued to lean on Villetard's shoulder. It was then that her idly straying eyes fell on the document lying before him on his table. The signature arrested her attention.

Another might not so quickly have perceived what was instantly obvious to the Vicomtesse. The occupation that for some considerable time now she had been following had cultivated her observation and had sharpened her power of swift inference. The glance that saw the signature read the date, and instantly she expressed the result of the addition of those factors.

'Camille Lebel is here in Venice!'

That exclamation of surprise at once fired a train in the no less quick wits of the chargé d'affaires. He flung himself back in his chair the better to look up at her.

'You know Camille Lebel?' For all its interrogative note, it was an assertion – and an amazed assertion – rather than a question.

'Know him?' There was an unmistakable significance in her glance. A little smile, bitter-sweet, curled her lip. 'Faith, I have some cause to know him, Villetard. To know him very well. In a sense I am his creation. It was he who made me Vicomtesse de Saulx.'

She saw amazement change to horror in that pallid, sardonic, upturned face.

'And you ask me if he is in Venice? You ask me that? Name of God!'

He was on his feet suddenly, thrusting away her arm, sending his chair crashing over behind him. 'Then who in the devil's name is this scoundrel who impersonates him? Who is your Monsieur Melville?'

She shrank before the fury of his aspect. 'Mr Melville? Mr Melville, Lebel! Are you mad, Villetard?'

'Mad!' he roared. 'I think they must all have been mad here. What is it? A legation, or a lunatic asylum? What was that fool Lallemant doing that he never suspected this? And – my God! – what were you doing that you never discovered it before?' He strode upon her furiously, a man out of his senses with rage and fear.

She retreated before him again. 'I? What had I to do with it? How was I to discover it? It was never whispered even that Melville called himself Lebel.'

'No.' Villetard remembered with what specious cunning that swindler – whoever he might be – had insisted upon the secrecy of his supposed identity. He curbed his anger before the urgent need to think. He stood still, his head in his hands, and fell to muttering.

'Bonaparte has always believed Lallemant to be a fool. My God! That doesn't begin to do the fellow justice. This man here during all these months! The secrets of the legation all open to him! The havoc he may have wrought! Rocco Terzi's end is explained, and Sartoni's. God knows whom else he may have betrayed.' He looked at her with fierce, brooding eyes. 'I marvel that he should have spared you.' Then, swift suspicion mounting in him to renew his rage, he advanced upon her threateningly once more. He took her roughly by the shoulder. 'Will you tell me, in God's name, why he did. You were not by any chance in this with him, you little trull? Answer me! Do you take the pay of both sides like every other damned spy I've ever known? Bah!' He flung her from him. 'Your neck's not worth wringing. I've other work to do. There's this order of release. Sacred name! What am I to say to the Little Corporal? He will break me for this, unless... By God! I'll have this rascal before a firing-party, anyway.'

He turned from her, and strode for the door. She heard him on the landing outside bawling furiously for Jacob. He came back wild-eyed, leaving the door open. He waved her out.

'Away with you! Go! I have work to do.'

She did not wait for a second bidding. It was not only that she had become afraid of him. She had become even more afraid of something else. His threat to have the false Lebel before a firing-party brought home to her how she had inadvertently betrayed Marc-Antoine, in what danger she had placed him. She fled, calling herself a fool for having talked so incautiously. Villetard's first exclamation should have warned her.

As she crossed the Corte del Cavallo almost at a run, she had no thought or care for what Marc might be, or for her duty to the side she served. All that she considered was that she had placed him in deadly peril. Through her brain like a reverberation rang Villetard's words: 'I marvel that he should have spared you. Will you tell me – in God's name – why he did?'

It was the question that she now asked herself. Being what he was, he must have known her for what she was. Why, then, had he not denounced her to the inquisitors of state? If his having spared her was not all the reason why now she must make every effort to warn him and save him, negligent of consequences to herself, at least it was an additional spur to the one that her heart must in any case have supplied.

As eleven o'clock was striking from Madonna dell' Orto, and pealing over Venice from its other belfries, she stood undecided on the fondamenta where her gondola waited. Where was he? How was she to reach him? From the stormy scene with Villetard came recollection that the chargé d'affaires had said that during the time of his disappearance he had been at the Casa Pizzamano. If that was true, even if he were not there now, the Pizzamani would know where he might be reached.

At about the same moment that she was being handed aboard and bidding her gondolier to take her to San Daniele, Marc-Antoine was landing with Domenico on the steps of the Casa Pizzamano.

He had lost no time once the order of release was in his hands, for he realized the danger of delays. So as to be ready for action as soon as daylight came, he had wrested that same night from the Doge, in exchange for the note from the legation, the warrant that should open the door of Domenico's prison on Murano.

The news of the captain's home-coming ran through the palace like a fired powder-train which increases in crackling vigour as it flares. From porter to chamberlain, from chamberlain to lackeys, from lackeys to serving-maids, the rumour ran; so that before they had reached the salon the house was agog with it, to an accompaniment of fleet steps, slamming doors and excited voices.

Francesco Pizzamano with his Countess and Isotta came to the two men where they stood waiting. The Countess sped ahead of them, and father and sister yielded glad precedence to the mother, who in tears gathered to her bosom the son whom yesterday she had accounted doomed. She crooned over him as she had crooned over him when he was a babe, so that he was brought himself to the very brink of tears.

Tears were in the eyes of Isotta when she kissed him, and of the Count, who took him to his heart. Then, that transport easing, all asked him at once by what miracle he was delivered.

'Behold the miracle-worker,' he said, and so drew attention at last to Marc-Antoine, where he stood in the background, a grave spectator.

The Count strode to him and embraced him. The Countess, following, did the same. Last came Isotta, slim and straight, with very wistful eyes, to take his hand, hesitate a moment, and then set him trembling by a kiss upon his cheek.

Francesco Pizzamano dashed what remained of tears from his eyes. But his voice faltered and broke as he cried: 'I possess nothing, sir, that is not yours for the asking.'

'He may take you at your word,' said Domenico, with cryptic humour, in an attempt to steady these emotions.

Marc-Antoine stood forward. 'Lord Count, this is less of a deliverance than an escape.' He raised his hand to stay an interruption. 'Have no fear. It is not an escape for which Venice will be held responsible. It is covered by an order from the French Legation, bearing the signature of the chargé d'affaires. I wrung it from him in my superior capacity as the plenipotentiary Lebel.' Then he smiled a little. 'At this time yesterday I was persuaded that I had played the part of Lebel in vain for a whole year. Now I discover a sufficient reason for it.' Then he resumed his earlier tone. 'Because an accident may at any moment discover the deception, Domenico must lose no time. The gondola that brought us from Murano will take him on to San Giorgio in Alga and the Admiral, so that he may be conveyed to Trieste and thence journey to Vienna, to lie there until all is safe again.'

Joy in his preservation outweighed the pain this severance must otherwise have caused. There was instant agreement and instant bustle of preparation. It was Isotta who undertook to supervise the packing of his necessaries. She departed on that errand almost in relief to escape from the presence of Marc-Antoine, a presence which today should have been to her as the opening wide of the gates of happiness and fulfilment.

When at the end of a half-hour she came back to inform them that all was ready and that Domenico's packages were being loaded in the gondola, the lackey who held the door for her followed her into the room to announce at the same time that Madame la Vicomtesse de Saulx was below asking to see Messer Melville immediately. The servant took it upon himself to add that the lady seemed deeply agitated.

The announcement made a curious hush in that room, a hush which had no mystery for Marc-Antoine. He was less concerned to speculate why the lady should seek him here than to be thankful for her presence.

He begged leave to have her introduced, and in a complete and rather constrained silence they awaited her coming.

She entered breathlessly. She checked a moment within the threshold, her anxious eyes questing this way and that until they rested on Marc-Antoine. Then, with a little gasp, she gathered up her flowered panniers, and fluttered across to him.

'Marc! Oh, God be thanked!' She caught him by the arms in her excitement, disregarding utterly the other tenants of the room. 'My dear, I have done a dreadful, dreadful thing. It was an accident. A miserable accident. You'll never suppose that I would consciously have betrayed you, whatever I had discovered. You know that I am incapable of that. I did not know that you were impersonating Camille Lebel. How could I? And I told Villetard... No, I didn't tell him. It came out by accident. I was unaware of what I was really telling him. I have let him know that you are not Lebel.' Thus, breathlessly, confusedly, in her anxiety to announce and to explain, she got it out.

Marc-Antoine caught her wrist. He spoke sharply in his alarm.

'What exactly have you told him?'

She explained it all: the document she had seen, and the manner in which the truth had been surprised from her. To Marc-Antoine it was instantly clear. To the others it was but a deeper mystification. Then came her more definite warning, the announcement of Villetard's avowed intentions.

'You must go, Marc. I don't know how. But go. Don't waste a moment.'

He had recovered and now preserved his momentarily shaken calm. 'We have a little time. Villetard must first procure an order from the Doge; then find men to execute it; and finally these must discover me. I told him that I was to be found at the Inn of the Swords. So that is where they will first seek me; and this must create delays. Without wasting time, then, we need not be precipitate. Your warning, madame, is a very noble amend for an error you could not avoid.'

'As to that, I only pay a debt. I perceive now that I owe you for having spared me.'

She would have said much more had she obeyed her impulses. She would have put into words some of the tenderness that was in her eyes as they now regarded him. But the presence of those others, of whom she seemed at length to become aware, imposed restraint. He had not attempted to present her to them. Now that she became conscious of their presence, she perceived the omission and begged him to correct it.

'Ah, yes.' There was an oddness in his manner. He looked at Count Pizzamano and the others, particularly at Isotta, who shared the general sense of mystery. 'Your pardon,' he begged of them, and then to the Vicomtesse: 'By what name shall I present you to these good friends of mine?'

'By what name?' She was bewildered.

He smiled. 'Just as you know that I am not Lebel, so I also know that you are not the Vicomtesse de Saulx.'

There was a little cry from Isotta. Convulsively she gripped the arm of her brother, who knew so well what was passing in her mind.

The Vicomtesse recoiled a pace, amazement and fear in her delicate countenance. Instinctively at once she became the secret agent, on her guard. Instinctively she gathered up her weapons. Her manner changed. The fond, natural child vanished, giving place to the sophisticated woman of the world. Her eyes narrowed.

'And how long may you have been of that opinion?' she asked him.

'Of that conviction from the moment that I met you. Indeed, from the moment that I heard you named.'

The hard, unfaltering stare of those narrowed eyes was evidence of her self-control, as was the hard laugh that seemed to brand his words an impertinence. There was not a quaver in her faintly scornful voice.

'I scarcely know how to set about dispelling so extravagant a delusion. I can only assert that I am certainly the widow of the Vicomte de Saulx.'

'The widow?' interjected Count Pizzamano.

The interjection did not draw her glance. She kept her eyes on Marc-Antoine whilst answering: 'He was guillotined at Tours in ninety-three.'

Gently smiling, Marc-Antoine shook his head. 'I have the best of reasons for knowing that that is not the case, although your friend Lebel believed it.'

Her fear deepened under his odd gaze, half-humorous, half-sad. But resolutely she stood her ground. She tossed her head a little. 'Even if it were true that the Vicomte de Saulx was not guillotined, would that prove that he is not my husband?'

'Oh, no, madame.' He came forward. He took her hand, which in spite of her angry fear she relinquished to him, for there was something compellingly gentle in his manner and pitiful in his eyes, as if to express regret and ask forgiveness for what he did. 'What proves it is that if he had married anyone half so charming, it is impossible that he could have forgotten it. And I can positively assure you that he has no recollection of the marriage. Can it be that, like you, he suffers from a bad memory? For you appear completely to have forgotten what he looks like.'

She drew her hand out of his clasp. Her lip trembled. His words, without meaning to her, gave her the sense of being in a trap. She was bewildered. She looked round and met a curious smile from each of her three observers. The only one who did not smile, whose glance reflected something of the gentle wistfulness in Marc-Antoine's, was Isotta: an Isotta who in these last moments had lost her listlessness, whose eyes, that lately had been so dull, were shining now as with an inner light.

Then the poor, dazed Vicomtesse found that Marc-Antoine had recaptured her hand. Very straight, his chin high, he seemed suddenly to have become protective. So much was she conscious of this that her impulse was to bury her face upon his breast and in the shelter of it yield to the weakness of a woman who is lonely and frightened.

He spoke to the others, quietly firm. 'She shall not be further harassed, further humiliated. It is a poor return for what I owe her.'

The Count and Domenico both bowed as if in understanding and acknowledgment.

'Come, madame. Let me reconduct you.'

Still bewildered, faltering a little in her step, she obeyed the suasion of his hand. Glad to obey it; glad to escape, although she did not know from what. All that she gathered was that sense of his protection, and in that she readily went out with him and down the stairs.

In the vestibule he addressed the liveried porter.

'The gondola of Madame the Vicomtesse de Saulx.'

She looked up at him appealingly as she stood waiting at his side.

'Marc, what is it? You know that I do not understand.'

'Understand this, that in me you have a friend who will always treasure the memory of the debt in which today you have placed him. We part here, Anne, and we may never meet again. But if ever I can serve you, send me word to Avonford in Wiltshire. I will write it for you.'

He stepped into the porter's lodge, and on a sheet of paper supplied by the under-porter, he wrote rapidly in pencil. He handed her the sheet. At the sight of what he had written her face turned bloodless. She looked up at him with an expression that was akin to terror.

'This is impossible. You are mocking me. Why?'

'To what end should I mock you? That is less impossible than it may seem when you consider how Fate links us through Lebel. Oh, yes, I am Marc-Antoine de Saulx, my dear. I was not guillotined, and I never married. Now you understand.'

'And in all these months…'

'It has been my privilege to observe my widow. A unique experience. Come, child, your gondola waits.' He led her out to the marble steps. 'Let us at least part friends, my vicomtesse.' He bowed and kissed her hand, then steadied her as she stepped down into the boat.

As the gondola glided away, be stood a moment looking after that little crumpled heap of silks and laces, upon the cushions of the felza.

Then it occurred to him that even now he did not know her name.

Chapter 39

Departure

When he came back to the salon, Isotta, warned of his approach by his brisk step, was standing near the door.

With a laugh that was almost a sob she stepped straight into his arms, and frankly and openly before them all she kissed him on the lips.

'That is for the mercy that you practised, Marc.'

He kissed her in his turn. 'And this is for the love I bear you. Each an earnest to the other of what must follow.'

The Count advanced, smiling through a natural impatience.

'Let it suffice for today if you are to make sure of the sequel,' he said. 'You have no time to lose, Marc.'

'And I will lose none. Life has just become of great importance. I must preserve it, so as to enjoy the fruits of a Venetian year that yesterday I deemed so barren.'

The Count sighed. 'Fruits gathered in the twilight of our Venice.'

'But from a tree that flourished whilst the sun was high, and rich with the fragrance and sustenance that Venice sheds upon her fruits. That will remain, Lord Count, as long as memory survives in man.'

Rapid steps approached the door. A lackey opened it, and Philibert precipitated himself, plump and breathless, into the room.

'Monsieur! Monsieur!' He ran to Marc-Antoine. 'Save yourself, monsieur. Monsieur the Major Sanfermo is at the Inn of the Swords with six men, waiting to arrest you.'

'Then, how did you get away?'

'He sent me, monsieur.'

'Sent you?'

'To tell you that his orders are to seek you at the Inn of the Swords and that if you should not be there he is to await your return. Faithful to those orders he awaits your return. Wherefore he begs you not to return; but to depart at once from Venice; because in the nature of things he will be unable to wait at the inn for ever. Those are the Major's exact words. So save yourself, monsieur, while there is time. I've brought a valise with some clothes for you.'

'Oh, most thoughtful of valets. You see, Domenico. We had best be going.'

'Where do we go, monsieur?' Philibert inquired.

'We? Do you come with me, then, Philibert?'

'Certainly, monsieur. Anywhere, if only you will abandon this habit of disappearing.'

'Very well, my lad. It will be England, I think.' He turned to Domenico. 'I am in your hands now. You will have to be my sponsor to your friend the Admiral. After that, if he will send us in a galley to this British squadron at Pola, I'll be your sponsor there, and carry you back with me to Avonford.'

'It is more alluring than Vienna, if you can suffer me.'

With a hand on Domenico's shoulder, he put an arm round Isotta's waist, and drew her to him.

'Suffer you! You are a hostage: to be redeemed by your parents when they come to exchange you for their daughter.'

Domenico looked at his father. 'I warned you, sir, that he might take you at your word when you told him that you possessed nothing that was not his for the asking.'

In the breathless moments of farewell, Isotta appeared utterly to have forgotten that once she had harboured a notion of taking the veil.

Rafael Sabatini

Captain Blood

Captain Blood is the much-loved story of a physician and gentleman turned pirate.

Peter Blood, wrongfully accused and sentenced to death, narrowly escapes his fate and finds himself in the company of buccaneers. Embarking on his new life with remarkable skill and bravery, Blood becomes the 'Robin Hood' of the Spanish seas. This is swashbuckling adventure at its best.

The Gates of Doom

'Depend above all on Pauncefort,' announced King James, 'his loyalty is dependable as steel. He is with us body and soul and to the last penny of his fortune.' So when Pauncefort does indeed face bankruptcy after the collapse of the South Sea Company, the king's supreme confidence now seems rather foolish. And as Pauncefort's thoughts turn to gambling, moneylenders and even marriage to recover his debts, will he be able to remain true to the end? And what part will his friend and confidante, Captain Gaynor, play in his destiny?

'A clever story, well and amusingly told' – *The Times*

Rafael Sabatini

The Lost King

The Lost King tells the story of Louis XVII – the French royal who officially died at the age of ten but, as legend has it, escaped to foreign lands where he lived to an old age. Sabatini breathes life into these age-old myths, creating a story of passion, revenge and betrayal. He tells of how the young child escaped to Switzerland from where he plotted his triumphant return to claim the throne of France.

'…the hypnotic spell of a novel which for sheer suspense, deserves to be ranked with Sabatini's best' – *New York Times*

Scaramouche

When a young cleric is wrongfully killed, his friend, André Louis, vows to avenge his death. Louis' mission takes him to the very heart of the French Revolution where he finds the only way to survive is to assume a new identity. And so is born Scaramouche – a brave and remarkable hero of the finest order and a classic and much-loved tale of the greatest swashbuckling tradition.

'Mr Sabatini's novel of the French Revolution has all the colour and lively incident which we expect in his work' – *Observer*

Rafael Sabatini

The Sea Hawk

Sir Oliver, a typical English gentleman, is accused of murder, kidnapped off the Cornish coast, and dragged into life as a Barbary corsair. However Sir Oliver rises to the challenge and proves a worthy hero for this much-admired novel. Religious conflict, melodrama, romance and intrigue combine to create a masterly and highly successful story, perhaps best known for its many film adaptations.

The Shame of Motley

The Court of Pesaro has a certain fool – one Lazzaro Biancomonte of Biancomonte. *The Shame of Motley* is Lazzaro's story, presented with all the vivid colour and dramatic characterisation that has become Sabatini's hallmark.

'Mr Sabatini could not be conventional or commonplace if he tried'
– *Standard*

TITLES BY RAFAEL SABATINI AVAILABLE DIRECT
FROM HOUSE OF STRATUS

Quantity	£	$(US)	$(CAN)	€
FICTION				
ANTHONY WILDING	6.99	11.50	15.99	11.50
THE BANNER OF THE BULL	6.99	11.50	15.99	11.50
BARDELYS THE MAGNIFICENT	6.99	11.50	15.99	11.50
BELLARION	6.99	11.50	15.99	11.50
THE BLACK SWAN	6.99	11.50	15.99	11.50
CAPTAIN BLOOD	6.99	11.50	15.99	11.50
THE CAROLINIAN	6.99	11.50	15.99	11.50
CHIVALRY	6.99	11.50	15.99	11.50
THE CHRONICLES OF CAPTAIN BLOOD	6.99	11.50	15.99	11.50
COLUMBUS	6.99	11.50	15.99	11.50
FORTUNE'S FOOL	6.99	11.50	15.99	11.50
THE FORTUNES OF CAPTAIN BLOOD	6.99	11.50	15.99	11.50
THE GAMESTER	6.99	11.50	15.99	11.50
THE GATES OF DOOM	6.99	11.50	15.99	11.50
THE HOUNDS OF GOD	6.99	11.50	15.99	11.50
THE JUSTICE OF THE DUKE	6.99	11.50	15.99	11.50
THE LION'S SKIN	6.99	11.50	15.99	11.50
THE LOST KING	6.99	11.50	15.99	11.50
LOVE-AT-ARMS	6.99	11.50	15.99	11.50
THE MARQUIS OF CARABAS	6.99	11.50	15.99	11.50
THE MINION	6.99	11.50	15.99	11.50
THE NUPTIALS OF CORBAL	6.99	11.50	15.99	11.50

ALL HOUSE OF STRATUS BOOKS ARE AVAILABLE FROM GOOD BOOKSHOPS OR
DIRECT FROM THE PUBLISHER:

Internet: www.houseofstratus.com including author interviews, reviews, features.

Email: sales@houseofstratus.com please quote author, title and credit card details.

TITLES BY RAFAEL SABATINI AVAILABLE DIRECT
FROM HOUSE OF STRATUS

Quantity	£	$(US)	$(CAN)	€
FICTION				
THE ROMANCE PRINCE	6.99	11.50	15.99	11.50
SCARAMOUCHE	6.99	11.50	15.99	11.50
SCARAMOUCHE THE KING-MAKER	6.99	11.50	15.99	11.50
THE SEA HAWK	6.99	11.50	15.99	11.50
THE SHAME OF MOTLEY	6.99	11.50	15.99	11.50
THE SNARE	6.99	11.50	15.99	11.50
ST MARTIN'S SUMMER	6.99	11.50	15.99	11.50
THE STALKING-HORSE	6.99	11.50	15.99	11.50
THE STROLLING SAINT	6.99	11.50	15.99	11.50
THE SWORD OF ISLAM	6.99	11.50	15.99	11.50
THE TAVERN KNIGHT	6.99	11.50	15.99	11.50
THE TRAMPLING OF THE LILIES	6.99	11.50	15.99	11.50
TURBULENT TALES	6.99	11.50	15.99	11.50
NON-FICTION				
HEROIC LIVES	8.99	14.99	22.50	15.00
THE HISTORICAL NIGHTS' ENTERTAINMENT	8.99	14.99	22.50	15.00
KING IN PRUSSIA	8.99	14.99	22.50	15.00
THE LIFE OF CESARE BORGIA	8.99	14.99	22.50	15.00
TORQUEMADA AND THE SPANISH INQUISITION	8.99	14.99	22.50	15.00

ALL HOUSE OF STRATUS BOOKS ARE AVAILABLE FROM GOOD BOOKSHOPS OR
DIRECT FROM THE PUBLISHER:

Order Line: UK: 0800 169 1780,
              USA: 1 800 509 9942
              INTERNATIONAL: +44 (0) 20 7494 6400 (UK)
                    or +01 212 218 7649
              (please quote author, title, and credit card details.)

Send to: House of Stratus Sales Department   House of Stratus Inc.
            24c Old Burlington Street   Suite 210
            London   1270 Avenue of the Americas
            W1X 1RL   New York • NY 10020
            UK   USA

PAYMENT

Please tick currency you wish to use:

☐ £ (Sterling)   ☐ $ (US)   ☐ $ (CAN)   ☐ € (Euros)

Allow for shipping costs charged per order plus an amount per book as set out in the tables below:

CURRENCY/DESTINATION

	£(Sterling)	$(US)	$(CAN)	€(Euros)
Cost per order				
UK	1.50	2.25	3.50	2.50
Europe	3.00	4.50	6.75	5.00
North America	3.00	3.50	5.25	5.00
Rest of World	3.00	4.50	6.75	5.00
Additional cost per book				
UK	0.50	0.75	1.15	0.85
Europe	1.00	1.50	2.25	1.70
North America	1.00	1.00	1.50	1.70
Rest of World	1.50	2.25	3.50	3.00

PLEASE SEND CHEQUE OR INTERNATIONAL MONEY ORDER.
payable to: STRATUS HOLDINGS plc or HOUSE OF STRATUS INC. or card payment as indicated

STERLING EXAMPLE

Cost of book(s):...................... Example: 3 x books at £6.99 each: £20.97
Cost of order: .... Example: £1.50 (Delivery to UK address)
Additional cost per book:.............. Example: 3 x £0.50: £1.50
Order total including shipping:........... Example: £23.97

VISA, MASTERCARD, SWITCH, AMEX:

☐☐☐☐☐☐☐☐☐☐☐☐☐☐☐☐☐☐☐

Issue number (Switch only):
☐☐☐

Start Date:
☐☐/☐☐

Expiry Date:
☐☐/☐☐

Signature: _____

NAME: _____

ADDRESS: _____

COUNTRY: _____

ZIP/POSTCODE: _____

Please allow 28 days for delivery. Despatch normally within 48 hours.

Prices subject to change without notice.
Please tick box if you do not wish to receive any additional information. ☐

House of Stratus publishes many other titles in this genre; please check our website (**www.houseofstratus.com**) for more details.